BY KATE WESTON

You May Now Kill the Bride

Murder on a School Night (YA)

Diary of a Confused Feminist (YA)

YOU MAY NOW KILL THE BRIDE

YOU MAY NOW KILL THE BRIDE

A NOVEL

KATE WESTON

RANDOM HOUSE
NEW YORK

A Random House Trade Paperback Original

Published in the United States by Random House, an imprint and division of Penguin Random House LLC, New York.

RANDOM HOUSE and the HOUSE colophon are registered trademarks of Penguin Random House LLC.

LIBRARY OF CONGRESS CATALOGING-IN-PUBLICATION DATA
Names: Weston, Kate, author.
Title: You may now kill the bride: a novel / Kate Weston.
Description: First edition. | New York: Random House, 2024. |
Identifiers: LCCN 2023057100 (print) | LCCN 2023057101 (ebook) |
ISBN 9780593731536 (trade paperback; acid-free paper) |
ISBN 9780593731543 (ebook)
Subjects: LCGFT: Thrillers (Fiction) | Detective and mystery fiction. | Novels.
Classification: LCC PS3623.E8725 Y68 2024 (print) | LCC PS3623.E8725 (ebook) |
DDC 813/.6—dc23/eng/20231211
LC record available at https://lccn.loc.gov/2023057100
LC ebook record available at https://lccn.loc.gov/2023057101

Printed in the United States of America on acid-free paper

randomhousebooks.com

2 4 6 8 9 7 5 3 1

FIRST EDITION

Book design by Ralph Fowler
Photograph of invitation by Photoguns / Adobe Stock

YOU MAY NOW KILL THE BRIDE

Hiya, hens!

I'm not sure that you're all getting my WhatsApp messages (I'm sure if you were, people would be being much more helpful!), so I thought it best to follow up with an email!

As you know, this Friday is approaching fast! And of course everyone can't wait to give Tansy the send-off into married life that she deserves! (RIP Tansy's single girl era!)

Just a few things to cover before our weekend of fun:

- We'll be arriving at the Camp Chakra retreat in the Kent(ish) woods at 10 A.M. It's a short drive from London (only two hours), so please have breakfast before we leave. There's really no excuse for crumbs in the luxury minibus that my darling Jeremy has hired for us! He's done such a nice thing; it would be a shame if he didn't get his deposit back!

- The camp is strictly no alcohol, no electronics, and no sugar. So please turn your phones off when we get there—there's no signal in the woods anyway, Team Bride! And NO CONTRABAND!!! We're detoxing, not retoxing!

- Re: the above point—might I suggest that those of you with little blessings like myself enlist the nanny to do some extra hours this weekend? Honestly, if we're leaving the men in charge, who knows what might happen. And no one wants to come back to bloody Chernobyl! Am I right, ladies?! Hahaha!

- We're going to be having the most blissful time: yoga sessions, sound baths, crystal healing, a cacao ceremony, and a craft, which as those of us actually reading my WhatsApp messages know is still TBA while we wait for a few—very busy, I'm sure—people's votes. Please, it's either flower crown making or macramé. And we're at an extremely tense 50/50 at the moment!

- Please come prepared to be a team player, and to help our beautiful blushing bride feel as relaxed as possible at *such* a stressful time for her. Remember: this isn't about you, so leave your Tinder dramas at home (Lauren and Dominica)!

And finally, this is all going to cost a little extra because we do obviously want to make sure that Tansy has the most wonderful time, don't we?! So please could you transfer an extra £200 to me by the end of the day. No one wants to be the one that lets her down, do they?!

Can't wait to see you all on Friday, 8 A.M. sharp!

SMOOCHIES
Saskia
Xxx

PS Please can everyone in the WhatsApp chat for Farah's hen do *next* weekend pay attention! I've asked some questions in there and I haven't had answers from everyone. I know this is a busy time (we're right in the thick of hen season!), but Farah's planning a whole other wedding and has managed to be perfectly active in Tansy's WhatsApp chat. We all need to pull our weight here, people. BEWARE, I will hunt you down this weekend and I will get answers out of you if you don't reply by then (whether you're in a downward dog or getting up close and personal with your chakras!).

LOVE AND LIGHT
xxx

Sent from my iPhone 15 Pro

CHAPTER ONE

The black minibus trundles down the tree-lined Kent lane, weaving between green fields of grazing cows. There's the occasional farmhouse in the distance, but civilization is fading farther and farther away. Inside the minibus, Girls Aloud's "Love Machine," from the Ultimate Hens Spotify Playlist, blares out over the noise of twenty excited hens, many of whom are still enthusiastically waving inflatable penises about an hour and a half into the journey, despite the early start time.

Saskia sits at the back of the minibus, presiding over the festivities, still hammering away at the WhatsApp group for the very hen party that they're already on. She can see people ignoring her texts, people who don't appreciate the importance of running a tight ship. This is exactly how *people* end up drinking Blossom Hill directly from the bottle on the pavement outside a club they're too drunk to get into. And that will NEVER happen on her watch. Not again. She cannot associate herself with that behavior now that she's a businesswoman with two children, a house in Holland Park, and two thousand followers on Instagram. What would it say for her new high-end events planning business if her first hen do in her official capacity is absolutely feral? Especially with this one being so public.

When Tansy's engagement announcement went viral just hours after posting, it made perfect sense for Saskia—as one of Tansy's oldest and dearest friends—to plan the hen do. Tansy agreed almost immediately, realizing that with Saskia's elite organizational skills, she was of course the best person for the job. But now that the whole run-up to the wedding is so high-profile, with thousands of followers watching on, Saskia needs to make sure it remains classy. At least she knows they're relatively safe in the woods. No internet connection and no alcohol. The perfect scandal-free time. They just have to get there without anyone tagging her in pictures of inflatable penises on Instagram.

"Ooh look, I'm quite beautiful!" Tansy pipes up next to her, trussed up in her "Bride-to-Be" sash and "Same Penis Forever" tiara. The armor of the British hen do.

"Stun-ning!" gushes Eva, Tansy's newest and youngest friend.

Tansy tilts the phone so that Saskia can see the bridal filter they've been taking endless selfies with. Not only has it added a veil to her head, but it's also contoured her cheeks, made her eyes fifty percent larger, and given her fresh lip fillers.

"A natural beauty!" Saskia chimes, without a hint of irony.

"God, I would kill for some lip fillers, but they're so NOT organic. I mean, everyone says twenty-six is too young to start on them anyway. But I definitely need to get *something* done before I'm thirty," Eva chatters. "Otherwise you just start decomposing, apparently."

Thirty-four-year-old bride-to-be Tansy says nothing. She simply continues beaming into the camera with the sort of contented smile that can only come from someone unaware that macramé is afoot. She met Eva—a content creator and the reason her engagement post went viral—six months ago at an ayahuasca retreat, where they developed such a powerful bond that Eva tells anyone who'll listen that she considers it more of a soulmate situation than a friendship. Since then, they've hung out together at Tansy's successful vegan café nearly every day.

Looking at Tansy's face IRL, Saskia thinks she could certainly do with a wellness break before the big day. She thought a plant-based diet was supposed to be good for your skin, but Tansy's definitely looking a little pallid these days. It must be the stress of the wedding getting to her. In Saskia's opinion, everyone should have a meditation teacher like she does.

She glances down the bus at the other women she and Tansy grew up with. Lauren, Farah, and Dominica are all slumped in their seats, glued to their phones but ignoring her messages, just like she knew they would. They've been friends for over thirty years, but Saskia is definitely proof that nature trumps nurture. They all had almost exactly the same upbringing and spent every day of their childhoods together, but look at how much higher she's flown. Sometimes she pictures herself as an eagle, soaring above her friends in the world of upper-class bankers' wives and boutique business owners. At least Tansy's marrying someone with a trust fund and his own vegan brand, an entrepreneur. And she's definitely keeping better company with Eva, aka @evabliss, who's got hundreds of thousands of Instagram followers and the type of skin Saskia pays forty thousand a year for.

Dominica, a divorce lawyer, is getting into the spirit of the weekend by frantically trying to send as many emails to her clients as possible before her phone signal disappears. Today couldn't be a worse day for her to be going away somewhere phones are banned. One of the celebrity divorces that she's currently working on broke in the news this morning when a mystery woman came forward with a story about the footballer husband's addiction to buying strangers' knickers online. And now Dominica feels the kind of restless excitement she always gets when she knows she's about to take half of everything a cheating arsehole has earned. She'll be extra pissed off at Saskia and Tansy if she misses a chance to get even more money out of the wanker.

She's tried to be pleased for Tansy, but every time she's met Tansy's fiancé, Ivan, he's been a massive dickhead. As someone who considers herself an expert on divorce, Dominica predicts that their relationship will be ripe for one around three months after the wedding. Especially as they've only been together for four months. They met at Tansy's café, where it sounded very much to Dominica like Ivan simply harassed her into both stocking his vegan products and going on a date with him. Then he proceeded to propose out of the blue on their three-month anniversary. Tansy says the rushed wedding is because "he's just so passionate," but Dominica can smell an entitled love-bomber a mile off. It's just so Tansy to throw herself into a legally binding contract without considering the consequences.

Dominica secretly hoped it would never get as far as the hen do, but now that it has, she doesn't understand why they can't just have a normal one, with strippers and cheap wine. Sure, there's no guarantee that everyone'd still be on speaking terms at the end of it, but that's the nature of the beast. Why should she be punished just because Tansy lost it two years ago and decided to live a pure and vegan existence, declaring alcohol a poison for her body? Somehow they've all been conned into spending a fortune on a weekend at some wanky wellness retreat, giving a month's worth of wages to some spaced-out rich woman who set up a business on her estate but won't give out the Wi-Fi code.

At the top of Dominica's screen, another message from Saskia pops up, which she tries desperately to ignore while she carries on with her emails.

URGENT MACRAMÉ QUESTION!
Does anyone have an allergy to hemp cord?

This whole weekend is going to be both joyless and irritating.

"I will happily strangle myself with the hemp cord if she sends any more texts," Farah mutters behind her, making Lauren snort in the next seat along.

"The fact that she thinks she can boss us around when she hasn't even bothered with our Christmas Day walk the last two years is frankly insulting," Dominica complains.

Every Christmas since they were fourteen, the friends have snuck out after Christmas lunch to drink, smoke, or do whatever it takes to make the rest of the day with their families bearable. It's become a cherished tradition.

"She does have her own children now. The whole point of the walk was to get away from our parents and get inebriated enough to survive the day. Can't really do that if you *are* the parents," Farah points out.

"I don't care! It's sacred!" Dominica whispers sternly.

This year it was weed gummies ingested in a hailstorm at the local park, the only notable effect of which was Lauren finding the King's Speech disproportionately hilarious.

The women return to their phones. Lauren stares at hers, her brow furrowing, but what's on her screen isn't business, it isn't time-sensitive, and there are just two sentences that she keeps reading over and over again, trying to find a hidden meaning.

Heya, this is your weekly check-in! How are you doing? Jx

Lauren's been considering whether to respond for an hour now. Since the second service station break that they've had in this hour-and-a-half-long journey (because it turns out not everyone's had a pelvic floor coach like Saskia). Despite the fact that Lauren normally replies to Joss's messages as soon as she gets them, there's something about it today that feels different. Maybe it's that she and Joss haven't been together now for five years and yet she still loves him. Maybe it's that she wonders whether these messages are what's actually preventing her from moving on. Or maybe it's because Joss's girlfriend, Eva, is sitting at the back of the bus next to Tansy taking bridal selfies, while his younger sister, Farah, is sitting right next to Lauren.

Surely Joss must know that she's on a minibus with his girlfriend right now. Unless he's forgotten that Lauren is also friends with Tansy. Maybe she seems so sad and lonely to him that he's simply forgotten she even has friends. She debates telling him to stop pity-texting her; cutting the cord and breaking away from him and their relationship, or lack of it. She hovers her finger over the screen with purpose, but never actually makes contact.

Lauren watches a thousand TikTok videos a week about women freeing themselves from men who are bad for them. Surely she can be one of them? She can dance in streams and drink green goddess smoothies! She can be a new woman, free of the unrequited love that grinds her down! FREE YOURSELF, LAUREN!

I'm good, she types. *Thanks for checking in. How are you? Lx*

Dammit. So close. And what is she thanking him for? DON'T FUCKING THANK HIM, LAUREN, FOR CHRIST'S SAKE! The truth is that even if she did try and cut him off, he's too embedded in her life. It was Tansy, one of Lauren's own best friends, who introduced Eva to Joss, declaring them "absolutely perfect for each other." Ironic, really, that they're spending the weekend celebrating Tansy's love life when she absolutely decimated Lauren's. But in that special Tansy way, she has absolutely no idea what she's done.

Despite herself, as the bubbles appear on the screen to indicate that Joss is typing a reply, Lauren feels a deep happiness and hope spreading through her. What could he be writing? Would she still sext him right now? she wonders. If he sent her a saucy message, would she respond in a frantic, overheated manner? Despite her proximity to both Eva and Farah? Yeah, she probably would, actually. But as her phone beeps again with his text, a crushing blow is delivered to her fantasies.

Cool. Spk soon.

Urgh. Lauren knows that *Spk soon* means *Spk when I next throw you a bone of attention.* It's the worst and most transparent way to end an interaction. She hates herself and her eagerness once more. He's not even wasting his vowels on her. She vows not to jump for that bone again. No, next time she *will* ignore him with poise and conviction. She will be a woman in a TikTok video in yoga pants, freed from her lovelorn prison.

She looks toward the back of the bus, where Eva is laughing with all her perfect teeth on display, and tossing her perfect glossy hair over her shoulder. How could she ever compete with that? At least none of her friends know that she's still in love with him. She'd never live that down. Dominica would just be plain furious, and Farah was grossed out enough when they were together, God knows what she'd do if she knew that Lauren was still besotted with him. Every time Tansy or Farah describes Eva as "just perfect" for Joss, it's another punch to her heart. It feels as if Tansy's ditched her for Eva too sometimes. Lauren's barely seen her since Eva came into her life, and they used to hang out all the time.

So now she's trapped in a minibus with said perfect woman while no one knows how long Joss has kept stringing her along, always going back to her, or how much time Lauren spends trying to convince herself that it's completely normal to masturbate at least three times a week over a man she hasn't been with for five years.

She's broken out of her self-hating trance by Dominica leaping up with delight in the seat next to her.

"Yes! I've got you, you dirty bastard! You're going to be so fucking poor! It's always their egos that betray them in the end!" She punches the air with glee.

Next to Lauren, Farah also jumps, having been totally consumed by her spreadsheet. She knows it's probably bad form to be planning her own wedding on another woman's hen do. But she's been waiting two years for this, since long before Tansy even knew Ivan existed. And anyway, if you ask her, it's bad form to plan a shotgun wedding just weeks before one of your oldest friends marries the man she's been with for a decade. Now she has to make sure that her wedding is bigger and better than Tansy's, or else what's the point? She couldn't believe it when Tansy's engagement picture went viral.

"What's happened?" she asks, twizzling the huge cushion-cut diamond around her ring finger in the way she's been doing for the last two years, hoping it will catch the eye of whoever she's talking to.

"Andrew Donovan, that shitty football bastard. I'm representing his wife in their divorce and I've finally got what I've always suspected: proof of sexy DMs between him and a fan where he's inviting her up to his hotel room." Dominica turns her phone round to show both Lauren and Farah. "This as well as knicker-gate should see her financially supported for the rest of her life."

"The marriage wrecking ball strikes again," Farah mutters.

"Like a bull in a marriage shop," Lauren quips.

"People like me fuel your industry," Dominica says, pointing at Farah.

"Incorrect. I don't work in the tabloid side of journalism. I stick to more long-form investigations," Farah says, pursing her lips. It's the response she's given Dominica many a time now about her job at a highly respected women's magazine.

"Either way, you'll want me on your side if either of you are ever in need of a divorce," Dominica says.

"Toby and I won't," Farah says. "Might I suggest you offer your services to the shotgun bride at the back, though."

"Meow," Lauren and Dominica chime.

"Just saying what we're all thinking," Farah says, spinning her massive ring again to make the point. "Fools rush in."

"And so do psychopaths," Dominica says, thinking specifically of Ivan.

"Such great news for you that this man was cheating on his wife," Lauren says to change the subject. She finds it uncomfortable when they bitch about Ivan so close to Tansy. She also finds it uncomfortable when everyone brags about their jobs, because she knows that they think her job in marketing for a cosmetics company is shallow and frivolous, though they're more than happy to accept the freebies.

"Now to phone the wife . . ." Dominica adjusts her excited expression for a more somber one and presses call on the number of the WAG in question. "Danni, I'm so sorry to be doing this to you so early in the morning. Before I start, how are you doing, my lovely? . . . I know, it's hard, isn't it? . . . I know . . . I'm so sorry . . ."

Lauren and Farah go back to their phones, both of them in their own versions of hell as they stare at their screens. A groan fills the bus just as Dominica hangs up her call, indicating that the signal has finally disappeared, and Saskia watches her fellow hens' mounting distress. She knew it was going to cause a scene, but really, if they can't spend one weekend away from their phones, they should look at whether they need to do a full-time digital detox. If she can cope, as a new business owner and with children to care for and a house and staff to run, surely they can too.

The trees at the sides of the road become denser, blocking out the light. On the screen of Eva's phone, a dancing brunette bride in an ivory lace gown stays frozen, her face pixelated into a melted blur, the bridal version of *The Scream*. Tansy looks down at her own phone. One message looms on it from an unknown number.

It's not the first message she's received like this; she got one last night just before she went to bed. She didn't sleep at all after that, and now, reading this new message, she feels a clawing in her throat and a familiar tightness in her chest.

I know your secret and I'll tell your fiancé unless you follow my instructions.

Do everything I say, and he never needs to know.

CHAPTER TWO

1993

Dominica's already sick of this stupid dress and these stupid shoes. Everything is uncomfortable: the shoes feel stiff, the dress feels scratchy, the headband that her auntie made her wear feels like it's squishing her brain from the sides. She already hates school and she's only been here for an hour and a half. She sits herself on the little bench at the corner of the playground, picking out a stone that's trying to sneak between the rigid leather of the T-bar on her shoe and her white, holey patterned sock. She refuses to suffer any more discomfort today.

Across the playground she sees two girls playing hopscotch. One of them has blonde hair so bright the sunlight's bouncing off it, and she remembers from the register that she was called Tansy. Her name stood out because it seemed a little silly, like Pansy but Tansy isn't even a flower. The other girl's got long mousy brown hair and big green eyes, and Dominica remembers her name too, it's Lauren. Everyone else here already knows each other because they went to nursery together. She's the only one who's new. The only odd one out, despite her auntie saying that everyone starts a new school at this age. In fact, everyone else sorted it out aged three and now, at the tender age of four, it's already far too late for Dominica to make friends. She liked her old school, her old life. She hates this one.

She watches as two more girls join the game of hopscotch, one of them with long dark hair, the other ginger with a smattering of freckles across her nose. She doesn't know who they are; they must be from the other reception class.

She looks back down at her foot, focusing on doing her shoe back up. The stiffness of the new leather makes it quite the task, and her tongue pokes out the side of her mouth, deep in concentration, as she passes the leather tab through the shiny buckle. Suddenly screams fill the playground. Dominica looks up to see a boy running in circles around the girls, waving his hand in the air. It takes her a while to work out what's happened, but it looks like he's stolen a hair clip from the one with the mousy hair. She's trying to get it back, but he's just laughing at her, his mates in hysterics while the girl starts to cry. Dominica watches for a second before deciding that the stone in her shoe was her first victim and this boy will be her second. She remembers him from the register too. He's called Greg; he had a snot bubble as he answered yes to his name.

She stands up and marches over to the group. Without thinking, she grabs Greg's head and pops it under her arm, the way her big brother used to do to her sometimes, before . . . She starts rubbing at his scalp aggressively with her knuckles, channeling all her anger into it.

"OI! GET OFF ME!" he shouts. His mates freeze around him in silent, scared shock.

"Give her clip back," Dominica replies calmly. She stops rubbing his head but keeps him in the headlock, her chubby little fists clenched and ready for a fight.

Dominica's got a lot of anger bottled up. Anger about missing her brother, and the way her parents have barely looked at her since he died. Anger that they've had to move here where she doesn't know anyone because her parents couldn't even bear to be in their house anymore, constantly surrounded by memories of him. She'd be happy to take it all out on this kid.

"FINE!" Greg shouts frantically. He holds out the hand with the clip in it, and the ginger girl takes it from him, a wide, gappy smile spreading across her face. She gives it to her friend, Lauren with the mousy hair, who replaces it on her head straightaway, as if afraid that someone might steal it from her again any minute. But that definitely won't be happening on Dominica's watch.

"Thank you," the red-haired girl says, putting her hands on the hips of her red-and-white checked school dress. "That'll learn you, Greg Thomas!"

Greg squirms, still under Dominica's arm, and she decides she should probably let him go, even though he doesn't deserve it.

"Jesus! No reason to strangulate me!" he says, his voice nasal and snotty as he rubs at his neck.

The boys walk away, Greg muttering petulantly. They look as scared of Dominica as she hoped they would be. She turns back to her bench. Maybe she'll take off these stupid shoes for a bit. So what if her socks get dirty? Her parents will never notice anyway.

"Hey!" the ginger girl calls after her. "Do you want to play? We're doing hopscotch!"

Dominica turns and considers this, looking the girls up and down, with their matching shoes and socks, and the identical ribbons in their hair.

"OK." She shrugs. This doesn't have to be a commitment, just one playtime.

"I'm Saskia," the ginger girl says. "And this is Lauren, Farah, and Tansy. Me and Farah are best friends and Tansy is Lauren's best friend but I'm also Tansy's best friend."

Dominica frowns in concentration, trying to keep up.

"What's your name?" Saskia shields her eyes from the sun and squints at her as if looking her up and down.

"Dominica," she says, her chest puffed out like a proud robin. The girls assess her for a bit while she stares right back.

"I always get first go!" Saskia shouts by way of approval, as she runs to the start of the hopscotch. "I'm really good at this game!"

"She is," says the girl with straight dark hair—Farah, Dominica remembers Saskia calling her. She leans in with a whisper. "And even if she wasn't, she doesn't like it when people disagree with her."

CHAPTER THREE

Twenty women stand in varying degrees of hen party hysteria, waiting to be allocated to their yurts. Since they had arrived at Camp Chakra and discovered that the whole sober hen do thing was absolutely not the joke they had hoped it was, two inflatable penises have spontaneously deflated. At the front of the flock—her tiara and sash still intact—Tansy can't shake the feeling that it's most likely one of the hens sending the texts. Who else could it be? Only her closest friends would know any secrets about her. It just depends on which secret it is they're referring to.

A small, long-haired yet somehow also balding man, wearing what looks like a hessian sack, stands next to her. He introduced himself and his wife earlier as the owners of Camp Chakra, and she tries to look thrilled as he pulls back the flap of her bridal yurt with great gusto, revealing its psychopathically white interior, paired with hundreds of spring flowers. She rewards him and the thrilled hens with what she hopes is an expression of gratitude and excitement, despite feeling intensely anxious. Any excited gasps that the hens hear are in fact just her attempting to inhale a decent breath.

At the back of the group, Dominica, Lauren, and Farah try not to engage too much with the overexcited flapping of the rest of them.

"Ah, look, it's the set of *Midsommar,*" Farah sighs at the reveal of the bridal yurt, safe in the knowledge that nothing so creepy will be happening on *her* hen next weekend.

"I thought men into wellness were supposed to be Adonises?" Dominica whispers, narrowing her eyes scathingly at the diminutive sack of a man they've all been introduced to as Felix.

"Maybe he was the original Adonis and he's lived this long because of all the wellness?" Farah suggests as Lauren stifles a snort.

"Christ, imagine the state of a penis that's over two thousand years old," Dominica says.

Lauren can't help staring at Eva. Seeing her face close up in real life, she can now be sure of something quite disturbing: Eva appears to have absolutely no pores. None whatsoever. How is this possible? She takes a sip of the wheatgrass shot she was handed upon arrival, but it's so gross she can barely bring herself to swallow it.

On seeing Lauren's face contort with disgust, Dominica and Farah simply tilt their arms sideways, tipping their untouched shots onto the grass in synchronization.

"Feels good to be giving back to nature," Dominica says.

"Selfless," Farah agrees.

"Nature deserves better than that." Lauren scowls. "Always me that takes the hit, isn't it?"

"Someone had to be the sacrifice," Dominica quips. But Lauren wonders why it has to be her. At least it wasn't a blood one. This time.

Tansy is now being led into the yurt by Saskia, who's determined to make sure that she's front and center at all times during the weekend. As if the tiara and bride-to-be sash don't already single Tansy out, Saskia has even requested that Eva be beside her at all times, documenting the entire thing with a disposable camera.

"So retro." Eva scrolls the little wheel after taking a shot of Tansy lying provocatively on the big white bed, surrounded by *Midsommar*'s rejected props.

"I am triggered by that child's insistence that everything from our youth is retro. What generation even is she?" Dominica looks cattily at Eva in a way that suggests she's jealous of her lack of Botox and number of Instagram followers, making her practically untouchable in Saskia's eyes.

"Gen Z?" Lauren whispers, unsure.

"She's quite nice really, definitely the best girlfriend Joss has ever had anyway," Farah says. "You've seen some of the wet blankets he's brought home. At least this one's got something about her."

Lauren thinks her wheatgrass shot's about to come back up.

"Obviously I'm not talking about you, Lauren," Farah adds ever so slightly too late, placing an arm around Lauren's sagging shoulder.

Saskia watches on proudly as everyone exclaims at the bridal yurt's beauty. She's very pleased she's not had to tell anyone off yet as well. It's lucky for her she can't see Farah, Dominica, and Lauren hanging back, whispering about cults and goat sacrifices.

Tansy tries to settle into her yurt while the other twenty thirsty and bemused hens are shown to theirs, but the knowledge that those messages are lurking on her phone, and that someone here might have sent them, is making for a somewhat unrelaxing time. At least Eva's gone to her own yurt now rather than constantly wielding that camera in her face.

She considers each of her closest friends to work out if any of them could have sent the messages, but it really depends on which of her secrets the mystery texter is talking about. Ivan's been very vocal about how poisonous he thinks Botox is, so she hasn't told him she's had it—could it be that? Surely no one would go to all this trouble over something so minor. She's only had it a few times anyway, to look her best for her big day. It could be the fact that her café is on the brink of financial collapse, despite her pretending for months that it's thriving. But Ivan already knows about that.

Which leaves her to wonder whether it's one of the much bigger secrets. The ones she shares with her oldest friends. The secrets that are much worse than a bit of Botox. Surely it can't be, because the only people who know are Dominica, Farah, Lauren, and Saskia. And if anyone ever found out what they did, all their lives would be ruined as well.

"Now don't worry, I've got everything you need for the weekend in this bag!" Saskia says, making Tansy jump. She gestures to a Mulberry holdall that at first glance when Tansy opens it seems to contain the entire Lululemon spring/summer collection and nothing else.

"Oh wow, thanks!" Tansy says, trying to sound more excited than she feels. The last thing she needs is Saskia thinking she's ungrateful and going all martyred, talking about everything she's done for her.

She wonders if she should tell Saskia about the messages. Saskia's really good at problem solving, and she feels like the closest thing to a grown-up out of all of her friends. Tansy watches her joyfully prancing around the yurt without a care in the world and thinks it's definitely the right thing to do. Saskia will one hundred percent fix it and then, unburdened, Tansy can joyfully prance around the yurt too.

Unless Saskia's the one sending the messages? No. Tansy shakes herself. Saskia would never risk her perfect life; it's her entire personality. Besides, she's far too classy to engage in something so demeaning as blackmail.

"Saskia . . ." Tansy begins, trying to get her attention, but Saskia's on a hen do organizer roll and won't be distracted.

"Don't worry about anything this weekend! Everything's covered!" she sing-songs at her.

"Yeah, about that. Um, Saskia, could you come here for a minute? There's this little thing, I just . . ."

Saskia stops prancing, realizing from the tone of Tansy's voice that there's a problem. "What's the matter?" she asks, really hoping she's not got the Lululemon in the wrong sizes. That would be catastrophic.

"It's . . . I've been receiving these messages."

Tansy hands Saskia her phone and sits patiently while she reads the texts, pausing afterward with a thoughtful expression on her face.

"Are these the only ones you've received?" she asks, her tone practical and calm.

Tansy nods, chewing on her lip in a way that makes Saskia itch slightly.

"And do you know what the secret is?" she asks as Tansy's teeth sink further into her bottom lip. She digs out a small tube of Paw Paw gel and hands it over. This is something Saskia first started doing twenty-five years ago with a far-less-fancy Lipsyl tube. The brand may have changed but the gesture is still the same, born of a motherly, slightly irritated kind of love for her friend. Tansy takes the tube without thinking and opens it, squeezing a blob onto her finger as she replies.

"I sort of wondered . . . if maybe it was one of . . . *our* secrets." She gestures between her and Saskia, a gloop of Paw Paw on her finger. "You know."

Saskia sits in silence for a second, trying to maintain a calm exterior while the threat of her entire life crashing down on her becomes a very real possibility.

"They haven't actually asked for anything yet, have they?" She studies the messages. "But surely it'll be about money. It's always about money."

"So what do I do?" Tansy asks, distorting her mouth while she rubs the Paw Paw onto her lips. If they want money, she thinks, they can't possibly know how much trouble the café is in.

"Nothing," Saskia says. "I'll tell Jeremy and we'll see what he says. He's good with this stuff. But for now, do nothing. We don't negotiate with blackmailers."

"I don't know," Tansy says, wearily. "All of this got me thinking. I shouldn't have secrets from Ivan. I should just tell him everything, you know? The two of us are in it for life. I can trust him."

"Everything?" Saskia asks, irritated. Why did Tansy even bother asking her advice if she isn't going to follow it? "Even the bits that could land people in prison?"

"Even those. Especially those," Tansy says. "He needs to know all of me before we get married. All the things I hold within me, all the secrets. Whether they're mine or other people's, they're about to be his too. I need to share the burden with him before we make that lifelong commitment."

"I think that's a little hasty, not to mention risky," Saskia says.

"Why risky? Ivan loves me, every bit of me, inside and out. That includes my flaws. If I tell him, I know he won't betray me. I trust him," Tansy says innocently, eyes wide.

That's because you've known each other for five minutes, Saskia thinks. He hasn't even had time to notice any flaws.

"Why don't you at least wait and see what Jeremy advises? Just until the end of the weekend?"

"OK," Tansy says, after a tense minute for Saskia. "But what if they send me the instructions while I'm here and I don't have any signal? I'll miss them, and they'll tell Ivan whatever it is anyway, and then everything will be ruined by the time I get home."

Saskia looks at her for a second before pulling out her own phone. "I'm going to share the Wi-Fi code with you. Don't tell anyone that we have one. Felix and Florence gave it to me in case of emergency only—like the nanny needing me. Give me your phone and I'll put it in there for you. And if you do get any more messages this weekend, then at least we know it's not one of your hens, because no one else has signal."

"Thank you," Tansy says, actually hoping to hear from the black-mailer again now so she can rule out her friends.

"Of course," Saskia says brusquely, pulling her into a hug at the same time. "Just keep me informed. We'll figure this out together."

Tansy already feels better, but she can't shake the horrible feeling of adrenaline flooding her veins. A couple of yurts away, she can hear Dominica, Farah, and Lauren getting ready for their first calming vinyasa session, and she could have sworn one of them just uttered the word "vodka." Maybe that's what she needs. Something to steady her nerves and help her forget that despite this being her hen do, she may never make it down the aisle. If there was ever a time for her to fall off the wagon, now really feels like it should be it.

She's vaguely aware of Saskia talking about the Lululemon outfits. She's holding up items and telling her what to wear, even down to her underwear, and explaining how the bag has been curated for her optimum experience.

"Right!" Saskia places the garments she's chosen for Tansy on the bed. "I'll leave you to get ready and round up the troops!"

"Great!" Tansy says. "And Saskia? Thank you. I really appreciate all of this. It's perfect, really it is."

Once outside the yurt, Saskia takes a second to steady herself. She can't believe what she's just heard. She can't believe that for the sake of her wedding, Tansy might be about to ruin all their lives. But then Tansy's always been too ditzy to see how her actions affect others.

Two yurts down, Dominica has returned from an unsuccessful march around the camp to try and find signal, and is now standing on her bed waving her iPhone at the sky. She refuses to believe that they can be only two hours away from London without a single bar of connection.

"There's something incredibly sinister and unhinged about taking a group of women to an area of woodland with no phone service," she grumbles while pulling on her Sweaty Betty shorts with her free hand. "And I KNOW she's seen *The Cabin in the Woods* because we all watched it together and then had to sleep in the same bed that night. Remember?"

The Lycra of her tight shorts slaps against her thigh as she tries to wrestle into them. A red welt appears almost instantly to mark the sting.

"God, even the clothes we have to wear for this are against me," she grumbles.

"You seem to wear them to spin without any complaints," Lauren points out, furious that the three of them are having to share a yurt with absolutely no alone time all weekend while Tansy gets one all to herself. Just because she's the bride.

"Spin is CIVILIZED!" Dominica pouts. "We BRUNCH afterward. Speaking of, pass me that vodka, I cannot be cat-cowing without hydration."

Lauren takes a swig from one of the many hip flasks the three of them packed for the trip, then hands it over. The more she drinks, the easier she'll find it to interact with Eva like a normal human and ensure she doesn't arouse suspicion or stare at her like some kind of obsessive fan. She especially doesn't want to have Eva's perfectly sculpted downward-dogging arse in her face right now. If it has to happen, it can at least be a bit blurry.

"Tansy better appreciate this," Dominica mutters.

"I'm sure she'll find it transformative," Farah says.

"Honestly, guys, she'll reach a higher state of being," Lauren adds, quoting Tansy herself after she came back from the ayahuasca retreat.

"Just so long as it doesn't give Saskia any weird ideas about my hen do," Farah says, knowing full well that she's made her preferences very clear. She wants it in Ibiza, staying on the classy part of the island of course, and for there to be a lot of Whispering Angel. She's quietly confident that there'll be no chance of another dry affair.

Dominica and Lauren briefly exchange a glance of recognition about exactly how much money they've had to part with for Farah's "completely surprise" hen do, and exactly how much she's banged on about the whole thing. Farah's quest for perfection around this wedding feels particularly jarring when they can both still remember a time she would drink cider and blackcurrant from a plastic pint cup and call it a cocktail.

Farah misses the conspiratorial look between her two friends, too wrapped up in her own thoughts. At least this weekend will give her some inspiration for an article about overpriced wellness experiences that feel like hell. She's already pitched it to her editor, Rebecca, using the Wi-Fi code she watched Saskia slyly punch into her phone earlier—the absolute lying snake. She refuses to tell the others, though, in case they blow the secret. Dominica for one would be on it all the time.

"YES! He's offered a settlement!" Dominica shouts, getting the smallest whisper of signal while balanced precariously on the edge of the bed. "Oh! It's only ten million. Who the fuck does he think he's playing with?" She takes another gulp from the flask and begins composing the fiercest response this man's lawyers will ever receive.

Lauren doesn't want to let on, but she's had signal this whole time. For some reason her service provider works out here. Good old Giffgaff. It's just that there's no one she's expecting messages from. She even checked her work email earlier, but it seems the world of makeup marketing is carrying on without her just fine. The most exciting email she'd received was someone asking her if she was suffering from erectile dysfunction, when what she's actually suffering from is a complete absence of any erectile at all.

She feels like most women succeed in either their career or their home life—case in point: Dominica is thriving in her career but isn't even remotely interested in getting laid as far as Lauren can tell, and Farah is getting married yet hasn't written an article that's gone viral for years. The women who are really hateful, of course, manage both. Like Eva.

"Is everyone ready in here?" Saskia's head appears through the tent flaps without warning, prompting all the occupants of yurt number three to jump.

Dominica does a sliding tackle face down onto her phone and hip flask, covering them with the full weight of her body. In a somewhat misguided attempt to make it look natural, she tries to raise one of her legs from her face-down position. It's not a graceful movement and everyone present stops to marvel at the spectacle.

"Just stretching my glutes!" she shouts as Saskia sweeps her eyes over the other two, looking as if she doesn't want to know.

"Class starts in five, so outside in two minutes sharp?" They all smile and nod as she ducks back out of the yurt and closes the flap before moving on to the next unsuspecting hens.

"Someone needs to put a bell on her," Dominica sighs, pulling herself up off the floor, gathering her phone and hip flask.

"Why don't yurts come with locks? We're really just out here in the woods with no security," Farah points out, checking that her hair and outfit are perfect, and engagement ring straight.

"This is hell," Lauren sulks, lunging to ensure that her leggings aren't nestling into her vagina, even though they very much feel like they are. She would pay a considerable amount of money she doesn't have for leggings that are guaranteed never to do this. She bets Eva never gets camel toe.

The flaps of the yurt rustle slightly, but this time they're prepared, all contraband safely tucked in their luggage.

"Guys," Tansy hisses from outside. "Can I come in?"

"See, the bride-to-be has an understanding of boundaries and polite behavior." Dominica points toward the flaps. "Of course, wifey, come on in!"

"Thought I'd sneak in while Saskia's busy rounding everyone up," Tansy whispers.

"You've given her such a gift, letting her organize this. All that bossing around is like a wet dream for her," Dominica says.

"Do you remember how she used to divide up the Sylvanian Families between us when we were little?" Tansy says.

"The Sylvanian dictator." Lauren nods.

"It was vicious." Farah shakes her head. She's reminded of the wedding dress that she made for one of the rabbit family out of a paper doily, and briefly wonders if she has a picture of it anywhere to send to her dress woman.

"Pre-vinyasa vodka?" Dominica offers Tansy the hip flask and nearly gasps when she actually takes it.

"PLEASE!" Tansy whispers.

The other women stare in shock as she takes three long glugs before wiping her mouth. Dominica feels a faint hint of anger. If the bride-to-be is drinking, then why the hell are they on this spirulina boot camp?

"It's easy to forget that Saskia used to be the one sneaking booze around in hip flasks for us, isn't it?" Tansy asks, unaware of all three of them feeling various levels of contempt for her.

"Back when she used to use her organizational skills for good rather than evil." Dominica nods. "Sorry to address the elephant in the yurt, but are you drinking again?"

"I thought this whole thing was because you were sober," Farah adds.

"Are you OK?" Lauren chimes in.

"Not drinking again, just, I dunno, really fancied one right now. You know? It's just a blip." Tansy shrugs, knowing they must be thrilled she's fallen off the wagon. They've always behaved as if her sobriety was a direct slight on them.

Farah thinks this might be an even greater betrayal than when Tansy signed and shared a petition calling for the cancellation of the "toxic" women's magazine that Farah works for. Farah was almost out of a job because of that. Tansy obviously hadn't realized it was her magazine—it was just another example of her having her head in the clouds and fucking up people's lives because of it. Farah constantly has to remind herself that they've been friends for so long, and Tansy never *means* any harm. Besides, after all these years, there are too many things tying them together. They are forever enmeshed in each other's lives.

"Please just tell me before I go back out there." Tansy takes another glug of vodka. "Flower crowns or macramé?"

They all stare at her with faux pity as Lauren loops a comforting arm around her shoulder.

"It's macramé, I'm so sorry, babe."

Tansy flings her head back, draining the last of the vodka, then straightens her yoga pants and heads toward the yurt flaps.

"Better get on with it then, I guess. At least it's a little less *Midsommar* than the flower crowns." They all titter, grimacing at her. "Thanks for the vodka!" she shouts over her shoulder, heading out to her fate.

"Any time," Farah calls after her sarcastically, turning the empty flask over in disbelief. "That fucking dozy cow."

"Well, look who finally got her personality back. I say this with love, but I'm just wondering if she could possibly have done it before we were dragged to this hippy boot camp," Dominica suggests, her irritation getting the better of her.

"I guess the bright side is that fun Tansy's back," Lauren says.

"I was starting to forget she was once the most fun among us," Dominica says. "Tansy is a case study in why you do need alcohol to have a good time. She used to be . . . legendary."

"You could always rely on her to know where the best parties were." Farah nods.

"Do you think she's OK?" Lauren asks, as the three of them stand staring at the swaying flaps that Tansy has just retreated through.

"Maybe she's having second thoughts," Farah suggests, eager with hope.

"I would be if I were marrying Ivan," Dominica reasons.

"But she loves him," Lauren says.

"Lauren, he pinched your arse at his own engagement party," Dominica snaps.

"Yeah, but he thought I was a waitress that he knew and was joking around with," Lauren says. "He explained that to Tansy."

"Honey, no," Farah says as kindly as she can, because sometimes they both despair at how naïve Lauren can be.

"Even if that were true, it still wouldn't be OK." Dominica arches an eyebrow.

"But Tansy was all right with it," Lauren says.

"Yes, and Tansy also believed him when he said that the hot woman coming out of his flat one morning a couple of weeks after they got together was reading the gas meter," Dominica says.

"Hey, gas women exist." Lauren boops Dominica on the nose. "BAD FEMINISM!"

"She was wearing a sequined jumpsuit," Farah says, opening another hip flask.

"OK, fine, he's a shit. I just miss a time when we used to be able to be happy for each other. Don't either of you?" Lauren pleads.

"We're very happy for each other." Dominica looks confused.

"Yeah, we bitch about each other as a mark of that happiness," Farah concludes, and the two of them fall about laughing while Lauren's left staring sadly into the distance.

She knows that they both call her basic and naïve behind her back, but that's just love, right? Besides, they're the only real friends she's ever had.

On the way back to their yurts after their first yoga session, Tansy feels calm, free, and like she's finally ready to put the messages behind her, at least for the weekend. She knows what Saskia thinks, but she's sure the best thing to do—the thing that Ivan would appreciate the most—is just tell him. If anything, sharing these secrets will make them stronger. And if he goes to the police and she loses everything, then he's not the man she thought he was and it's no more than she's deserved all these years anyway. Acceptance is the key to healing.

She takes a quick look at her phone, feeling such a sense of resolution and harmony that even the sight of another message doesn't have the same effect as it did before.

> *Drop £5,000 into this account by the end of the weekend or I'll spill.*

The decision is made quite simple by this text. With the café on the brink of bankruptcy, she doesn't have five thousand pounds, so she can end this right here, right now. Honesty and love are more important than money anyway. If Ivan really loves her, everything will turn out all right, no matter what the secret. And the good news? Whoever sent this message has signal, so they're not on her hen do. She can still trust her best friends.

> *I don't have that money,* she types. *I'm just going to tell him myself. It's time I was honest and faced the consequences of my actions.*
>
> *I hope you find peace.*
>
> *Love and Light x*

CHAPTER FOUR

1996

"Um, I . . . Saskia . . . I . . . I . . ." Lauren looks over to Dominica for some courage, trying to finish her question. They've practiced this, she knows she has to be brave, and she IS a brave girl. She can do this! "Saskia, I was wondering if this time maybe I could be someone other than the badger family?" She looks down at the Sylvanian Families characters that she's been lumbered with since the dawn of time. "You know I'd much rather be the bunnies, especially as mummy bunny has the two babies. And I feel like it's mean that I'm always stuck outside in the badger sett, which isn't even a sett, it's just the inside of an elastic band laid out to look like a hole that they live in. Everyone else gets to be the animal they want to be and I . . . The badgers don't even have furniture . . ." She trails off, seeing Saskia's face start to redden with fury, her eyes narrowing and dimpled little fists clenching.

"But I'm always the bunny family," Saskia says as if it's just common sense. The mother bunny in her floral dress and apron, and her two baby bunnies, safely nestled in their carriages, are clutched tightly in her pudgy fingers.

The bunnies live in the big house, while the badger doesn't have a home because they've run out of Sylvanian Families houses between them, and Lauren's mum could only afford to get the badgers, not their house. Despite Lauren's suggestion that maybe the badgers could be guests staying in the big house, Saskia never goes for it. She says the biggest family is in the big house and no one else, and that's just how life works.

"I do think though that sometimes you could do better sharing," six-year-old Dominica says fairly, standing next to Lauren with her hands on her hips, trying to show a united front with her. They've discussed how today is the day that Lauren is finally going to stand up to Saskia, and get out of the badger sett and into the house.

"I just think if Lauren wants a house, Lauren should bring one round," Saskia says.

"Saskia!" Dominica and Tansy say all at once.

"You know her mum's single and has no money," Tansy mumbles.

"Just because your parents are rich doesn't mean everyone is," Dominica chastises.

Lauren sits awkwardly on the brink of tears, stroking the soft face of the badger and cuddling him to her cheek.

"What do you think, Farah?" Dominica asks. "It's your house."

Farah stares down intently at the panda in her hand, aware of Saskia's eyes boring into her. They're supposed to be best friends. She can't cross her. But she can't help wondering if it is a little unfair on Lauren.

"Don't know," she says, fear of being on the wrong end of Saskia's rage preventing her from saying anything else. Saskia told her earlier that she's got her a new Polly Pocket for her birthday because she's such a good friend, and she doesn't want her changing her mind about giving it to her.

No matter whose house they play at, Saskia always seems to find a way to be in charge anyway. They're all sure that Dominica's house would be the only place she couldn't, but they never play at Dominica's house. Dominica's parents never talk to the other parents or invite the girls to play around there, and whenever they see them, they look sad. The other girls' parents have told them that they're sad because Dominica's brother died in some kind of accident before they moved here and they need space. Although the girls don't fully understand it, they know that Dominica's house is out of bounds and never to mention her brother. Farah even feels bad mentioning her own brother, Joss, sometimes, but he can't be avoided because he always seems to hang around just to annoy them, even though he has his own friends to be a loser with.

"Lauren can be my hedgehog family in the bakery this time if she wants. I don't mind being the badgers for a change," Tansy says kindly. Tansy thinks this is a nice thing for her to do and it makes Lauren happy, but she's completely oblivious to the fact that it makes Saskia very unhappy. Farah clutches her panda close to her chest and braces herself.

"But she can't do the voice! You do the voice!" Saskia exclaims in anger. "And it makes sense for you to have the bakery because you want one when you're a grown-up!"

"Lauren can do her own voice," Dominica says sternly, her fists clenched, ready to fight for Lauren's right to be the hedgehogs.

"I CAN," Lauren says in a high-pitched, robotic squeal. The way she thinks a small spiky animal would sound.

"FINE!" Saskia concedes, huffing and puffing while she puts the baby rabbits into the bath. "Enough about the hedgehogs. Mrs. Rabbit has to get the kids to bed now because she's very tired."

"And Mrs. Hedgehog needs to start baking more cakes because the animals ate them all today. Especially you, Mr. and Mrs. Badger!" Lauren says in her hedgehog voice, putting some plastic baguettes into the tiny oven. She's thrilled to finally be out of the badger sett and somewhere she has more props.

The girls continue playing, mainly oblivious to Saskia's mounting rage. She can't believe that people aren't sticking to their animals or listening to her.

"Hello, Mr. Squirrel!" Tansy says, walking Mrs. Badger over to Dominica's squirrel.

"Oh, Mrs. Badger, you look pretty today!" Dominica responds.

"STOP! STOP! STOP! What are you doing? Are you trying to make Mr. Squirrel be having an affair with Mrs. Badger?!" Saskia squeals. "That's SILLY!"

Dominica's about to protest that actually their Sylvanian Families could use a little excitement in their lives. She's recently started watching *EastEnders* in the evenings and her eyes have been opened to a whole new world of chaos and high drama.

"Girls! Dinner!" The call from Farah's mum comes drifting up the stairs and into Farah's perfectly pink bedroom.

Without a second thought, the five of them ditch their Sylvanians and thunder out of Farah's room. Farah's mum always makes the best dinners. Actual Birds Eye fish fingers, not like at Lauren's house, where her mum has to buy the own-brand ones with less breadcrumbs on them so they're always just naked, ordinary bits of fish by the time they come out of the oven, and at Farah's there's always Little Gems or Club biscuits for pudding.

On the landing, they bump into Farah's older brother, Joss. Lauren looks down at her hands as they pass him, only looking up when she senses his eyes on her.

"Have you been playing with the silly animals again?" he asks her.

"Yeah, so stupid, right?" Lauren says, abandoning all her beliefs and principles because she wants Joss to think she's cool but she doesn't know why.

"So stupid. I knew you were into cooler stuff than them," Joss says. "You can come and have a go on my PlayStation instead if you want."

Lauren beams at him.

. . .

The five girls return from dinner high on the additives and sugar from an unexpected treat of Party Rings, and settle back down to the world of Sylvanian Families. But as she looks down at the hedgehogs' bakery, Lauren screams.

The other four jump up and race over to her, peering into the bakery in dismay. Mrs. Hedgehog is lying on her back on the floor, pins in her eyes and chest, with big red marker pen splotches over her frilly white apron.

"WHAT HAPPENED?!" Lauren wails.

"THERE'S BEEN A MURDER!" Farah screams, covering her eyes so that she can't see Mrs. Hedgehog's poor mutilated figure.

"MY HEDGEHOG!" Tansy shouts. "MY MUM BOUGHT ME THAT!"

The girls gather round Tansy as she cradles Mrs. Hedgehog in her arms, weeping over the brutal slaying of her favorite Sylvanian Families figure.

"Don't worry, Tansy," Dominica says, frantically pulling pins out of the hedgehog. "We can fix her."

"Maybe the red bits are just jam?" Farah says innocently.

"Mrs. Hedgehog loves to bake," Lauren concurs.

"Poor Mrs. Hedgehog," Saskia says.

It's only Dominica who narrows her eyes, knowing full well that Mrs. Hedgehog didn't do this to herself. Mrs. Hedgehog was hurt by one of the girls; she just needs to find out who.

CHAPTER FIVE

Twenty exhausted women traipse through Camp Chakra's Wellness Woods toward this evening's activity—the Cacao Circle. In stark contrast to the cocktail-making classes and strippers of the hen parties they're used to, these hens are about to embark on a sober and spiritual journey together. Or that's what Saskia thought anyway, but it seems some members of the group are much less sober than she instructed. She's already had to tell Florence—the owner of Camp Chakra—that Tansy's fall from downward dog earlier was due to the heavy weight of the tiara she insists on wearing, and not any illicit substances that would get them thrown out and banned from Camp Chakra for life. She'd never be able to show her face in the W11 postcode again if that happened. Her business would be ruined.

Saskia leads the group to the cacao space, getting more and more annoyed. She can't actually believe that she's done all this for Tansy and now she's *drinking*. One threatening message and she's fallen off the wagon. And it's not like vodka's going to help the situation, is it? It's so very Tansy to get blackmailed for something that's probably only about her and to drag the rest of them into it by threatening to spill all their secrets.

Saskia hasn't told the others yet: she doesn't want the cavalry losing its collective shit when she can probably talk Tansy round herself—or at least she could have if Tansy hadn't chosen this weekend to get pissed for the first time in two years. Knowing what a loose cannon she is when she's drunk, she might even share the secret that's just between her and Saskia, not thinking about the consequences. Because as usual, it's all about Tansy "doing the right thing," the eco-warrior princess who starts every morning alternating iced water and vegan bone broth.

Saskia can't even use any of the pictures that Eva's taking for marketing or Instagram because Tansy's still insisting on wearing that ghastly tiara. How did it even make it onto the bus? Who was responsible? She *will* find out. If only people had read her emails and Whats-Apps properly, they would have known that they were eschewing the whole naff penis vibe in favor of more subtle bride- and bridesmaid-to-be sashes. Penises are hardly ethereal, are they?

Farah walks at the back of the group with Dominica and Lauren, watching as a glow surrounds the hens up front as they reach a clearing. Twenty-two golden floor pillows are laid out in a circle, bathed in the pink light of the evening's sunset. In the center of the circle, orange flames lick at a cast-iron cauldron filled with the ceremonial cacao. Waiting at the head of the circle stand Florence and Felix in white linen outfits, ready to greet the hens in a way that only two rich white people with a Jesus complex can.

"Welcome to the Cacao Circle!" Florence announces, spreading her arms wide like an eagle, as if to embrace them all. Dominica thinks she just looks like a twat.

"This is a chance for you all to really get in touch with what's going on deep inside of yourselves!" Felix talks with his hands clasped together in the sweaty and excitable way that a dirty old man might when stumbling upon a dance class. Dominica suspects that he'll be in the news in a few years' time either for being the leader of a cult that takes advantage of vulnerable women or, at the very least, accused of some kind of sexual harassment.

"Please, take a cushion and be seated. We'll wait for everyone to get comfortable before we begin." Florence gestures expansively to the floor pillows.

Dominica, Farah, and Lauren are already three sheets to the wind. When they try to sit down, they fall into each other like dominos. Only Saskia seems to notice, narrowing her eyes at them. It's her own fault though: if you give starving people only rabbit food, they will turn to hard spirits and get wasted.

"Dare you to spike the cacao," Dominica whispers, passing Farah the hip flask. She knows that out of the three of them, if it's not her that does it, it'll be Farah. Lauren's an unpredictable dare, depending on how reckless she's feeling, and she's got an anxious look in her eye tonight that suggests that even if she were to spike the cacao, she'd confess two seconds later for fear of being arrested by the wellness police. Dominica's already being watched too closely by Saskia, who obviously expects shenanigans. But Farah, when she's not obsessing over her wedding, and if she's had enough to drink, will take a reckless challenge and perform it with the subtlety of a feather drifting to the ground.

"Oh please! That's easy!" she hisses in Dominica's ear while Lauren stares on open-mouthed.

Dominica hasn't heard Farah talk about her own wedding for hours now. It's honestly a joy to have her pissed and behaving more like herself. Even if she will go straight back into bridezilla mode when she sobers up. It wasn't a surprise that her perfectionist, overachieving friend wanted the perfect wedding, but it was alarming for Dominica to see someone so career-driven and capable transform into the sort of person who loses their mind over a sugared almond once that ring was placed on her finger. She'd heard it happened, but she just hadn't expected Farah to be one of them.

"But what if there are pregnant people here, or alcoholics?" Lauren whispers anxiously. This level of overthinking is exactly why Dominica didn't dare her.

"Everyone here with the exception of Saskia has drunk vodka from us today. There's no way *any* of these bitches are pregnant," Dominica says, gesturing to the group.

"Pregnant?" pipes up Helen, one of Tansy's university friends, on hearing her trigger word.

Helen and Tansy's other uni friend, Jen, started drinking their own contraband on the minibus after ranting in the WhatsApp group that if they were taking a weekend away from their children, they were going to make the most of it, so help them God. And Saskia actually seems slightly afraid of their wild frazzled-mothers-without-nannies energy, so she leaves them to it. There's no question that either one of them could take her in a fight. Actually, come to think of it, Dominica's a little scared of them too.

"Who's pregnant?" Jen leans in. "Don't do it. It's a trap!"

"No one's pregnant. Farah's just going to spike the cacao," Dominica whispers back hurriedly.

"Oh yes!" Jen and Helen squeal in tandem. "Thank fuck!"

"OK, fine, you're right, I see no possible problems with this," Lauren says, her eyes darting from side to side.

The women huddle together in a small gaggle of mischief before releasing Farah toward her task. She strides confidently over to Tansy, Eva, and Saskia, handing the three of them penis straws that Jen has just produced from her cleavage. Dominica watches Saskia's troubled reaction with glee. There was a time when Saskia would have drunk a Bacardi Breezer through a penis straw without even realizing what it was.

Farah proceeds around the group, giving out the straws to everyone, explaining that it simply isn't a hen cacao circle without a penis straw. On her way back, she walks directly through the center of the circle, casually tipping the contents of her flask into the cauldron as she passes. In response, the cauldron fires up and she leaps back.

"This thing's a safety hazard!" she squawks at Florence and Felix before scurrying back into her place, patting down her eyebrows in case of rogue embers. "I'm getting married soon! I COULD HAVE LOST MY EYEBROWS!"

Saskia, still holding her newly acquired penis straw between thumb and forefinger, marvels at how some people can make even the most spiritual of activities a common mess. She had thought with all the wedding planning Farah might be starting to develop a little class.

With everyone seated, the last glimpse of pink sun disappears behind the shining green branches of the trees and the group sit huddled under blankets on their cushions, the air turning colder around them. They wait expectantly, all hoping that this won't take too long and doesn't involve any kind of howling at the moon. Lauren finds herself admiring the way the pink light bounces off Eva's perfectly shiny hair while slowly stroking her own lank bird's nest.

"HMMMMMMNMMMMMMMNMNMNNNNNNMMM-MMMMMmmmmUHMMMMMMMMMMMM," Felix suddenly blurts out.

The noise has the effect of making everyone jump. Florence joins in at a higher pitch, which makes Jen and Helen titter and snort. Across the circle, Tansy seems to be drunkenly swaying in time with the hums.

"Oh God, she's hum-onizing," Farah whispers while Lauren and Dominica struggle to contain their giggles either side of her. Saskia shoots them a glare, but Florence ignores them and carries on with the humming. At the same time, she and Felix begin drumming on the bongos at their feet, prompting an eye roll from Dominica. She'd clocked those drums when they sat down but had hoped they were a prop and not for actual usage.

"Hmmmmmmm and now Florence is going to serve the cacao. Hmmmmmmm." Felix seems to be trying to make the words fit in with his humming, giving the whole thing the air of a low-budget boy band on a nineties shopping center tour.

Florence rises in time with the drumming and Dominica mentally adds "Felix making the woman serve" to her list of reasons why he's problematic and has probably got a cult of women locked away in a bunker somewhere, sewing him more hideous hessian sacks to wear.

Florence hands around small earthenware mugs that Saskia's seen in a Notting Hill boutique. She silently approves but can't believe she's going to have to put a penis straw in one like a complete philistine.

"We gather in celebration of Tansy and her upcoming nuptials to our brother Ivan," Felix starts as Florence returns to her floor cushion next to him.

Dominica screws her face up at the thought of anyone calling Ivan their brother.

"Cacao ceremonies originated with the Mayans and Aztecs. They are an ancient tradition, a space for us to set intentions, to meditate, to dance, to celebrate, and to pray. We pray for Tansy and Ivan's continued love and growth and offer you all an opportunity to say why you're grateful for Tansy."

Lauren wonders what qualifications Felix has that give him the right to be messing with something that he's already described as an ancient tradition. She imagines Mayan and Aztec ghosts busting through the night sky to punish him for misusing their cacao ceremony for his own clammy-pawed gain.

"And now, we and the spirits invite you to drink from the ancient cacao," Florence says, as across the circle a gurgling sound comes from Helen's phallic straw. She clearly hadn't realized that you were supposed to wait to be told to start and has already reached the bottom of her cup.

Felix starts a low chant, hitting his drum softly, and Florence joins in, adding a ghostly harmony. The whole thing gives Lauren the heebie-jeebies, while Dominica and Farah simply rage at having paid these charlatans so much money. Despite the cynicism around the circle, however, the mood does appear to change.

A light breeze hits the women, the dark sky and its stars drawing in, a twinkling roof over their small forest clearing. Around them the noises of the night—birds, scratching forest animals, and a rustling of leaves—become pronounced against the backdrop of Florence and Felix's ghoulish chanting, and in the darkness, the bonfire flames lick at the shadows.

Felix sways gently. "We invite you to close your eyes so that you can really focus inwardly on this moment of reflection. Or if you'd rather, you can stare at the flames, meditating on the power of nature. Nature is king and fire is its throne," he announces. "Tansy is going to visit you all with an embrace, and you must tell her why you're grateful for her."

The fire hisses and spits as the group stare at it, with the exception of Saskia and Eva, who've closed their eyes, clearly far less afraid of appearing like dickheads than the rest of the group.

"Tansy, come to me!" Felix commands, and Tansy, on the verge of hysterics—the vodka hitting hard—rises and walks toward him. He takes her hands earnestly before she leans down to hug him. "I am grateful for Tansy's beauty and grace," he shouts, holding the embrace a tad too long. Dominica shudders.

"I am grateful for Tansy's kindness and her generosity of spirit!" Florence adds, and then resumes humming.

Tansy proceeds around the circle, embracing the hens one by one, cacao in hand.

"I am grateful that Tansy gives love as powerfully as she receives it!" Eva says, making Dominica do a small sick in her mouth.

"I am grateful for Tansy's friendship!" Saskia declares, the least imaginative one yet.

Lauren, Farah, and Dominica realize that they're going to have to think of something to say, fast, as everyone else in the circle seems to be positively spewing out their reasons to be grateful for Tansy.

"I am grateful for Tansy's humor!" Farah announces, and she and Tansy share a smirk.

When Tansy comes to stand in front of Lauren, clasping her arms around her, Lauren feels a rising panic, knowing she has to speak. She's convinced she saw a small flicker on Tansy's face as she leaned in.

"I am grateful for Tansy's smile," she says sweetly.

Tansy moves on to Dominica while Lauren hates herself.

"I am grateful for the tampon that Tansy gave me when I got my first period while wearing new white Tammy Girl trousers," Dominica says, embracing Tansy tightly.

As Tansy progresses to Jen, across the circle Saskia opens her eyes, resting a stern glare on Dominica, while Lauren and Farah giggle. But really, Dominica cannot be doing with this bullshit. Not even Tansy is taking it seriously, so why should she?

When everyone has made their declaration of gratitude, Tansy returns to her original place, thoroughly embraced. Across the circle, Florence stands and raises her arms above her head. Clearly taken by some urge, she starts dancing like a woman possessed.

"We invite you to connect with your inner child; move in whatever way you feel inspired to. Feel the peace of dancing to your own beat in a completely unselfconscious way. For among the trees, we do not fear judgment," Felix says, as if excusing Florence's cringeworthy, overdramatic movements.

Dominica, Farah, and Lauren make eye contact, casting great judgment. They watch as Jen and Helen briefly look at each other before launching into the big fish, little fish dance of their youth. Across the circle, Tansy laughs into her hands, covering her face. Her shoulders are shaking, jerking in the flames, while Eva and Saskia on either side of her are fortunately distracted, performing their floaty, ethereal dances.

Lauren finds it hard to lose herself when they're in the middle of a deserted woodland at night. She stares out into the endless darkness of the woods, thinking that there's absolutely no way she's about to close her eyes and start writhing around near an open flame. Plus anyone could be hiding out there. Who's going to save them if they get attacked while everyone's prancing around like fannies? She wonders if she's perhaps had a smidgen too much vodka. She does have a tendency toward paranoia when drinking hard spirits. But it's hard not to be paranoid when all around her are frenzied drunken limbs, and two idiots with bongos thumping to the tune of her banging, anxious heart. She wonders if she should be using her Giffgaff signal to text Joss now. Finally tell him how she really feels before she's dragged to her death or ripped apart by wolves.

Tansy's shoulders are still shaking, her hands over her face. Across the circle, Lauren laughs back at her, enjoying the fact that her old friend appreciates the hilarity of the situation. But when they make eye contact, instead of seeing joy and humor in Tansy's eyes, Lauren sees panic and confusion. It takes her a minute to join the dots, but then she realizes: Tansy's not laughing, she's coughing, and she can't seem to stop. But the sound isn't penetrating the loud pounding of bongos or the now aggressive chants of Felix and Florence as they become fully possessed.

Tansy glances around her, wide-eyed with fear, clawing at her neck. In the light of the fire, Lauren notices the swelling of her lips, and the redness creeping across her face. But everyone else now has their eyes shut, taken by the spirits of the forest, or at least pretending to be. Tansy starts frantically clawing at the tiny bag containing her EpiPen that she carries around with her everywhere, and Lauren knows she needs to get to her. She tries to bat her way through the dancing hens, desperate to get people to hear her, to understand that there's a problem with Tansy, but everyone's wasted. She watches helplessly as Tansy clutches Saskia's forearms, but Saskia doesn't even open her eyes, she simply carries on dancing.

Against the backdrop of pounding drums and flailing arms, Lauren finally reaches Tansy, delving into the bag for the EpiPen but finding it empty. Tansy is bent double, the air wheezing out of her. Lauren grabs Saskia and Eva, trying to get their attention; she screams and shouts and waves to make people open their eyes. Finally Saskia opens hers and turns to her, her expression aghast.

"Where's her EpiPen?" she shouts as the rest of the circle finally realize what's going on.

"It's in the bag!" Dominica yells, racing across from the other side of the circle as if her presence can take charge of the situation. "It's always in her bag!"

"It's not there!" Lauren screams. "IT'S NOT IN THE BAG!"

"Doesn't anyone have a spare?" Farah pleads.

But it's too late. Tansy falls to the muddy ground, her eyes wide open, a trickle of vomit sliding down her chin. And the women know without a doubt, even before any of their shaking hands reach for a pulse, that their friend is dead.

CHAPTER SIX

Blue lights flash, illuminating the woods. In the center, nineteen sobbing hens are being interviewed by police officers while a cordon is drawn around the twentieth: the deceased bride-to-be. The women sit numbly on muddy logs, tears streaming down their faces, their eyes vacant with disbelief. Apart from Saskia, who is wailing and shouting, ordering the police to do their jobs and the paramedics to just do SOMETHING.

"I don't understand what happened. What was in the cacao that she was allergic to? They had a list of all her allergies. Where was her EpiPen?"

"She was just coughing. That was all. I couldn't do anything," Lauren whispers, staring at the people in white suits buzzing around them.

Farah comes and stands next to Lauren, placing her hand on her shoulder as the police begin erecting a tent around Tansy's lifeless body. Even Saskia and Dominica stop asking the questions that no one has any answers to and go to stand with them, watching as their friend who just minutes ago was preparing for her wedding is covered in white tarpaulin.

"I didn't realize what was happening. I didn't know she was coughing; I didn't see the swelling at first. I would have moved faster." Lauren stares in disbelief.

"The penis straw? Was it the straw?" Farah frets. "Or what was in the flask?"

"No, Far, she won't have been allergic to that," Dominica says, her tone more gentle than usual. "She's used penis straws before. And the flask was vodka, she was drinking that all day."

Lauren looks around the group, her eyes eventually settling on Eva, who, despite knowing Tansy for the least amount of time compared to everyone else here, appears to be crying the most.

"I want to wake up tomorrow and find out this is all some kind of awful cacao dream," Farah says. She looks around her at the weeping hens with a terrible sinking feeling as her phone vibrates in her pocket with what must be texts from Toby. Joss will have told him.

"Excuse me!" Dominica catches the eye of two passing police officers, aware that absolutely no one else is going to do anything productive. It's always down to her. "What happens now? Do we need to give statements?"

Dominica needs to focus on the practical: she doesn't have any other way of coping. If she stops, she might get annoyed by the over-emotional displays from people who haven't known Tansy anywhere near as long as she has. Or she might become overwhelmed by her own grief. The female officer gives the four women sympathetic looks as the hens around them grow increasingly hysterical, making Dominica wince.

"We're still not sure what's happened, I'm afraid. We won't know more until the postmortem, but you all say she had allergies and she was looking for her EpiPen, so it's most likely she was allergic to something she ate or drank."

"Why didn't we notice?" Farah gasps, tears rolling down her cheeks, as Saskia marches angrily over to Florence.

"How did this happen?" Saskia's voice can probably be heard for miles around. "WHO WAS RESPONSIBLE?!"

Florence looks petrified. Lauren, Dominica, and Farah move to stand beside Saskia, because they can't leave her to avenge Tansy's death alone, but Dominica's not sure Florence is the one to blame.

"This isn't helping anyone," she reasons calmly.

Saskia glances at the other women helplessly, a flicker of herself as a younger child coming into view. The stubbornness, the rage, the insistence at always getting her own way, no matter how impossible.

"What do we need to do now?" Dominica asks a detective wearing a suit and a long mac.

"The owners are arranging for your minibus to come back and collect you all. They want to help you get home as soon as possible. There's really nothing else you can do here," the detective says gently.

Dominica nods. "Thank you, officer."

Lauren tries to absorb some of Dominica's strength. It's something she's always lacked, but for Tansy's sake, she needs to try and figure out what the hell happened. If she weren't so caught up in her grief, she might have clocked the detective's kind brown eyes and tortoiseshell glasses, the kind that would usually send her weak at the vagina. But as it is, she doesn't notice a thing.

Felix finishes the phone call he's been making and claps his hands to get the group's attention.

"We'd like you all to go up to the house, where your minibus driver will pick you up in about an hour and a half," he says. "If we head via the camp, you can grab your things on the way."

Nineteen grief-stricken hens start to leave the forest, one hen down.

CHAPTER SEVEN

The windows of the old farmhouse glow yellow with a warmth that's not replicated inside. Within its idyllic walls, the shaken party sit in a spacious wood-panelled living room, shivering with shock and confusion. They silently sip cups of hot, sweet tea, waiting for the minibus's arrival, the occasional sniff and text alert the only things to puncture the silence.

At least at this time of night traffic won't be so bad, Saskia thinks. Like Dominica, it's all she can do in times of crisis: think of the practicalities and organize things. The day she found out her dad had died, she set about organizing a funeral for a man she hadn't seen since she was twelve, after he left her and her mum alone and penniless. They'd had to sell the house, her horse, everything. Yet still, when she heard about his death twenty years later, her first response was to take control of the situation. Standing alone at the window now, she watches as the blue flashing lights illuminate the woods. Florence and Felix are still down there with the police, helping them with their inquiries. Although Saskia thinks they'll be mostly covering their arses. They claim to be all earthy and spiritual, but she suspects their chief concern is that this might hurt their business. And Saskia's going to make sure that it does.

Across the room on one of the spotless white sofas, Eva's scrolling through pictures of her and Tansy on her phone and weeping. Next to her, Farah puts an arm around her shoulders, while Dominica and Lauren sit shell-shocked, staring at the cups of tea they've been handed. Tears splash into Lauren's one after another.

"I should be comforting you. You knew her for way longer than I did," Eva sobs to Farah.

"You were very close," Farah says, sniffing gently.

"It's just, when we met at the ayahuasca retreat it felt like we'd known each other for years. Like maybe we were friends in a previous life. I felt more like myself with her than I ever have before," Eva says. "Maybe the ayahuasca just helped us to find each other. You know?"

"I don't," Dominica whispers, ever rational despite the tears teetering at her eyelids. Farah glares and she adjusts her tone. "You two were very lucky to have met each other."

"Oh God! What about Ivan?" Eva wails. "Do you think he knows yet?"

"They'll probably be telling him now," Dominica says. "Someone from the police will go to him and explain what's happened."

At this, Eva starts sobbing even more loudly. Farah keeps her arm around her shoulders while she stares at her phone. There's far too much for her to process right now. Questions and thoughts piling up like a to-do list at the forefront of it all.

"I need to get some tissues and call Joss. I'm a mess," Eva says, getting up delicately and turning to Dom and Farah. "Thank you."

Lauren thinks she's never seen anyone who's less of a mess in her life. She feels a different pang of sadness as the realization hits her that Joss won't be there for her in her hour of need. Eva will be the one he comforts. When Lauren really needs him, when all she wants is for him to wrap his arms around her and let her cry into his chest, she'll be lucky to mop up even the slightest crumb of his affection.

"Poor Ivan," she says.

Farah and Dominica exchange a look that makes Lauren glance back down at her phone, pretending that she has someone to talk to rather than just staring at it, willing Joss to text her instead of talking to Eva.

"I imagine some kind of self-pitying Instagram post will be imminent," Dominica whispers to Farah, making sure the rest of the party can't hear her remark.

"Dom!" Lauren chastises immediately, moving away from them to go and stand with Saskia at the window, watching the scene in the woods. She wishes Dom wasn't like this sometimes. She knows it's a defense mechanism, but it appears heartless.

"You and I both know that he's going to do a huge gross post about it. He's going to optimize this for likes and for self-promotion. And then ultimately he's going to be using our friend's death to get pussy," Dominica continues, in a louder whisper this time.

"Urgh," Farah sniffs. "I hate that it's true. She deserves so much better. That man is a real arsehole. And you just know some naïve woman will fall for his sob story."

"We must protect Lauren at all costs," Dominica murmurs back with genuine concern.

They assume that Lauren hasn't heard them over by the window, but she has. She pretends she hasn't just like she always does, though, standing next to Saskia looking out into the night.

"It's just awful," Saskia mutters to her. "I can't get my head around it."

While obviously Saskia *is* thinking about how awful it is that Tansy is dead, the other implications swim around her brain. Her friend died at the party she organized. The inaugural party for her events-management company. She knows she needs to be smart about this. Her finger hovers over the Holland Park Mums WhatsApp group, where most of her social business gets done. Without further hesitation, she takes decisive action, composing a message about what's happened. She knows these women will support her through this. She can rely on them to see it as the tragic incident it is, and make sure the word is spread in the correct way. Then, once they find out what killed Tansy, Saskia will throw a benefit gala in her honor.

Farah and Dominica eventually cease bitching about Ivan—venting their grief in the best way they know—and join Saskia and Lauren over by the window. The four of them stand silently, perfectly aligned between the light green (Farrow & Ball) wood-panelled shutters, their ghostly reflections visible within its glass panes. Farah begins twirling her engagement ring around her finger in a way she always hopes looks absentminded, soothed by its twinkle in the window.

It's Dominica who reaches out first, linking Saskia's fingers with her own, and then Saskia takes Lauren's hand, before Lauren reaches for Farah's without even looking, their fingers joined in exactly the way they have done for years. At the other end of the line, though, the fingers on Dominica's free hand twitch, reaching out for a grip that'll never be there again. As they stand together like this, they feel uneven, Saskia no longer sitting perfectly in the middle of their friendship group. Despite the way their friendship has changed over thirty years, with all the frustrations and bitchiness they've been guilty of at various points, the bond between them still exists. It may be a little more ragged than before, frayed by squabbles, long-held grudges, and secrets, both private and shared, but it's always stayed strong.

"We need to be careful," Saskia says quietly, hoping to remain discreet.

"Why?" Dominica asks, knowing exactly what Saskia's saying. She feels a hint of irritation at being told what to do, can hear it creeping into her voice.

"Well, what if one of us slips up when we're talking to the police about Tansy?"

Dominica snorts. "Sorry, you actually think that while talking to the police about something completely unrelated, one of us will suddenly accidentally spill our darkest secret and ruin all our lives?"

"Do you think we're stupid?" Lauren adds, spurred on by Dominica.

"You can't blame me for worrying. I've got so much to lose now." Saskia frowns.

"Oh, and the rest of us don't have anything?" Dominica hisses. "I could be struck off! Farah would definitely lose her job, and Lauren, well, I mean she'd . . . be in trouble too."

Thanks, Dom, Lauren thinks. Final confirmation if ever she needed it that her friends don't view cosmetics marketing as nearly as important as their own jobs.

"Don't worry," she whispers angrily. "None of us have any desire to spill the secret, break the pact, or ruin your yummy-mummy status."

"I'm getting married in less than two months," Farah says through clenched teeth. "Bizarrely, doing something that might jeopardize that isn't on my bucket list."

Saskia keeps her head up, her nose firmly raised in the air, determined not to let them see that they've bothered her, that they've in any way cracked the surface of the person she's taken years to carve herself into, the person she needs to keep hold of.

Dominica rages silently in her head. She can't believe Saskia thinks her life is so much more valuable than theirs. What does she do that's so life-changing compared to the rest of them? Besides, she barely even knows them anymore. She only reappears in their lives for weddings and hen dos. The rest of the time she's so busy living her fabulous life they may as well be strangers.

"The thing is, someone knows," Saskia starts, her mouth stretching and straining as she forms the words. "Tansy was being blackmailed. She had these texts from someone saying they knew her secret and they were going to tell Ivan."

The other three women turn to her slowly. She knew that would get their attention.

"What secret?" Dominica grits her teeth.

"It might have been something else," Farah says.

"It must have been," Dominica agrees. "There's no way anyone else could know."

The women fall silent, hands gripping tighter, anxiety vibrating between them as they contemplate the fact that their lives have been turned upside down and things might yet get worse. As they stare out of the window, orange headlights appear at the end of the long drive-way, approaching the house. The minibus. They can finally get out of here and back to civilization to process their loss.

"I can't leave her," Eva's voice trills behind them. "I can't just go back to London and leave her by herself!"

The women at the window spin round to stare at her. Mascara is trailing down her face, and the tip of her nose is somehow redder than it was when she went out to make her phone call. She looks desperate. All four of them eye her with suspicion, because who is Eva, really? This woman so new to their group and yet so entwined in it.

"The police won't be removing her body until at least tomorrow," Dominica says, feeling more detached from her grief the more she talks about process. She knows from one of her friends who works in wills and probate that these things can take a long time.

"Then I'll stay until tomorrow," Eva says. "She shouldn't be on her own."

She's never been on her own, though, not when the five women are bonded so tightly that even when one of them pulls away, they're still a unit. Linked forever by their past.

"I'll stay with you," Dominica says.

"Then I'll stay too," Saskia declares, in a tone that brooks no argu-ment. If any of them were about to question her loyalty to this group, she's putting a stop to that right now.

"Me too," Farah says. "We can't leave our girl alone. And Joss would never forgive me if I left you here." She rubs Eva's shoulder.

"And me," Lauren adds, even though she's sure that no one's listening.

"That's settled then," Saskia says, taking charge. She must remember to add this to her WhatsApp group. "I'll go and speak to Florence and explain to her that we're staying and that we're sleeping in the house. The least they can do is put us up for the night, after everything that's happened."

A knock at the living room door startles them all, and they turn to see the detective with the tortoiseshell glasses, flanked by Felix and Florence. His commanding presence makes them stand up straighter.

"I'm DI Ashford and this is DS Castle," he announces, gesturing to his younger female colleague. "We need to speak with you all regarding the death of your friend. We've been unable to retrieve an EpiPen at this stage. Could we just clarify what she was allergic to?"

"There should never have been anything in the cacao that she was allergic to in the first place," Saskia snarls in Felix and Florence's direction. "Peach was her worst. Why would that be in it?"

"That's what we're here to find out," DI Ashford says, pushing his glasses up his nose.

"Surely you should be asking the people who made the cacao then?" Saskia says disdainfully.

"Are you saying there *were* peaches in it?" Dominica presses, confused.

DI Ashford looks uncomfortable. "We can't give any more information at this stage I'm afraid," he says, shutting her down. "But we do need you all to stay here a little longer. We'll want statements from everyone, particularly those who knew about her allergy and the EpiPen."

"Everyone knew," Farah says. "And surely the EpiPen just fell out of her bag somewhere around camp?"

"As I say, we haven't been able to locate it. Is it possible someone else had it?" DI Ashford speaks casually enough, but his questions prompt Saskia to screw up her face in anger.

"What, and you think one of us simply *forgot* we had it?" DI Ashford says nothing. "You can't think one of us is responsible for her EpiPen going missing. I'm phoning my husband. You wait till he hears about this. He's got friends in the force, you know, VERY high up in Scotland Yard. And they'll be none too pleased to hear about this!"

But the rest of the women say nothing, contemplating the threatening messages Tansy was receiving yet knowing they can't tell the police about them. They have too much to lose.

CHAPTER EIGHT

2003

"Why is it always me that ends up stealing the booze when it isn't even my house we're hanging out in?" Dominica huffs, sneaking back into Farah's bedroom with a bottle of peach schnapps unsubtly concealed up her jumper.

"Because you're the only one of us that can lie without your face going red or collapsing into a fit of giggles every single time. Or wetting yourself." Saskia looks pointedly in Lauren's direction.

"It was ONE time," Lauren defends herself. "You knew I'd drunk almost a whole bottle of Sunny Delight, and Tansy made me laugh. Also, I was like FIVE years old or something!"

"It was last year," Tansy sniggers, but gives Lauren an affectionate squeeze.

"It was a year and TWENTY DAYS AGO. And SHUT UP!" Lauren folds her arms across her chest and glares at them all. She wishes they wouldn't do this. What if Joss heard?

"It's OK! What happens between us stays between us. Anyway, no amount of pant pissing can possibly be as bad as the story about how Simon Hallow broke his penis while having a wank in the boys' changing room." Dominica pulls the bottle out from under her jumper and takes a swig, then instantly regrets it.

"I just hate the word 'wank.' It's so . . . ewwwwww." Saskia takes the bottle from Dom and grimaces. "I think you're supposed to have that with lemonade or something."

"Definitely," Farah agrees, looking disappointed at her friend's efforts. She would never have left the job half done.

"Is it not enough for you that I've come up with hard spirits? Now you're saying you want a mixer too? It's only a week ago that I saved you from getting grounded when I snuck you home and distracted your parents while you were wasted." She points at Saskia. "And Farah, didn't I stop your brother from seeing you that time you were covered in your own vom? You know he'd have told your parents and you'd have been grounded forever." Dominica grabs the bottle back off Saskia and spitefully takes a sip before passing it to Tansy. "Must I always be the savior?"

"But you're just so good at it," Farah retorts. "Besides, I don't think it's fair to bring up the time I was covered in vom, because it was my worst day ever."

"You got a B on a test and drowned your sorrows," Saskia says. "It's really not so bad."

"I CANNOT TALK ABOUT IT!" Farah raises her hand to block out the memory.

"What if I'm allergic?" Tansy asks, cradling the bottle of schnapps nervously in her black-polished fingertips. "ARGH, but I wanna get wasted so baaad."

"You're allergic to everything." Dominica rolls her eyes.

"I've got a spare EpiPen in case you ever have a reaction when I'm with you," Lauren says, gesturing toward her bag.

"I knew you loved me the most," Tansy says, hugging her before raising the bottle to her lips.

"Hang on. How come I don't get first sip? It's my house! That's my parents' schnapps you've stolen!" Farah snatches the bottle back from Tansy before she has time to take a swig. Tansy's pissed her off already today by coming in with a new fringe when Farah was excited about showing everyone her DM boots. Everyone knows a fringe blows everything else out of the water. And it even looks good on her: if any of the rest of them tried it, it would look like a cry for help. She knows Tansy doesn't do it on purpose, but it's annoying always having to take a backseat to her beauty.

"You've stolen what?!" Joss's head pops around the door and Lauren feels her stomach flip at the sight of his cheeky smile and his green eyes glistening with mischief. Her cheeks burn and she tries to hide them so no one notices.

"Ewww, get out!" Farah shouts, throwing a heart-shaped pillow toward his head.

"Look, you've got two options," Joss says. "Either you share the goods, or I tell Mum and Dad." Lauren pleads with whichever gods decide these sorts of things to make Farah let him stay. "And FYI, you're being so LOUD, there's no way they're not going to hear you if you don't shut up."

All five girls stop where they are, frozen with fear.

"Fine," Farah sighs. "But you need to like, just, NOT be annoying."

"Yes!" Joss flops down onto the beanbag next to Lauren. "Like I'm the annoying one when she's constantly getting straight A's and making me look bad."

"And yet you're still somehow the favorite," Farah sighs while Joss beams.

The heat of Joss's body next to her makes Lauren feel flustered, and she remembers the other evening. Her mum was working nights again and she was sleeping over at Farah's. She'd been in the bathroom cleaning her teeth when Joss walked in, and she'd nearly choked on her toothbrush. He came and stood next to her, an amused expression on his face. She hadn't been at all prepared when he took the toothbrush out of her hand and kissed her. It wasn't how she'd thought her first kiss would go, with toothpaste around her mouth, but at least her breath was fresh. Ever since then, all she's wanted is for it to happen again. As soon as possible. Farah would kill her if she ever found out, though.

She watches him as he raises the bottle of schnapps to his lips, taking in the way his jaw bobs as he drinks, tracing the path of the liquid as it goes down his throat. He lowers the bottle and brushes back a lock of dark hair from his face, his green eyes meeting hers, as Lauren realizes that she's been staring at him with her mouth open. He smiles, his dimples popping just like they did after they kissed.

"I heard that there won't be ANY PARENTS at the party tonight," Saskia says, jolting Lauren out of her trance. She's sitting in front of Farah's mirror, trying for the twentieth time that day to do black-winged eyeliner on her right eye so that it matches her left, which actually went really, uncharacteristically well.

"As if," Dominica says. "We're fourteen, they're not going to leave a house of teenagers without any supervision."

Farah snatches the bottle out of her brother's hand, trying to ignore the smirk on his face. As usual, she suspects he knows something they don't, and she hates it.

"Johnny Graves has already had sex with three older girls. His parents really don't care what he gets up to. I bet they do just go out," Saskia says, presenting it as carefully formed evidence.

"Ha! SURE!" Joss blurts out as if he can't keep it in any longer. "Johnny Graves doesn't even KNOW three girls."

"Exactly," Dominica says.

"Hey! Don't AGREE with him!" Farah says. "It'll only encourage him."

"Encourage me to do WHAT? Be right more?" Joss knows he's winding her up. Lauren wishes he'd stop it, despite how sexy his little smirk is, because Farah's going to kick him out if he carries on, and she's enjoying being next to him. She likes spending time with him. It's not just that he's hot, it's that he's actually really caring and considerate. He always asks how she is—she can't remember the last time one of the girls asked her that.

"All I'm saying is that I've heard he's definitely not as experienced as he lets on," Dominica says.

"Oh? And who did you hear that from?" Saskia arches an eyebrow at her, then turns back to the mirror, inspecting her handiwork.

"Here." Tansy passes Saskia her blusher. She knows Saskia can't afford things like makeup at the moment because her mum's still paying off her dad's debts after he left, so she often shares with her. She also occasionally gives her clothes that she says don't fit her, but Saskia knows they do and she's being kind. She's in no position to decline, though.

"Just rumors at school." Dominica looks shifty, which makes the rest of them lean in.

"He's in a band, though," Farah says. "And girls literally fall over guys in bands, don't they? And he is kinda hot."

"Oh?" Saskia turns, her lips pouted in a kissy shape. "OH MY GOD! FARAH FANCIES JOHNNY GRAVES!" she shrieks while Dominica covers her ears.

"Um, yeah . . . I mean, we've just been talking a bit . . . on MSN in the evenings, you know . . ." Farah shuffles in her seat and downs more schnapps to help with her confession. It's something that doesn't come easily to her.

"You've been flirting?" Dominica joins Saskia in her excitement.

"I mean, yeah, he just talks to me a bit, sends me song lyrics and stuff, and he asked if I was going to be there tonight and when I said yes he said cool," Farah admits shyly.

"ARGHHH!" Dominica and Saskia scream and leap on top of Farah. Joss mock-screams and piles on too. Lauren wonders if it would look weird if she were to throw herself on top of Joss.

"OH MY GOD! EW! JOSS! FUCK. OFF," Farah shouts, pushing him off them.

"Oh my God, he's been messaging me too!" Tansy says suddenly, halting the excitement and making them all turn around. "He was saying that he wanted to spend some time with me tonight to get to know me a little better or whatever. But I didn't realize you liked him too. You should totally go for it, I'm not that bothered."

At once, Farah feels all her confidence and excitement about tonight's party being replaced by a sense of embarrassment and rage. How could she have been so stupid as to think he actually liked her? She's got no chance now, especially with Tansy's new fringe.

"Nah, it sounds like he likes you way more," she says. "He never said any of that stuff to me. You go for it."

"Are you sure?" Tansy asks.

"Yeah, course!" Farah tries to sound as unbothered as humanly possible.

"Hang on! He's been messaging both of you? So he's a player then, right?" Dominica asks, directing her question to Joss.

"Oh, I'm sorry, now you want me to speak? Now you actually want my opinion?" he asks.

"Don't make me beg." Farah rolls her eyes at him. "Just spill."

"What am I? Your boy correspondent?" Joss shrugs. "I dunno, man. He's never really seemed like that big of a deal to me."

"He sounds like he doesn't know what he wants," Dominica says, disappointed with Joss's answer and remembering every single copy of *Just Seventeen* she's ever read.

"OH MY GOD, HE'S JUST TEXTED ME!" Tansy says.

Farah curses the fact that her parents won't let her have a mobile phone. If she did, maybe he would have texted her too? Or maybe not, who's she kidding. Why go for her when he can have Tansy?

"OH MY GOD!" Lauren and Dominica scream, huddling round and poring over the text message.

Farah tries to join in behind them, not letting on that she feels so crushed. For her it was a huge thing, a boy finally paying her attention. She even thought she might finally get to one of the bases—she didn't care which one, she just wanted to be in the game. But then there's Tansy acting as if it doesn't even matter. She can have anyone she wants because she's so beautiful. Why couldn't she just have gone for someone else? Why can't there be ONE thing Tansy doesn't overshadow her on? Just one! She hates feeling jealous of her friend, but she can't help it.

"I dunno. I'm still not convinced," Saskia notes. "He sounds like a little boy. And we should only be spending time on men."

Everyone pauses to consider this very important point, except for Joss, who bursts into hysterics.

"MEN! You're fourteen!" He knows he's going to get kicked out, so he takes a last sip of schnapps and stands to leave.

"FUCK! OFF! JOSS! GET OUT!" Farah says, throwing a cushion at him. To be fair, it's nice to have something to take her rage out on.

"OK! OK!" He holds his hands up. "I'll leave you guys to talk about . . . MEN!"

Farah throws another cushion at him as he departs, and it smacks against the closed bedroom door. Lauren lets out a small accidental sigh she hopes none of the other girls hear.

Farah watches as Tansy grabs the bottle of peach schnapps from Dominica. Rage still burns within her. Why can't Tansy just back off? Why is she always the one that boys want?

"Wait, are there actual peaches in here? Because I'm definitely allergic to those," Tansy says, narrowing her eyes at the bottle.

"I'm sure they're not *actual* peaches," Farah says. Tansy won't look so pretty if her face swells up or she gets one of those nasty rashes. "It's mostly alcohol and sugary flavoring."

She watches as Tansy shrugs and takes a giant swig from the bottle.

"What happens if you have peach anyway?" Farah asks, suddenly nervous, coming to her senses and realizing that she doesn't want to hurt her friend.

But it's too late. Tansy's lips have already started swelling, Dominica's phoning 999, and Lauren's grabbing the EpiPen before Farah's even had time to consider her actions.

CHAPTER NINE

In the peachy morning light, a low mist swirls around the woods. The tent that was erected around Tansy's body pokes crudely out of the trees. There's just one police car down there now, all the blue flashing lights and chaos of last night cleared away. Lauren watches from the padded window seat of the guest room she slept in, her knees pulled up to her chest, her oversized jumper stretched over her leggings. She inhales the cold, damp air through the open window, feeling its freshness hit her lungs.

At first when she woke up she couldn't remember anything that had happened. She lived for a few seconds in blissful ignorance and a four-poster bed, not even questioning why the view from her window wasn't the usual bin storage unit, or why she couldn't hear the drunks still up from the night before, vomiting. After the police had questioned them all last night, the minibus containing the other hens left at around 2 A.M., while Lauren, Dominica, Farah, Saskia, and Eva stayed on at the house. It felt to Lauren like they were all determined to prove themselves as Tansy's best friend.

She's surprised she managed to sleep at all after everything. She spent most of the night watching her phone. She couldn't believe Joss hadn't texted her yet to ask if she was OK. But she could hear Eva on the phone, wailing through the wall, so of course he was too busy with her.

Feeling her phone vibrate next to her leg now, she experiences the smallest glimmer of hope before reminding herself that it's probably just Saskia or Dominica again. They've been sending logistical texts all morning about how they're getting back today—apparently Jeremy's driving over to collect them. It's an act Saskia obviously considers chivalry but the rest of them know to be Jeremy simply exerting his wealth, superiority, and manliness with a Range Rover big enough to fit them all in. She turns the phone over, bracing herself, but instead she sees Joss's name, shining out at her like a mirage. Is she hallucinating? Could she have wanted something so much that she's willed it into existence? The phone vibrates again, and a second message from Joss appears on the screen.

Are you OK?

I'm here for you. Whatever you need x

She's waited years for him to send her a message saying something other than a version of "How are you?" Now that she's got it with that second text, she has absolutely no idea how to respond. She just sits staring at it, her finger hovering over the screen, hope threatening to spill out of her, all the while knowing it's Tansy's death that's caused this.

A soft knock at the door makes her jump. If anyone else could see her now, they'd tell her to get a grip, that his super-fucking-hot girlfriend is just in the next room and it doesn't matter what she replies, he is never in a million years going to dump Eva to get back together with her.

"You up, babe?" She recognizes Farah's soft voice through the oak door. Even more reason not to be mooning over her brother's messages.

"Yeah, come in," Lauren shouts back, not moving from her window seat.

The door creaks open and Farah's face appears. She pads in, closing it behind her. She's already dressed in a similar outfit to Lauren, except she's got a full face of makeup covering her eye bags and tear-stained cheeks. She looks ready to face the day, while Lauren knows she looks ready for absolutely nothing.

"Hey, how did you sleep?" she asks in a voice that sounds as tired as Lauren feels.

"Not great, you?" Lauren chews one of her nails so hard she nearly draws blood.

"Not the best," Farah admits, perching next to Lauren, crossing her legs, her feet tucked underneath her bum. The two of them sit staring out of the window for a minute in companionable silence, something they've always been good at. Or at least they were before Farah got engaged and started spending every moment talking and thinking about her wedding.

"Saskia's taken over Florence's kitchen," Farah says. "She's making some kind of weird wheatless, fun-less pancakes like a woman possessed and forcing everyone to eat."

"Always being mother," Lauren replies in a way that sounds sarcastic even though she didn't mean it to. She stares back out at the woods. "I just can't believe it. I can't believe she's gone."

"I know," Farah replies sombrely, a hand on Lauren's bended knee. "I don't get why the police are behaving like they think someone stole her EpiPen."

"Right? Why would any of us do that? We were her friends." Lauren hugs her knees tighter, thinking about the messages, and the possibility that someone could have been intentionally responsible for Tansy's death. "And how did the peach even get in the cacao anyway? I couldn't taste any."

"No, me neither," Farah says, pausing thoughtfully. "I just can't get my head around the fact that that's it. One slip and now she's not going to be marrying Ivan in a couple of weeks, or doing dress fittings, wedding breakfasts, reception wine tastings . . ."

"She's not going to be wearing that beautiful dress or going on that honeymoon," Lauren starts, but her voice breaks. Tears she wasn't aware she still had left teeter on her eyelashes.

"She's not going to be at my wedding, or my hen do next weekend. I'm going to be getting married without her," Farah adds, her eyes glistening with moisture.

She watches Lauren as she stares out of the window, and wonders if this is the best moment to do this. But she needs to: there's not much time. She can't let the dominos start to fall, because if they start, they'll keep falling, and she'll be ruined in ways she can't even begin to think about right now. She's already so heavily in debt with this wedding that if anything's cancelled or moved, she could be in serious trouble. She's just being rational—Tansy's already dead, she can't save her. But she can save herself.

"Listen, I was thinking, you're good at knowing what to do in these situations," she begins, and Lauren tenses at the change in tone, knowing her friend well enough to predict what's coming. "What do you think we should do about my hen do? And the wedding? Is it weird to get married so soon after . . . because so much stuff is paid for and we won't get refunds this late in the day and I just . . . I mean, we could even have the hen do in Tansy's honor. It could be a chance for us to take some time away together, process everything."

Farah has absolutely no intention of turning her hen do into a grief fest, but she's not about to let Lauren know that. She can feel her stress rising as she talks, making her cheeks flush. She's struggling to hold her voice steady because her brain's pulsing with the thought of it all coming crashing down around her.

Lauren stares at her for a moment. Why do her friends always do this? They come to her with some kind of moral question, but they don't actually want the answer. They just want her to give them her blessing, to tell them that what they're doing is perfectly fine, even when it's not. She hates confrontation, and her friends think she's not judging them because she never says anything, but internally she absolutely is judging. And right now, if it weren't for the fact that Farah's voice is breaking with emotion and her cheeks are red with the strain of trying not to cry, she'd think she was being a selfish monster. To be honest, maybe she still does.

"I know it's weird and it might not feel like the most natural thing to do," Farah goes on, "but we need each other now more than ever. We can use it as a chance to get away and recalibrate. We've been through so much; we need to learn how to live now . . . without her . . . But I don't want the others thinking I'm insensitive . . ." She trails off and starts fanning her face, looking like she might burst into tears at any moment.

Lauren knows that what Farah means is that she wants Lauren to convince the others that she's not being insensitive. She can't believe what she's hearing. Is Farah really worrying about her own hen do right now? When their friend is dead?

She hugs her knees closer, trying to shield herself from the discomfort of the conversation and Farah's expectant eyes boring into her. She hates this, but she knows she's going to have to say something soon.

Farah raises her eyebrows as if coaxing her to hurry up and make up her mind. She needs Lauren onside if she's ever going to get the other two to agree to it.

"I mean, I know this probably all sounds a bit heartless. I'm just so totally gutted about Tansy, completely heartbroken. I just need to focus on something else. You know? It's so weird to think that she won't be here anymore, obviously. She won't be at my wedding; she won't be my bridesmaid . . ." Farah trails off and Lauren chastises herself for suspecting it's because she's thinking about how being one bridesmaid down throws off her configuration walking down the aisle, and that she'll have to pay for a dress that no one will be wearing now. Then again, no one would be surprised that she's thinking it—ever since Farah got that ring on her finger, she's been like a woman possessed.

"The hen do especially could be such a healing trip for all of us. I just think, what would Tansy have done in this situation?" Farah tilts her head and leans in, reaching over and gently brushing a bit of sticking-out hair behind Lauren's ear, a familiar gesture so steeped in kindness and normality that Lauren almost feels bad for judging her.

To be fair, Lauren knows full well that Tansy would have gone ahead with her hen do. She would have said it was a celebration to honor whichever one of them had died, and isn't that exactly what Farah's suggesting now? Tansy had a habit of not noticing she'd done the wrong thing; she was too caught up in her own world. It never seemed malicious, though, and they always forgave her, but certainly in recent years she'd got worse. They'd all at some point or another fallen victim to her thoughtlessness, but it was hard to be cross with someone who was so generous in other ways. She'd more than once covered Lauren's share of the rent when she was struggling for work in the old days.

"Yeah, I know what you mean. It's hard to know what to do, though, because Tansy's not coming back." Lauren feels like she needs to remind her friend of that fact—that Tansy hasn't just popped to the shops—but at the same time she can't be bothered to argue with her. "I'm sure Saskia will be sorting it already anyway."

"Oh my God, has she messaged?!" Farah asks, clutching her chest. She can feel the palpitations gathering pace at the thought of the domino effect already in action, and all the other things that might now have to be rearranged. The figures on her wedding spreadsheet rapidly increasing as she heads for complete financial ruin. So many of those deposits were non-refundable. So many of the payments made were already far more than she could afford. The things she'd had to do to get that money.

"No! I just meant that she's probably thinking it through. You know what she's like. Prepared for anything." Lauren really hopes this is the end of it, because she doesn't feel ready to answer any more questions in a way that will satisfy Farah. She thinks she's only got wrong answers left in her repertoire. She can't believe Farah could think for a second that they've all been messaging about her hen do at a time like this.

They're interrupted by their phones beeping.

"Speak of the devil," Farah says, gesturing to a text from Saskia on her phone. "I think we'd better go downstairs before she comes to round us up."

"I'll see you down there. Just got some things to do first," Lauren says vaguely.

Farah nods and walks out of the room, relieved to have a moment to process the incredible mess she's in, leaving Lauren now practically in the fetal position on the window seat.

Once the door's closed, Lauren stares back down at the text from Joss. Maybe she should just cut her losses, tell him she loves him. Life's short, the last twenty-four hours have proved that, and it's what Tansy would have done. She starts typing out the sentiments that she's kept secret all these years. Her heart thumping in her chest, her fingers shaking with fear and anticipation at what he might say to her. And then she deletes the entire thing and simply writes: *Thank you x*

Always fucking thanking him for the tiniest scrap of attention, but never saying what she really feels.

She pops on some lip balm and mascara and braces herself for Saskia's bossiness—the grief edition—while they wait for Jeremy's massive status car to arrive. Her phone beeps again and she's surprised to see Joss's name back on her screen.

Let me know when you're back and I'll come right over x

She reads and rereads the text. She's never wished more that she was in her grotty flat rather than a sprawling country estate. She wonders briefly how long it'll take to accompany Tansy's body back to London. Thank God she didn't follow all that TikTok advice.

Yes please, I could use a friend. Xx

She hesitated over the word "friend," but she needs to be casual about it; she can't go straight in thinking this is him coming over for anything more. They've known each other a long time, they have a history, he probably just wants to check she's OK. But that said, this is everything she's ever wanted. Everything she needs. Finally.

Her phone vibrates again almost immediately.

Sorry that last text was meant for Eva.

But I can come over if you need? When you get back.
Just let me know.

Oh God, the embarrassment. Of course she doesn't want to be some kind of sloppy seconds. She's not so desperate to be alone with him in her flat, just the two of them.

Yes please, she types. *Thank you, I will.*

She struggles to think of a time when she's hated herself more.

CHAPTER TEN

Farah hovers over the motorway service station toilet, trying her hardest to piss without any of her flesh so much as grazing its disgusting seat. It would be easier if her hands were free, rather than clutching the small Nokia burner phone as she balances, but she's been frantic the whole drive, worrying about what she's going to do with it. She's too nervous to put it down anywhere in case she forgets it.

Ever since the detective's announcement and Saskia's bombshell about Tansy's messages, the panic's been rising within her. That, combined with her financial worries, built to a climax while she was trapped in Jeremy's pristine tank-like car on the motorway. She'd felt as though the walls were closing in, her throat becoming increasingly scratchy and tight. She knew she needed to be alone to get rid of the phone somewhere anonymous, and the service station seemed like the best place to do it. But now she's here, she doesn't know how to dispose of it in a way that she can be confident no one will find it.

Her initial plan was to put it in one of the sanitary bins and destroy the SIM card, but then she remembered an article that she'd worked on a while back about what happens to menstrual waste. They can't process anything in those bins that isn't a tampon or a pad. Leaving a phone there would be the surest way for it to be found by someone.

She feels bad about it, of course she does. But Tansy was always going on about how well the café was doing, and she and Ivan seemed to have so much money. Farah thought £5,000 would be nothing, from the way she talked about the business. And really it was Tansy's fault that Farah had to go so extra in the first place. If she hadn't decided to have her wedding at the same time as Farah's, Farah wouldn't have had to throw so much more money at it. Especially as Tansy had freebies coming out of her ears after her post went viral. Really, Farah was just claiming compensation. Tansy was supposed to assume the texts were referring to the Botox she hid from Ivan, or one of her other silly secrets of recent years. And Farah couldn't have known that she would actually end up dead.

Having finished her wee as hygienically as possible, she knows she has to move fast if she's going to find somewhere else to dispose of the phone. She pulls up her leggings and flushes in one movement, then quickly washes her hands and doesn't bother drying them.

"Going to get some fresh air and stretch my legs. See you outside!" she shouts to the others, all still sequestered in their cubicles. She darts swiftly out of the door before one of them gets any ideas about joining her.

She races through the busy service station foyer, weaving in and out of the people milling around in a daze after spending hours cooped up in their overheated cars. In her attempt to get out before anyone sees her, she pushes through a family of five whose mother looks on the brink of meltdown. She feels bad about it but doesn't have time to apologize.

Outside, she shoves her tortoiseshell sunglasses over her reddened eyes and walks back in the direction of Jeremy's Range Rover, frantically searching for bins on her way. But there's never one when you need it, is there? She can see the car from here and thankfully no one's miraculously made it back there before her, so no one will see her if she heads off in a different direction. She loops around slightly to the right, spotting a bin in the distance, looking over her shoulder as she approaches, afraid of being watched. But apart from a family picnicking out of their car boot on the glamorous car park asphalt, there's no one to be seen. As she reaches into her pocket, her fingers clasped around the phone ready to take it out, a voice behind her makes her jump.

"Farah?" Jeremy's so-posh-it's-barely-comprehensible accent has its usual grating effect on her.

She spins around, face-to-face with his slicked-back dark hair and green eyes watching her like a hawk.

"What are you doing over here?" he asks.

"Looking for the car?" she says as if it's obvious. "Is it not just up there?"

"Back that way." He points behind her. "You walked right past it."

"Oh," Farah says, hoping she conveys shock. "Could have sworn it was over here. My sense of direction's so bad!"

"Ha!" Jeremy says jovially. "Saskia's terrible too. Must be something about you girls!"

He smiles at her in the smarmy, sarcastic way he's prone to when mocking them all for simply being female. It makes her literally want to smack him in the face; it always has done, ever since he came to their first shared house together and made fun of it.

When Jeremy and Farah arrive back at the car, she sees that everyone else has already returned and Eva's crying once again.

"Oh Eva," she says comfortingly, going to put her arm around her shoulders. As Joss's sister, she feels like she has a duty of care toward the girl, but she also finds all the crying incredibly jarring. If nothing else, it's making the rest of them feel like they aren't crying enough. Like they all need to be keeping up in the grief Olympics, especially considering how much longer they knew Tansy.

No one can tell how much Dominica's crying on account of the chic oversized black-rimmed sunglasses that cover most of her face.

She's never been one to show emotion, and she's already displayed far too much in the last twenty-four hours for her liking.

"I just . . . It's like a nightmare!" Eva weeps, clutching her phone.

Farah can see that Saskia and Dominica—despite the sunglasses—look furious, while Lauren stares blankly at her phone.

"What's happened?" she asks, studying their expressions.

"Ivan's posted about Tansy," Dominica says, gently prying the phone out of Eva's fingers and passing it over to Farah, the sun bouncing off her dark lenses.

On the screen is a picture of Ivan and Tansy from their engagement party, along with the lyrics from the wartime song "We'll Meet Again."

"It's just heartbreaking!" Eva says.

Dominica holds back from pointing out that people write song lyrics as captions when they don't have original thoughts or emotions of their own.

Lauren simply wonders why he's chosen a picture where half Tansy's face is obscured by his arm, despite his own face being fully visible and quite possibly airbrushed.

"I really think we need to get going," Jeremy says, butting in with a self-importance that gets Dominica's back up on a good day. "The sat nav's saying there's traffic in town now."

"He's right," Saskia says. She does a quick head count, doing a double-take when she counts one fewer than she expected and gasping to stop the air from tumbling out of her lungs when she remembers why. "The last thing we need is to be stuck in a traffic jam for hours after everything we've been through."

Dominica climbs back into the car to avoid calling Jeremy a pompous twat anywhere other than in her own head, and the others follow suit. Lauren glances at Eva's screen and sees a text from Joss appear just as Eva closes it.

I know baby. Just come home to me xx

She studies Eva's exhausted face as they settle back into the squeaky leather seats of the Range Rover and can't help noticing she's even a beautiful crier. Hag.

Dominica also studies Eva's face, but she's wondering whether it could have been Eva sending Tansy the messages. After all, what do they really know about this woman? And more to the point, what does she know about them? Her phone beeps for the millionth time this morning. She knows who the message is from, and she knows that he's panicking, but she simply doesn't have the mental capacity today. She does her seatbelt up and ignores the vibrations in her pocket.

CHAPTER ELEVEN

Lauren shoves the last bit of dirty (or clean; she's not entirely sure because it all just mixes into the same pile on her bedroom floor) washing into the laundry basket and sits on it to try and stop it all from spilling out. After flinging bleach down the toilet and cleaning the hair out of the bath plug, all that's left to do is dust off the one expensive candle she owns and light it. Oh, and get the Aesop hand soap out of the cupboard, of course. That'll need a dust-off too because she can't remember the last time she had occasion to roll it out. She wonders if it was when she had everyone round for a bridesmaid planning meeting for Farah a month ago. The same planning meeting where Tansy arrived late and revealed that she and Ivan had just got engaged. She'd wanted to tell them all in person and thought Farah would be thrilled to have another friend to experience all the giddy bride-to-be-ness with. It hadn't occurred to her that Farah might feel exactly the opposite, or that Farah, being Farah, would have planned everything so meticulously that any kind of disruption would throw her off dramatically.

She remembers Farah looking like she was going to fling Tansy off the balcony as she tried to keep everyone excited about the seasonal tablescapes she'd spent weeks preparing and was so proud of, while Tansy danced about excitedly showing everyone her ring. Farah's bridezilla behavior ramped up even more after that.

When no one's been round in a while, her flat truly starts to give off the vibe and smell of someone who owns multiple cats, though she's quite sure that no living thing could survive in here except for her and some very persistent black mold. Even that plant she had recently died within three weeks. Fortunately she's acclimatized to the level of neglect and negative energy that hangs in the atmosphere.

The last time she and Joss were alone here was definitely before he started going out with Eva. Lauren had been seeing a surfer guy for a couple of months and told everyone she really liked him despite knowing that he was going back to Australia. So when they inevitably broke up and he did of course go back to Australia, Joss came round to comfort her and the two of them ended up having sex. All part of her cunning plan. A month later, Tansy introduced him to Eva and that was that. No more sleepovers. Maybe they could have got back together if it weren't for Tansy. Or maybe not. As much as Lauren tries to deny it, Joss and Eva really do appear to have found love.

Her phone goes off and she sees the message that deep down she'd suspected she might get.

> *Hey, I'm sorry but I'm not going to make it over after all.*
> *Eva really needs me.*

She stares at the words. Of course he's staying with Eva. Eva who seems to have a PhD in the perfect emotional response to grief while still remaining attractive. Who *is* she anyway? Lauren doesn't trust her, and it's not just because of Joss. Well, maybe.

She goes to the kitchen and looks around for something to do that isn't just replying to him straightaway like a doormat. Opening the fridge, she sees it's empty aside from a few slices of pizza from two days ago and half a lemon. All of it from a time when Tansy was still here, she thinks, tears pricking at her eyes.

Her phone beeps again and she knows it's going to be another text from Joss, some pathetic excuse to try and keep her onside. It's like he wants to keep her in his pocket for later. She's become his spare.

Angrily, she ignores the beep and grabs the lemon. Standing at the tiny counter space with its peeling surface, she begins hacking away at the hardened flesh with a blunt knife. She's not even sure what she's doing. Gin, maybe? She thinks she's got some gin, just definitely no tonic. Fine, gin and a slice of lemon it is. Her phone beeps again and her rage increases. Gin and a slice of lemon and no texting Joss back. That's it, he's blown his last chance. She's not even going to look. If it weren't for the fact that she's in about five different wedding and hen do WhatsApp groups right now, she would definitely throw her phone out the window or shove it in the freezer or something.

Walking past the phone to get to the bottle of gin, though, she catches sight of the screen. In a split second, a flicker of the eyes, she sees all she needs to convince her to take a look. Her fingers reach for the phone before she has time to engage her brain and stop herself. A self-destructive muscle memory that she can't ignore.

> *I'm really sorry xx*
>
> *Could we do something in the week? Maybe I could take you for dinner or something? We could have a proper catch up like we used to? Xx*
>
> *Don't be cross at me Lozzie . . . xx*

Oh not cross, she replies, *sorry just got distracted by grief. Dinner sounds good, I could definitely use a chat. I miss Tansy.*

She knows she's laid it on a little thick. She wants to make him feel guilty, for him to realize that while he's with Eva, she's grieving a friend she's had for over thirty years. That's twenty-nine years longer than Eva was friends with her. And she's proud of her response, because at least she didn't thank him.

His reply pings through.

Tuesday? We'll go to that pasta place you like, my treat.

Before she can stop herself, she's typed: *Thank you.*

For fuck's sake. Throwing herself down on the sofa and pulling a blanket over her tired limbs, she thinks about getting a bottle of wine so that she's not just drinking straight gin with dried-up old lemon, but she doesn't fancy going out in the dark on her own. She's still feeling hugely on edge after what happened. Instead, she opens the Deliveroo app and finds a wine delivery service; she's not going outside just for a couple of bottles of Campo Viejo. She shivers as she thinks about the peach in the cacao, the missing EpiPen, the messages Tansy was receiving . . . her thoughts on a loop with the accompanying buzz of anxiety.

She heads to the kitchen, debating what she has that might double up as a weapon. The knife barely cut through the lemon, so although it's a good showpiece, it's not much use. In the end, she simply grabs the toaster and heads back to the sofa, cradling it. It's the heaviest appliance she owns.

She flicks through TV channels until she gets to a reality talent show that can suck her attention, giving her just enough stimulation to stop her from thinking relentlessly about Tansy and murder, the shortness of life, and the meaning of existence. She also scrolls through Eva's Instagram, wanting to investigate, trying to find something to confirm her suspicion that the influencer's not trustworthy, that she might have been blackmailing Tansy. But really, she's just sabotaging her own self-esteem once again.

CHAPTER TWELVE

2015

Lauren could have sworn she heard voices, but everyone else is out tonight. She told them she was going to a party, but in truth, without a job, she's been too poor to go anywhere. Staying in her room is the only way she can afford the rent. Hopefully not for much longer, though, because Tansy's new boyfriend, Rob, is a TV exec, and his company is looking for a runner. Tansy said he'd promised to give Lauren a recommendation. Working in TV is Lauren's absolute dream. She's applied for so many runner positions and been turned down that she was beginning to think it'd never happen. They've always gone to interns, already working in the industry for free. It felt like there was no way in for her until Rob came along. But now, for the first time in months, she feels hope that she might actually have a chance at getting the career she wants. Maybe a chance at turning her life around.

She sits up in bed at the sound of a man's voice again, trying to work out who it is. It's only 9 P.M., so someone's home early. She must have fallen asleep after crying over the end of *She's All That* when she realized she was never going to get someone like Freddie Prinze Jr. She can't even get Joss to commit to her properly. Her life is a sham. She feels something on her cheek and realizes a slice of pepperoni from the pizza she fell asleep eating has welded itself to her skin.

The voice travels up the stairs toward her. Definitely a man, but she can't hear any of the girls. What if it's an intruder? She reaches over and turns up her curling tongs to their max setting. She doesn't want to call the police in case she's being overdramatic, but she's also not going to investigate without protection.

The tongs now fully heated, she heads out into the hallway, brandishing them in front of her like a red-hot poker, ready to defend herself and her property. She hasn't gone far, though, when she hears the familiar tinkle of Tansy's laugh and sees the light under her door. Of course, it was Rob. He and Tansy must have come home early. She turns on her heel, ready to return to her pit of misery, but then hears her own name and freezes like a meerkat, not making a sound so that she can listen to the conversation in full.

"I just can't imagine Lauren working with that Magda woman. She's so savage," Tansy giggles.

"Magda's incredible. A real force of nature. But she's so good at her job because she takes no prisoners. That's how she's risen so high in TV so quickly. She could be a great role model for Lauren," Rob says, making Lauren smile.

Then she hears Tansy snorting with laughter.

"What?" Rob asks.

"Well, I mean . . . it's Lauren . . . I mean, she's just kind of . . . fragile. Like she cries at the drop of a hat. When Take That split up, she actually phoned that helpline they set up! My God, please promise me you'll look after her if she gets the job."

"Oh really?" Rob says.

"Well, yeah, especially working for someone like Magda. She gets upset so easily. She wouldn't do well with someone like that shouting at her. But that's part of why we love her so much, you know? She's a delicate soul, not like the others," Tansy goes on breezily. "Saskia and Dominica would give as good as they got with someone like Magda, and Farah would just make sure everything was so irritatingly perfect she couldn't criticize a single thing. Lauren, though . . ."

Lauren hates that she feels tears prickling at her eyes as if proving Tansy's point. Why is she saying these things to Rob? She knows how much Lauren wants that job. And also, Lauren wasn't the only one of them who phoned the Take That helpline. Farah definitely did, and according to Joss, she slept with a picture of Mark Owen under her pillow for a month.

"I'm sure she'll be fine. Especially as you'll look after her, right? For me?" Tansy putting on a baby voice as she says this makes Lauren want to launch in there and stab her in the face with the curling tongs.

"I see," Rob says. "I just wouldn't want to recommend someone who wasn't up to the job. I've got a reputation, you know. I'm kind of a big deal . . ."

"I know you are, big shot," Tansy says teasingly.

After that, the only things Lauren hears are the noises of kissing and gasping. The sounds of the two of them having sex. She can't believe Tansy's been so thoughtless over something so important to her.

Rob's uncertain tone replays in Lauren's head over and over as she heads back to her room to rewatch Freddie Prinze Jr. She'll never forgive Tansy if she's screwed this up for her. Never.

Lauren's standing in the kitchen, squinting in the morning light, waiting for the kettle to boil, as Rob comes past in his boxers. For a moment she considers not talking to him; she can't bear talking to the boyfriends in their pants. It's so awkward. Is she supposed to pretend that they're not just there with everything on show? But he grabs a glass off the side and comes to stand next to her, glugging down water. It would be weird for her not to talk to him now. Especially as he's doing her a favor with the job thing—as long as he still is after what Tansy said last night.

"Hey," he says while she stares intently at the boiling kettle.

"Hey," Lauren replies, trying to keep her eyes firmly up and away from his ample pant package. She knows she's going to have to dismantle all the bad work Tansy did on her behalf last night. She's going to have to seem businesslike and together, career-focused. "How's it going? I don't suppose you got a chance to do that recommendation for me?"

"Oh, about that." Rob's eyes don't reach Lauren's face as he talks. "They've actually already filled the position. I'm so sorry. I just wasn't fast enough. Things move quick in TV . . . it's . . . uh . . . cutthroat!"

"Oh right, yeah, no worries," Lauren says, staring back at the kettle. She hates that she can feel tears forming at the back of her eyes. But she won't give in to them. She can't be that pathetic person Tansy was describing last night. And even if that is who she is, she can't let him see it. She refuses to prove anyone right.

"Hey, look, if something else comes up—" he starts to say, but she cuts him off, sick of people's bullshit.

"Yeah, no worries." She's relieved when the kettle finally comes to a boil and she can busy herself with her coffee-making ritual.

She can feel him awkwardly shuffling off, back up the stairs. She hears the click of the bedroom door followed by the jarring tinkle of Tansy's laugh. Her best and oldest friend, and the person in the world who's betrayed her the most. She can't believe what she's done to her, just casually ruining her life with one careless comment. What kind of friend does that?

CHAPTER THIRTEEN

Farah sits across the desk from her boss in her huge glass office, trying to keep a neutral expression on her face. Rebecca said she wanted an update on the undercover article that Farah's been working on for her, which immediately set alarm bells ringing in her already frazzled head. She spent ages freaking out over what she was going to tell her, about why progress on it had stalled. But to her great relief, since she's been in here all they've discussed is Tansy. Like everyone else, Rebecca must have heard the news from either Ivan's or Eva's now viral grief posts on Instagram, and she's summoned Farah in here under the guise of official business because she wants to know more about it.

Behind her desk, Rebecca sits with her arms crossed, her huge thick-framed glasses perched on her nose, giving her the look of a stylish owl. Farah can feel the disappointment radiating from her, as if the story of one of her oldest friends dying from an allergic reaction isn't quite the scoop she'd hoped it would be. A small, terrible part of her did consider giving Rebecca a juicy tidbit about the text messages, or the detective's suspicion around the missing EpiPen. That might at least have got her boss off her back about the article, the one she's pretty sure is the only thing still keeping her employed. With the magazine in trouble, they're laying off almost all full-time staffers, and Farah knows she has to pull out the big guns to stay. But she just couldn't bring herself to use Tansy's death as some kind of story. At least she's still got some morals.

"How awful for you all, absolutely terrible," Rebecca says with a sincerity that makes Farah almost think she means it. "And such a small slip. Where was her EpiPen?"

"It must have fallen out of her bag at some point. We were all pretty plastered and downward-dogging all over the place." Farah finds herself sniffing. "We tried so hard to find it."

"God, you poor things, just horrific. I can't even imagine. And wasn't it supposed to be *your* hen do next weekend?" Rebecca moves on at speed from Farah's friend dying.

"Yes," Farah says, trying to keep her tone measured, because the other disaster this morning was a text from Saskia explaining that they were going to have to move her hen do. Not even a phone call, a text! If she's not careful, she's going to burst into tears, and she knows that tears make Rebecca uncomfortable.

"Just awful," Rebecca repeats, her red lips pursed back together in seconds, but she's clearly already distracted, their conversation having not revealed any scandalous details. She's even begun clicking on emails on her computer and swirling her mouse around. "Is there time before the big day to reschedule?"

"I hope so," Farah says, but she's already worked out that there isn't without moving things like dress fittings and hair and makeup trials, all of which cost money that she no longer has.

She honestly doesn't understand why they can't go away this weekend. Surely having something nice to do and celebrating her upcoming wedding would be a great mood lifter for the group. Tansy lived in the moment, flitting from one event to the next, never worrying what other people thought of her or what was appropriate. To be fair, this often annoyed her friends, but if her death has taught them anything, it's that they should live life to the fullest. And honestly, it's the least they could do after Farah forked out hundreds of pounds for the hen do so they could go to Ibiza even when people said they couldn't afford it.

"Well, I'm very sorry for you," Rebecca says. She clasps her red-manicured fingers together and gets ready to change the conversation to what she's really asked Farah in for this morning. "The surrogacy piece. Where are we? What's the update?"

For the last six months, Farah has been working on an exposé uncovering a surrogacy ring in the UK that's illegally trading babies for money. It was only a month ago that the CFO finally agreed to give her the budget to go undercover at the agency, making her own enquiries to try and gain some proof for what they all suspect has been going on. She was thrilled to be embarking on some proper journalism for the first time in ages, at least to start with.

"I'm still waiting for my appointment," she says, shifting in her seat.

"Gosh, wouldn't you think that with these people paying so much money, it would all be a bit quicker? Honestly, I'm quite shocked. Have they sent you a date?" Rebecca asks, her expensively highlighted hair swooshing over her shoulders.

"Yes, but it's not for another few months," Farah replies quickly.

"Well, maybe that's just as well. We may not even need that appointment," Rebecca says. "Don't ask me how, but I've managed to obtain something quite valuable to us in this investigation. In the next couple of days, we should be receiving a list of all the people who have used the service in the last ten years. Obviously we cannot tell *anyone* about this. No one in this office aside from you and me can know. The moment I get it, I'll be sure to send it straight over to you."

"Wow." Farah sits very still, taking it all in. She might not need to go to the clinic? She might not need to go undercover? "How did you—"

"Like I said, I can't tell you where it's come from." Rebecca looks firm, her eyes fixed in a hard stare. It's not the expression of someone who's about to help bring down a huge illegal surrogacy ring. Farah guesses it's not stylish to look excited these days. "Once we have the list, we can approach the people on it, try and get them to confirm what's gone on. We'll offer anonymity, obviously, and money as an incentive, which is where the twenty grand you were given for going undercover comes in. We'll need you to use that."

"Of course." Farah hopes she's looking grateful. After all, this article could be huge for her. If she can do it, if she can get the proof and get the story, it'll be one of the biggest exposés on surrogacy ever. And just the kick they need to save the magazine, and Farah's job. But the money might be an issue.

She didn't really think it through at the time, but now that the article is within reach, Farah realizes the gravity of what she's done. She really, really needs this job. It's never been a big-money career, but that was never the point—it used to be about the thrill of a good story, the glory of her colleagues' and friends' approval. She was the star of the office. But in the last few years, she hasn't had anything worth writing about. Her ideas dried up, her clicks were minimal, and Rebecca's disdain has been growing with every week, as has the looming threat of redundancy. So much hinges on this, not least the last scraps of loyalty and respect from her boss, and now Farah might have scuppered it all for herself.

"Right, I'm going to lunch," Rebecca says, leaning down and grabbing her bag as the clock ticks over to 1 P.M.

Farah used to be invited for lunch, but that stopped months ago. She knows she's on the way out if she doesn't nail this story. She heads back to her desk as Rebecca sweeps out of the building in her chic black shirtdress. Once she's sure she's in the clear, she opens up the wedding spreadsheet—not the one she shares with Toby, with just the costs they've paid for and what they haven't—but the real one. The one with the *actual* costs, as well as the loans and the maxed-out credit cards that she's taken out to make this dream wedding a reality. Her eyes zoom in on the sum that she added to the sheet last week. The one that came from the company bank account to hers and then straight out to the florist. She'd hoped that with Tansy's help she could at least pay five thousand of it back before anyone noticed. It wasn't the whole amount, and she still had no idea where the rest of it was going to come from, but at least it would have been a start. Now, though, without Tansy she's got nothing.

Her eyes scan the rest of the sheet, pausing at the money she put into the hen do. Money that has now just gone. She wanted to have the kind of do that people would be jealous of, that people would see pictures of and want to re-create. After years of being a loyal friend, never complaining, going to other people's weddings and paying a fortune for hen weekends, she wanted *her* time and she wanted it to be really special. Why shouldn't she have that? She looks at the other deposits on the spreadsheet highlighted in purple, huge five-figure sums that are all non-refundable, and grits her teeth. She's fucked, and if anything else moves she'll be even more fucked. She'll have to some-how hold Rebecca off until she finds a way to get that money.

She can't help it, the stress gets the better of her and she picks up her phone, firing off several angry texts to her friends about the Ibiza weekend before she closes her spreadsheet, stands up from her desk, and marches purposefully out of the office. She needs to get rid of her other phone, the burner, and the SIM card as quickly and neatly as possible. It's been wearing a hole in her bag all morning, like a bomb that's about to go off.

Outside, she walks down the Strand to a small set of steps. At the top is a square that she knows will be quiet. On her way up the steps, she stops briefly, completely alone. She takes the phone out of her pocket, removes the SIM card, and scratches at it with her house key until its surface looks damaged. Then she puts the phone on the ground and stamps on it repeatedly and aggressively until its screen and buttons smash. It takes a few goes to crack the old Nokia—it's built like concrete—and she hurts her foot, but eventually it's done. She continues up the stairs to the square, where all she can see is an old man in a suit eating sandwiches from a small plastic box. Passing him as if on her way somewhere important, she tosses the SIM and the phone into a nearby bin. As she walks away, she feels a relief she thought would never come.

Dominica reaches the office after a successful morning in court and flings her phone down on her desk. She can't believe that Farah's kicking off about them moving her hen do. Of *course* they weren't going to be able to go to Ibiza the week after their friend died like that. They can't just up and leave the bloody country. How can she even think about her wedding when Tansy's dead? She's behaving like a spoiled little bitch. Has being a bridezilla taken over her senses so much that she no longer feels fear or grief?

Dominica had been in a reasonably good mood before she received that text from Farah, all in block capitals, explaining that the entire run-up to her wedding was now ruined and she wasn't even sure she wanted to get married anymore. Which is attention-seeking bullshit, of course, but Farah's occasionally prone to that if things don't go exactly the way she wants them to. She pretends to be so cool and calm, but the people who really know her, who have known her all her life, know that isn't the case. Her lip twitches on the right-hand side when she's stressed and trying to hide it, for example. Dominica remembers the first time she noticed that, after Tansy lost her virginity the same day Farah got a journalism work experience placement. And since her transition to bridezilla, she's barely even mentioned Toby. Sweet, funny

Toby, her actual groom. He's always been quiet, but recently he's completely faded into the background of her plans, as if Farah considers him some kind of wedding bonus rather than a main component. Dominica doubts he'll be getting anything *he* wants at the wedding, if he can even remember that he has preferences in the first place.

Her secretary comes in, placing some fresh files on the desk ready for her next appointment, just as Dominica's phone starts to buzz so vigorously it's in danger of dropping off the table.

"Hello," she sighs, answering the group FaceTime.

"What the fuck is going on?" Farah falls straight into her rage. "Saskia's just texted me asking if I'd be OK if we had my hen AFTER the wedding. HOW IS THAT A THING? Is this it now? Is my wedding just going to be whatever scraps of joy we can salvage in this mess?"

"I mean, Tansy is actually dead," Lauren says calmly.

"OF COURSE I KNOW TANSY'S DEAD! FOR FUCK'S SAKE, LAUREN!" Farah shouts into the screen, and the two of them can see right up her nostrils.

"HEY!" Dominica scolds back, using her best family court voice. "Don't shout at Lauren! None of this is her fault!"

Lauren looks on the verge of tears, and as usual Dominica feels compelled to leap to her defense, though what she really wants to do is tell Lauren to pull herself together. It annoys her how much she lets people walk over her.

"Sorry, Lauren," Farah says. "I just mean that yes, our friend has died, but doesn't that mean we need some time together to recuperate? To heal?"

Dominica knows she means *don't I deserve to be pampered and fawned over like the princess bride-to-be that I am,* because everything since Farah got engaged has been about her wedding. She just can't believe she's made Tansy's death about her wedding too.

"I mean, even Joss was saying to Eva that he thinks I deserve that. EVEN JOSS! And he point-blank tells me I'm a prick three times a day and has done since he could talk!"

And yet it hasn't sunk in, Dominica thinks cattily. She loves Farah, but in this moment she is behaving exactly like an entitled prick.

Dominica searches her desk for her emergency vape or a rogue packet of cigarettes from one of the many nights she's ended up back in her office, pissed, doing unspeakable things on her desk with unspeakable people. Finding a cigarette, she pops it in her mouth and heads outside, ready to take her frustration out on her poor lungs. When she dies young or gets that cat's-bum mouth old smokers get, she'll be sure to tell Farah it was her fault.

"Are you not worried about the murderer?" Lauren asks in a small voice.

"Why is everyone assuming it's murder?" Farah asks. "It was an allergy!"

"Because someone was blackmailing her, we couldn't find her EpiPen, and I don't think cacao's supposed to have peach in it," Dominica says, trying not to snap.

"Oh my god, Dom, don't smoke, it's so bad for your skin," Lauren says, sucking on a cigarette outside her dusty office block in Shoreditch.

"Pot, kettle . . ." Dominica says, lighting up and exhaling the smoke into the phone screen.

"I'm not smoking until after the wedding," Farah says, taking a cigarette out of her pocket and lighting it up there and then. "BUT YOU SEE WHAT THIS HAS DONE TO ME?! Anyway, Lauren, you don't actually believe that it was murder, do you?" She screws up her face and Lauren and Dominica squint at her.

"Er, well . . . I mean, I don't know?" Lauren says awkwardly.

"Besides, if it was, then who did it?" Farah inhales crossly on her cigarette before folding her arms and staring into the phone screen expectantly. "Saskia? Couldn't bear that Tansy was embarrassing her, so she offed her?" She laughs like this is ridiculous, which it normally would be, if their friend hadn't maybe just been murdered at her own hen party.

"I mean, I wouldn't put it past her . . ." Dominica mutters.

"Well, we don't know, do we," Lauren says. "It could have been any of those people we were out in the woods in the middle of nowhere with!"

"But *why* would someone want to murder Tansy?" Farah asks.

"Not to speak ill of the dead, but she did often piss people off without realizing," Dominica says.

"Dominica!" Lauren protests, but then relents. "I guess she sometimes didn't realize when her 'floaty and cool' behavior was getting people's backs up. Like when she went on that date with a farmer and talked about being vegan for the whole thing and he pointed out that people like her were the reason his farm was probably going to have to close down in the next two years."

"Or when Saskia had that massive posh housewarming party so she could make friends with her Holland Park neighbors and Tansy got drunk and told some Neighborhood Watch guy about the time at uni when Saskia got caught by the police urinating on the street and had to pay a hefty fine," Dominica laughs.

"Oh, that's less funny, though," Farah says. "Saskia's still not been allowed into the Neighborhood Watch group. She tells people it's because she's too busy, but it kills her."

"Poor dear," Dominica says sarcastically. "What a terrible hardship that must be."

"Has anyone actually heard from the police since the weekend?" Farah asks.

"Nope," Lauren says.

"Me neither," Dominica says.

"Well then, they'd surely be a bit more vocal if they really thought it was murder!" Farah says.

"They have to do a postmortem to establish cause of death before anything else," Dom says knowledgeably.

The women suck on their cigarettes in silence. Farah hates the way Dominica lords it over them sometimes. She's watched *Silent Witness* too; she knows what a postmortem is.

"Anyway, I told Saskia no, to the hen do after the wedding," Farah says. "She said that you guys will plan something else but I just wanted to point out that the wedding is only two months away. AND I don't want a puffy alcohol face for the big day, so please, whatever it is you're planning, don't make it too close to then. Capiche?"

"Yes, ma'am," Dominica says, rapidly losing patience.

"Sorry, so neither of you are actually worried about the murderer?" Lauren asks, lighting up a second cigarette straight from her first.

"I mean, not really," Farah says. "Tansy had an allergic reaction and her EpiPen fell out of her bag somewhere when she was pissed. I just think murder's a bit dramatic."

"But the police seemed . . ." Lauren sees how annoyed Farah looks so stops talking.

Dominica glances up from the phone and feels a jolt of adrenaline as she sees him approaching across the courtyard, his blue jacket blowing in the wind, brown shoes clacking on the cobbles.

"What'll happen with the funeral?" Lauren cuts through her distraction. "Surely we need to know when that is before we plan dates for the hen do?"

Farah's face starts to turn a little red and Dominica knows her stress levels are about to implode as she faces the possibility of fitting in another event before the wedding of the century. She also knows she needs to end this call before he reaches her; she can't risk them noticing him.

"I don't know," she says hurriedly, exhaling smoke. "But I think that'll depend on when they're done with the body. They'll probably have more questions either way, though, so we need to be prepared for that."

"Do you think Saskia's going to give us another lecture on not accidentally slipping up and telling anyone our darkest secrets?" Lauren asks flippantly.

"Probably." Dominica rolls her eyes. "As if after nearly twenty years one of us would just forget to keep quiet. Anyway, guys, I have to go. My next client's here," and she hangs up on them abruptly.

She stamps out the cigarette under her black LK Bennett heel. When he reaches her, a broad smile on his face, she knows he's about to mention it, using it to his advantage in one of their games that he's so fond of.

"Naughty girl—don't think I didn't see you smoking," he teases, leaning against the side of the building. He nods toward one of the narrow alleyways leading off the courtyard. It's not glamorous, but it's a place they've been to before, far enough away from Dominica's office to mean none of her colleagues will see them there.

With a swift look around, Dominica darts down the alley. She needs to be quick before her next meeting.

"I've got ten minutes," he breathes into her ear, his green eyes sparkling with mischief. "And I've got some sexual tension that I really need to dispose of before my next client."

"Oh great, that's really romantic," Dominica says.

"Dom, we both know you're not here for romance. You're here for a hard cock and a good time."

"Correct," she purrs.

As he pushes up against her, pawing at her like a rabid bear, she thinks of what the others would say if they knew what she was doing right now.

. . .

Dominica is on her way back to the office when she gets the text from the detective at Scotland Yard who she used to sleep with. She'd asked him to keep an ear out for anything to do with Tansy's case. Opening his text, she feels her heart stop, the words jumping out and practically smacking her in the face.

The DI thinks it's murder. Peach was only present in the victim's cup. EpiPen yet to be found. You'll all get called in soon, but you didn't hear it from me. Delete this text when you've read it.

CHAPTER FOURTEEN

2016

"HAPPY WEDDING DAY!" Lauren screams as soon as the door to Saskia's hotel room opens. "Oh!" She deflates slightly at the sight that greets them.

Dominica, Farah, Tansy, and Lauren had expected to be the first here, what with Saskia telling them to arrive at nine, but as the door opens wider, the four of them can see that her other bridesmaids, Verity, Lavinia, and Anastasia—the Holland Park contingent—have obviously been here for ages.

"Come in," Verity says with a tight smile.

Since moving in with Jeremy last year, Saskia's spent more time with her new friends than her old ones. When she announced that she was getting married, Dominica, Farah, Tansy, and Lauren were of course expecting to be her bridesmaids. What they weren't expecting was for there to be three other bridesmaids, and for those bridesmaids to completely take over. Dominica had even started referring to the four of them as the B-list, while Lavinia and her tribe were clearly A-list.

"Oh, hi!" Lavinia looks disconcerted to see them. As if they're somewhere they weren't invited.

The contrast between the two groups could not be more obvious.

Lavinia, Verity, and Anastasia in matching silk Team Bride robes with their names delicately embroidered across the back, their hair already set in rollers and their makeup halfway to being done. While Dominica, Lauren, Tansy, and Farah all display the telltale signs of hangovers, including Dominica's gigantic pair of oversized Chanel sunglasses, Tansy's panda eyes, and Farah's traces of smudged and persistent red lipstick from last night. Lauren stands sucking on a huge strawberry lace to try and combat the low blood sugar that hangovers give her, while Dominica has a packet of cigarettes in her pocket ready to dole out during the first black coffee of the morning.

"Here she is!" Tansy exclaims at Saskia's reflection in the huge gold mirror she's sitting in front of in her white silk bridal robe.

The four of them walk through the pristine suite, the only things in the room that aren't made of white silk or smelling like a floral meadow.

"You're glowing!" Lauren gushes as they reach Saskia at the giant mirror.

"Really beautiful!" Farah agrees.

"Oh my God! Look at you four!" Saskia's mum emerges from a hair and makeup fog to hug the women one by one. "Gosh, Farah! I always assumed we'd be at your wedding first. You and Toby have been together such a long time."

"Haha, yeah," Farah says, biting at the remnants of red lipstick. This isn't the first time someone's made this comment in the run-up to Saskia's wedding.

"Well! I'm sure it'll be you next." Saskia's mum winks and walks off back to the Holland Park A-team.

"How do you look so good?!" Dominica peers over her sunglasses at Saskia, the glare of the sun-drenched room almost turning her to dust like a vampire.

"I only had one glass of wine with dinner last night," Saskia says, plucking a grape from the bunch in front of her. "I didn't want to feel rough on my big day."

"No one wanted to ruin Saskia's big day by being hungover, did they?" Verity says from behind them, bringing Saskia a glass of fresh orange juice. Her voice is sickly sweet but she knows her words are venomous.

"Right," Dominica says, while the other three smile and nod sheepishly. Lauren wonders if she might actually be sick any minute, and the only things in her eyeline that would take the hit are white.

"Two hours until kick-off! I hope you're all going to be ready in time," Anastasia says from her seat next to Saskia, where she's being preened and primped by a makeup artist and hair stylist.

"We brought our stuff with us," Dominica says, the only one of them with the confidence to speak up around the three witches of west London. "We presumed we'd all be getting ready together."

"Mmm." Verity puts on her best fake show of concern. "It's just a little bit small in here." She gestures around the substantial suite. "And we thought maybe we'd get ready in here and you guys could get ready in there." She points to a small room just off the suite, barely big enough to house them all. "You can do your own hair and makeup, right?"

Dominica's about to open her mouth to speak again when Lavinia starts talking over her. "It really is the best option, especially to keep things stress-free in here for Saskia," she says, ignoring Dominica's incredulous expression. "Which as her friends is obviously what we all want, right?"

"No stress or fuss for the bride," Anastasia parrots.

"Right," Farah says as the four of them look at each other in confusion.

Undeterred, Dominica stares straight at Saskia, but her friend doesn't turn around. She knows Saskia can hear everything that's going on, but she's pretending she can't for some reason. Dominica's eyes burn into the back of Saskia's now entirely blonde head, not a hint of her beautiful red mane left in sight since her big west London makeover, and thinks that just because she's the bride doesn't give her carte blanche to be a prick.

"Right then, if that's what you want, Saskia, we'll head into that small room there. IF THAT'S WHAT YOU WANT?" She says the last bit as clearly and loudly as she possibly can, just trying to get a response from Saskia, trying to get her to own that she's being a complete dickhead right now. But Saskia simply goes on showing the hair stylist a strand of her hair that seems to have come dislodged from her curlers.

"She's a bit busy," Anastasia says.

"Come back when you're ready," Verity echoes.

"FINE!" Dominica says, turning abruptly on her heel and stomping out, Tansy, Lauren, and Farah following close behind, throwing death stares back at Saskia.

"We'll order champagne for breakfast and charge it to the happy couple," Farah mutters on her way out.

"This is so not what love's supposed to be about," Tansy says slyly.

"Farah! Oh my god, I so thought it would be you and Toby getting married first! What happened? Is he just not the marrying type?" Saskia's cousin says, spotting them on her way past.

"Haha! Yeah! Right!" Farah says, her teeth already gritted to the hilt.

"Can you believe the nerve of that fucking prick?" Dominica says, draining the table's bottle of red into her glass. "And then she puts us BEHIND THEM IN THE PHOTOS!"

Tansy, Lauren, Dominica, and Farah have been seated at a table together for the reception, but it's quite a way from the top table. It feels like the final insult in a day full of insults, including (but not limited to) being put at the back of all the pictures, having to get ready on their own, and being ushered so far off to the side of the congregation during the ceremony that they were practically out of the church.

"They won't last," Lauren says sagely, eyeing the other bridesmaids, who are of course just next to the top table, with their Holland Park husbands who are all the spit of Jeremy. "They're not forever friends like we are. We've known her all this time, they're just new and shiny. She'll regret those pictures when she's older and barely remembers who they are. They're just a novelty."

"It's like now she's met Jeremy and she's rich again we're nothing to her," Tansy says, narrowing her eyes. "Material things can only make someone so happy, you know."

"It's weird, when you see him with his family and friends he doesn't seem that posh because they're all just like him. He just seems like a regular prick," Farah says, squinting at Saskia's brand-new husband across the room. She's had far more champagne than she intended to already and they're not even at the speeches yet. She's lost count of the number of people who have expressed surprise that Toby hasn't popped the question yet, staring at her ring finger in search of a diamond then giving her a sympathetic look, or worse, telling her that getting married isn't everything and just because she and Toby aren't the type doesn't mean they're any less in love. Oblivious to all of this, Toby's been having a great day.

"A plethora of pricks," Dominica observes. She's really held herself back today, when on any other day she would have stood up to Saskia, for the sake of the others as much as herself.

"His friend told me he's got a fear of pubes," Tansy says, closing one eye to try and improve her vision while she takes a drink.

"When were you talking to his friends? Which friend?" Dominica frowns, nervous about any of them fraternizing with the other side.

"The best man, when I gave him a blow job in the disabled loo,"

Tansy says casually, downing the rest of her glass as if washing her mouth out.

"TANS!" Lauren scolds her in a whisper. "That's Lavinia's husband!"

"Hahahahahaha," Dominica cackles, almost falling off her chair and being steadied by Farah's unsteady hand.

"He didn't mention it." Tansy shrugs. "I thought I was just doing my duty as a bridesmaid."

"You're bad," Farah says, tapping her arm with proud affection. Fuck the smug already-married people, she thinks.

"Oh God. What are you four up to? You're looking decidedly dangerous," Joss says as he and Toby arrive back from having a smoke.

"Just talking about how Jeremy has a fear of pubes," Farah tells them as Toby sits down next to her, slightly propping her up in the process and giggling at her revelation.

"Oh wow, that's gotta be tricky," Joss says. "So, Saskia has to have NO pubes then."

"I hadn't even thought of that." Tansy's eyes sparkle.

"Trust my brother to have turned the conversation to who does or does not have pubes," Farah says, despite being the one who told him about it in the first place. "Where did your date go anyway?"

"She has departed," he says, taking a sip of his whisky. "It wasn't really working out."

"You didn't even make it to dessert!" Farah scolds.

"I'm just not a commitment guy!" Joss says, catching Lauren's eye across the table as she swoons at him in his suit. Officially the hottest she's ever seen him look.

"Dessert isn't a commitment," Farah chastises in a way she often finds herself doing with her brother.

Across the room, the tinkling of a fork against a crystal champagne glass casts a ripple of silence and the whole room stops, turning to the top table.

"This'll be good," Dominica mutters as the best man stands up. "Oh look, Tansy, it's your new friend!"

With the room completely silent, the best man and Tansy's toilet companion stands to address the reception.

"Farah! Gosh, always thought you two would be married first!" Saskia's uncle Derek whispers on his way past her.

"Yes, yes, hahaha." Farah raises her glass to him as he passes and downs her champagne. When she does get married it's going to be the biggest wedding any of these fuckers have ever seen.

"Ladies and gentlemen, we'd like to kick off the speeches now. So if you could all make sure you have a glass of something, the groom would like to say a few words first."

Dominica's eyes roll back in her head at the patriarchy of it all. Every single man at that top table will speak, but not one woman will be permitted to address the reception. If she was getting married, she'd never let that happen.

Jeremy stands, rebuttoning his suit jacket and adjusting his cufflinks in the way expensive men do, as if flashing their wealth from their wrists, then slicks back his already far too slicked hair.

"Crumpy and I would love to thank you all for coming today," he begins in his public-schoolboy voice. No one knows why he calls Saskia Crumpy. It's got nothing to do with her name and none of them have been able to work out where it came from or why it's acceptable for him to say it in public. Apart from the fact that posh people just do this. They just give someone a random name and think it's funny. "When Crumpy and I first met, I'm not saying she was on the poverty line, but she was living in a house share in east London, hahahahaha." Everyone in the room laughs, with the exception of Dominica, Tansy, Lauren, and Farah, who only moved out of that place last month. It was a lovely house, with a cleaner who came once a fortnight, and a small but well-tended garden, close to London Fields and Broadway Market. Now a pretty expensive area to live in, actually, Farah thinks bitterly.

She's pleased Tansy gave one of those women's husbands a blowy. Probably the first thing Tansy's done in a while that hasn't pissed her off. Especially considering that on the day that Farah was FINALLY promoted at work last week, Tansy said that was such great news because she was opening a fucking café and now Farah could bring all her important sources there. As if Farah would bring anyone to a vegan café. Tansy was just pissing all over her news, again, with her own announcements. It's like she does it on purpose.

"I remember thinking, 'God, I have got to get her out of this hell-hole!' And so I did. I saved this little scrap! I brought her back to Holland Park and dedicated my life to giving her the life she deserves. Because our Crumpy deserves one hundred and ten percent!"

"You can't get more than a hundred percent," Farah whispers bitterly, swigging wine. "One hundred percent is complete."

"Prick," Dominica mutters. She hates the way Saskia's smiling up at him admiringly while he patronizes her.

Across the reception, while his wife is enthralled by Jeremy's bullshit speech about his own bullshit greatness, his best man winks in Tansy's direction, prompting all the women at the table to wink back at him. He does a double-take and has the decency to look shaken by the response.

"Saskia, you make me proud every single day, but especially today. I know that every day with you I will be living my best life, smashing my goals and achieving that bonus. Hahahaha!" As he laughs at his own pitiful joke, so do several of the other finance bros in the room. "You've made our house a home. Crumpy, I love you, and I can't wait to get you up the duff so we can have our own mini Crumpys and Lumpys!"

There's a collective "aww" around the room that thankfully covers the gagging of Dominica, Farah, Tansy, and Lauren.

"So much of posh weddings are about the woman producing an heir." Dominica looks disgusted. "It's gross."

"I'm going back out for another cigarette," Joss says as soon as the speeches are over. "This whole thing's very 'get married, procreate, and die.' I feel claustrophobic."

As he stands up, Lauren knows that she's going to find a reason to sneak off in about ten seconds and follow him out.

"Dare you to go over, hug Jeremy, and spit in his champagne without him noticing," Dominica says to Farah.

"I'll shake his hand but I shan't hug him," Farah compromises, squinting.

"Deal," Dominica says as Farah stalks off on her mission, Toby egging her on.

"I need a wee," Tansy says, laughing. "I got a bit distracted when I was in the loo before."

Walking across the dance floor, she sees her blow-job buddy leaning over to give his wife a loving kiss and does wonder if she should feel a little bad about having just sucked him off. But really it's not her problem, is it? She's free and single and he literally presented himself to her. She can't go checking every man's availability before seizing an opportunity that they're ready and willing to give. Besides, Lavinia's a real bitch.

In the toilet she's relieved to be away from all the posh people, especially the rival bridesmaids, and to momentarily escape the disappointment of seeing one of her best friends not only marrying a posh twat but turning into one as well. As she flushes the toilet, she hears a door slamming and the noise of someone crying. Before leaving her cubicle, she peers under the door, nervous that it might be the best man's wife, having discovered their escapade. But it's not her; instead it's Saskia's wedding shoes that she sees. Adjusting her dress swiftly, Tansy rushes out to her aid.

"Saskia! What's up?" she asks. "What's happened?"

Saskia simply shakes her head. Tansy goes back into the cubicle to fetch some toilet paper. Handing it over, she puts an arm around her friend's shoulders. Saskia blows her nose and looks up at her, eyes glassy.

"Oh Tansy! You have to promise not to tell anyone!" she says.

"I promise," Tansy agrees, nervous about what could be wrong with her friend on the supposedly happiest day of her life.

"It's Jeremy! I just found out he . . . he . . ." Saskia can't get the words out for crying. She flings her head onto Tansy's shoulder, wailing while Tansy gently strokes her hair.

"Whatever he's done, you can leave, you don't have to stay," Tansy says, but Saskia stops crying abruptly and stares up at her like she's mad.

"I can't leave . . . I can't leave my life!" she wails, before throwing herself dramatically back into Tansy's arms and continuing to sob.

Across the hotel, in the gift room, Lauren and Joss shag among the presents, Joss propping Lauren's arse on an 8L, cast-iron Le Creuset casserole dish.

CHAPTER FIFTEEN

Three weeks after Tansy's death and just one week after they were finally able to lay her to rest, the four women stand in a sunny London square, once more on the precipice of a hen do.

Since Tansy's death was declared a murder investigation, the police don't seem to have made much headway. All the women know from countless interviews with them is that the peach was only present in Tansy's cup—not any of the others—and that the lost EpiPen is yet to be found.

Despite the fact that they're still none the wiser as to who murdered Tansy, the women wait nervously (and who can blame them) outside a swanky London hotel, ready to embark on a weekend of spa treatments all in aid of spoiling Farah. In spite of her protestations that there was no time before the wedding, she's managed to find time for today's treat with just her closest bridesmaids before her dress fitting tomorrow. It was Saskia's idea, to try and soften the blow of cancelling Ibiza.

"TA-DA!" Saskia says, spreading her arms in front of the boutique Georgian townhouse hotel.

"WOW!" Farah hopes she sounds enthusiastic, because internally she's feeling more than a little disappointed.

When they told her that she was going to be having a spa do at a hotel in London, with a small, perfectly curated group of her hens, she had assumed it would be somewhere fancy—maybe the Savoy or Claridge's. But this isn't either of those. It's nice enough, but it's not going to look as impressive on Instagram as the Savoy would have done. How are people supposed to be jealous or feature her hen do in one of those "Top 10 London Wedding" articles if she's just in a random hotel that no one's ever heard of?

"And this is just part one!" Saskia announces, as if unveiling a big cake. "Part two next week will be HUGE!" Dominica watches on admiringly as the lie falls seamlessly out of Saskia's mouth.

They all know that there's currently absolutely nothing planned for next weekend, which is when they've promised Farah a much bigger part two to this charade.

"Jeremy's paid for us all to stay the night—and you, missy, are sleeping in the bridal suite! Isn't that wonderful!!" Saskia forges on with her faux positivity.

Her friends all stand grinning at Farah encouragingly, but she doesn't buy it. She knows that they know this is a shit substitute for the incredible designer villa with live-in chef that they'd booked in Ibiza. The villa you have to reserve two years in advance. She also knows they know that anything they could come up with now will be a poor second. The stakes were high and they went far too low.

Saskia's aware that this isn't what Farah wanted, but she does think she could look a little more grateful. It's not been easy to plan Farah's hen dos, especially with her business in the shadow of Tansy's murder. She would have thought they could *all* be a bit more grateful, actually. Especially Farah: she's normally far more well-mannered.

"We're starting with massages and facials!" Lauren says excitedly.

"And then moving on to Prosecco in the jacuzzi and whatever other treatments you want," Eva says cheerfully. It's taken a while, but Eva's tears do seem to have finally dried. At least in public anyway.

Lauren can't bloody believe she's at another hen do with Eva. Fair play, she's dating the bride's older brother, but does she have to *always* be here? Rubbing her beauty and her boyfriend in Lauren's face all day? She probably looks incredible in a bikini too. Lauren just doesn't need that.

"And we're booked in for dinner at the restaurant tonight. Apparently the chef's Michelin starred or something. The bar's great." Dominica waves her hand airily.

"Wow," Farah says, feigning excitement about this hotel that she's never heard of and certainly never seen a celeb checking into. But as they go inside, she concedes it is quite chic. There's a chandelier in the entrance hall, and it's decorated tastefully. There's that at least. Maybe she could say it's exclusive and that's why no one's ever heard of it. A secret that only the highest class of people know about. She could put this place on the map. "Who else is coming?"

"It's just us," Dominica says, gesturing to the five of them.

"And Jen and Helen," Saskia adds, which even Dominica and Lauren look surprised by.

She points into the reception area, where Jen and Helen are waving excitedly. Farah tries to look pleased to see them, but she doesn't really understand why they're there. They're Tansy's friends; she only hung out with them once or twice before Camp Chakra, so why would Saskia think she wanted them at her hen do? If Jen and Helen are here, then why couldn't she have had Tina and Izzy, who she actually lived with at uni and still speaks to regularly?

"A small group definitely minimizes the chance of anyone else getting murdered," Dominica says a little too loudly, her words echoing around the marble-floored, wood-panelled lobby, gaining the attention of the other people waiting there.

Farah grits her teeth. None of *her* friends are murderers, not like Tansy's clearly are. Which is exactly why Jen and Helen shouldn't be here. Is it really a "perfectly curated" group? Or have people been scared off by Tansy's murder? She feels her fists clench, thinking about all the other hen dos that she's been forced to attend for people who "couldn't make it" today, and considers sitting them out in the hallway for the reception. She's going to adopt a zero-tolerance policy for those who don't come next week for sure.

Besides, what are people afraid of? It's not like lightning is going to strike twice, is it? Surely someone getting murdered at a hen do isn't a regular occurrence? So why would it happen again?

"Just think of it as a small but perfectly formed group of people that we know aren't cold-blooded killers!" Dominica whispers into Farah's ear.

"I still reckon it was someone at the camp that killed her," Eva says, her eyes tearing up again at just the mention of it.

"Felix and/or Florence if you ask me," Jen says, nodding sagely and sniffing.

"Felix was pretty shifty." Eva nods, sniffing in synchronization.

Dominica still doesn't trust Eva; they really don't know her that well. She catches Lauren looking like she's thinking the same as Eva wipes her watery eyes.

"I can't find a motive for them, though." Helen shakes her head. "I've been doing some research, trying to work out who it might have been, and those two were obviously first on my list."

"She's become the hairdressing version of Nancy Drew," Jen says. "By day she's giving wolf cuts, by night she's googling murder."

"Surely that's just going to make the police think you did it if they ever look at your search history?" Dominica says sensibly.

"Oh my God, but she has actually found some huge stuff out. Tell them!" Jen says excitedly.

Farah wonders if this is why the two of them are on her hen do, just so that they can do more amateur detecting like twats, and if that's the case, they can turn straight back around and go home. She will uninvite them herself. Is it too much to ask for just one day to be about her and her wedding? After everything she's been through?

"Tansy didn't have any money!" Helen blurts out. "Her business was going under. The café may be shut because she died, but even if she'd survived, it would have closed within days. I walked past the other day and there was a sign from the bank on there, and when I did some digging, it turns out she was bankrupt!"

Dominica frowns. She's not even sure why Jen and Helen are here—she thinks Farah's hung out with them maybe twice? She watches Farah's lip twitch whenever they talk.

"I called Ivan the other day," Helen says. "Boy, is he a mess! Did you see his Instagram post?"

"No?" Lauren says.

"Look!" Jen says, scrolling through her phone. "He reckons this pigeon he keeps seeing in the park is Tansy reincarnated."

"That pigeon's got one leg and mange." Dominica narrows her eyes. "It's not a reincarnation, it's an insult."

"Reincarnation doesn't happen that quickly," Eva says seriously, blinking. "That pigeon's fully grown; she would only just have been reborn."

"Honestly, he's all over the place," Jen says. "I genuinely think he's one of those people that in a few years' time we're going to find out has had an anatomically correct sex doll of Tansy made and is just living with it like it's a real person. Anyway, Helen's working on a system to find out who the murderer is."

"Oh?" Saskia asks curiously.

"Yeah, I mean I can't say too much obviously," Helen says. "But if the peach wasn't in everyone's cup, then it either has to have been added to her empty cup or her full cup. I've got several theories as to how it might have got in there. I just need to act each one out and time them and the speed of the reaction, and then I reckon I can crack it."

The women stare at her, momentarily taken aback by the logic of it all.

"Aaanyway, should we maybe go into the spa? I'm guessing they're waiting for us," Farah says, trying to move on. All she's ever trying to do is move on. If she keeps moving, maybe she can forget the fact that the hair and makeup trial she cancelled so that they could go away next weekend has cost her another three hundred pounds.

"Of course!" Saskia says, clapping briskly.

"You are so brave." Eva clutches Farah's hands in her own and stares deeply into her eyes. "The way you just carry on. So, so brave," she repeats mournfully.

Lauren wants to tell her to shut up. She's barely heard from Joss since the Saturday after Tansy's death, and he never came good on his promise of dinner. The only time she's seen him was at Tansy's funeral last week, where he was surgically attached to Eva, though he did manage to send her a text asking if she was all right, obviously. Every time Eva speaks, Lauren edges closer to wondering why he's with her. What could they possibly have in common? Lauren once read him his horoscope over coffee, and he called it woo-woo bullshit for gullible people with no meaning in their lives. And now he's dating someone with a prescriptive knowledge of reincarnation.

"Thank you," Farah says, trying to look her most grateful.

"SELFIE!" Eva shouts, pulling her into an Instagram story with a tacky hen-do filter, complete with L plates and penis straws, that makes Saskia itch just to look at it.

As Farah pulls away, she feels her phone vibrating in her pocket. She knows already who it's going to be, and she doesn't want them hounding her all day, the same way they've been hounding her for the last few days. The only way to stop them is to respond right away. She turns away from the group, opening the text. Sure enough, it's from Rebecca.

Don't forget what I need you to do for me today.

Great, Farah types. *Thanks for the hen do wishes.*

Rebecca replies immediately. *I mean, I'd have thought you'd be a bit more grateful considering the alternative. Unless you have that money for me?*

Farah had eventually been caught out by Rebecca when she had cornered her this week. The list of people who had used the illegal clinic had arrived, and Rebecca had asked where the twenty grand undercover money was. The only problem was that the money was still gone. Farah hadn't been able to replace it after borrowing it to pay the florist. After what had happened with Tansy, she hadn't been able to think of a new plan to retrieve even a portion of it. Eventually, with no alternative, she had to confess. She was sure she'd be fired but was surprised when Rebecca made a deal with her instead: there was something she needed Farah to do. Something that would not only save Farah's job, but also save her from the possibility of being prosecuted for stealing from the magazine. The only problem was that what Rebecca wanted in exchange was going to cost Farah dearly in other ways.

CHAPTER SIXTEEN

The women sit around the jacuzzi in their bathing suits, working away at their fourth post-pamper bottle of Prosecco. Each of them has the kind of glow that could be attributed to either a hydrating and exfoliating skin treatment or being incredibly pissed. It's hard to tell the difference.

"This is so relaxing!" Eva leans back against the side of the jacuzzi. She's just posted a selfie of her with the others captioned: *These ones.*

Lauren keeps giving Eva's perfect bikini body envious, almost to the point of mournful, looks and Farah really wishes that she could be just a little bit more resilient. She and Joss broke up ages ago; she needs to buck up and move on. She's an adult woman after all, and lately Farah's been growing really tired of her shit. Lauren's life is easy, all she does is send mascara to influencers. Sometimes Farah wishes she had a job like that, one with less at stake.

Across the jacuzzi, Dominica's on her bloody phone again. Even when she's submerged in water, Farah thinks, she just can't switch off from work. And Saskia's still sipping the same glass of Prosecco she had two hours ago, only deigning to dip her feet into the jacuzzi. It's Farah's hen do, for Christ's sake. Can't she just let go and have fun this once?! Five glasses down and feeling belligerent, Farah wonders if her friendships are just a constant stream of irritation these days. If they didn't have this huge secret and long past bonding them, would they even still be friends? But imagining life without them seems impossible, especially in the wake of Tansy's death.

"I know it's not Ibiza, but we have so many nice things planned for you," Saskia says, at last topping up her glass. "We're going to spoil you rotten before the big day. And we're going straight from brunch here tomorrow to the dress fittings! We're all *so* excited to see your finished dress and try on those gorgeous bridesmaid dresses again!"

Saskia actually thinks those dresses are the most disgusting things she's ever seen in her life.

Dominica downs her drink and taps out a reply to the frantic texts she's been receiving all day, at the same time thinking she might vomit if Saskia crawls any farther up Farah's arse. Surely the point of being friends with people for so long is that you can tell them when they're being a dick. And Farah is being a nonstop bridezilla dick. You'd think the death of her friend would at least have curbed her diva tendencies.

"OMG, yes! Are you ready to try on your dress for the final time before the big day?" Lauren asks with so much glee that Dominica actually feels a bit queasy.

"I can't wait!" Farah's thrilled that *finally* they're treating this like a proper hen do. "I've made some small changes to it that I'm so excited for you guys to see. Just to make it a little more special!"

Saskia's quite sure that whatever she's done to the already OTT dress will be far too much. Surely the only thing left to add is flashing fairy lights or something. And no one wants a flammable bride, especially not after what happened to Tansy.

"That's so exciting!" Lauren says.

"Oh my God, I actually had something I wanted to ask you, Eva. While we're talking about the dresses." Farah now feels drunk enough to face the delicate subject. She's spent the last three weeks trying to work out the best way to phrase it, though she still chokes on the words. "Now that Tansy's . . . no longer available for bridesmaid duties . . . I wondered if you . . . well . . ."

Lauren attempts to keep the wide smile on her face, but she's afraid she knows where this is going, and she can't bear it.

"Oh?" Eva asks, getting her phone ready to film whatever momentous question Farah's about to ask her in case it makes good content. Lauren realizes she's caught on camera in the background and tries to look as sexy as possible.

Dominica's also caught in the background, but she's not going to make any apologies for her scowling face. She can't believe Farah's doing this. Just let the fourth dress go. So what? Tansy's gone, surely her life was worth more than an empty bridesmaid dress.

"I was wondering . . . I know you were so close to Tansy, and obviously you're with my brother, and I think it would be such a beautiful tribute if you stood in for her on my big day, as my fourth bridesmaid. I know you'll do her proud and that she'll be smiling down on you."

Smiling down on you from WHERE? Dominica thinks. What a load of old shit. If Tansy can see this, she'll simply be wondering how Farah could just replace her like that. Dominica suspects Farah's only done this because she wants the bridesmaids to be even. She remembers her saying that she's lucky she has four best friends, otherwise she'd have to find someone else to even the numbers because everyone needs to walk down the aisle in twos.

Saskia's all for keeping things just so and Eva *would* look stunning in the pictures, but she does wonder if this is a little distasteful so soon after Tansy's death.

Lauren stares at them all, wondering if anyone's going to point out that Eva and Tansy are different sizes. Unless that dress has already been altered, surely it still needs to be done. And Lauren was given strict instructions by Farah not to gain or lose any weight because the dress wouldn't fit anymore and there was no time for alterations. Not to mention that she and Eva wearing the same dress, probably next to each other, is also her idea of hell.

Farah can feel her friends looking at her in disbelief, but she has to do what she has to do. She needs to get the money back to Rebecca by any means necessary, and last night she had the bright idea of simply asking her friends to make a small contribution to their dresses. After all, she's heard other people do it all the time. It's the least they can do really, considering how much she's already paying for. And with each dress costing hundreds of pounds, she can't afford to have one go empty.

"OH MY GOD, I'D LOVE TO!" Eva raises a hand to her weepy face as she films herself, and Jen and Helen clap in the background. "Oh God, wait, hang on." She presses the stop button on her camera. "I just need to do that last bit again; my pixie ear was sticking out." She adjusts her hair over her perfect ear and presses record again, raising her hand to her face to capture the incredibly genuine real-time emotions that she's feeling. "Can you believe that in an alternative universe, Tansy would be married now?" she says sadly.

"To Ivan, though." Dominica grimaces.

"She never had the greatest taste in men even before Ivan," Saskia says in a rare moment of candor.

"God, yeah," Farah says despite herself. "Do you remember that guy Luke she went out with who was a photographer? He was hot but kind of lecherous and definitely shagging at least three of the models he photographed. Even though she wouldn't have any of it."

"Oh my God, I remember Luke!" Saskia says. "He seemed so cool and attractive but was such a creep."

"Such a creep." Lauren shudders, though secretly she remembers thinking he was quite nice really.

"She always saw the best in people," Saskia says.

"And situations," Farah finds herself agreeing.

"Like when Saskia's mum wouldn't let her go to Glastonbury and we couldn't go without her, so Tansy set up a tent in her back garden and we watched it on TV," Lauren says.

"She really got the vibe right." Dominica nods. "And she was good at a party."

The women find themselves uncharacteristically weepy. Even Dom looks like she could shed a tear, while Eva has obviously welled up and spilled over already. Such is the danger of a daytime Prosecco binge.

"Remember opening night at the café?" Lauren says.

"She was so proud," Dominica says.

"So proud." Helen and Jen nod in agreement, their foreheads furrowing.

"We were all proud of her," Farah says, swept away by memories. "What she did with that café was amazing."

"It was as beautiful as her," Lauren says.

"No, nothing was as beautiful as her," Dominica says. "Nothing could be."

Saskia, who hadn't managed to make it to the café opening, simply nods. "She'd have looked stunning on her wedding day."

Eva lets out a small wail alongside her sobs, which snaps Farah back out of it, feeling irritated once again at how Tansy is dominating another part of her wedding preparations. She scowls and takes a glug of Prosecco.

"There'd be no bride more perfect," Jen says, sniffing loudly as Helen puts her arm around her shoulder.

Farah feels her jaw clench. All she can do is nod along, keeping her mouth firmly shut in case she accidentally screams something about how *she'll* make the most perfect bride too. She can't believe they're all crying about how beautiful Tansy would have looked when it's *her* hen do.

"She would have looked incredible in her bridesmaid dress too," she says, trying to bring the topic back to the matter in hand. This is her day.

"It'll be an honor to wear her dress, Mrs. Farah Winters!" Eva says, squashing Farah into another selfie.

"Oh, you're taking his surname then?" Dominica asks, and Saskia shoots her a look. She knows that Dom's about to start her usual rant about how the guys never take the woman's name. Why does she need to ruin a perfectly lovely moment?

"Well, yes. I mean, I just wanted to do something to mark the fact that I'll be a married woman, you know?" Farah says.

Dominica decides not to say anything else, because Farah's already wound so tightly and she doesn't want to push her over the edge. But Lauren's surprised that Farah's changing her name, not least because it's the first hint of Toby being an actual part of the wedding that they've heard for a while. Sometimes it feels like Farah's marrying herself.

"Did you consider a double barrel?" asks Saskia Bardon-Burnett.

"I did, but could you imagine Farah Innes-Winters?" Farah asks. "Also takes up extra space on a byline."

"You're changing it for work as well? When you've already established your career in your name?" Dominica realizes she can't just sit by and watch her do this after all.

"Why does it matter so much to you?" Farah asks, irked.

"I just don't see why you're giving a man this much power over you and ultimately your career!" Dominica says.

"I can very easily communicate to everyone that I have a new surname. I have social media; my wedding will be all over that. It's not like people who like my work won't know that I've got married!"

It's not as if anyone within a ten-mile radius of her will miss the news, Lauren thinks, the bitterness bursting like a confetti cannon in her head.

"It's her decision, Dom," Saskia says protectively. "And I think it's lovely that she's changing it. It's such a nice symbol of their love for each other."

"Beware, though, it's a lot of boring admin," Jen says wisely, pissing Farah off even more.

Dominica smiles in as tolerant a fashion as she can muster. She knows that she's in the right, that she just wants what's best for Farah's career, but she can't be bothered to take on Saskia right now. She holds back from pointing out that it's not really a symbol of their love for each other if Toby's not doing it too. It's just a one-sided, unequal symbol of centuries of female oppression.

"Guys! You'll never guess what I saw in the spa reception when we were coming in!" Jen shouts drunkenly, breaking the tension.

"WHAT?" Farah turns to her, a little angrier than she meant to be, still on edge from Dominica sharing her opinions as usual.

"Fanny eggs!" Jen shouts.

"OMG!" Eva claps her hands with delight.

Lauren and Dominica sit blank-faced.

"Pardon?" Dominica says.

"They're called yoni eggs, they go in your vagina," Farah explains. "They're supposed to promote healing and improve pelvic floor function. There's a mixed view on whether they're actually just really bad for you. I wrote an article on them a while back. Nice to know you all read my work."

"I used one in pelvic floor training after the babies," Saskia says, prompting Lauren to spit her Prosecco into the jacuzzi.

"You did?" Farah tilts her head in surprise.

"I tried one during this yoga thing I went on. It was like, yoga in a room with baby goats and a yoni egg." Eva nods and Lauren screws up her face. Of course Eva has a hench pelvic floor.

"That's a lot more going on than I can deal with," Dominica says, making a swirly gesture with her hand in Eva's direction. "And Saskia, I am shocked."

"I honestly found it very beneficial. Childbirth really messes with your pelvic floor. I can promise you that having an eight-pound baby tunnelling out of there is far worse than a little jade egg that helps everything ping back into shape." Saskia turns to look at Farah. "You'll be getting to all that soon enough!"

"SASKIA! You can't assume someone's going to have children just because they're getting married," Dominica says.

"I mean—" Farah starts, but gets cut off by Saskia, who's thoroughly pissed off at being talked to like she's insensitive.

"I'm not assuming! She told me herself that they were going to have them!"

The rest of the women turn to Farah to see her wearing a sheepish expression.

"I did," she confesses.

"Why didn't you tell me? You're telling Saskia about your reproductive choices now instead?" Dominica narrows her eyes.

Lauren stares at them both, indignant, very much on Dominica's side. They barely ever see Saskia, unless it's a hen do or a baby shower or some other big life event. Why would Farah choose to tell her but not them? Lauren talks to Farah and Dominica every day. She's not a fair-weather hen party friend like Saskia.

Saskia tries to ignore the fact that Dominica's being extremely rude about Farah's choice to confide in her about something she is *obviously* the best person to go to for advice on. If she'd talked to Dominica about it, she'd probably have sent Farah articles on getting her tubes tied or told her that children ruin your career.

"I would have done, but you judge me for EVERYTHING these days," Farah says, rolling her eyes.

"I do not." Dominica screws up her face dismissively and pours herself more Prosecco.

"You literally just judged me for changing my name after marriage." Farah blinks at her.

"Yeah, but that's a poor business decision," Dominica scoffs, and leaves out the fact that so is having children.

"You didn't tell me, and I don't judge anyone," Lauren says, the hurt radiating from her.

Farah simply stares at her. She didn't tell Lauren because Lauren would just give her the pitiful look that signifies she's thinking about how she'll never have children with Joss. And that's the last thing Farah wants to be thinking about.

"That's so exciting! I could be Auntie Eva! I can't wait to see Joss holding a baby, my ovaries will just FLIP!" Eva says as Lauren's will to live simply departs the scene.

Dominica is rendered silent thinking about what a catastrophe it would be for Lauren if Eva and Joss had a baby.

"I just wanted to ask Saskia some logistical questions," Farah says. "You know, from someone who's done it."

"Don't do it, you'll never piss right again," Jen announces before jumping out of the jacuzzi and heading off toward reception. "I'm off to get us some healing eggs!"

"Anyway, there's no telling what might happen," Farah continues. "We might not be able to. Although I guess we could adopt, or there's surrogacy . . ." She trails off.

"Tricky in this country, though, it's basically illegal to pay for it," Dominica points out. Always on the job. "You have to find someone willing to do you one hell of a solid."

"Yeah, I guess," Farah says.

"I might go and see if I can find more Prosecco," Dominica says, tapping away on her phone. "We've drunk the four bottles they left us. I can't believe they'd provide so little."

"Oh, Jen can get it," Helen says. "She gets the discount for everything after all. What with her husband being a part owner."

Suddenly everything becomes clear to Farah, Dominica, and Lauren. Jen and Helen are there because Jen gets them a discount, and as usual Saskia's been bigging up her and Jeremy's generosity. Why is it that rich people are always the stingiest?

"No, I'd rather go," Dominica says pointedly. "I could use the air."

CHAPTER SEVENTEEN

Dominica doesn't go to find Prosecco. She knew he was acting oddly today, texting her frantically even though he knows where she is and who she's with. And now she finds out that he's *here*, upstairs in a room, waiting for her. She never had him down as a risk-taker. She always thought he was smarter than that.

She stands in the lobby, waiting for the jarringly modern lift to arrive—clearly not an original feature—swaying slightly drunkenly in her spa robe. His latest message is a picture of his cock next to a glass of champagne—her two favorite things, according to him.

Fine, she responds, *you win. I'm on my way up.*

I can't believe you'd pull something this risky.

Riding up to the third floor in the lift, she stares at her phone as he sends a thumbs-up in return.

The elevator doors open and she can see that the door to his room's already ajar. She can't believe he's being so irresponsible. The rooms they're all staying in are just at the other end of the hall. What if one of them drunkenly came up to get something and spotted him? He'd better not be thinking about leaving that room at any point, but he'd also better not be planning on staying the whole weekend.

She looks both ways before darting inside. Once there, she pulls across the safety catch and double bolts the door just to be sure.

"Paranoid much?" His voice comes from the bed.

"Well, at least one of us doesn't want to blow up everyone's lives," she says sternly.

"Ooh, I love it when you tell me off!" he says lasciviously. "How long before they notice you're gone?"

"Probably about half an hour," Dominica says, approaching the bed. "They're already wasted. They're getting some vaginal eggs to experiment with."

"Do I want to know what that is?" he asks, raising an eyebrow.

"Little stone eggs that go in your vagina, supposedly to heal you," she says vaguely.

"I've got a stone that'll heal you . . ." he says, his fingers brushing the hair off her face and tracing over her alcohol-swollen pout.

"You keep talking like that and you'll never put that stone any-where near me again," she laughs.

The two of them stay locked in eye contact as he continues tracing her lips. Dominica trails one finger down his chest, along his stomach, and to the crotch of his trousers, then slides down his body without kissing him. She teases him with her lips, making contact with his skin but barely brushing it as she runs her hand up and down his leg, stop-ping at the fly before tearing the trousers down. He groans as her phone lights up with messages from the other hens asking where she's gone.

CHAPTER EIGHTEEN

Down in the spa, sprawled on a sunbed at the side of the pool, Farah's finally feeling wasted enough not to care what Dominica or anyone else thinks of her life choices. She cannot believe she kicked off so much about the name thing. But then that's Dominica all over, she's always got something to say about what everyone else is doing but never takes any risks of her own. In fact, she never even tells anyone what she's up to half the time. She's so bloody secretive. Why *would* Farah tell her she was planning on having kids?

Anyway, she also didn't tell her because she's not actually planning on it, not yet anyway. She needs her job to be more secure before she thinks about starting a family. And right now, it's very insecure. She's been trying to ignore all the texts from Rebecca and enjoy her day, and now that she's so drunk she can't read them, she's finally doing just that.

"Oh, there you are!" Saskia exclaims as Dominica walks back into the changing room. She nods toward where Farah is currently attempting to drain an already very empty bottle. "Where have you been?"

"Just went to find more Prosecco." Dominica holds up the two buckets in her hands. "Ended up getting lost and waiting at the bar for ages."

Saskia eyes her friend's flushed cheeks suspiciously but accepts her excuse nonetheless, because what else could she have been doing? Anyway, it was probably good that she and Farah had a bit of time to cool off. She knows that Dominica's little outbursts are just because she cares about them all so much, but with Farah so highly strung already, she should have known it wasn't the time.

"Here you go!" Dominica puts the Prosecco in front of Farah, who looks up at her bleary-eyed. "Peace offering. Sorry for being an old nag about the name. It's just because I want the best for you, you know that, right? And sometimes I forget that not everyone feels the same as me. I'm sorry."

Farah pulls her in for a very sloppy hug and Lauren notices that Eva's filming the whole exchange like some kind of weird friendship perv.

"That's so cute, you guys!" Eva says, and they turn around, realizing that they're on camera. "POSE!"

The two of them make peace signs, a symbol of their truce.

"When you've been friends as long as we have, a bit of bickering's nothing," Farah slurs.

Lauren smiles knowingly. Farah and Dominica have been bickering for as long as she can remember. They once didn't talk for a whole week after a particularly vicious argument over the best *Bake Off* contestant. It's almost become a sign of affection as they get older, though Lauren wishes they would save it for the less exciting Bread Week.

"Oh God, are these them?" Dominica is eyeing up a tray containing stone eggs of varying size and color, each of them labelled with their names.

"They are!" Jen says. "The spa technicians have picked out the ones that will work for each of us."

"How can they tell?" Lauren whispers, anxiously biting her lip. "Are there actually people that can tell the size of your vagina just by looking at you?" She glances at one of the technicians breezing through in her white uniform. "Are they sizing me up right now?"

"Duh, no," Jen says. "I just gave them basic info about each of you, like your age and if you'd had any children, and they came back with these. That's how they do it. Saskia, I presumed because you don't have a C-section scar you had natural births like me. So we've got the bigger eggs."

"What's the difference between the colors?" Dominica asks.

"Jade does physical healing, rose does emotional healing," Eva says wisely.

"I gave them everyone's names and they made a judgment on whether you're a rose girlie or a jade girlie," Jen says, smiling at Dominica, who stares at her rose egg, perturbed.

"Maybe they sensed you needed some healing for your cold, dead heart?" Farah says, tilting her head playfully.

"I don't even have a heart to heal," Dominica quips in response.

"What do we do with them?" Lauren asks, studying her small rose egg quizzically.

Dominica knows that rose is the right color for Lauren, which is further proof that it's definitely not the right color for her.

"You just put them in and then take them out twenty minutes later," Saskia says.

"Do you clench?" Lauren asks, whispering again.

"Actually, I've just remembered from that article I did that people found they caused thrush," Farah says, leaning back on her sunbed and groping for the Prosecco again. "I do *not* want thrush for the wedding. I'm out."

"Oh go on, just take a Canesten." Jen narrows her eyes at her.

"Honestly, guys, I'm like so prone to it," Farah says. She's not about to get thrush because this woman she barely even knows is instructing her to put a rock up her fanny on *her* hen do. More Prosecco.

"Same," Helen says. "I'm out too. I've literally only just got over one dose. Also, this whole mass vaginal egg thing feels a bit . . . I dunno . . . icky."

"LOSERS!" Jen teases. "I mean, I was thinking we go and put them in in the cubicles. I wasn't about to do it out here in the open."

All the women except Farah and Helen take their eggs into the changing cubicles. They emerge shuffling and shifting around weirdly, with the exception of Saskia, who's clearly done it so many times that she feels completely at home with a lump of rock in her fanny. What the other women don't know is that Saskia's egg is in fact concealed safely in her robe pocket.

"OK, start the timer!" Dominica shouts. "Team Fanny Egg! Let's go!"

"Wait! I feel left out now!" Helen says. "I'm going to do it!"

"Yeah, you are!" Jen cheers her friend on as Helen rushes into a cubicle.

"Farah?" Eva points to the remaining egg.

"Still a no from me." Farah narrows her eyes. "Doing fanny eggs with my brother's girlfriend also just feels kind of weird, you know?" She wrinkles her nose at Eva and Eva wrinkles hers back.

"Ew, you're right." Eva looks disgusted at herself. But then she shrugs. "It's in there now, though. And actually it doesn't feel too—"

"Please God, no," says Farah, cutting her off. "I don't want to hear about it . . . from any of you! And don't you be texting him about it. I don't want this to become some weird sex thing between the two of you." She mock-gags in disgust.

Lauren thinks how Joss would laugh about the vaginal eggs. He'd find it really silly, not sexy.

"I've done it, but I'm just going to stay in here because it feels weird," Helen calls from her cubicle.

"I never knew she was such a prude," Jen says.

"I've started the timer," Saskia says. "More Prosecco for everyone?"

"Yes!" Jen shouts.

"Please, but just slide it under the cubicle door," Helen says. "I'll stay in here and continue my investigations."

Farah can't believe that Helen's still banging on about her "investigations" with a rock up her fanny.

Saskia gets up and goes over to the table in the changing area. But as she reaches for a bottle, she loses her footing on the wet poolside and slips. It's in that moment of confusion and trying to right herself that the egg falls from her robe pocket, landing with a heavy thud at her feet on the tiled floor and rolling unceremoniously into the pool with a *plop*. The other women are completely silent as the egg sinks to the bottom.

"What was that?" Helen asks from inside her cubicle.

"Saskia just laid an egg," Farah says, looking at her questioningly.

"A hen through and through," Dominica adds.

"Oh my God," Saskia says, mortified.

"Did it just clean fall out of your fanny?" Jen asks, blinking.

Saskia realizes that none of them know what's really happened. She still has a chance to get away with it; she'll just lose her dignity instead.

"Er, yes, I guess so," she says, before laughing heartily in an attempt to cover up her embarrassment.

The other women follow her lead, falling about with hilarity on their sunbeds.

"I thought your pelvic floor was trained and tight!" Dominica sniggers, at which point there's a thud from Helen's cubicle and the women see her legs sprawled on the floor, her feet poking out from under the door.

The laughter only intensifies at this.

"Babe, did you legit just fall off the bench laughing?" Jen asks between gasps for air.

"Oh my God, if I laugh any more, my egg's going to pop out too," Eva says.

At this, the hens go into further hysterics, but as the laughter dies down, Saskia realizes that Helen's still on the floor. Her legs not moving.

"Are you going to get up, Helen?" she asks, thinking of the germs that must be down there.

The other women turn to look in the direction of the cubicle, the last tinkles of laughter dying out.

"Hels?" Jen asks, standing up. "Are you OK?"

The silence of the spa develops its own echo, the rhythmic rumble of the jacuzzi bubbles filling the dead air. The smell of bergamot is suddenly overwhelmingly cloying as Jen heads toward the cubicle.

"Hels?" She knocks on the door as the other hens look on confused.

When there's no response, she pokes Helen's leg, and everyone stares, expecting to see the telltale movement of her toes, or her calf kicking out.

"HELEN?" Jen's shouting louder now, hitting Helen's foot.

A buzzer goes off to signify it's time to take out the eggs, slicing crudely through the air, making them all jump, and yet Helen's legs stay still.

Jen pushes the door open and for a moment there's silence as the women strain to see what's going on.

It feels like hours, but it can only be seconds before Jen falls to the floor next to her friend. "HELEN!" She emits a scream that echoes around the spa, bouncing off its pristine white walls, the scented candles flickering in its wake.

The entire hen party leaps up and races to the cubicle, hearts thudding and skin prickling. Jen's kneeling on the floor, Helen's head in her lap, her face blue, lips parted, and eyes wide.

"SHE'S DEAD!" Jen screams. "HELEN'S DEAD!"

CHAPTER NINETEEN

Lauren waits for the lift, struggling to hold all the bags she somehow ended up collecting for Dominica and Saskia.

"Are you OK?" Joss's voice behind her makes her jump, and she drops the bags. She could have sworn she was the only one up here.

"Joss! What are you doing here?" She tries not to sound too excited to see him. Especially after the way he pied her off after Tansy died.

"Sorry, I didn't mean to scare you. Just grabbing Eva's things for her. She called me and I was in the area so I thought I'd come and see if I could help somehow." He gestures to a massive bag that's far bigger than anyone would need for one night away. Despite his burden, though, he leans down and picks up some of Lauren's bags to help her. She's furious to find herself swooning.

"Right, same, I mean, getting my own things," Lauren says, gesturing to her suitcase.

"You all right?" he asks.

"Yeah, fine. I mean . . . not *fine*, but you know . . ." She realizes she's actually shaking as she grasps the handles of Dominica's bag, and she does feel a little dizzy. "I didn't know Helen that well, she was really more Tansy's friend. Only met her a few times. Not that that makes it any better that she's dead . . . Obviously she shouldn't . . . be dead." She's aware that she's babbling.

"Er . . . yeah," Joss says.

The lift makes a pinging noise to indicate that it's arrived, and he stands back to let her get in first. His dark wavy hair looks especially floppy today as it catches the light, and she watches as he reaches to press the button for the ground floor, his muscular arm framed by the sleeve of his white T-shirt. The doors close, and it's finally just the two of them for three whole floors, everything Lauren's ever wanted. But despite this, she can't seem to think of a single word to say to him, the shock of what's happened preventing any sense from coming out of her mouth.

Joss reaches over and places his hand on her shoulder; it's a friendly gesture, and she tries not to swoon at the unexpected joy of it.

"I . . ." She thinks about how Eva's taken up all of Joss's attention with her grief lately, and wishes she too was one of those people who could cry on the spot. It's not that she doesn't feel sad, just that she feels detached from the sadness somehow; from all feelings, in fact. "I miss Tansy," is all she can think to say. And she does, she misses her all the time. Until Eva came along, they had spoken nearly every day. Lauren had already been feeling abandoned, and now she'll never get to speak to her friend again.

It's enough for Joss to step toward her, pulling her in for a hug. She feels the relief of his strong arms sliding around her.

"I really am here if you need me, you know," he says into her hair. She feels the breeze from his words tickling her ear. Suddenly she feels incredibly horny, somewhat inappropriately considering she's just been in a room with a dead body. Maybe it's the shock. "I know I'm with Eva now, but that doesn't mean I can't be there for you. I *want* to be there for you."

Lauren tries to subtly inhale him, holding in what she really wants to shout, which is: "I NEED YOU! DUMP YOUR GIRLFRIEND AND RUN AWAY WITH ME TO MY TINY ONE-BEDROOM FLAT WITH ITS MOUSE INFESTATION."

"And you don't need to worry about Eva. She knows, and she understands. She doesn't feel threatened or anything. She understands that you don't really have anyone else."

Oh God, the worst. Lauren has never felt so fucking pathetic in her life. The other woman pities her because she's so lame. Of course Eva doesn't feel threatened by her! Eva's a perfect twenty-six-year-old model and Lauren's an average thirty-four-year-old with recurrent cystitis and now probably thrush too. She wants to tell him to piss off and that he and his smug girlfriend can absolutely go fuck themselves.

"Thank you," she says instead. "I really appreciate that."

She will NEVER respond to his texts within seconds or fall into his hugs gratefully or needily again. NEVER!

He hugs her tighter and she crumples into him. Maybe just this one last time then, she thinks. Her stomach flips as she feels his solid chest against her cheek. He's always worked out, even as a teenager, but since he started going out with Eva, she feels like he's got even sexier. She guesses that's what happens when your girlfriend's so young and hot. She wonders how long it'll take before nuzzling into his armpit becomes creepy. But instead of him trying to shrug her off, she feels his chin come to rest gently on her head and his hand on her back. A slight movement of his thumb, almost imperceptible, but then she's sure. His fingers travel to her side and he caresses her waist gently. She worries that if she looks up, she might find she's imagined the hand, taken its movements the wrong way. But she feels he might actually, definitely be doing that thing where a man gently runs his thumb over your back, or hand or thigh or whatever, in a way that he can later pretend was accidental just in case he gets rejected.

She stays completely still, not wanting to ruin the moment, hoping the lift doors never open. His other hand goes to her head, stroking her hair, his fingers drifting down and landing on her cheek. It's a light movement, but one that Lauren can be very sure she hasn't misunderstood. He tips her head slightly upward, and their eyes connect just as a dinging noise echoes around the lift. He jumps away from her; the doors open, and he's out into the lobby while she's left stumbling to regain her balance. By the time she's made her way out to join the others, he's already got his arms around Eva. Lucky bitch, she thinks. As she watches him lovingly comfort his girlfriend, it feels as if she imagined everything that happened just seconds ago.

Everyone sits on sofas in the lobby, waiting for the police to do their thing. As Dominica comforts Jen, her arm around her shoulders, she becomes increasingly irritated by Jeremy, who's pacing around, his hand on his chin, repeating details with the authority of a man who's watched too much *Poirot* and is one flicked mustache away from becoming irrevocably insufferable.

"I just need everyone's name and contact details, and we'll need you all to come down to the station to make your statements within the next few days," DI Ashford says.

"Are you sure you don't need them to make statements now?" Jeremy asks. "Isn't that a bit sloppy? There's already been one murder; surely it's safe to assume this could be a second."

DI Ashford ignores the slight on his expertise. "With all due respect, we won't know that until we get a toxicology report and do an autopsy. We've cleared the scene and we've got forensics down there now. As long as everyone gives their statements over the next few days, it should be OK."

"Jen's the one who found her," Dominica says to Jeremy. "And she's in no state to be making a statement." She gestures to Jen trembling next to her in a foil blanket.

"I'm going to ask my mate, he's a chief inspector at Scotland Yard. I'm sure he wouldn't agree with this method," Jeremy says, taking out his phone and scrolling through his contacts.

Lauren feels a bit sorry for DI Ashford, but he seems to be dealing with Jeremy's pomposity well. Saskia stares at her husband with simpering admiration; she loves it when he asserts his authority. Meanwhile, Dominica wonders how much longer she can stand listening to his voice before she tells him to shut the fuck up and let people who know what they're doing get on with their jobs. She opts instead to sip at the glass of brandy the bar manager gave her earlier for the shock.

Having managed to slip away from the others, Farah takes a deep breath. She told DI Ashford she needed a minute to phone her fiancé and get her things together. She even turned on the waterworks to show him how upset she was, before escaping to her room.

It wasn't just an act—she really did need a moment to compose herself—but, selfishly, it isn't just about Helen, or at least not in the way everyone thinks. Another woman is dead, and it happened on *her* hen do. Farah was already feeling the judgment for not moving her wedding after Tansy's death, and now she knows she'll be under even more pressure. A double murder investigation is scary enough, but the prospect of having to cancel is, to Farah, maybe even scarier.

She sits on the bed in her suite and pulls up the spreadsheet, her breath ragged, tears rolling down her cheeks as she tries to convince herself that even if the worst happens, things could be OK. But the numbers are bigger than her, so big it almost doesn't feel like real money anymore. But it is. If she can't have the wedding now, there'll be no wedding at all. She'll spend her whole life paying off the wedding she never got to have. And if she can't get what Rebecca wants, then Toby will leave her when he realizes just how far she's gone to have the day of her dreams. As she runs her eyes down the spreadsheet she knows so well, she unravels further with every line.

Her phone beeps beside her and Rebecca's name appears on the screen like a threat.

Have you done it yet?

Farah stares at the message, feeling rage rising in her. She cannot let her wedding be cancelled. No matter what else happens over the next few weeks, she needs to get married. She needs to have the wedding she's planned, or else all this will have been for nothing. And she won't let that happen.

She stands up from the rose-petal-covered bed, feeling every inch not at all the relaxed and blushing bride she planned to be. All she wanted was the money to make sure that her wedding was better than all those other ones she's sat through, all those years of other people's disbelief that Toby hadn't asked her yet. Now look at the mess she's in. Weeks from her wedding with another dead hen and even more stress.

She needs to get back downstairs, it's not a good look for her to be missing. She gathers her things and heads out into the hallway. She's wiping the tears from her eyes as she rounds the corner, and puts her shoulders back when she sees him waiting for the lift.

"Toby?" she asks, confused. "What are you doing up here? I thought you were meeting me downstairs."

He appears slightly startled, but nevertheless moves straight to give her a hug.

"I came to find you of course," he says.

CHAPTER TWENTY

"SURPRISE!" the women all shout as Saskia enters her own balloon-filled living room at 2:30 on a Saturday afternoon.

"Wow!" Saskia does an admirable job of looking as if she wasn't expecting any of this.

In truth, she picked everything out herself: the "Hello Baby!" balloons, the flower arch around the front door, the artisan cakes, the party games, including "Guess the Food" (using organic baby food, of course), and the artfully assembled boards of everyone's baby pictures for "Guess the Baby." And every guest will be leaving with a small basket containing a biscuit shaped like a stork and some baby-blue marshmallows. It's obvious to everyone in attendance that this entire thing is her handiwork, but they're far too polite to point it out. It's all so extra that Dominica's surprised there's no real-life stork roaming about the party.

Dominica promised Farah, Tansy, and Lauren that she wasn't going to spend today at war with the self-appointed A-team, Verity, Lavinia, and Anastasia, who are all also, conveniently, pregnant. It's as if they've perfectly timed their menstrual cycles and husbands' ejaculations to ensure their waters break within seconds of each other. The whole thing makes Dominica feel a bit sick.

"Oh my God, you're such a huge, beautiful mama!" Tansy exclaims, causing Verity to look down her nose at her and Dominica to gag a little.

"Thank you, darling," Saskia is used to this kind of thoughtlessness from Tansy. She certainly takes being called huge much better than the other pregnant women in the room would have done.

"Congratulations!" Lauren says as Saskia reaches her for a hug.

Upon scanning the list of gifts for the baby shower, Lauren found only one item she could actually afford on her assistant's wage, which was a small plush rabbit. She hastily plonked it in a sparkly blue bag and hoped it was hidden far enough down the pile of gifts that if there was some kind of mass public unwrapping session they would never get to it. Most of the stuff on the list was wildly expensive and unnecessary. She doesn't understand at all why a baby needs to have Gucci shoes.

"You look incredible!" Farah says breathily, studying Saskia's glowing skin and the fact that even in this heat, when many of her contemporaries are struggling, she hasn't got even an ounce of swelling around the ankles.

"I know!" Saskia says, grinning. "Pregnancy yoga is such a blessing! And we've all been going to hypnobirthing classes together. It really is just a joy to be pregnant with your pals. You guys definitely need to do it when the time comes. It's so rewarding, and it's made me feel completely in touch with my womanhood."

Dominica looks at her as if she's completely insane. She can't help wondering why all these women are so obsessed with having babies. Treating each other like cattle. "Ooh, look at your glossy pregnancy mane." It's ridiculous. Women have come so far, and people like Saskia just reduce it all to spewing a man's offspring out of their vagina and feeding it from their udders. She remembers twelve-year-old Saskia announcing that she intended to be the youngest female prime minister. She was going to do incredible things. All now thwarted by Jeremy and her new life with the Holland Park Witches. She quit her job the moment they got engaged and spent all her time just waiting around to get pregnant. Dominica herself feels like she's in touch with her womanhood just fine without having to spawn, thanks very much. Especially as she's on track to be made partner at her law firm before she's even hit thirty.

"I'm going to blame pregnancy hormones for that," she mutters through gritted teeth to the others as Saskia moves on to a heavily fillered blonde, who's wearing more diamonds on her fingers than Lauren's ever seen in her entire life.

Lauren takes Saskia's comment like a slap to the face. When is she ever going to find someone to have babies with? She can't imagine loving anyone as much as she does Joss, and he doesn't want to have children with her. He doesn't even want to be her boyfriend. What if she never feels completely in touch with her womanhood?

Meanwhile, Tansy's taking in deep breaths of the air around her, hoping to inhale some pheromones. She feels so connected to her womb with these women. Just being close to the miracle of life is making her feel more fertile. Even if she has performed oral sex on one of their husbands.

Farah looks at the incredible maternity clothes being worn around the room and knows that if she and Toby ever get to the stage where they're having children, there's no way she'll be able to afford YSL pregnancy wear. Unless she comes up with the scoop of the century, it'll be Primark for her. Although it could be a long time before Toby gets there anyway; he seems in no rush. Just the other day, he described getting a houseplant together as "a really grown-up decision."

"Oh my God, sit! SIT!" Lavinia trills to Saskia. "Come join us in the mothers' nest!" She gestures to the area of the sofa that she, Verity, and Anastasia have filled with cushions and cuddly toys.

"Mothers only!" Verity giggles.

"Oh! I'm a mother!" says another woman hopefully.

"Pregnant mothers!" Lavinia quickly clarifies, to make sure this woman knows she's not welcome.

Dominica, Lauren, Tansy, and Farah all have the same thought at the same time: they're pleased that Tansy sucked Lavinia's husband's dick.

"Ooof!" Saskia says, landing on the sofa clutching her bump.

"Is he kicking?" Verity asks solicitously. "Chelsea's newest footballer!"

"Just stopped!" Saskia says, flashing everyone a grin. "He's been dancing around in there all morning!"

After two rounds of "Pin the Nappy on the Baby," it's time to open the presents. Lauren's got the measure of these women enough now to know that they're going to sit and unwrap every single one painstakingly and shame anyone who hasn't done a good enough job. She's wondering if she can make up a reason to leave. A family emergency, perhaps.

"PRESENTS!" Lavinia squeals, clapping her hands.

"I just need to pop to the loo!" Saskia says, prying herself off the sofa.

"Good idea," Lavinia says, starting the task of raising herself too.

"You go down here and I'll take the upstairs one. And there's plenty more loos for anyone that needs one!" Saskia says, the two of them waddling out of the sitting room.

"I could use the loo too, actually," Tansy says, a few moments after they've left.

"Me too!" Farah says. "You go upstairs and I'll go downstairs, and I've got ten thousand more loos for anyone that needs one because I'm so rich!" she adds in a whisper, mimicking Saskia's casual brag.

Tansy heads out of the living room and through the tiled hallway, past the giant vases of flowers that sit precariously on tall tables in the middle of the space. The whole house is very far from baby-proofed. Climbing the wide staircase, she marvels at the fact that one of them has a house this massive. She doubts it's eco-friendly.

Upstairs, she realizes that she can't actually remember where the loo is, and starts pushing open random doors to try and find it. She presumes she's found the right one when she hears noise on the other side.

"Won't be a minute!" Saskia's voice tinkles.

"No worries, Mumma! You take all the time you need!" Tansy says.

When Saskia opens the door, she looks slightly flustered. "God, so sorry," she says. "It takes ages to just lower yourself down there, you know!"

She pats her bump and moves to walk away, but her Birkenstock sandal gets caught on the edge of the door in her flushed haste, and she falls against the frame. Tansy gasps, immediately leaping to her aid. She knows how bad it is for pregnant women to fall over. Fortunately, she grabs her just in time and Saskia sort of bounces against the wood.

"Gosh, that was close!" Saskia says, straightening up. "Could have been a disaster." But as she grins to demonstrate that everything's OK, a look of horror settles on Tansy's face.

A sense of impending doom washes over Saskia as her hands, followed by her eyes, scan down to her bump. The side closest to the door frame has dented inward, so that it looks as though a huge portion of it is missing. Hastily she grasps it and pops the silicone back out, but she knows it's too late.

"What the hell?" Tansy whispers once Saskia's shuffled the two of them away into her bedroom. "I don't understand. Why are you faking being pregnant? There won't be a baby at the end of it. What are people going to think when you don't go into labor like EVER?" She looks as confused as she feels, her eyes flitting back and forth with every new thought. "Does Jeremy know?"

"Yes, of course Jeremy knows!" Saskia hisses in a harassed way, pacing back and forth with her hands on her lower back for support. "Look, I can tell you everything, but you have to promise not to tell anyone. I especially need to make sure that Dominica doesn't find out. What we're doing, it's not legal. And I know she could get struck off for being involved in something like this. So please, for her sake and mine, don't say anything. OK?" She looks so desperate that Tansy simply nods.

"After we got married, obviously I just wanted to get started on having babies right away. But remember what Jeremy told me on our wedding day? That he'd suffered testicular trauma and wasn't sure he'd be able to father a child?"

Tansy narrows her eyes as if struggling to remember. "Yes! The rugby ball to the nuts!" she says eventually.

Saskia can't believe it took her so long to recall a conversation they had less than a year ago in the toilets at her wedding.

"So he's infertile and you're pretending to be pregnant? But what happens after you're supposed to have had the baby and there's no baby . . . Oh my God, are you adopting! That's so lovely! But why not just say?" Tansy looks even more confused. "You're not doing a Madonna, are you?"

"No, we're not adopting," Saskia says. "We still wanted the baby to be, you know . . . one of us . . . but Jeremy wasn't keen on the idea of a sperm donor. I had all these perfectly respectable options, but he said there was no way in hell he'd let another man's sperm enter his wife."

"Seems a bit . . . er . . . controlling," Tansy says.

Saskia ignores her. "There was really only one other possibility if we were going to have a baby that at least sort of looked like us. We combined my eggs with one of the donor sperm deposits, and because

Jeremy wasn't comfortable with it being inside me, we paid for a surrogate."

"So why not just tell people that?" Tansy asks.

"Because paying for surrogacy in this country, especially the amount of money we're talking, is illegal," Saskia explains patiently. "We found a clinic that took money under the table in return for a reliable service. So that we'd know that the womb carrying our child was of a high standard."

Tansy holds herself back from a long speech about how people aren't cattle and how gross it is to refer to someone only by their reproductive organs.

"It was a fix, something that meant that we'd get our baby and I could even be pregnant at the same time as my friends. All our children can be friends! It was such a happy coincidence that we all got pregnant together!"

"Except you're not pregnant," Tansy says.

Saskia can't believe that Tansy's suddenly behaving like she has some kind of moral authority in this situation.

"It's still our baby at the end of it," she says, irritated.

"I just don't get why you'd go to all that trouble to do something illegal. I know surrogacy can be great. I'm not saying it isn't a beautiful way of having a child. But doing it like this? All because Jeremy can't swallow his pride when you're perfectly capable of carrying a baby. He's depriving you of the experience you've wanted since you were a kid. You used to stuff Pound Puppies up your jumper and pretend you were pregnant all the time! It just feels so . . . sad!"

Saskia can't believe how dense Tansy is being. She doesn't know what it's like. Saskia needed a child, and this was the only way Jeremy would do it. She did what she had to do to secure the future she wants, for her and their unborn baby.

"And what about the person that carries and births your baby?" Tansy asks.

"They get handsomely rewarded," Saskia says. "And when he's born he just gets passed straight on to us."

"And no one knows? None of those women downstairs know?"

"Correct."

"Right," Tansy says. "So this is massively illegal, I'm the only one that knows, and I can't tell anyone?"

"Correct," Saskia says again.

"And you've just been wearing a fake bump this whole time?"

Saskia nods.

"So you've never felt your baby kick?" Tansy looks at her sadly.

"No," Saskia replies, tears forming in her steely eyes.

"I think this might be the saddest thing I've ever heard," Tansy says.

"Look." Saskia grips her arm. "You can't tell anyone."

"Of course," Tansy agrees in her usual breezy fashion.

"I mean it." Saskia clutches her arm tighter. "If you do, I'll know it came from you. And if other people find out about this, my life may as well be over. So yours will be too."

Back downstairs, Saskia takes up her position in the nest again, next to the other mums-to-be, while Tansy looks around at the storks, the baby-blue decorations, the scan pictures blown up. Everything looks so perfect, but it's all a lie.

CHAPTER TWENTY-ONE

Lauren has been awake in her damp and moldy flat staring at her phone since 6 A.M., after about two hours of sleep. While obviously Helen's death is at the forefront of her mind, her time in the lift with Joss, especially how close he came to kissing her, replays over and over in her head. Her thoughts keep wandering from Helen's poor family to thinking about what could have happened if the lift hadn't arrived at its destination when it did. In the fantasies she's had about it since, she imagines sexily reaching across him and pushing the stop button before ravishing him on the lift floor.

She stares at her phone as it beeps almost constantly with messages from the other women. None of those messages are from the person she most wants to hear from. She knows she should be thinking about Helen, and is nervous about the bad karma she's racking up by only focusing on what happened between her and Joss. She's thought about going to get her aura cleansed, but it's probably so toxic by now that it's beyond help. She tries once again to focus on the sadness of Helen's death, but ends up staring at her phone, willing a text from Joss to appear, hating herself.

Finally deciding that a watched pot won't boil, she heads to the toilet to take the wee she's been needing for hours now. Just as she leaves the kitchen, she hears her phone chirp. She skids back into the room, sliding across the cheap, peeling laminate floor, and grabs the phone off the side, only to droop with disappointment when it's Saskia's name that she sees there rather than Joss's. Taking the phone with her, she heads back to the toilet. She's not going to give herself a UTI for Saskia.

SASKIA: *We need to talk. Meet at the café on Old Ford Road in 1 hour.*

DOMINICA: *Copy.*

LAUREN: *Yep.*

FARAH: *Erm, don't forget it's dress fittings today? At eleven?*

DOMINICA: *We're still doing that after yesterday?*

FARAH: *I've already moved them once. I can't move them again without being charged.*

SASKIA: *Of course.*

Lauren finds it desperately sad that they're using the WhatsApp group Tansy was a member of. She scrolls back to see her last message to them from the night before her hen do.

> *Guys I am SO excited about tomorrow! I can't wait to see you all!*
> *Xxxxxxxxx*

Underneath she'd posted a series of GIFs from the film *Bridesmaids* that couldn't have been further from the hen do she was getting but were still funny.

Another message goes off while Lauren flushes the toilet. This time it's their *other* WhatsApp group, the one without Saskia in it that they started around the time of her wedding. They set it up primarily to bitch about the other bridesmaids, but it made sense to carry it on afterward because there was so much of their lives that Saskia no longer seemed interested in. Tansy's still in that WhatsApp group too, and Lauren's heart aches at the knowledge that she'll never again message to make fun of the Hags of Holland Park.

FARAH: *You hadn't forgotten, had you?*

DOMINICA: *No, of course not.*

LAUREN: *What Dominica says.*

FARAH: *I can't believe Saskia forgot.*

DOMINICA: *You can kind of understand it after yesterday though.*

LAUREN: *Do you think we should reschedule? Given what's happened?*

FARAH: *We barely knew Helen. What was her middle name? What was her job? Did she have siblings? I bet none of you know the answers to those questions. I'm not rescheduling.*

Lauren stares at her phone in shock, unsure how to respond to Farah's little tirade. When she hears the phone chirp again, she's almost scared to look. Relief floods her when Dominica's name appears on the screen.

> *Oh my God Lauren, how is it possible that Farah's become more intense about her wedding after this?*

She's a woman possessed, Lauren types.

Dominica agrees. *Truly frightening.*

CHAPTER TWENTY-TWO

The café on Old Ford Road was the place where they would all de-brief on a Sunday morning after a big night out. Back then, it used to be a greasy spoon run by a sweet old East End man who wore a white jacket and called everyone *sweetheart* and *darlin*. But now it appears to be the most tasteful patisserie the area has ever seen.

"God, I hope he retired and is living happily in the sun some-where," Lauren says, looking around, worrying that the gentrification her generation are responsible for may have ruined the man's liveli-hood.

"He probably died," Dominica says bluntly. She's wearing a pair of black Ray-Bans and a black roll-neck, and when she takes the Ray-Bans off, she looks tired and hungover.

Dominica's phone has been beeping almost constantly this morn-ing; she's had to put it on do not disturb so that the others can't see how many messages she's getting and start asking questions. She's sur-prised: she would never have had him down as one to panic unneces-sarily. Thank God she knows how to keep her emotions in check and her secrets secret. She'd just always assumed that, given who he is, he did too.

"Finally, here she is," Farah says, spotting the top of Saskia's expen-sively highlighted head through one of the front windows. She's been fidgeting and checking the time since they arrived, despite the fact that it's still two hours until their dress-fitting appointment.

Saskia sweeps through the café door, her shoes clipping across the black and white stone flooring, Prada sunglasses firmly fixed on her face. She's wearing black cigarette trousers with a white blouse, giving her the air of someone who has their shit together even this early on a Sunday morning.

"Black Americano, please, I'll be over there with my friends," she calls to the barista, breezing past the counter.

She pulls out the empty seat and tips it forward to get rid of any crumbs before sitting down. Her sunglasses stay *in situ* until she's completely settled, then she whips them off, exposing her heavily concealer-ed eyes.

"Well, what a fucking shitshow," she says. "How's everyone doing?"

At this unexpected question, the other women all blink in disbelief. Dominica's so startled she feels her teeth set on edge, and Farah stares down at her engagement ring, clenching and unclenching her fist to make the sparkle pop.

Saskia leans forward and lowers her voice as if she's in some kind of spy novel. "Jeremy was on the phone to his contact at Scotland Yard this morning—" she begins.

"I know how she died. I've got a friend on the force who feeds me information sometimes if I need it for a case," Dominica butts in. "Helen's vaginal egg was poisoned with arsenic."

The barista, who has approached with Saskia's coffee, puts it down hastily and backs away.

"Obviously it doesn't look great for those of us who were there," Saskia says, trying to regain control of the situation.

"Obviously." Dominica nods like she's in no mood to be told how to conduct herself legally by Saskia.

"Things just got serious," Saskia continues. "They're going to delve into our pasts. Two people murdered, and we were there for both of them. We need to be prepared. If they go back far enough, they'll get to when we were sixteen. And if they get there, they could figure it out."

"How?" Dominica squints at her like she's being stupid. "It would be a huge leap to make. And they're not exactly concerned about something that happened nearly twenty years ago that has already been laid to rest. They're concerned about two people being murdered now. So unless any of us did the murdering, we've got nothing to worry about."

There's a momentary awkward silence as the women shuffle in their seats.

"All the same," Saskia says, "I'd rather we make sure we know what we're saying if someone brings it up."

"Just say 'yes, that was very sad' or something. It's not a big deal. Don't be weird about it," Dominica says.

"I can do that," Farah says.

Lauren feels like what happened back then actually was a massive deal, and it makes her wonder if her friends are psychopaths when they talk like this. They all stare at her. She really resents that they think she'd be the first to crumble under pressure. She knows how to keep a secret way better than any of them. "What? I'll be fine. Say nothing and act normal. Business as usual for me."

"Well, exactly," Saskia says, a little flustered.

"That's that then," Dominica says, tilting her head to Saskia in a challenge, as if to say "I told you so, dare you to mention it again."

"I can't believe we're having this conversation right before my dress fitting," Farah mutters into her latte.

"Do they have any leads?" Saskia asks Dominica, ignoring Farah and swallowing her pride.

"Not that my friend could tell me. But obviously we're all suspects." Dominica is thrilled that she gazumped Saskia with her information. Finally the guy she was shagging at Scotland Yard who was way too into her has come in handy for something.

Lauren's face turns pale and her jaw drops. *All* of them are suspects? There's a spiky silence around the table while the women sit for a second, not making eye contact with each other. Farah stirs her coffee more aggressively and for far longer than any cup of coffee warrants.

"You'll stir all the flavor out of that if you're not careful," Saskia snipes. Farah drops the spoon and glares at her like a petulant child.

"Did Jeremy's friend have any intel?" Dominica asks, revelling in the knowledge that he clearly didn't. She just wants to hear Saskia admit it.

"He didn't say. He probably doesn't want to bother me with too much unnecessary detail because I'm so busy." Saskia puts her nose in the air, taking a sip from her coffee.

"Yes, of course, no one needs unnecessary detail," Dominica parrots back at her. She can't believe Saskia thinks she's busy. Like she thinks the PTA and a vanity events-planning business are more time-consuming than the twenty divorce cases Dominica's currently bashing through.

"Where would someone even get arsenic from?" Lauren asks.

"I don't know," Dominica says. "Google it."

Lauren narrows her eyes; she's not about to start googling how to buy arsenic when she's a suspect in a murder that was committed with arsenic. She's not that stupid.

"I'm going to go with Jen when she gives her statement tomorrow, if anyone wants to come too," says Dominica. "Give her some support. We might not have known them well, but we all know how tough it must be for her losing a friend like that."

"Good idea," Saskia says, bristling at being told what to do, while Farah and Lauren nod. Dominica's surprised she can find the time.

"We need to get going if we're going to make our appointment," Farah says, breaking the silence. "I can't miss another one, there's only a few weeks until the wedding."

"Right, yes, of course," Saskia says.

"Do you think we should maybe postpone next—" Lauren doesn't get to finish the question, because Farah cuts her off.

"No," she says bluntly. She pushes out her chair and gets up. "Come on, let's go, we can't be late. I'll get charged if we miss this one."

The other women look around them feeling slightly dazed, but they stand up and follow Farah. Dominica takes her phone out, trailing slightly behind so that she can check her messages. There's a barrage of texts from *him*, but it's one of the emails that grabs her attention. One she's been waiting on for a while—three months, to be precise—since she acquired some information during a divorce case that piqued her curiosity. And now, here it is, sent to her by a private investigator: a document she's been trying to uncover for so long she thought this day would never come. And at the top of that document, standing out on her screen in bold, and highlighted for ease, is exactly the name she was expecting to see.

Jeremy Bardon-Burnett

CHAPTER TWENTY-THREE

2005 Part One

Dominica pulls her top back on and combs through her hair with her fingers. He's already standing by the door, fully dressed. She feels exposed, the sinking pang of failure hitting her as she sees the way he's pulled the duvet over the bloodstain. To look at the room, you'd think nothing had happened here at all.

Shame fills her right to the brim as she turns to look at him, but he doesn't return her eye contact. And why should he? He's Greg Thomas, the captain of the football team; any sixteen-year-old girl would be lucky to lose their virginity to him. But rather than it being a sexy and sophisticated encounter, Dominica bled all over his sheets.

"I should go out first," he says. "Then you count to a hundred and come out after. Probably best we don't tell anyone about this."

"What about the sheets?" she asks, picking at her nails and staring at the floor. "I can wash them if you like?" The searing pain in her vagina demands that she goes home, but she feels like if she stays maybe she can redeem herself somehow. Also it's not like home offers any more emotional comfort or warmth than here. Surely there has to be a way to get back to how they were. He's gone from telling her how sexy she is to barely even registering her presence.

"It's fine. I'll sort them," he says brusquely, and then looks back at her as if finally feeling the tiniest bit of empathy. "Look, if it's any consolation, you've definitely got the best tits I've ever seen," he compliments without any hint of irony or self-awareness.

Not once has he asked her if she's OK or questioned if the blood that made him recoil might be causing her any kind of pain. She thought he was different, she thought he really cared about her. And now he's behaving like a stranger. He opens the door and looks both ways before disappearing out into the corridor, taking no responsibility for his part in what happened. She'd been led to believe that losing her virginity would help her feel more accomplished somehow, but instead, she's never felt more humiliated.

Having spent all her time with Greg trying to make sure she came across as sexually experienced and some kind of minx, the fact that she's just bled all over his bed is beyond disastrous. It's obvious their relationship is over, and probably so is her life. He doesn't have to remind her to keep this to herself; there's no way she's telling anyone about it.

Losing her virginity might be the biggest and most disappointing anticlimax she's experienced to date. She knows this wasn't his first time. The whole school knows this wasn't his first time. There's an entire wall in the boys' toilets devoted to Greg's conquests; a picture of it circulated round the Nokia camera phones of Year 11 only last week. She was just foolish enough to believe that after weeks of texting and MSN conversations in the dead of night, he actually really liked her. She wanted to believe she meant something to him. She needed to be something special to someone.

She thought post-coital you were supposed to feel full of love and happiness and a kind of warmth. She just has a searing pain between her legs and an urge to punch things, specifically parts of Greg's body.

.   .   .

Dominica finally makes it back downstairs to the party, after sitting on the toilet for ten minutes splashing water on her burning vagina. She tries to convince herself that it'll be all right. If he's not going to tell anyone and neither is she, maybe she can pretend it never happened. That would be OK, right?

Then she sees him and realizes he's already way ahead of her in that respect. In full view of everyone in the living room, he's sitting on the sofa with Tansy straddling him, her tongue down his throat.

CHAPTER TWENTY-FOUR

The hens pile wearily into the small pink-and-gold-decorated wedding boutique. No sooner has the door closed than a woman in her sixties with platinum-blonde hair piled on top of her head, and a tape measure around her neck, comes racing out to meet them. The thick green-rimmed glasses perched on her nose wobble slightly as she moves.

"DARLING!" She embraces Farah like an eagle suffocating its prey. "You poor thing! What a terrible time you've had over the last few weeks! I simply cannot imagine what you've been through. At a time that's supposed to be so filled with joy as well."

"Thank you, Cynthia." Farah accepts the hug gratefully, feeling as if no one else has really considered that all these murders are ruining her wedding run-up. At least it seems like Cynthia gives a shit about what is supposed to be the happiest time of her life.

"You poor, poor darling. Come! I've got champagne, and all the dresses are ready for you." Cynthia ushers them all across the shop floor, through some thick gold curtains, and into the beautifully mani-cured dressing room.

Everything's set out in an Instagram-perfect way so that brides can take pictures with their bridesmaids in the huge gold-edged mirrors and really cherish the beautiful moments. Two younger assistants are busying themselves around the dresses, but when Cynthia clicks her fingers, they immediately hand everyone a flute of champagne.

"Now then, what order would you like to do things in today? How about bridesmaids first, then we have the big reveal after we've dealt with the supporting actresses?" Cynthia suggests.

Dominica screws her face up at being called anyone's supporting actress, and Saskia simply stretches her lips into what she thinks is a smile but isn't. Lauren looks around, marveling at the decor, and sips at a glass of champagne that she didn't think she'd be able to manage after yesterday but as it turns out is going down a treat.

"Agreed," Farah says. "Bridesmaids first, then we can do the grand finale."

"Girls! Fetch the dresses!" Cynthia says to her assistants, clapping her hands.

Cynthia's been making and altering wedding dresses for the last fifty years, since she was a teenager, according to her website. She's so popular that she can pick and choose her brides and has an impenetrable waiting list. Unless you have enough money, that is. And Farah made sure she had enough money.

The assistants rush to get the dresses, handing them out to Lauren, Saskia, and Dominica. The assistant holding Tansy's dress stands looking confused, the terrible moment stretching on and on.

"Girls! I told you, we won't be requiring that dress anymore!" Cynthia snaps. "Put it out the back! QUICKLY!"

"Oh no, it's OK," Farah says. "My sister-in-law's going to be my fourth bridesmaid now."

At this Cynthia looks positively scandalized. Lauren feels slightly sick at the mention of Eva as Farah's "sister-in-law."

"She should be here any second. I'm afraid it does mean that the dress might need some alterations, though," Farah goes on. "But I thought in the circumstances you wouldn't mind."

"Oh yes, of course!" Cynthia says so enthusiastically that they all know this is a complete pain in the arse for her. The shop buzzer goes before there's time for any more passive aggression.

Farah can tell from the others' faces that they're not impressed about Eva being a bridesmaid, but she needs someone to wear the dress and contribute to the cost. Speaking of which, she realizes she hasn't actually mentioned to the others yet that she's going to need them to pay.

The assistant who doesn't have their dead friend's dress in her hands heads to the front door to let Eva in.

"I'm so sorry I'm late!" Eva says, rushing into the dressing room.

Her face is blotchy and her eyes are red, clearly from the crying that she's been doing since yesterday. When Tansy died, they assumed her endless tears were because the two of them were so close, but given that yesterday prompted the exact same response, when *none* of them really knew Helen that well, they're beginning to wonder if she's simply a complete and utter drama queen.

"We should get on," Farah says. "We've only got two hours."

Even Saskia thinks that really two hours should be plenty of time to try on some dresses, but she says nothing, simply grabs her hideous lavender outfit and heads obediently into a changing room.

Once all the bridesmaids are closeted in their cubicles, Farah begins to talk to Cynthia about the terrible time she's had sorting out flowers because the ones she wants in her bouquet aren't in season and apparently no matter how much money she throws at her florist they're saying that they simply can't make it happen.

"You've already had so much else to struggle with, you don't need issues with the flowers as well. You poor, poor dear," Cynthia says, pouring more champagne into her glass.

"I just feel like it's time the universe gave me a break, you know?" Farah says, sipping the champagne gratefully, pleased that she finally has someone to talk to who isn't going to make her feel bad for complaining about flowers when two people have died.

Dominica throws open the door to her changing room, partly in disgust at the dress and partly with irritation that Farah's behaving as if her wedding is a giant hardship for her. She's had enough of people losing their shit over a single day of their lives. The other three doors open much more gently, and all four women stand there in their puffy-sleeved dresses complete with lace fringing between the cake-like tiers.

Saskia thinks these dresses must be a sick joke, while Lauren's not really noticed what she's wearing because she's too busy being annoyed about how much better Eva looks in it than she does. Dominica wants to know why all bridesmaid dresses have to be an uncomfortable penance for being a good friend to someone.

"Oh God, you all look so beautiful!" Farah exclaims. "I really mean it! GORGEOUS!"

"WONDERFUL! STUNNING!" Cynthia shouts, and her assistants nod along eagerly.

"Do they all fit OK?" Farah asks, getting closer to the hens to inspect the dresses. "Lauren! Have you lost weight? You were given strict instructions not to! Cynthia? Does Lauren's dress look a little loose around the arms?"

"I don't know." Lauren stares at the puffy sleeves, wondering how anyone could even tell. "I'm not sure . . ."

"Don't worry darling, we can just nip those in, no worries at all!" Cynthia says quickly, pinning the apparently massive arms of Lauren's dress.

"The other two seem fine," Farah says. "You'll definitely look better with hair and makeup!" she adds to Dominica and Saskia without so much as a hint of self-awareness. "Eva's just needs taking in around the waist and letting out around the chest."

"You've got the most perfect figure I've ever seen! Gorgeous!" Cynthia says, marveling at Eva as the assistants crowd around this case study of perfection.

"Great," Lauren says, smiling through gritted teeth.

"Wonderful! Ladies, get changed and we'll crack on with the main event," Cynthia announces. Then she turns to Eva. "Except for you, dear. If you'd just go through to the back there with my assistant, she can get your dress all pinned up and ready to be altered. You really do have a dream figure, though; it'll be an honor!"

Farah starts clapping and jumping at the mention of her own dress fitting and Saskia joins in, while Lauren looks again at her sleeves, confused about how she's supposed to get the dress off without stabbing herself with the pins. Dominica simply stands wincing at the whole affair. Had she known that today was going to be so screechy, she might not have drunk so much last night.

In their normal clothes again, the three women gather on a crushed-velvet sofa, listening to the sounds of Farah getting into her dress. There's a banging and rustling from the bridal changing room that makes them all fear for what they'll have to do on the big day without Cynthia there to help.

"Do you think Farah's OK?" Lauren whispers, sipping her champagne.

"Well, planning a wedding's stressful at the best of times, and this is the worst of times," Saskia says, tapping away at something on her phone.

"I mean, she was stressed before anyway because she said she felt like Tansy was stealing her thunder." Lauren says the thing that no one has dared mention since Tansy's sad departure.

"She waited years for Toby to propose and Tansy only met Ivan a couple of months before they got engaged," Saskia reasons. "I can see how that would grate a little. But she surely can't hold it against Tansy now."

"What are we going to do about next weekend?" Dominica whispers. "She's expecting a big hurrah and we haven't found anywhere yet."

"I'm scared," Lauren says. "I don't think we should do it."

"For God's sake, Lauren!" Saskia hisses.

"She has a point," Dominica says. "Two out of two have ended in murder. Even I'm getting a little edgy."

"I know what you mean, but you saw her earlier when Lauren suggested postponing," Saskia whispers. "She's clearly having some kind of crisis; we need to do SOMETHING. Have neither of you ever heard the expression third time lucky?"

"For us or the murderer?" Dominica hisses.

"Look," Saskia says, "I get your point, but do either of you want to be the one to tell her?"

"We'll get killed if we don't and killed if we do," Dominica says sagely, and Lauren nods.

"What if it was just a small group of us again?" Saskia asks.

"It was a small group of us before and someone still died," Lauren says, nervously chewing on the inside of her cheek. "Which makes it all the more concerning, to be honest."

"OK, let's look at this sensibly," Saskia says. "We were all present both times, all of us, and Jen. So that means the murderer has to be . . ." She hesitates as she realizes that what she's saying sounds impossible. "OK, so it has to be someone who was there yesterday."

"Jen didn't do it, she was gutted," Lauren says.

"Do you ever wonder about Eva, though?" Dominica mutters. "What do we really know about her?"

"And those text messages Tansy was getting . . ." Lauren trails off.

"But we can't not invite her, she's Farah's 'sister-in-law'!" Saskia exclaims.

"We could tell her it's cancelled?" Lauren offers innocently.

"It has to be someone else," Saskia says. "Why would she sabotage Farah's wedding like that?"

"OK, well, obviously it wasn't me," Dominica says. "I work in the law."

"Absolutely not me," Saskia adds.

"And it wasn't Lauren." Dominica laughs at the thought and Saskia joins in. Lauren thinks that her being the murderer would really show them.

"Right, so that leaves . . ." Lauren points toward the changing room.

"OH MY GOD, GUYS, I'M SO BEAUTIFUL!" Farah suddenly shouts. "I CAN'T WAIT FOR YOU TO SEE THIS!"

There's a shocked silence among the women until Saskia elbows the other two.

"CAN'T WAIT!" she shouts, with Lauren and Dominica mumbling other excited phrases. As they stare at each other, their eyes wide, Farah's phone beeps in her open bag on the sofa, and a message appears on the screen from Toby. Dominica doesn't mean to look, but it's right there and she can't help but see what it says. Saskia and Lauren find themselves also accidentally glancing in that direction.

> It's fine honestly, you probs need to stop saying how good it
> is that Tansy's wedding isn't happening tho.

"Jesus Christ," Dominica mouths.

"You don't think she could have been so annoyed about Tansy's wedding that she . . ." Lauren blinks, just as there's a loud banging noise from the changing room followed by an eerie silence. The three women stare at the door, frozen.

"I'm sure it's fine. You can't die in a bridal shop," Lauren whispers. But she sounds very unsure of herself.

"The sewing tape?" Saskia offers at the same time that Dominica blurts, "Pins."

The three of them assess the closed changing room door, waiting for any sign of life. When no such sign is forthcoming, they all slowly rise from the sofa. Saskia's finger hovers over the emergency call button on her phone while Dominica picks up the empty champagne bottle, and they creep toward the door.

"MY GOODNESS, YOU LOOK RADIANT! INCOMPARABLE! A BEAUTY!" Cynthia screams in delight, making them all jump away and race back to their seats, knowing that any minute now the door's going to fly open and Farah will sweep out, eager for them to cry and cheer and praise her perfect dress.

"We keep an eye on her and we keep an eye on Eva," Dominica whispers through a gritted smile.

"You're being ridiculous," Saskia mutters back.

"I don't want to die before the next season of *Grey's Anatomy* airs," Lauren adds to the mix.

"Oh guys, while we're here," Farah's voice comes from behind the changing room door, "I just wanted to let you know, things are a bit tight at the moment, so would it be OK if you contributed a little bit to your dresses? Should only be a few hundred each."

The three of them nod, eyes still wide. There's no way they're going to say no to a potentially murderous bride.

"Of course," Dominica replies, nudging the other two.

"No problem!" Saskia adds.

"Sure!" Lauren chimes.

"Great, thanks! I knew you'd understand!" Farah says, just as the door opens and Cynthia's delighted face appears.

"Ladies! YOUR BRIDE!" she announces as Farah steps out in an abundance of lace, a white veil pinned into her hair.

"STUNNING!" Saskia shouts.

"AMAZING!" Dominica exclaims.

"OH, YOU LOOK BEAUTIFUL!" Lauren screeches.

In fact, none of them are really taking in the dress at all. All the emotions they expected to feel—the love and pride and happiness for their friend—have been completely overshadowed by fear.

CHAPTER TWENTY-FIVE

Farah's been trying to ignore Rebecca's glares across the office all day. She's attempting to concentrate on this story about older brides, the women who are doing it for the second, third, fourth, and in one case tenth time. She knows that these women have lost their first husbands or been through traumatic divorces, but still she can't help but feel jealous of them and the excitement around their upcoming nuptials. None of them are spending their time pre-wedding in police interview rooms, are they?

When Lauren started to suggest that they move Farah's hen do a SECOND time the other day, she thought she was going to lose it. And no, the spa trip didn't count. She's waited to be a bride for over ten years—since she first met Toby—and now that it's finally happening, all of it's been overshadowed by Tansy's wedding and then Tansy's death and now Helen. *Helen,* a friend of Tansy's they didn't even really know! She doesn't mean to sound heartless, but Tansy spent her whole life stealing Farah's thunder; how is she still managing to steal it from beyond the grave?

She knows she shouldn't be thinking like this. She's just stressed. It feels like the wedding disasters are mounting up the closer it gets to the big day.

Noticing the time, she stands up and grabs her denim jacket from the back of her chair.

"Gotta go and give this statement to the police." She rolls her eyes at her desk buddy. "Should be back after lunch."

She can feel Rebecca's eyes on her as she walks across the office. Her boss has been watching her since she found out about the money, a stern reminder of the £20,000 that she needs to find from somewhere or face the consequences. Like she could ever forget. When her phone beeps with a message from Dominica, she's relieved to have something to do while she's being observed so closely.

Remember, you don't know anything about H.

Farah heads into the waiting lift. She can't believe Dominica thinks they need reminding that they're not supposed to know how Helen died. Just because they're not lawyers doesn't mean they're stupid.

Helen shouldn't even have been there on Saturday; she'd still be alive if she hadn't been. But it's entirely Saskia's fault that she was. And now, because of that, even Toby suggested yesterday evening that they move the wedding. As soon as he said it, Farah's stress levels simply boiled over. He couldn't understand why it made her so angry and it caused a massive fight, because he doesn't realize that if they do move it, she'll be instantly bankrupt. But there's no way she can tell him that, not after all the lies she's spun him. As far as he knows, the most lavish parts of the wedding and all the expensive dress fittings are favors she's called in from the magazine and colleagues she's worked with over the years. He's never questioned it. Or looked into her biggest lie: that the castle is actually costing them twenty grand more than she told him it was.

When she saw the place featured as a wedding venue in *Vogue,* she knew she needed to get married there. It would be the perfect showstopper. All those people who had joked about her and Toby would eat their words when they saw it. But if they postponed the wedding now, people would think he'd got cold feet. Worse, if he found out how much debt they were in, he might *actually* decide he didn't want to marry her. And Farah would be heartbroken.

Heading through the glass barriers in the lobby and out onto Fleet Street, she looks enviously at the people standing outside pubs having lunchtime drinks in the sunshine. Turning down the alleyway next to the Cheshire Cheese, she feels a prickling on the back of her neck but puts it down to the darkness of the space and carries on going. It's only when she heads into a second passage that she hears the sound of footsteps and senses someone behind her. Her steps quicken, but so do the steps behind her. She tells herself it's overdramatic to be this scared, it's just someone else trying to get from A to B as quickly as possible like her. Even so, she doesn't look back for fear of who she might see there and rustles in her bag for something to defend herself with. Finding only her cigarettes, she tries to light one without stopping, wishing she'd stuck to the main roads rather than a series of alleyways and narrow closed-off paths surrounded by building works. She thinks about changing her route, but that'll take ages and surely she's just being silly. She's on edge after everything that's happened.

The footsteps get louder as she tries to speed up. The noise bounces against the chipboard walls of a tunnel-like structure created under the scaffolding of an office block construction site. The space is darker than the other alleyways, only lit by the bright sunlight at the other end that Farah now races toward as a beacon of safety. She feels as if her legs are dragging as she tries to move them faster, willing herself closer to the end of the tunnel, imagining the point where the sun beams down on her face and she's safe. She takes a pull on her cigarette, hoping it'll calm her nerves, but her breath's too shallow to take it in, the walls closing in on her as the footsteps behind get so close she knows they're either going to pass her or stop her. She blinks, willing it to be over, the clack of shoes now directly behind her. A hand reaches down and grasps her shoulder, and she spins around. She tries to jab at them with the lit cigarette, but it falls through her shaking fingers to the ground and she jumps back, freeing her shoulder from the hand's clawed grasp.

"Farah!" Jeremy's voice booms as she registers his face and blue suit in the darkness. She looks down at the brown shoes that pursued her.

"Jeremy!" she says in a strangled half-scream as she tries to compose herself.

She doesn't want to let on that she was terrified, but she can feel her heart hammering away in her ears, the noise of blood pumping directly to her brain. She can't think of a single time the two of them have been alone together or even really spoken that much, so she finds it a little bit jarring to be in such close quarters with him now, not to mention that he actually touched her. It's like he's never heard of personal space.

"Gosh, I thought I was going to have to run after you then!" he says, his laughter echoing off the chipboard. He looms over her, his hands in his pockets rustling coins or keys or something in that way men do when they want to cement a certain status. "How's it going?"

"Good, thanks. Just off to see your wife at the police station, actually," Farah says, trying to edge away but coming up against the chipboard.

"Ah yes, I thought you might be," Jeremy says. "That's why I followed you down here. I just wondered if we could have a little chat." It doesn't appear to be a question. "I heard something this morning from a friend on the board at your magazine. Something about an article you're writing that might make things rather difficult for Saskia and me were it to appear. I'm sure you didn't realize what you were doing when you started writing it, but now that you do, and you understand the repercussions it could have for us, there's no way you'll continue with it . . . yes?"

She racks her brain, trying to work out who he might know and why they would have told him. Only a handful of people know about the article, and they're all sworn to secrecy. She hasn't even told Toby what it is she's working on. It should never have left the building.

"No idea what you're talking about," she replies, staring behind him, willing someone else to come down the alleyway to ease the tension.

"Excellent. I knew it must have been some sort of misunderstanding. Of course you wouldn't be part of it. To double-cross Saskia like that would be catastrophic for your friendship, wouldn't it?" He stares at her.

"Of course," Farah says, feeling a lump form in her throat.

"Glad we understand each other. It's such a risk for you anyway; a bit of a legal nightmare really. There's absolutely no truth to it, so at the very least you'd get done for defamation. Obviously no one wants to see your career suffer like that." He flashes a dangerous smile. "And that's if we're playing by the book."

"I understand." Farah says.

"Great, fabulous." He slaps her on the back before leaning closer. "Certainly I think a woman in your position should be focusing on making sure everything runs smoothly for her big day. It'd be a shame if anything ruined it."

"Right." Farah gulps. "I should really go. The police are expecting me."

"Of course, of course," Jeremy says, stepping aside. "Lovely to see you! I'm around these parts a lot, so I'm sure I'll bump into you again soon."

Once she's out in the open, with plenty of people around her, she pulls out her phone.

Rebecca, we've got a big problem. It's Jeremy.
He knows and he's threatened me.

And this is my problem how?

Please. We have to stop. He says he'll sue for defamation.

They always do.

*I can do an article about Tansy instead. An article about
a bride being killed on her hen do! That's bound to get hits!
Please . . . my career will be over. He'll ruin me.*

*Darling, so will I. You've stolen company money. All I have
to do is tell one person and you'll be sacked and prosecuted.
Unless you like the sound of a prison wedding?*

Dominica almost chokes on her takeaway coffee when she sees Jeremy
following Farah. She's just about to call out to Farah and catch up with
her, but something about the way he's pursuing her with such purpose
makes her hang back, instead following at a distance, trying not to be
noticed. She catches snippets of their conversation, but she can't get
close enough to hear the whole thing, not without alerting them to
her presence.

She ends up pressed against the corner of a bit of chipboard a little
way down the makeshift alley, their voices traveling toward her amidst
the clanging of builders moving things on the scaffolding above them.
The words she does catch paint a picture that is enough to concern
her, though. It sounds like Farah's writing an article and Jeremy isn't
happy about it. It stands to reason that a journalist might have found
out the same things that Dominica has, but surely if she was going to
write about it and expose it on such a large scale she'd notify Saskia first?
Surely she hasn't lost her way so much she's forgotten about loyalty?

She strains, trying to hear more, but the builders have got noisier, laughing and joking, shouting to each other over the clanking of the steel posts. It has to be the same thing Dominica knows; what else could it be? She needs to talk to her contact, find out how the press could have got hold of it. If something's going to be revealed, she needs to get Saskia out of there faster than she'd planned. There's no way Saskia knows about what Jeremy's doing: she's just an innocent bystander to the crimes of her husband. And now Farah's got herself involved and is probably being threatened by Jeremy. Why is Dominica *always* having to save them all?

CHAPTER TWENTY-SIX

Lauren's had countless breathless dreams since Saturday about having sex in a lift with Joss. She's telling herself it's a trauma response to Helen and Tansy's deaths so that she feels a little less pathetic. But as she walks into the police station ready for her interview, she finds herself looking around her like a meerkat, hopeful that he might have come to support Eva. She's not sure why she's so excited about seeing him here; he can't exactly shag her in the police station waiting room, across the cold metal seats. She really just wants him to look at her and think she's sexy, maybe get a little hot under the collar . . . But that's ALL. Definitely, no more than that. She wonders how strict they are about the use of those interrogation rooms. Focus, Lauren. Helen's dead. Tansy too.

She can't see Joss though, or Eva for that matter. Was all the preparation she put in for this interview for nothing? Has she got perfect hair for no reason?

"Finally, Lauren!" Saskia gasps, her voice cutting through Lauren's foggy-headed fantasies. "The detective was waiting for you. He's just taken Eva in. He said as you were late he'd do you after."

"I need to head off," Farah says, emerging from the toilet and making Lauren sidle a little closer to Dominica for protection.

After their concerns about Farah the other day, none of them have said anything more, but Lauren's not volunteering to be alone with her. Rationally she knows it's ridiculous: they've all known her since they were kids. She's Farah! Right?

She realizes Farah's staring at her impatiently because she's trying to say goodbye and Lauren's just standing silently wondering if she's a killer.

"Sorry! Hi! Bye!" she says, giving Farah a nervous hug.

Dominica says goodbye while scrolling down her inbox. She can't believe she hasn't had an immediate response to the email she sent after overhearing Farah and Jeremy's conversation.

"I mean, I thought the idea was that we were going to debrief afterward," Saskia says with the tone of a disapproving teacher. "But whatever you want to do is fine."

Lauren finds herself glaring at her. Why would she prolong time with the person they think might be the killer?

"I've got this whole pesky job thing I have to get back to. Not to mention the whole getting married soon thing," Farah says, looking harassed. "Sorry."

"OK, well, that's probably for the best anyway, because we'll be talking very important hen do details!" Saskia trills.

"YAY! Don't worry, I've got my passport ready and waiting!" Farah says, beaming because FINALLY someone's prioritizing her wedding.

"Oh." Dominica, Saskia, and Lauren all look shifty, nervous that not being able to take her on a hen do abroad will be what gets them slain. Lauren watched a documentary the other day about killer brides-to-be who just sort of pop under the stress and become serial killers. She's been doing her research.

"What?" Farah asks, twigging that none of them are looking at her. She narrows her eyes in a way that prompts shudders of terror in all of them.

"Look," Dominica says, advancing toward her. The bravest of the lot. "There's no easy way to say this, but the police don't want us leaving the country, so we're going to have to do something UK-based."

Farah says nothing. Saskia admires how she's really using the whole "silence as power" thing. It's almost impressive how awkward she's made this whole situation.

Lauren worries that Farah's about to launch at them in a murderous rage. Surely they're safe in a police station, though? Dominica cannot believe that Farah still thought after everything that happened that they were going to be leaving the country. Has she become that far removed from reality in her little bridezilla bubble?

"Are you fucking joking?" Farah asks slowly, deliberately, so there can be no mistaking her tone. She blinks slowly, disappointment radiating from her eyelids.

"Um, no?" Dominica says as Saskia puts a tentative arm around Farah's shoulders. Lauren doesn't know how they have the guts. She feels like a baby goat that's just picked a fight with a bull.

"Look, I know this isn't ideal, but with everything—" Saskia begins.

"WHY IS IT ALWAYS ABOUT HER! WHY CAN'T IT JUST BE ABOUT ME FOR FUCKING ONCE?!" Behind the reception desk, police officers are staring, wondering if they need to intervene. "After everything, with all this going on, *everything* I've got to deal with, I thought I could rely on you all to let me have ONE nice weekend away from the stress and drama!"

Dominica wonders what kind of hen do Farah thinks would contain a lack of drama. It's certainly never been known in her lifetime.

Saskia attempts to reason with her again but gets brushed off. Before anyone can say anything else, Farah's storming toward the automatic doors. Only held back by the slowness with which they open. It takes so long that the moment there's a tiny gap, she inches her way through, positively throwing herself down the stairs on the other side in a rage.

"See you Saturday," Dominica calls after her, raising a hand to wave goodbye.

The three of them look at each other. They knew Farah's bridezilla attitude had got out of hand. But could it really have got THAT out of hand?

"Fuck, she is pissed . . ." Lauren is distracted by Joss appearing round the corner with a coffee in hand.

"I think she's just feeling the pre-wedding pressure," Saskia says, as if such a huge blow-up were completely normal.

"Was that my sister just storming out?" Joss asks. "What happened? I presume it was wedding-related."

"She's annoyed that we can't go abroad on the hen do," Dominica says.

"Ah. You've activated Princess Farah. She'll get over it once she accepts that she can't have exactly what she wants." Joss shrugs.

Maybe, Saskia thinks, they've all been a little hard on her. She's still their friend, they should trust her more, surely. Dominica thinks people need to get some fucking perspective. It's just a wedding.

Lauren's already moved on, studying Joss's face for any kind of recognition that something's changed or that he even remembers being in the lift with her on Saturday, but he seems completely unmoved by her presence, barely noticing her.

"Heya! What did I miss?" Eva's voice from behind Joss makes Lauren jump. She marvels at how incredibly perfect Eva looks in a tracksuit with her hair pulled up in a bun. She hasn't made any effort and yet she's stunning, while Lauren's worked on her look for hours and feels like melted candle wax.

She watches as Joss puts his arm around Eva, kissing her on the cheek and staring at her with such love.

"Lauren?" DI Ashford calls, snapping her out of it.

"Hi," Lauren says. She could have sworn that she saw the detective just checking her out. Maybe she should flirt with him in front of Joss. Is that childish? Fuck it, she'll do it anyway.

CHAPTER TWENTY-SEVEN

"Unfortunately it does look as if Helen's death was definitely murder," DI Ashford says. Lauren tries to make sure that she rearranges her expression into one of shock. "Which makes it even more likely that your friend Tansy was murdered too."

Lauren feels tears pricking at the mention of Tansy, but she tries to hold them back. She's done well at keeping it together so far. Dominica really needn't have sent her quite so many texts about not letting on what they all already know.

"Can you think of anyone who had a grudge against either of your friends?" he asks.

"No." Lauren shakes her head. "I didn't really know Helen; I think I met her maybe twice before Tansy's hen do. But Tansy, definitely not. Everyone loved her." She decides not to mention the number of times Tansy pissed her off, and the others too.

"And aside from the people you've already listed in your statement, was there anyone else you remember being at both hen parties?"

"No." She feels very sure of that, despite the possible liters of alcohol that she'd consumed at the time.

"No one on the staff maybe?" DI Ashford asks.

"No." She frowns, wondering why he's pressing the point.

"OK, that's probably all. But here's my card if you think of anything else." He hands her the card and she takes it politely, putting it in her bag, then stands up, pulling her skirt down and feeling suddenly shy as she realizes he's looking at her legs.

The two of them head back out to the waiting area, Lauren ready to flirt with DI Ashford for Joss's benefit. But when they get there, she's disappointed to see that he and Eva have already left.

The three women walk out of the station and into the hot afternoon sun. There's a small pause where they all enjoy the fresh air before Saskia ruins it.

"Guys, we need to talk about Farah's hen do," she instructs. "It's in four days and she'd *kill* us if she knew we don't have anything sorted."

"Maybe literally," Dominica interjects. "But actually, we do have a plan. I think we've sorted the perfect weekend."

"Oh, but so have I, and I think mine will be way better," Saskia says smugly. "It's at the Ritz."

"We're going to Blackpool," Dominica says at the same moment, with conviction.

Saskia's mouth drops open. "I beg your pardon?"

"Lauren and I figured it'd be good to get her out of London, and we thought you were a bit snowed under, so we've arranged it all. We leave on Saturday morning." She goes on without taking a breath so that Saskia doesn't get a chance to butt in. "We know Farah wanted something abroad, so we thought what's better than the beach? Plus it's something we can all afford after not getting our full deposit back for Ibiza. We're going to be arriving at midday, and I've booked us into a nice but affordable hotel. It's just going to be us and Eva. Farah's other friends don't fancy a hen do with us for some reason." She shrugs. "Eva's called in some influencer favors. We just need to do a lot of posting on her account for the brands that have given us freebies. Shouldn't be a problem, right?"

"Right," Lauren confirms.

"We're going to start the weekend by pedaling a party bike along the seafront before our pole dancing class—very chic now, apparently—then we'll grab dinner and finish off the evening at the Adonis Arena Cabaret before heading home on the Sunday morning, probably somewhat worse for wear but fulfilled by the experience."

Saskia looks as if she's just been slapped around the face with a wet fish.

"And Eva says this is *all* very chic?" Saskia asks.

"It's kitsch." Dominica smiles.

"What if *we* die, though?" Lauren gulps, still focusing on the fact that the rest of Farah's friends aren't coming because they're so afraid of being murdered. "There's no way I'm sharing a room with Farah."

"You cannot still SERIOUSLY think Farah did it," Saskia says.

"I mean, brides can really lose it before their big day," Dominica says. "I watched a documentary on killer brides the other night—"

"ME TOO!" Lauren says. "With the woman who killed someone with her cake topper?"

"Fierce use of a plastic effigy of yourself." Dominica nods.

"I really do think we've all lost our shit," Saskia says. "Why would she do anything to sabotage her own hen dos and wedding? And why would she kill Helen, someone she barely knew?"

Lauren realizes that Saskia actually has a really good point there.

"Either way, it's a rock and a hard place: go to Farah's hen do and risk being murdered, or don't go and risk her coming after you and killing you herself with her bare bridezilla hands," Dominica reasons.

"Does anyone even know if Toby's having a stag do?" Lauren asks, as if suddenly remembering he exists.

Everyone looks around blankly, shaking their heads.

"Right, I'll send you the money and sort out the nanny." Even as she's saying it, Saskia can't believe the words coming out of her own mouth. "How are we getting there?" Her face begins to glow with the smallest glimmer of hope that the transport situation at least might be acceptable.

"Train," Dominica says bluntly. "And not first class. I've already booked the tickets." She looks Saskia directly in the eye—a challenge—and gives her a small, smug smile. "It's all we can afford at this stage."

"Right, well, that's that then." Saskia looks down at her phone. "Oh gosh, is that the time? I should get going. Sorry, I know I said we'd have a debrief, but I'm sure we all did fine. I should be getting to Mabel's ballet recital."

"OK, see you Saturday!" Dominica says cheerfully. "Meet in the Costa at Euston."

Saskia shudders, but nevertheless gives them both air kisses before heading toward her convertible BMW.

Lauren glances at her own phone. She got excited when she felt it vibrate, and she was right to be. It's Joss.

How are you doing? You looked really well today.

Really well? she thinks. Is that his way of saying she looked hot? Is this him admitting there *was* something between them on Saturday? And then her phone buzzes again. He's sent her a flame emoji.

Dominica links arms with her. "Wine?" she suggests. "I feel like with everything, we haven't really had a chance to chat lately."

"Oh absolutely," Lauren says, a huge smile on her face, barely taking in what Dominica's saying because all she can think is that Joss has just called her hot.

Dominica looks at her friend, feeling confused, but then gets distracted by her own phone, where the words *I need to see you, he's hungry* sit underneath a picture of a very recognizable erect penis in the also very recognizable location of her office.

"Oh God, I have to go," she says. "It's work. I'm so sorry! Another time?"

Lauren's too busy formulating her response to the flame emoji to really care.

CHAPTER TWENTY-EIGHT

Dominica closes the door to her office. Her assistant told her someone was waiting in there for her, but she already knew exactly who it was and what they wanted.

"Don't you ever have to work?" she asks, as her desk chair spins round. Upon it her male visitor appears to be naked but for his tie and a pair of long white socks.

"Some things are more important than work," he says.

Dominica really disagrees with this sentiment but carries on anyway.

"You know you shouldn't just be hanging in my office on your own. I've got confidential documents in here. I'm working on a massive case at the moment, very high-profile. I can't believe my assistant let you in."

"Oh, I'm well aware how powerful you are. And as for your assistant, I think we can both agree I'm very persuasive when I want something." He raises himself from the chair, a cheeky, boyish smile on his face. She can see there's one part of him that certainly doesn't need persuading.

"Well, I guess you're right about that," she says, locking the door behind her and slinking out of her jacket. She struts toward him, losing an item of clothing with every step.

A vibration flows through her desk as she straddles him, making her look over distractedly at her illuminated phone screen. She squints over his shoulder so that she can read the news alert that's popped up, and when she does, she stops still, his erect penis standing between the two of them awaiting action.

"He'll get a complex," he says, referring to it like it's a sentient being.

"They've arrested someone for the murders," Dominica says, reaching out and grabbing her phone from the desk, his angry cock forgotten. "I need to call the others."

His clothes are on and he's out of the door in seconds.

Farah starts the group FaceTime from behind her desk and isn't surprised when all the women pick up immediately.

"Have you seen the news?" Everyone speaks at the same time.

"Who is it?" Farah asks, a steely look in her eye that suggests that now the perpetrator has been caught, she will be making them pay for everything they've done to her pre-wedding glow time.

"It doesn't say," Saskia says. "But the police must have known they were going to arrest someone when they were questioning us—they wouldn't have released the information that quickly if they'd only just found them. Maybe something one of us said led to them formalizing the charges, but they would have definitely been questioning them for a while before making an arrest and making it public like this."

"Oh my God, can you imagine if the killer was there at the same time as we were?" Lauren says, shuddering melodramatically.

"Yeah, Loz, they've been in the same place at the same time we were a few times," Farah snaps.

"Oh yeah." Lauren looks hurt and Dominica gives Farah a stern stare.

"Sorry. Bit stressed," Farah says. Lauren smiles tolerantly, though really she thinks Farah's being a cow.

"How are we going to find out more?" Saskia asks.

"I'll talk to my contact," Dominica says.

"I'll talk to mine too," Saskia adds swiftly before her eye is caught by something on the screen. She leans in and squints. "Dom, is that a condom on your desk?"

The other two women also lean in, peering at where Dominica's hand is placed on the desk, very clearly next to an unwrapped but not yet unraveled condom, its teat protruding. Dominica looks down slowly, knowing she's going to need to come up with an excuse pretty quickly.

"Yeah, it's evidence in a case," she says smoothly.

"Gross." Farah makes a face.

"Used?" Saskia asks.

Lauren simply sits with her mouth open.

"The case is confidential," Dominica says. "Look, I'll get on to my people, Saskia you get on to yours. And we'll see who comes up with what."

She hangs up the call so abruptly that the other women are left looking slightly shell-shocked.

The moment Dominica hangs up, Lauren continues her text conversation with Joss.

What are you doing now? she asks.

> *I'm a bit busy now, but should be free in an hour or so if you need to talk?*

I'd really like that, she replies, *especially given . . . everything. The bar by my flat?*

> *See you there.*

She hopes that by suggesting the bar, she's made it obvious how she wants the evening to end. She brushes off any thoughts of Eva. Where Joss is concerned, there's no point trying to be reasonable, fair, or moral. Besides, aren't her friends always talking about how much of a doormat she is? It's time for her to take what she wants, just like everyone else does.

Stopping off at the flat on the way, she gives it a quick tidy, hiding any evidence of her solitary, slightly feral life. Then she heads down to the bar. She's definitely got time for one wine before he gets here. Dutch courage.

She sits on a high stool at the bar and checks her work emails, responding to three flagged as urgent about an advertising campaign for a new mascara. She knows what the others think of her job, that it's not as valuable as being a journalist, a lawyer, or a mum/entrepreneur. But actually what she does is everywhere and none of them even realize it. They see celebs posting about beauty products but they never link it back to Lauren. She's sick of her friends behaving like she's not as important as them. This career wasn't her first choice, but it's not her fault she ended up in it. If it weren't for Tansy, she could be working in television now.

Joss's name pops up at the top of her screen, giving her hope that maybe he's nearly here. But when she clicks on the message, that hope is crushed.

I'm so sorry, Eva needs me, the news about the arrest has really shaken her. Can we postpone? Xxx

Of course. This is so Joss. He never does what he says he will, never follows up. He's flaky and she doesn't know why she's wasting her time with him. She can't believe she's fallen for it again.

As if he can read her mind, he sends another message.

Please don't be angry. I'm here for you. We can text? Xxx

Text? Yeah, great, that's exactly what Lauren's vagina wants her to do right now, *text* with someone she's been secretly in love with for almost her whole life. Maybe this is some kind of karmic intervention for her lusting after a man with a girlfriend. Though at the risk of sounding like a toddler, SHE HAD HIM FIRST.

She downs the rest of her twelve-quid glass of wine, raging and ready to tell him exactly what she thinks of him. Enough is enough. She's moving forward, breaking free. She starts typing, feeling a fury in her belly as she expresses herself freely and without compromise—and then deletes it. Actually, silence speaks volumes. She doesn't need to reply. She never needs to reply to Joss again. What if she just moves on RIGHT NOW? Yes. STRENGTH! COURAGE! GHOSTING IS GOLDEN!

She slides off her stool. She can do this. She doesn't need him. If she hurries, she's got time to pop to the Co-op and pick up a meal for one and a bottle of Blossom Hill before *Love Island* starts. What a life.

Walking out of the bar, she's so busy living her new and empowered life where she lets nothing stand in her way that she doesn't notice a man coming toward her, looking at his phone. She crashes headfirst into him and, filled with embarrassment, immediately starts apologizing. She can already feel an egg forming on her forehead from headbutting his incredibly solid shoulder, and she stands rubbing it for a while before she finally looks at him properly—at his dark floppy hair and his brown eyes behind tortoiseshell glasses—and realizes it's DI Ashford.

"Lauren?" he asks as she squints at him. "Are you OK? I'm so sorry! My fault! I was looking at my phone!" He holds it up. "Friend just told me he's going to be late."

"Not just you." Lauren holds up her own phone. "Friend just can-celled."

"Oh God, your head. You've got a bump!" he says, noticing where she's rubbing. His brow furrows and he pushes his glasses up the bridge of his nose.

"Ah, honestly, don't worry," she says. She's trying to be stoic about it because outside of a police scenario, DI Ashford is even more attractive than he was before. "I'm fine! Very strong skull!"

"Looks like we've both got a bit of unexpected time to kill, and I'd like to check that I haven't concussed you," he says. "Can I buy you a drink?"

"I'm not sure wine's good for concussion, but you may, DI Ashford," she says, hoping she's coming across as coquettish. Fuck Joss. This is a sign from the gods. Or maybe from Tansy.

"Please, now that we've caught our culprit, call me Tom," he says.

The pair of them head into the bar and he pulls out a stool for her in a way that manages to be both gentlemanly and non-patronizing. Is this love?

"What can I get you?" he asks.

"A glass of Sancerre would be great, please," Lauren says, asking for the £12 wine she's just finished. He doesn't even seem fazed.

Her phone vibrates again and she sees Joss's name flash up on the screen. She puts it on do not disturb and flings it into her bag.

CHAPTER TWENTY-NINE

2005 Part Two

"Look! Tansy's getting action!" Lauren appears at Dominica's side and nudges her. Tansy's still snogging Greg. It's been minutes and she hasn't come up for air.

Dominica blinks away the tears that are threatening to form in her eyes. She won't cry over him. No way. She's not letting him win. She's really confused, though. She definitely told Tansy she fancied him. That she was so clichéd she actually had a crush on the captain of the football team. And now look. Last time Tansy got off with someone Dominica fancied it was just a coincidence, Tansy didn't know she liked him. But now? Dominica remembers the entire conversation they had. She can't believe it. Although it would be incredibly like Tansy to have simply forgotten.

"Isn't that sweet! Don't they make the cutest couple!" Lauren says dreamily.

Dominica tries to act naturally. There's no way she can tell any of her friends about her and Greg now. She's just lost her virginity to him and two minutes later he's getting off with one of her best mates.

"Cute," she says, feeling a panic rise within her, needing to step in and protect her friend despite the fact that Tansy has double-crossed her.

"What's happening?" Joss appears behind them.

"Tansy's snogging Greg," Lauren says in the girlie voice that Dominica only ever hears her use when she's talking to Joss. It's so obvious that she fancies him. Whenever Dominica's mentioned it to Farah, she gets really defensive and says it would just be "too gross," but Dominica reckons Joss actually fancies Lauren too.

"Shot?" Saskia appears next to her, a jelly shot in each hand, just as Lauren disappears into her Joss bubble where she can't see or hear anything that isn't him.

Dominica takes both shots and downs them one after the other. Saskia chastises herself: she should have known better and brought more than two.

"That guy's such a snake," she slurs into Dominica's ear as the two of them head back to the kitchen in search of more jelly shots.

"Oh yeah?" Dominica asks.

"Yeah, this girl on the netball team gave him a blow job, like, three weeks ago, and afterward he just ditched her, even though she thought they were getting along."

Dominica realizes she should have run Greg past her friends before she lost her virginity to a dickhead.

"Gross," she says. "We need to tell Tansy that. Who was the girl?"

"Um, well, it was kind of me, but let's not tell anyone. I'm too embarrassed," Saskia says.

Dominica looks at her, shocked. Saskia wouldn't normally engage in anything with a guy unless she'd secured some kind of commitment. How does Greg do it?

"You're right, though, we should tell her. Let's just not tell her it was me," Saskia says. "We need to wait for her to stop being attached to his face first."

The two of them stare through the doorway into the living room, where Tansy's finally come up for air and is twirling her hair and throwing out all her best cute laughs.

"She looks happy," Saskia observes reluctantly.

"Yeah, but it doesn't make a difference if he's going to fuck her up in the end," Dominica says through gritted teeth.

"What's going on?" Farah asks, appearing beside them. "Oh my God, guys, Tansy literally walked in the kitchen and said: 'I fancy Greg!' and two seconds later they were getting off. I swear she is just so beautiful it's sickening. Whenever I say I fancy someone all that happens is they look at me like I've got three heads and run really far away. You know, I actually had a kiss with Greg once, but he never spoke to me again after. It was in Year 7."

Saskia and Dominica look at each other and then back at Farah.

"Why didn't you tell anyone?" Dominica asks.

"I was totally embarrassed. He said I was a bad kisser. Tell no one," Farah says. "I've been practicing since then obviously. I know I'm better now."

Dominica clenches her fists and jaw in synchronization. How dare he treat girls like this? She glances toward Tansy. Greg's standing up, telling her he's going to get her a drink.

"NOW!" Dominica says. "We have to act now!"

The girls race over to Tansy, leaving Lauren behind with Joss. Farah follows even though she doesn't know what's going on, because it looks like drama is afoot.

"GUYS! DID YOU SEE?! I KISSED GREG!" Tansy squeals in their faces, grabbing Dominica by the hands.

Dominica looks her directly in the eye and realizes that despite her telling Tansy that she fancied Greg only a week ago, Tansy has not retained that information at all.

"Babe, look, I'm not saying this to be a dick, but Greg is not the one," she says, and Saskia and Farah nod in agreement.

"What? Why?" Tansy looks miffed.

"He kisses and shags and gets blow jobs from girls and then he completely ditches them. He does it all in secret and makes them feel stupid. You should stay away from him. He'll use you and pretend in front of his friends like he doesn't even know your name." Dominica tries to be vague about it to keep their dignity intact, especially her own.

Saskia nods in agreement. "He's a bad egg," she says sagely.

"But he's kissing me in front of his friends now," Tansy says, wincing slightly. "So maybe this is different. Maybe he actually likes me."

Dominica's stumped. This is not the reaction to the sisterhood she was expecting from Tansy. Here they are trying to save her from humiliation and heartache, and she's just telling them that maybe it's different for her. The implication that he clearly didn't give a shit about them stings like a slap. Even though Tansy doesn't know it's them Dominica was talking about.

"I mean, not to brag, but he told the other guys on the football team that he'd fancied me for ages and thought I was really hot," Tansy says. "So, I dunno, I just feel like whatever rumors you've heard may be exaggerated."

Aside from Tansy's lack of solidarity, Dominica feels a raw burn in her vagina, reminding her of the way Greg treated her. She briefly feels stupid for thinking he actually liked her, but she didn't have the information and Tansy does. And if Tansy thinks that she and Greg are going to work out . . . well. There's not much else Dominica can do.

Tansy's frankly sick of the way Dominica and Saskia are always pissing on her good news. Whenever something exciting happens, it's like they have to be the overly cautious harbingers of doom. She's not letting it get to her.

Dominica, Farah, and Saskia look at each other, feeling themselves deflate. Greg reappears in the doorway, and they know they have to leave it there for now.

"You grab her keys, Farah, and I'll keep her propped up. Tansy, you can sweet-talk her mum if she's still awake, you're good at that," Saskia instructs.

They're outside Dominica's house. In an abnormal turn of events, Dominica got so drunk at the party the other four are having to hold her upright. Normally she can drink the rest of them under the table, so none of them are really sure what's happened tonight.

"Got them!" Farah whispers, triumphantly pulling the keys from Dominica's pocket. "Everyone ready? Stealth!"

"Snoonehome," Dominica snorts as Farah puts the key in the lock.

"Huh?" Lauren asks.

"SNOONEHOME," she shouts.

"She's saying there's no one home," Saskia translates as Farah opens the door into the dark hallway.

"Wow, yeah, I can see that," Farah says, looking down at the post accumulated on the doormat. She turns on the light, unveiling the terrible state of the house.

"Where's your mum?" Tansy asks.

"Left," Dominica says. "Dad came back, two of them just left."

Dominica's dad has been in and out of her life since her brother died when she was four. The girls knew that much, but they didn't know about this latest development.

"When are they coming back?" Farah asks, looking around at the mess in disbelief. Saskia's nose wrinkles at the stale smell around them.

"Never probably," Dominica says. "He died saving me, you know. They hate me."

The girls stand in silence. None of them have heard her talk like this before. She only ever mentions her brother vaguely, and even then it's something they know not to push.

"I'm sure that's not true," Lauren tries gently.

"They can't even look at me," Dominica spits. "That's why Dad kept leaving. Neither of them can bear to be near me."

"What about the rest of your family?" Saskia asks. "Is there anyone else who can help? Your auntie?"

"You're my family," Dominica says, eyes glistening as she looks round at them. "All of you are my family and no one else." Her chin drops onto her chest.

The girls exchange worried glances.

"Oh my God, what do we do?" Lauren mouths.

Saskia takes charge. "Right, Courtney Love, let's get you up the stairs and into bed with some water."

As they prop her up, two to each side, they notice the cups and plates everywhere, dirty clothes strewn about the house and red bills flung among the debris. How could none of them have noticed what was going on? How could they not have seen something was up?

"You know I love you all," Dominica slurs.

"We love you too," Tansy says.

"We do," Saskia agrees.

"So much," Farah adds.

"That's why we're taking you up to bed!" Lauren says.

At the top of the stairs, they head toward her bedroom. They've only been here on a few rare occasions, and their parents always told them not to hang around because Dominica's parents needed space.

Pushing into the room, they ease her onto the bed. Saskia gets her shoes and socks off and tucks her in while Lauren heads downstairs to get water.

"I meant it, you know," Dominica says, beaming at them all from under the duvet. "You're the only family I need."

They stay there all night, cleaning and tidying the house and making sure Dominica's not alone when she wakes up in the morning. And while they wait for her to wake up, they come up with a plan to help her. There's no way any of them are going to let her deal with this alone anymore. They're a team, they're in this together.

CHAPTER THIRTY

Lauren spent most of the train journey from London to Blackpool relishing the glory of having found out more information than either Saskia or Dominica from her one drink with DI Ashford the other night. She'd been able to discover that the person they'd arrested happened to be working in the kitchen at Camp Chakra and at the spa on the relevant dates, and it seemed she was some kind of super-fan of Tansy's. She was following both Tansy's Instagram account and the café's and she had sent Tansy several DMs that Tansy had ignored. Pre-engagement-post Tansy didn't have a massive following and she definitely wasn't the sort of person to reply to or even check her DMs.

Now that they're standing in the hotel lobby, Farah's really hoping they can finally stop talking about Tansy so she can actually enjoy a weekend that's just about her and her wedding. She couldn't believe it when she arrived at the train station earlier and there were only the four of them waiting there. She had thought that with the culprit safely behind bars more people might come, but no. The whole train journey she's had a flurry of messages with everyone's various excuses, but she's ignored them all. They can sweat. Were it not for the fact that it would mess with the table plan and she's already paid for the food, a lot of people would be uninvited to her wedding after this.

Having collected the keys from a desk that Saskia notes is blanketed in dust, Dominica leads them all down the heavily carpeted corridor in the direction of their rooms. She can feel Saskia following close behind her, and she's already heard the rustle of antibacterial wipes in her handbag. Wait until she finds out that they're sharing a room, she thinks, practically rubbing her hands with glee.

"OK, so it's two to a room. Lauren and Eva, you're together," she says.

She ignores the hurt expression on Lauren's face. She's hoping that Lauren and Eva being thrown together like this will help Lauren get over Joss, or at the very least accept that he's moved on. Especially now that she seems to be on very flirty terms with the detective, if the texts she was showing them on the way here are anything to go by. Besides, Dominica has her own reasons for wanting to spend some one-on-one time with Saskia.

Lauren tries desperately not to react to the news that she's sharing with Eva, but she wants to scream. Dominica might as well have just thrown her into oncoming traffic.

"Farah, you have your own suite!" Everyone waits for Farah to get excited, but she's just not. This isn't Ibiza. "Saskia, you're with me."

"Great," Farah says with a lack of enthusiasm that grates on them all after the effort it took to pull this together at short notice. Although Saskia's happily taking no responsibility for the weekend: a Blackpool hen is a poor fit for her company's portfolio.

"Eva," Dominica says, "you need to keep an eye on Lauren's drunk-texting later. Make sure she doesn't send anything too cringeworthy to the detective when we're not around."

"Rude," Lauren says, looking genuinely hurt.

Saskia tries to distract herself from how nervous it makes her that Lauren is getting close to the detective by focusing on all the hardened stains on the carpet. She's anxious about the things he might find out from her when she's drunk—because Dominica's right, Lauren is a complete liability after more than two glasses—or the things he might realize for himself if he spends too much time around them all.

"OK, we're fetching the party bike in an hour, so get yourselves freshened up and hen-do-ready. We'll meet back here in forty-five minutes!" Dominica says. "I'd suggest we wear our Team Bride T-shirts and tiaras, because if people at the bars know we're on a hen do, we'll get discounts. This is the hen-do capital of the UK, after all."

Once this is all over, Dominica's washing her hands of weddings for good. She's had enough. The way they're all behaving, it's like feminism never existed!

"Everyone say 'SAME PENIS FOREVER' for the 'gram!" Eva says, holding her phone up to take the first of the many boomerangs, Instagram stories, and product posts she's contracted to do this weekend, after getting them all a hen do on the cheap. Everyone poses ready with their T-shirts and tiaras.

Dominica hands Saskia their room key as the other hens disperse to get settled in their rooms. But Saskia doesn't take the key, instead just staring down at it like it's a bomb.

"Can't you do it?" She gestures at her other hand, holding her small Louis Vuitton case.

"Um, sure, but my hands are kind of full too, you know," Dominica says, knowing that eventually Saskia will crumble and she'll have won, getting her to touch the disgusting, smeary key with her actual fingers. It's a petty game, but Saskia brings out the petty in Dominica.

"Fine," Saskia says, holding the key with its sticky key ring—clearly soiled by years of hen weekends and grubby hotel trysts—between thumb and forefinger.

She unlocks the door as quickly as possible and heads straight into the room. Dominica trails behind, hoping that at some point the wine, shots, pole dancing, and naked men will chill Saskia out a bit. Maybe this is the weekend they'll get their old friend back. Or maybe it'll be the weekend they lose her forever. She's certainly hoping that at some point Farah will stop comparing their last-minute replacement to the Instagram-perfect do that she should have had. There's nothing anyone can do about that now, though, and they've tried their best. Bridezilla could show a little gratitude.

Forty-five minutes later, the hens are gathered in the hallway waiting for Saskia. They've all got their T-shirts and tiaras on, some inflatable penises have made it into the mix, and they're ready to have a classy, classy time. Farah's tiara obviously has a light-up banner on it that says "Bride-to-Be," in case there is any confusion about her status on this little weekend dedicated to her. The tiara did seem to cheer her up a bit, to the relief of the others.

"Come on, Saskia!" Dominica shouts. "We've got to go and pick up the party bike! We've only got two hours of drinking and pedaling on there."

"I'm ready!" Saskia trills, coming through the door in top-to-toe Sweaty Betty workout chic. While the rest of the group have got dressed up for a night out, Saskia's dressed like she's going to a Pilates class. "What?" she asks, seeing everyone's assessment of her outfit. "We'll be pedaling and then pole dancing. I'm not about to get my Viktor & Rolf sweaty. I'll just duck back here and change before dinner. Don't worry."

"OK," Dominica says. She's glad to see that Saskia has chilled out considerably since the shot of vodka she liberated from the minibar for her, but she's clearly got a way to go before she could be classed as enjoying herself. No one's really sure that can happen outside of a west London postcode anymore.

Saskia shoves her T-shirt over her workout top and places the bridesmaid tiara on her cap and then looks at them all expectantly. "Shall we?"

"We shall!" Dominica says, gesturing to the hotel exit. "To the party bike!"

"TEAM BRIDE! READY TO ROLL!" Eva hollers into her phone

screen while filming a video of them all waving at her, inflatable cocks aloft. "Off to show our beautiful bride-to-be how fun and cool a retro hen can really be! All while minimizing our carbon footprint and staying in the UK. Hashtag responsible henning."

At the word "retro," Dominica wants to smack Eva's phone right out of her manicured fingers. But she knows if it weren't for her and her influencer status, this hen do wouldn't be anywhere near as good as it's going to be. So she bites her tongue and accepts that everything that feels normal to her is retro to Eva.

Once everyone's happily installed on the party bike, and the health and safety rules have been read out by the facilitators, the women start pedaling. All except for Farah, that is, who refuses to pedal because she's the bride, and apparently brides don't do teamwork, they just drink. So she's currently sitting in the middle of the hens, downing Prosecco with her legs crossed. If she's being honest, she's a little disappointed there isn't some kind of throne she can sit on. Also, she's sure Eva knows what she's doing, but is this really considered cool? Surely cocktail-making classes with a saucy barman are more 'grammable?

"So it turns out that party bikes are a bit more of a workout than I thought," Dominica hisses to Lauren, hoping Saskia won't hear her. She's deep in conversation with Eva and Farah about how she can maximize her two thousand followers to start building her profile.

"I'm sweating," Lauren says, sipping her wine through a straw to rehydrate as she goes.

"At least the bride looks like she's starting to enjoy herself." Dominica nods at Farah, who has used the cushions from a couple of the empty seats to boost her position and raise herself up above the others.

"Very 'Princess and the Pea,'" Lauren says. "Thank God they made that arrest this week. I don't think I could have relaxed knowing the murderer was still out there."

"Me neither," Dominica agrees. "Especially given Bridezilla's behavior."

"I feel terrible for thinking it could have been her," Lauren murmurs, and Dominica shakes her head.

"It was a fair assumption, given . . . everything."

The two of them watch as Farah waves at passersby, behaving like pissed royalty. At anyone else's hen do she would have been taking the piss out of the bride-to-be for this kind of behavior; in fact she has done many a time. Dominica really hopes her self-awareness comes back after the wedding.

"Oh look!" Eva suddenly turns her phone away from Saskia and starts filming. "CHECK IT OUT, GUYS! THE BLACKPOOL TOWER! And our bride's having the time of her life!"

She pans the camera round to Farah, who is smiling with a penis straw in her mouth.

"Honestly, this is so great!" Farah says, clearly only for the benefit of Instagram, although she is starting to perk up a bit, and slur her words.

In the background, the party bike's playing all the Spice Girls' hits, of which it turns out there are many. Enough to fill this part of the journey anyway. Lauren feels her phone beep in her pocket and grabs it, nearly sending her drink flying. She realizes at that moment that she is no longer sober enough to multitask. Pedaling, drinking, and looking at your phone all at once is hard, it turns out.

"Oh," she says, without meaning to, looking at the text from Tom.

"Is that from DI Ashford?" Eva asks in a kind of drunken, slurred attempt at sexiness.

"Yep," Lauren says bluntly, disliking the way Eva has started using a matey tone with her. The last thing she needs is for her to think they're friends. But she's smiling at her phone nonetheless.

"He can detective-inspect me any day," Farah says, before wrinkling her nose, realizing that A, she doesn't mean that, B, she's on her own hen do and actually doesn't want anyone, ever, except for Toby, and C, she's clearly wasted already. She just hopes things between Lauren and DI Ashford don't get too serious before the wedding, because Lauren asking for a plus-one would really fuck with the numbers. The chef simply cannot make any more changes at this late stage.

"What's he saying?" Dominica asks. "Anything about the investigation?"

"Oh no, he never talks to me about that," Lauren says, brushing the thought away with a drunken hand. "He's just saying he hopes we have a nice weekend. I asked if he thought it was weird that we were still going, and he said it was probably about time we all let loose with some inflatable penises. He's very funny, you know."

"And do you think you'll shag the good detective?" Dominica asks.

"Dom!" Saskia exclaims. "But, well, do you?"

"I mean, surely something good has to come of all this," Farah sighs.

"I think I'll give it a good go," Lauren says, laughing, but then abruptly stopping when she sees that Eva is still filming.

"Obviously I've barely noticed, but he is quite fit," Farah giggles, just glad they're not talking about the murders for a change.

"He's been texting her the whole time we've been on this bike," Eva says.

Lauren turns to her, shocked. She thought she was hiding the screen, especially from Eva. What if Joss had texted and she'd seen it? Not that he'd be saying anything except "Are you OK?"

"You're definitely in there then," Dominica says.

"Not to be a whinger, but could at least one of you start pedaling again, please? I carry the emotional and physical weight enough at home, thanks," Saskia puffs.

Dominica snorts at the thought of Saskia carrying anything that doesn't sit in a Chanel or Birkin bag.

"Sorry, babe," she says, pushing on the pedals again while sucking pina colada through a penis straw. "You should ask if he fancies a fuck when you get back."

"She's right, you know," Saskia slurs, clearly more pissed than she's letting on. "You need to be forthright!"

"I am not going to send him that!" Lauren gasps, and then folds over in a fit of giggles, almost inhaling a feather boa.

"Give her a few more drinks and she'll do it," Dominica chuckles as Lauren starts pedaling aggressively, trying to block them all out.

"Show me on the penis where you'd like to touch him!" Eva flings an inflatable penis at Lauren, and everyone screams as she catches it. "You go, girl! CATCH THAT DICK!"

Once again Lauren prickles at how familiar Eva's being with her, though to be fair, she is pretty wasted. She hopes she doesn't try and have some kind of drunken deep and meaningful back in their room tonight. Or perhaps, she thinks, Eva's encouraging this whole shagging-the-detective thing because she actually feels threatened by Lauren? She shakes her head: probably not. But she knows she could definitely make Joss jealous if it gets back to him via Eva that she's really into this detective.

"He's just so lovely. Never met anyone like him, you know. So manly, with his big hands. I just . . . I'm totally going to shag him." She's exaggerating for Eva's benefit, and Eva laps it up.

"Big hands . . ." Saskia says, and she and Dominica collapse into a fit of giggles.

"I remember when I first had sex with Toby . . ." Farah attempts to change the subject to her fiancé, which is surely why they're all here. Not to talk about one of Lauren's hook-ups.

Dominica's shocked: it's the first time Farah's mentioned her husband-to-be in such a long time, she's surprised she can even re-member his name.

Lauren grabs her phone off the table in front of her and types out her sensible (so she thinks) response to Tom's message, adding a selfie of her cradling the penis like a precious baby.

All going as planned so far. I've made a friend!

She feels a smug satisfaction at the greatness of her text, which lasts only a few minutes before she realizes that actually maybe posing with an inflatable cock isn't the detective's sort of humor. After all, he does have a very serious job. Well, fuck it, she's sent it now, she can't take it back.

"What did you send him?" Dominica asks.

"Dick pic." Lauren points to her new penis friend as they all fall about laughing. She shows everyone the selfie she's just taken, which she thinks is probably a work of comedy genius.

"Loz!" Saskia snorts, surprising Lauren by using the childhood nickname she thought Saskia had long since abandoned and finding her text just as funny as the rest of them.

"You know, Tansy would have loved this," Eva says loudly over their guffaws. "She always said how much she wished you guys could hang out like you used to and just be silly."

The women all smile reflectively at each other, even Farah, despite the fact that the conversation's come back to Tansy *again*. She does wish she was here.

"To Tansy," Dominica says, raising her glass, before adding, "And Helen . . . To the fallen hens!"

The other women stand and join in with the toast. While normally most of them would feel queasy at the cheesiness of the gesture, it feels appropriate after the shocking events of the last few weeks and the amount of alcohol they've consumed in such a short space of time.

In their enthusiasm, they don't notice the bike coming to an emergency stop as the facilitators ram on the brakes. The hens are jolted forward, all of them falling to the floor, with the exception of Lauren, who's inexplicably thrown over the edge. The others drunkenly scrabble up to save her, faces aghast. But they're too late. She lands on the tarmac with a thud. The facilitator takes his foot off the brake in panic, and the bike lurches toward Lauren's prone body, prompting the women to scream. When it comes to a standstill again, one of its wheels is resting just inches from her leg.

The hens fall silent as they hang over the pointless railing that failed to stop Lauren's tumble. Lauren stares back up at them, lying on her back, still clutching the inflatable cock.

"Fuck," she breathes. "I could have died."

"Oh my God, you were nearly Brian Harvey'd!" Farah shouts.

"Who? What?" Eva asks, confused by a reference probably from before she was even born.

"Jesus, are you OK?" Dominica starts to climb off the bike.

"DON'T MOVE!" Saskia goes into mother mode while the other drivers on the road and the bike facilitators seem to have completely frozen. "She's fallen at least a meter and a half! She'll need an ambulance!" she shouts at the facilitators.

"Oh no, don't be silly. I'm fine!" Lauren says, sitting upright, completely ignoring Saskia. She stands and brushes herself off. "See, totally fine!" She waves the penis at them.

Dominica helps her back onto the bike.

"OMG, are you sure you're OK? You could have a concussion!" Eva says, settling her back on her seat.

"AREN'T YOU GOING TO HELP?" Saskia shouts at the facilitators, who are still immobile with shock. "WE COULD SUE, YOU KNOW!"

"We've just never been trained for this," says one of them, who appears to be about sixteen and has clearly never seen anything like it.

"You should always be prepared!" Saskia does a Girl Guide salute, and Dominica realizes quite how drunk she must be.

"Are you sure you're OK, Loz?" Dominica asks as the other women fuss around her.

"Totally fine. How badass is the detective going to think I am now, though? Me and my penis cheated death!" Lauren grins, and then realizes that most of Blackpool is currently staring at her like she's a museum exhibit. "Please, let's just carry on so these people stop looking at me."

The two facilitators seem to have been turned to stone.

"I'm sorry, did you not hear her?" Dominica instructs. "She said ONWARD!"

"And if you don't, well, we'll definitely be having a word with your manager about the safety precautions on this deathtrap!" Saskia adds.

"More booze?" Eva asks.

"MORE BOOZE!" Lauren replies.

"And make it free," Dominica says to the facilitators.

"Unless you want to be hearing from our lawyer," Saskia adds.

"That's me!" Dominica shouts while she and Saskia high-five.

"And I'll give you the WORST review when I post about it," Eva says, joining in with the high-fives.

Lauren finds herself staring up at Eva warmly, despite herself.

"Look, she's fine! Can we just carry on?" Farah says, trying to keep her temper under control. All she wants is an incident-free hen do that's not about someone else's tragic accident or death.

The others turn to her, slightly jarred by her lack of empathy, but Lauren doesn't want to cause a scene. She's too busy texting Tom to tell him how much of a stunt queen she is.

"ONWARD, DRIVER! FOR I HATH CHEATED DEATH!" she shouts, and the general public around the bike start clapping.

"What a hero," a guy passing them says.

"Fuckin' class," his friend replies. "Great rack too."

Luckily for him, the party bike has already started moving by the time the women realize what he's said. You should never anger a brood of pissed hens.

CHAPTER THIRTY-ONE

The Adonis Arena is, predictably, hot and sweaty, with sticky seats, an even stickier floor, and a tacky kind of moisture in the air. As the hens stand in the lobby, the events and alcohol of the day threaten to start taking their toll.

"Is anyone else feeling kind of sleepy after dinner and all the pole dancing?" Lauren asks, having polished off a bowl of pasta and half a pizza because she knows that when you're drinking as much as they all are today, you can't be fucking around and limiting your carb intake. Not if they're going to survive anyway.

"Exhausted! I still can't get over how great you are at pole dancing!" Eva says in a way Lauren finds incredibly patronizing. It's true, though, she was uncharacteristically good.

"Guess I just have a natural flair," she says faux modestly.

"We should go to classes together! It's a great way of keeping fit!" Eva suggests.

"Oh yeah, I'd love that!" Over my dead body, Lauren thinks. She hates that Eva's being so nice. Why can't Joss go out with someone who's awful? She's starting to realize why Tansy was always singing her praises, and it's even more annoying.

"Great! We must hang out more. I was thinking that just the other day. You're the only one I feel like I don't know that well, and I know you and Joss are super-close." Eva says it with a smile and without any hint that Joss may have told her that they used to date.

It makes Lauren realize that Eva's definitely never seen her as a romantic threat, and she's offended.

"Absolutely!" She smiles at her like she doesn't hate her.

Her phone vibrates, and she looks down at it, expecting to see a message from DI Ashford, but instead it's Joss's name on the screen. She glances at Eva, feeling a small amount of triumph, before opening the message.

Is Eva OK? I haven't heard from her all day.

Her face falls. She closes her phone and ignores the message. Fuck you, Joss, she thinks. Fuck you.

"Here, have a shot of tequila. It'll revive you!" Dominica says, appearing with a tray of shots minus the salt and lime because they're past the point of adding any extra complications. No one has the hand-eye coordination for that shit.

"Thanks!" Farah says.

Since Farah started drinking hard spirits, her mood has really improved.

"SAME PENIS FOREVER!" Saskia shouts, raising her hand. She's now so past the point of awareness that she feels freer than she has in over ten years. She realizes that she's reverted to being someone she hasn't been for a long time, but Jeremy isn't here to tell her off or judge her for it.

"SAME PENIS FOREVER!" they all chime in unison as another nearby hen party whoops along.

Fortified by the shots, the women head into the arena to face the naked, baby-oiled men that await them.

"Honestly, who knew you were so sporty, Lauren?" Saskia says.

Lauren's really enjoying smashing the perception that she's this pathetic, fragile being. She's proved she's far more resilient than they ever thought possible by both falling off the party bike and surviving and being a surprise pro pole dancer. She's relishing her new image.

"OK! Those are our seats." Dominica indicates some gilt-edged red velvet seats on the very front row. There's a medley of suspicious-looking stains on the fabric, and as Saskia goes to take another shot, she realizes that no matter where she looks, she is probably going to be in the direct eye of multiple penis storms. It's been years since she's seen one that wasn't Jeremy's, though, so maybe it'll be thrilling.

Without warning, Lauren starts to cry, having reached a level of overemotional inebriation that demands tears. She can't explain it; she's just wasted. She worries she's undone all her hard work.

"Oh no!" Eva says, putting her arm around her immediately.

"Woman down!" Dominica shouts, putting her arm around her as well.

"No no no!" Saskia joins the huddle.

"Oh for fuck's sake," Farah mutters, rolling her eyes.

"Farah!" Saskia shouts.

"What?" Farah slurs. Three tequila shots down and she's also reached the next level of drunkenness: an untamed, give-a-shit mess. "I finally get my hen do after all the drama, and now people are crying! THIS IS NOT HEN-DO BEHAVIOR!" she shouts in Lauren's face, her words blending into one, spit showering Lauren's already moist cheeks.

"Er, yes it is," Dominica corrects her. "Someone *always* cries on a hen do—granted, no one ever really understands what about, but there's always a crier. This IS hen-do behavior."

"SURELY IT'S SUPPOSED TO BE *ME* THAT CRIES, THOUGH!" Farah's shouting again, but no one really understands why.

"Well, dear, it sounds like you're having your own little breakdown over there," Saskia says, pursing her lips.

All the women stare at Farah, waiting for her comeback, but she's seemingly unable to think of anything. Eventually she stands up with great force, clutching an inflatable knob, and storms out of the auditorium, fighting her way against the oncoming lusty traffic with her blow-up accessory.

"Someone should go after her," Lauren says, sniffing, before having a small think about it. After all, she was the one crying and Farah was kind of a bitch. She also realizes Eva still has her arm around her and shrugs it off.

"I'm tempted to leave her to stew," Dominica says. "Are you OK, Lauren?"

"Yeah, I'm fine, that shot just triggered me," Lauren says. "You know tequila's always made me emotional."

"Maybe someone should go and talk to her." Saskia exchanges a look with Dominica that clearly says they both think Farah's being a tit but Saskia might be right.

"I'll go," Dominica says, standing up. "Check she's not smashing up the toilets in a rage or something. She's being fucking ungrateful and rude." She stalks off, handing her inflatable penis to Saskia on her way out.

Farah's locked herself in a cubicle and is sitting on the closed loo seat staring at her phone screen through her tears. Rebecca told her she had to do it this weekend. With Saskia drunk and away from her husband, it's the perfect time for Farah to get her to confess, or at least to tell her what she already knows and try and get more information out of her. But Farah just can't do this anymore. She's tried to pitch other articles, but her boss won't budge. She reads back the instructions from Rebecca on her phone, thinking of the consequences if she doesn't do what she's asking.

> *Just send me anything you can. Try and get voice recordings if poss. If you can't talk to your friend, try talking to her husband again, but record it this time with your phone. Rookie mistake not doing it last time. What he says can be used as a confession.*
>
> *If you can't do it within the next week, I'll have to tell people higher up about the money you've taken. They're starting to ask questions, you know. It's not fair on me.*

The ultimatum was sent earlier in the week, after Farah's run-in with Jeremy. Rebecca wasn't even remotely perturbed by Jeremy's threats, but she could see that Farah was, and since then she's upped the pressure.

Farah feels like she's in a nightmare of her own making. None of this is really her; she knows she's lost her way, but she can't stop. She's stolen from her place of work and blackmailed her now dead friend, all to get the perfect wedding. And now she has to betray another of her oldest friends. She's done so many things she's not proud of at this stage; surely she can just do one more to protect herself? If she doesn't, then Rebecca's going to make sure that rather than a castle and a white dress, she'll get a jumpsuit and a prison cell.

Even if she doesn't go to prison, she'll lose her job. Then she'll have no hope of paying off any of the wedding debt. Toby'll find out about the mess she's made, all the things she's done, and won't want to marry her anymore. And despite everything, the ridiculous wedding prep, he really is the most important thing to her. She just wanted to be the envy of her friends for once. After years of being the supporting actress, she was finally getting to be the star, but at what cost?

Maybe her best bet would be to get the confession from Jeremy like

Rebecca suggested. At least that way it feels a little less like a betrayal. Who's she kidding? It's still awful, it's just that using Jeremy to get the story feels marginally better than using Saskia.

She types out a short message to him saying that they need to talk and then moves to leave, but his reply is instant. Stopping her before she even flushes the toilet.

> *What would you like to talk about? We could start with whether my wife knew you were blackmailing Tansy before she died if you like?*

Farah thinks her heart might have stopped, the words on the screen blurring in front of her. How is it possible? How could he know about Tansy? What's he going to do? If he tells Toby or the others, then it's over. She's pretty sure no one will ever speak to her again, let alone marry her or be her bridesmaids. He's not doing that to her and she's not losing her job either. She grits her teeth. This ends now.

Enough games, she types. *Just tell me when and where and we'll talk.*

Feeling bold, she flushes the toilet and puts her phone in her bag, ready to deal with him later. She opens the cubicle door, prepared to face whatever happens next, and immediately sees Dominica leaning against the sinks next to a flurry of overwrought women fighting to get in their pre-show piss.

"Do you want to tell me what the hell's going on?" Dominica looks furious, tapping her fingers on the side of the sink and glaring at Farah with her eyebrows arched.

"What do you mean?" Farah asks. "Just got a little overwrought, that's all. I should probably apologize to Lauren."

"You fucking think?" Dominica asks sarcastically. "Yes, Lauren gets very emotionally delicate when she drinks, but we NEVER have a go at her! What the hell are you doing? Are you trying to push all your friends away before you walk down the aisle? You're acting as if you think this wedding is all you've got in life, like it's the most important thing to you, more important than any of us!"

"I—" Farah tries to stand up for herself, but Dominica steamrolls over her.

"In two weeks your wedding'll be over. You'll be married to Toby till death do you part. And then what? Who'll you have left to be your friends for the rest of your life? Because the way you're behaving, it'll be no one."

Farah and Dominica are locked in eye contact, while the other bathroom hens fall silent. There's a look of realization dawning on some of their faces as they glance around at their own friends. Some of the braver women make their escape from the most stressful toilet they've ever been in.

"I . . . didn't realize I'd been that bad," Farah says finally, suddenly taking a different tack.

"I don't know how you thought you were being, but it's been REALLY bad," Dominica says, not giving an inch.

"I'll go and apologize to Lauren," Farah says, knowing it's easier at this point just to give in.

She's never actually been on the end of one of Dominica's telling-offs before. They're usually reserved for the others when they're doing something stupid or behaving like a twat. Farah has never been the one to upset or offend. Having a long-term relationship with Toby since they were at uni probably helped—unlike Lauren, she didn't have relationship dramas, and unlike Tansy, she didn't cause them. She never even told her friends how much it hurt that Toby hadn't proposed. Not that they ever asked. And now that she's finally getting her big day, if they can't let it be about her just this once, are they really her friends at all? But this close to the wedding definitely isn't the time to fall out with them. How would it look for a bride to be without any of her besties? She trails out of the toilet behind Dominica, a sheepish expression on her face, while Dominica looks as proud as though she's just won another case.

Back in the auditorium, the lights have dimmed considerably. Saskia, Lauren, and Eva are all on their phones, their drunken faces lit up as they turn silently to watch her.

"I'm sorry, Lauren," Farah says before she's even sat down. "That was really insensitive and uncalled for. I'm just taking out my stress on everyone else." She looks sincere enough.

"No worries!" Lauren says cheerily. The post-shot tears never last long; it's mostly a knee-jerk reaction to the tequila burn.

"Sorry, everyone," Farah says. "I was being a twat."

"Weddings are stressful, darling," Saskia says, catching Dominica's eye and giving her an approving look.

"I think you're allowed a diva strop before your big day," Eva agrees, shrugging.

"What's a hen do without a little rumble anyway?" Dominica says.

"Right then, sit down. Show's about to start!" Saskia instructs.

"IT'S PENIS TIME, BITCHES!" Lauren shouts drunkenly, surprising everyone.

"Lord save us," Dominica whispers as a gaggle of old women push into the seats behind them at the last minute. They seem overly rowdy.

Smoke rises across the stage and misty lights gradually appear. The Adonis Arena is drenched in darkness and sexual tension. As the smoke continues to swirl around, Cardi B and Megan Thee Stallion's "WAP" begins to play. The OAPs behind start chanting, "There's some whores in this house, There's some whores in this house . . ." and the rest of the audience joins in. Everyone except for Dominica and Saskia, who can't bring themselves to chant the word "whore" even if the crowd demands it. The tension in the room builds as the music blends into 50 Cent's "Candy Shop" and the lights come up. Behind them the OAPs scream as their ringleader jumps onto her seat, ripping off her top in an act of dexterity Lauren thinks she herself would probably struggle with.

"TAKE IT OFF!" the OAP starts screaming in her bra.

There are flashes of something that looks like a sparkler as the stage erupts into light, and ten men all oiled up and wearing bow ties and arse-less chaps emerge through the smoke.

"It's enough to put you off knobs for life," Dominica observes.

"It just feels intimidating having them this close en masse, doesn't it?" Lauren agrees.

"Speak for yourselves!" Saskia exclaims.

The others turn to look at her admiringly, enjoying a flash of the woman they've missed terribly since she married Jeremy.

"SHHHHH!" one of the old ladies behind chastises. "It's time to concentrate."

They all stifle giggles, realizing that even the ringleader has settled and is staring intently at the stage. Then, quite without warning, one of the strippers scans the crowd and catches Lauren's eye. As he extends his big fake-tanned hand toward her, flexing his pecs, she tries to bury her face in her own cleavage while shaking her head. It comes across as faux reluctance—no one wants to be seen to be too keen to leap into the crotch of a stripper, do they?—but in Lauren's case she can genuinely think of nothing worse than being up there.

"YES, LAUREN!" Eva's shouting.

"UP! UP! UP! UP!" A chant starts in their row, taken up by the old ladies and then eventually the rest of the arena.

"GET UP THERE, YOU SILLY TROLLOP!" a jealous old lady from the row behind shouts right in Lauren's ear.

Farah realizes that Lauren's about to get the moment of crowning hen glory that should definitely be for her. She's not having anyone stealing her thunder, so she reaches across to the hand and grabs it, pulling herself up from her seat and climbing onto the stage. Lauren sits back in relief.

Farah ascends the stage to shouts from the OAP ringleader of, "LUCKY FUCKING CUNT!"

Within seconds, Farah's hands are covered in baby oil and she's got whipped cream on her nose. She's led to a chair, and five of the men begin gyrating, thrusting themselves at her. Dominica has a horrible feeling that they're about to lose their chaps, but at least Farah looks like she's enjoying herself.

Saskia thinks Farah would be very pleased with the way her engagement ring's glittering under the stage lights.

"TAKE ME INSTEAD!" one of the ladies behind is screaming from her seat. She starts shaking her walking stick at Farah, who apparently isn't moving fast enough for her liking. "LICK IT OFF HIM, YOU SILLY COW!"

Dominica turns round. "Hey, lady, sit the fuck down and stop shouting at my friend." The two women narrow their eyes at each other for a moment before they're distracted by the arena filling with the noise of screaming.

On stage, there's a crescendo in the music as the strippers rip their chaps off and one of them squirts cream on bits that definitely aren't savory. One of the old ladies faints and has to be carried out, but her friends are too engrossed by the strippers to notice.

CHAPTER THIRTY-TWO

Hours of grinding, gyrating, and baby oil later, the lights go down. As they all stand up and stretch, one of the venue workers, wearing a black T-shirt printed with a close-up view of a pair of pecs, comes to talk to the hens.

"The boys were wondering if you fancied joining them backstage before the next show for a drink. As a thank you for being such a good sport," she says, beaming widely at Farah.

"Absolutely!" Farah beams back at her.

"Oh my God, that would be SUCH good content," Eva says, pretending she didn't know this was coming; it was part of the deal, a little behind-the-scenes video of the strippers being charming and adorable. Something to get more people hot and bothered enough to come to the show.

"Great! Follow me, please! Bring everything with you," the venue worker says, eyeing the inflatable penises the hens have taken to fondly clutching to their bosoms like babies. In some cases, this might be because they're starting to feel a little sleepy. It's been a very active day after all.

The woman starts talking into her headset as they all troop up onto the stage and toward the backstage area. Feeling high on the effects of the show, Farah follows her joyfully, but when she looks down at her phone and sees three more messages from Jeremy, her mood sours.

Lauren's struck by how massive the stage is. She'd never realized quite how high it would be off the ground; it all feels a bit vertigo-y. While marveling at the scale and complexity of the strip show, her foot skids underneath her on a rogue pool of baby oil and she begins aquaplaning across the heavily lubricated floor, arms flailing, until Eva grabs her and brings her to a halt.

"Thanks!" Lauren gasps, as the two of them clutch each other and giggle.

Realizing with horror that they might actually be bonding, Lauren snaps out of it. If anything's ever going to happen between her and Joss, it's imperative that she *never* becomes friends with Eva. Although does she even still want something to happen with Joss? She startles at the thought that it might actually be possible to get over him, then looks down at her phone, disappointed to see that there's still nothing from DI Ashford since her last message. She fears the inflatable penis may have put him off.

Backstage, the hens walk through heavy gold curtains, past various pulley systems and oil-squirting machines, to a much bleaker, breeze-blocked corridor. Following the noise of men laughing, they head toward a changing room, where the assistant knocks on the door.

"Everyone decent?" she asks fruitlessly.

"Oh, absolutely not, darling! SEND THEM IN!" a posh male voice replies.

They all file into a room where nine men stand in various states of undress and gold Adonis Arena branded robes, excited to greet them. Even Saskia accepts their oiled-up hugs.

"Prosecco, ladies?" one of them asks.

Lauren, exhausted from the whole stripping shebang, eyes up a pile of what look like fur blankets in the corner and drifts over to them while everyone else gets settled.

"Just gonna head back out into the corridor to do a bit of behind-the-scenes filming. So I can show a little run-up to being in here with you guys," Eva says, heading out of the dressing room with her phone.

Saskia sits herself between two strippers who introduce themselves to her as Jimmy and John. Both of them have the kind of natural-looking fake tan that she absolutely needs to know more about. She can feel her phone beeping away in her pocket, but she's ignoring it. She's having a nice time.

"So tell me," she purrs at them. "Are any of you single? My friend over there could do with a good shag." She points to where Dominica's hunched over her phone, her brow furrowed. She doesn't appear to have heard her.

"SASKIA! They're not gigolos! That's so rude!" Farah exclaims before turning to the men. "I'm so sorry about my friend. She doesn't get out much."

"It's OK!" Jimmy giggles. "Actually, we're all gay. John's my husband."

"Apart from Clive," John says. "Clive's straight, but he's been married to his high-school sweetheart since he was eighteen."

"Yeah, and he's already left," Jimmy says. "Likes to get home and help with the kids on a Saturday."

"I need to take a call," Dominica says, jumping up and ignoring them all. "A client's about to do something very silly if I don't stop them."

The other women don't even seem to notice as she leaves the room. Only Lauren, from her pile of blankets, briefly wonders if Dominica should be doing anything work-related given how much tequila they've consumed. Before she has a chance to mention it, though, she's distracted by her phone vibrating. She gets excited wondering if it might finally be DI Ashford responding to her dick pic from earlier. But when she checks, it's not DI Ashford, it's Joss.

Still can't get over how hot you looked at the police station the other day.

She turns the screen off despite being immediately turned on, just in case anyone else can see it, and feels her cheeks stretch into the most ridiculous smile. This is finally it. He still likes her, SHE KNEW IT. She's watched plenty of videos about what a red flag it is when a man with a girlfriend comes on to you, but she's simply charging toward those flags, embracing them with all her might, all thoughts of DI Ashford seemingly left in the dust.

She's too excited to allow herself to feel guilty about double-crossing Eva. In her mind she's already planning her and Joss's wedding, and unsurprisingly, Eva isn't invited.

"Oops, need a wee!" Farah says, jumping up from her seat, where she's been giggling with one of the strippers. "Made me laugh so much I felt a little trickle!"

"Just down the corridor, to the left. Do *not* go right. This place is linked to the lap-dancing club next door. You go right, you end up in *there,* and it all gets very confusing once you're in. You'll get lost!" John warns her.

"Great! Thanks!" Farah says, clutching her phone on her way out.

"Do you think she's a bit better?" Saskia whispers loudly to Lauren as soon as she thinks Farah's out of earshot. "No more diva strops?"

"Uh-oh!" Jimmy says. "Have we got a bridezilla in our midst?"

"I mean, our friend got murdered by some poisoned cacao and then our other friend got murdered by a poisoned vaginal egg at Farah's first hen do last weekend. I think she just kind of had a meltdown," Lauren says from her fur pile.

The strippers have all stopped what they were doing and are staring at her open-mouthed.

"I beg your pardon?" Jimmy says.

"So two of your friends have been murdered?" John clarifies.

"And do they know who did it?" Jimmy asks.

"My God, I feel like I'm in a true crime podcast," John says, turn-

ing to Jimmy, the two of them not having even waited for answers to
their questions.

"You poor things!" Jimmy cries.

"Don't worry, they've arrested someone," Saskia says. "They've
been in custody since Tuesday."

While Saskia's busy giving the strippers a dramatic account of everything they've been through, Lauren texts Joss back.

> So did you x

She watches the little bubbles appear as he types, feeling her heart
race, the conversation in the background blending into a garbled blur.

> I wanted to come over the other day, by the way. Eva tagged
> along because I said I was going out for a walk. I couldn't get rid
> of her. I really wanted to talk to you alone. I miss you. I don't
> think Eva's right for me.

The last sentence sends Lauren slamming back to reality. She's heard
him say things like this before, always when he's been drinking, so she
can only guess that he's been drinking a hell of a lot. He's probably let
the freedom of a single night alone get to him. She sits and stares at the
message, taking it in. Embracing it. Knowing that by tomorrow he'll
probably regret sending it and pretend it never happened. That's Joss's
usual way, and it's these small glimmers of affection that keep her
hooked. As long as he still sends these messages, she'll never manage
to move on.

"Oh my fucking . . . What?!" Eva suddenly shouts, waking Lauren up
with a start. She must have fallen asleep after texting Joss back. She's
scared that Eva's somehow found out about Joss's texts, but she sees her

phone carefully snuggled next to her in the furs and thinks she's probably safe for now.

"What?" Saskia asks. "Where's everyone else?" She barely noticed
the others disappearing, immersed as she was in her conversation with
Jimmy and John. She's currently looking at photos of their frankly *gorgeous* wedding and is thoroughly enjoying herself.

"Look," Eva holds out her phone, and before Lauren even has a
chance to read the headline displayed on her screen, the strippers gasp.
"The person they arrested for the murders has been released. It says
the evidence was thrown out."

"Did the detective tell you about this?" Saskia turns to Lauren, an
accusatory look on her face.

"No!" Lauren says sheepishly. She doesn't want to admit that she
hasn't heard from him for hours.

"I don't understand. How have they just released the suspect and
not told us?" Eva asks.

"I guess they thought that whoever it was didn't do it," John says
reasonably. It prompts a glare from all three women.

"But if they didn't do it, then whoever did is still out there, and
they've been out there the whole time," Lauren says slowly.

At the thought of the killer back on the loose, the eyes of everyone
in the room seem to grow wider. The strippers start grabbing various
props to defend themselves with, John and Jimmy taking hold of some
especially phallic fake swords.

"Where are Farah and Dominica?" Lauren asks. "They've been gone
ages. Did you see them when you were out in the corridor, Eva?"

"No," Eva says, looking nervous.

"I'll text them," Saskia says with urgency, despite slurring her
words. "We need to find them and stick together."

"Oh, wait, I've got a message from Farah!" Eva says, raising her
phone triumphantly like a contestant getting a text on *Love Island*.
"She's lost. Says she's in some mirrored corridor. She must have taken

a wrong turn and can't find her way out!" She starts frantically texting Farah back to warn her about the released suspect.

"Oh God, the poor lamb! She's in the lap-dancing club!" Jimmy cries.

"What about Dom? Has she messaged yet?" Lauren asks with a sinking feeling.

"Not yet," Saskia says, staring at her phone with one eye closed, trying to keep control in the face of her own extreme drunkenness.

"We can take you through to the lap-dancing club to find your friend in there," Jimmy offers. "But it sounds like she's lost in the maze—the corridors where the private dance rooms are. It's a warren. The walls are mirrored to deliberately confuse people. Customers think it's for privacy, but really it's so they can be kicked out discreetly if they touch the women, and never find their way back in. But if your friend's had a bit to drink, she's got no hope."

"Here, everyone needs one of these." John hands out small plastic whistles shaped like penises. "We give them out to hens who want a souvenir at the end of the night. We can use them to find each other if any of us get lost."

"DON'T WORRY, FARAH, WE'RE COMING TO RESCUE YOU!" Saskia blows her penis whistle and shouts pointlessly at Eva's phone screen.

"Shots for courage!" one of the other strippers announces, pouring vodka into everyone's mouths as they form an orderly queue on their way out of the dressing room.

"This way!" John and Jimmy lead the group.

They all huddle together as they pass down a cold concrete corridor en route to the lap-dancing club. The wind echoes against the breeze-block walls, making them all shiver and clutch their feather boas tighter around their necks. A door to the left marked "Toilet" opens, the creak of its hinges making Eva scream and throw herself into Jimmy's arms.

"What's going on?" Dominica's voice comes from the open doorway as she surveys the tense gaggle. "Why do you look like the Famous Five getting ready to shoot a porno?"

"Where have you been?" Saskia chastises her.

"I was talking to my client and then I went for a wee." Dominica points to the toilet she's just come out of.

"Farah's lost in the lap-dancing club," Lauren explains.

"And they've released the suspect," Eva adds.

"What?!" Dominica's already looking it up on her phone. "And no one knows where Farah is?"

"She's trapped in the mirror maze!" Lauren says, as if Dominica would know what that was.

"We're doing a rescue!" Saskia gestures with her penis whistle.

"Right then!" Dominica grabs Saskia's arm and joins the group.

They turn right through a fire door, into a poorly lit corridor. Saskia touches one of the walls and notes that it's slightly furry, a kind of crunchy velvet wallpaper that feels like a sensory and sanitary nightmare. They emerge into a huge room with neon lights and small stages complete with poles dotted around tables. The hens stare at the beautiful women dancing on the stages, then at the sweaty-looking men at the tables below. Logically Saskia knows this is just the reverse of what they've been doing next door in the arena. It's just that men haven't had to deal with centuries' worth of sexualization and objectification, so this feels decidedly seedier.

"This is a LOT," Lauren shouts, referring to the weird strobing lights that don't seem to illuminate anything and the pumping music, so loud that none of them can really hear a tune.

"Yeah, we don't come in here much," Jimmy says. "It's kind of aggressively . . . vagina-y."

The hens stare at him as he realizes what he's said to a group of people who all have vaginas.

"We need to separate, we'll find her faster that way," Saskia shouts, and the others nod.

"Good idea," John yells back over what might be the soundtrack from *Moulin Rouge,* no doubt glad to move on from Jimmy's little vag-pas. "There are about ten mirrored corridors coming off this main room that all link together. If we take one each, we'll end up in the same place eventually anyway. Don't forget, if you need help, blow your whistle."

"Good plan," Saskia confirms, wincing slightly as she watches a woman practically flossing her butt with a pearl thong. She wonders briefly how they wash those.

The group scatters, each of them taking a corridor. Saskia uses the mirrors in hers to make sure no one else is around. She jumps when, after checking behind her, she sees someone in front of her: messy blonde hair and black-smudged blue eyes staring back at her, lipstick half rubbed off a pair of chapped, drink-stained lips. She stares, her head spinning, as the woman multiplies in the mirrors around her, and puts her hands out to protect herself before realizing she's in a corridor with infinite versions of herself. The woman in the mirror is almost unrecognizable to her, her ginger roots more grown out than usual, makeup far from immaculate. She feels her way along the wall, every movement causing a prickle down the back of her neck and a fear that someone else could appear in the mirror at any point.

Dominica walks deeper into the mirrored maze, aware that one of the doors from the private dance rooms could open at any time. With every step she feels the weight of the suspect being released, the feeling of danger getting closer as she hurries through the corridor, never able to outrun her own reflection. She needs to find Farah, quickly.

Lauren takes another turn in the maze, a chandelier sparkling from the ceiling above her, dulled with dirt and dust but multiplied infinity times by the mirrored walls. She clutches the penis whistle for safety, ready to blow any second. She hasn't come across anyone else yet in this hellish corridor, and if she does, she knows she'll scream. Her heart thumps in her chest, adrenaline coursing through her veins. She thinks she hears footsteps behind her, but when she turns, she can only see herself again. There are more versions of herself ahead, and to the left and the right, and she starts to lose track of which direction she was going in the first place. She knows they're all expecting her to wuss out, to get scared and run away. But she's going to be the one to find Farah; she *needs* to be the one who finds Farah first.

Turning the next corner, she jumps as the reflection of someone squatting on the ground appears. It's Farah, but she can't work out which way to go to reach her.

"FARAH!" she shouts, hoping to get her attention, but the music's so loud.

Or maybe, she thinks, the mirrors are a trick and Farah's not really there. Maybe she's miles away but being reflected into this corridor. She spins around, trying to make sense of how someone can look so close yet be so far from her grasp. Feeling her way along the wall, she comes to another corner and sets off down a new corridor. Now Farah's reflection is either side of her.

"FARAH!" she shouts again, grabbing the penis whistle from around her neck and blowing on it hard. "FARAH!"

Farah is crouching in the open doorway of one of the private rooms. She turns and stares at Lauren, but her eyes look blank and there are tear marks trailing down her cheeks. Lauren feels the telltale prickle on the back of her neck she hoped she'd never feel again.

"Farah? What's wrong?" She reaches her friend and follows her gaze, and all at once the world stands still.

Slumped on a small leather seat in the tiny mirrored room, trousers round his ankles, is Jeremy. His eyes are wide open, there's a massive wound on his head, and a half-inflated plastic penis dangles from his slack mouth.

CHAPTER THIRTY-THREE

Lauren and Farah stare straight ahead at Jeremy's clearly lifeless body, frozen with shock.

"What was he doing here?" Lauren asks eventually.

"I just found him like this," Farah whispers. "I don't know what . . . You don't think that I . . ." She turns to Lauren, appalled.

"Oh God, no!" Lauren says, putting an arm around her friend, trying to remind herself what Saskia said: that Farah has no reason to sabotage her own hen do. It can't be her, it just wouldn't make any sense. "Of course not! Just . . . I mean . . . Oh God, Saskia . . . Poor Saskia."

The two of them shift awkwardly next to each other. There's a spikiness between them that's never been there before. A sort of uncertain edge to the air as they wait there, unsure what to do.

"FARAH?" Dominica's voice echoes from around the corner before her reflection comes into view. "There you are!"

She races toward them, and before either of them have a chance to warn her about what's happened, she's gasping, her mouth flung wide.

"Fuck!" she yells, stepping forward to get a closer look. "Is that Jeremy? What's he doing here?" Like Lauren, she finds herself eyeing Farah suspiciously.

"Don't look at me like that! I don't know!" Farah shouts back. "Why would you look at me like that?!"

"I'm sure Dominica doesn't think you . . ." Lauren starts. "I mean . . . it's just you have been a bit stressed."

"Somewhat lacking in compassion," Dominica adds, peering at Jeremy's lifeless body again. "Are we sure he's . . . ?"

"I mean . . . I think so . . ." Lauren says, gesturing to the head wound.

"Just because I wanted a nice wedding and hen do that was actually about ME for a change, and was UNDERSTANDABLY stressed after everything that's happened, you think I killed our friend's husband?!" Farah shouts. "That would be quite the opposite of what I wanted, surely?"

Dominica and Lauren stare down at their feet, neither of them wanting to look at Farah or at Jeremy's cock-asphyxiated state.

"I can hear them!" Saskia's voice travels along the mirrored corridor, making them all jump into action.

"Shit!" Dominica launches into the little room to do something she's always told other people never to do and touch the evidence.

She grabs the inflatable penis, trying to yank it out of Jeremy's mouth, but it's stuck fast.

"Fuck," she grunts. "Help me!"

Farah and Lauren join in, but the penis doesn't move.

"Whoever did this must have blown it up from the outside once it was in his gullet," Lauren says. "We need to let the air out!"

Dominica wrestles with the stopper, and the air trickles slowly out of the penis, while the unmistakable clip-clop of Saskia's heels as she rounds the corner counts down the seconds to her life changing forever. The cock starts to decrease in size, but it's too late. Saskia's already there.

"What's going on?" she asks, hurrying forward, Jimmy and John right behind her. "Who's that? Why does it look like . . . ?"

Farah, Lauren, and Dominica know there's absolutely nothing they can do now. None of them know what to say. Not even Dominica, who can normally cope with any situation.

"NO! NOOOOOOO!" Saskia screams, flinging herself onto Jeremy.

Dominica attempts once more to remove the deflated and shrivelled penis. She tries mouth-to-mouth, but it's no use. The last thing that's going to help this situation is more inflation, after all.

"I'll call the police," John says.

"He's been deep-throated," Jimmy whispers distastefully before shoving his hand over his mouth and burying his head in John's baby-oiled shoulder.

"DON'T LOOK AT HIM!" Saskia screams. "EVERYONE STOP LOOKING AT MY HUSBAND!"

CHAPTER THIRTY-FOUR

It's been four hours now since they found Jeremy, and the hens remain huddled in the dressing room wrapped in foil blankets, some of them starting to grow restless. They're being kept under the watchful eye of the local police, who have been instructed that, as Jeremy's death is part of an ongoing case, they must wait for the arrival of DI Ashford and DS Castle from London before any questioning can take place.

In the meantime, the hens have closed ranks, crowding around Saskia, comforting her and forming a protective barrier in the way they have always done for each other. To look at them you'd never know that inwardly they're eyeing each other with suspicion, and wondering what Jeremy was doing here in the first place. Well, most of them are, anyway.

"Why did they release that woman?" Saskia cries. It's the first thing she's said in hours. "Did she do this? They need to find her!"

"We'll talk to the police. We'll find out," Dominica says, rubbing Saskia's shoulder.

Dominica's not really sure what good this bit of foil's going to do. She feels like a jacket potato. She was over this hen-do stuff a long time ago; she really just wants to go home. Instead she dutifully sits at Saskia's side, knowing that if ever there was a time when Saskia was going to need her old friends, it's now. In the back of their minds, Dominica, Farah, and Lauren all can't help thinking that Saskia's going to be better off without Jeremy. They'd never dream of saying it out loud, though.

"Did you know he was here?" Dominica asks gently, and Saskia shakes her head. Her sobs are muffled by Dominica's shoulder.

Lauren's not sure how long it's been since they found the body, but it feels like days. She's starting to wonder if they'll ever leave this back-stage area. She knows it's much worse for Saskia. She probably can't even begin to imagine a life without Jeremy. And what about the children? But she can't feel any sympathy for Jeremy himself, a man who tore their friendship group apart, who was patronizing and judg-mental, and sometimes downright nasty. A man who died as he lived: a massive penis. She eyes Eva suspiciously across the room. The younger woman is tapping away frantically on her phone, and Lauren wonders if she's texting Joss to tell him what's happened.

Farah sits in her foil blanket, staring at the scene in front of her, as-sessing her friends one by one. She feels her own phone vibrate in her pocket and pulls it out to see another barrage of texts from Rebecca.

Did you do what I asked?

Farah replies bluntly: *He's dead, Rebecca.*

"Why was he even here?" Saskia asks no one in particular, remov-ing her head from Dominica's shoulder. She stares straight ahead, her lips quivering, her eyes blank and misty. As if the shock has completely detached her from everything.

"The police'll find out," Dominica says, stroking her hair. "They'll find out what happened."

"But what about the children? Who's with the children?" Sudden panic fills Saskia's eyes.

"It's OK, they're with the nanny, remember?" Lauren says, reaching out and taking Saskia's hand. "I phoned her earlier and she's going to stay with them until we get back."

"I need to see them," Saskia mutters.

"Excuse me," Dominica asks one of the uniformed officers. "How much longer do we have to be here? My friend needs to be with her children, she needs to inform family members."

"We'll get you back to your children as soon as possible," a familiar voice says from the doorway, and Lauren turns to see DI Ashford standing there, along with DS Castle.

She looks at him hopefully, but he doesn't smile or give her a wave or anything; in fact he doesn't even look at her at all. She realizes that he has a job to do and that his job is very serious, but she can't quite associate the stern-looking detective in front of her with the man she was sending pictures of herself posing with giant penises just hours ago.

He introduces himself to the strippers, then makes his way over to Saskia and the hens, but continues avoiding Lauren's gaze.

"I'm sorry for your loss," he says, "but I'm going to have to ask you all to stay put a while longer so we can speak to you one by one and take your statements." He turns to the uniformed officer next to him, who looks positively affronted by his presence. "Please could we clear the crowd that's built up out front asap? We need to make sure that no one's filming or taking pictures; it needs to be a public-free zone when we move the body. We can't have anything showing up on social media."

"OH MY GOD!" Saskia claps her hand to her mouth. "They can't! They can't take pictures! I couldn't bear it if this ends up on social media or on some tacky tabloid site! This isn't what's supposed to happen. He's supposed to die old, in his sleep, and have a respectful full-page obituary in *The Times*! Not a sodding headline next to tits of the fucking week! HOW COULD THIS HAPPEN? HOW COULD ANYONE LET THIS HAPPEN? WHY DID YOU RELEASE THE SUSPECT?"

She leaps up and points accusingly around the room, her foil blanket scrunching at her shoulders. Her anger seems to be specifically directed at DI Ashford and the venue staff, as if Jeremy's death is their sole responsibility.

"Here, pet." John takes her pointing arm gently, and he and Jimmy settle her back into her seat.

"There, there," Jimmy says. "We'll look after you, love."

DI Ashford clears his throat. "The suspect was released earlier today after new evidence came to light that proves they had no interaction with the cacao and that in fact they were nowhere near the ceremony at the time. With the confirmation that the peach was only in one cup, it seemed impossible that they were involved. Nor were they near the eggs at the spa." He sounds robotic in the face of Saskia's grief.

"But now this has happened, after they were released," Dominica presses.

"They've been with family since they left the police station six hours ago. It's simply not possible that they were here. That was the first thing we checked," DS Castle confirms calmly. "We need to speak with all of you now to take your statements. An officer will stay in here with you while we interview you one by one."

Everyone sits in silence, Saskia with her head in her hands and the other women looking at one another, realization dawning.

"You think one of us did it, don't you?" Farah says. "As if one of us would *ever*!"

Lauren realizes that's why she hasn't heard from DI Ashford: with the suspect released, she's under suspicion again. She stares at him with the expression of a kicked puppy, trying to plead her innocence with her eyes, but he won't look at her.

"Who found the body?" he asks, and everyone points to Farah, who's still pissed off with the way her friends are behaving around her.

"Farah went missing in the club for ages," Eva says.

Farah glares at her. "Yeah, I got lost. Anyway, you went out way before me to film content," she adds defensively. "And I didn't see you out there, you know."

"Farah . . ." Dominica warns her.

"And *you* certainly seemed to find us quickly," Farah snaps.

"Lauren found you first," Dominica reminds her, pushing Lauren in front of the massive bus Farah seems to be piling people under at speed.

"Because I was lucky," Lauren says. "I was curled up in the coats the whole time. *I* never left this room!"

"Right, yeah, Little Miss Nervous never puts a foot wrong," Farah tuts. "You were in the toilet for about an hour during the show, though, weren't you?"

"I WAS OVERWHELMED AND NEEDED TO HIDE!" Lauren shouts. "THERE WAS A STRIPPER DOING A WINDMILL WITH HIS DICK!"

"Oh no, I'm Lauren, I'm overwhelmed by penises," Farah taunts.

"Dom, you went out for a while to take a call, did you not?" Lauren asks, arching an eyebrow.

Dominica blinks, clearly thrown. "The number of times I've stood up for you when people call you pathetic behind your back . . ."

The women are in a standoff, none of them paying much attention to Saskia, sobbing into her foil blanket in the corner, or the detectives who are clearly bemused by their behavior.

"Perhaps there's somewhere quiet DS Castle and I could talk to Farah to start with?" DI Ashford interrupts.

"The props room's free," says the venue manager, a woman with huge eyelash extensions. "I'll show you the way."

Lauren watches them go, filled with uncharacteristic rage after her friends' comments, though she is momentarily distracted by watching DI Ashford's arse as he leaves. She looks around at the other hens, seeing that with the exception of Saskia, no one else is crying. Even Eva doesn't seem to be doing her usual performative sobbing routine. She had met Jeremy a few times though, which is more than enough to determine that he was a real dickhead.

"What can we do, Saskia?" Lauren asks, feeling like she has to make up for their outburst.

Saskia just stares straight ahead. Lauren's not even sure she heard her.

"Did he have a lawyer?" Dominica asks, trying not to take out her fury at the other girls on Saskia. "Would you like us to call them? Really, I think the sooner they're involved the better, especially given how . . ." She trails off, because Lauren's looking at her as if she's being insensitive, but she knows that this stuff's important. She's just trying to look after her friend.

"Yes, it's in here, under the name David Bannerith." Saskia passes over her phone, briefly snapping out of her trance for a practicality. Dominica takes it and steps away to make the call.

"Mrs. Bardon-Burnett?" A police officer approaches her, his shiny black shoes clacking on the concrete floor. "Could we ask you to come with us back to the station in London? We can talk more easily there. And I'm afraid we'll need to take you through the formal iden-tification process," he adds delicately.

"Oh, um, yes." Saskia looks around for Dominica. She seems lost, for the first time any of them can ever remember. Even before she met Jeremy, she always had a kind of steely determination and sense of purpose. She knew what she wanted, and she always got it, whether it was a particular character in a game of Sylvanian Families or getting wasted on free shots. The only time she's ever looked this frail was when her dad first left, and she and her mum realized they'd been left to deal with the aftermath of his bankruptcy.

"Don't worry, I'm coming," Dominica says, appearing at her side with the phone in her hand. "And the lawyer didn't mind being woken up. He says to let him know when we're half an hour away and he'll meet us there. Given it's two A.M. now, we'll probably be there around six."

"Thank you," Saskia says, gripping her arm and looking her straight in the eye.

"You don't need legal representation," the officer says kindly.

"I just want to make sure that my friend's OK," Dominica snaps defensively.

"Of course," the officer says, but she could swear she saw him roll his eyes a little.

The other girls hug Saskia goodbye, but she's too spaced out to hug them back. She leaves with Dominica just as Farah returns, moving with furious speed, no doubt spurred on by rage at her friends.

"Lauren?" DI Ashford calls from the dressing room doorway. "We'll take your statement now, please."

"Sure." Lauren jumps up, hoping that this means he might finally look at her with something other than indifference.

The two detectives sit on chairs that Lauren recognizes as the ones the strippers were using on stage when they were completely naked, their sweaty balls smushed up against the back of them. She makes a point of not sitting too far back in the seat of hers, but then realizes that she's perched exactly where bare arse cheek and crack would have been anyway. It's a minefield. She wonders if she should tell DI Ashford and DS Castle, but she doesn't know how they'd take it.

"I'm DI Ashford, we've met before, at your previous interview." And the rest, Lauren thinks. But she guesses that wouldn't be considered very professional. "And this is DS Castle." He gestures to his female colleague, who she remembers from the night Tansy died. "We'd just like to go through your movements leading up to the body being discovered." He's seemingly unaware that next to him a fireman's uniform is draped on a mannequin, giving the terrifying silhouette of someone about to whack him with their long hose.

"We were invited backstage after the show, so we were hanging out in the changing room with the strippers," Lauren begins. "Farah left to go to the toilet but took a wrong turn and ended up lost in the lap-dancing club next door. So we went to go and rescue her. When I found her, she was just crouched in the corridor outside the room where Jeremy was. She was in total shock. So I went to her and that's when I saw him, in the room. He had blood on his head and the, um, inflatable hanging out of his mouth. Oh, and his trousers were, er . . . around his ankles."

"Was it just your hen group and the strippers that were backstage?" DI Ashford asks. Is it her imagination, or does he look a little bothered by this?

"Yes," she replies.

"Was there anyone else around when you found Farah?" DS Castle asks.

"No one," Lauren says. "I hadn't seen anyone down that stretch of corridor at all. Not since walking out of the main bit of the club where the stages and poles and stuff are."

"Great, thank you. And had you seen the inflatable penis before?" DI Ashford asks with an entirely straight face.

"We had loads of them," Lauren says without flinching. She can play this game too.

"OK, great, thank you." DS Castle scribbles this down.

"Can you think of anyone who would want to hurt Jeremy? Was he particularly liked or disliked?" DI Ashford asks.

Lauren knows she needs to be careful here. They all loathed Jeremy, of course, but he doesn't need to know that.

"I mean, I wouldn't say any of us knew him particularly well or spent much time with him. Apart from Saskia, obviously. We'd sort of lost touch with her a bit lately, you know, life and stuff. But Tansy's hen do brought us back together again. She wanted Saskia there and Saskia had just started this events business, so she offered to plan it. We were just happy to be reunited . . ." Lauren trails off, aware she's not really answering his question. DI Ashford raises an eyebrow, but nods to his colleague to continue.

"And do you know why Saskia's husband, the deceased, was here?" DS Castle asks. "I wouldn't invite my husband on a hen do if I was going on one."

"None of us knew he was here, not even Saskia. So it's a bit weird," Lauren says. "You might want to talk to their nanny. She was looking after the kids, and when I called earlier to break the news, I think she was shocked he'd even left the house. I mean, I know they've got a big house, but still, you'd think she'd have known if he'd gone out."

"That's useful. Thank you, Lauren." DI Ashford makes eye contact with her for the briefest second, and she feels victorious before he looks away again.

"No problem." She feels like smiling at him would be a bad shout. A man has just died.

"That's everything, I think," DS Castle says. "Thank you for your cooperation."

"No worries," Lauren says. "Should I send someone else in?"

"I'll come with you to get the next one." DI Ashford stands up and follows her to the door.

The two of them head out into the deserted corridor. As they walk side by side, their hands sway just millimeters from each other. Lauren wants to look at him, but feels suddenly shy, thrown by his distant attitude. She knows he's got a job to do, but she just thought there'd at least be some sort of acknowledgment. She brushes her hand subtly against his as if it could be an accident. At once, his fingers clasp around hers, and within seconds he's pulled her into a small, dark room. From the smell and the clutter she thinks it might be a cleaning

closet. Disorientated, she looks around as he switches his phone torch
on. It's exactly what she thought: she's standing next to a bottle of
Toilet Duck.

"I don't think we can do this anymore." He says it softly, just inches
from her face, still clutching her hand. "I really like you, but I can't
compromise the investigation."

They lock eyes. Despite everything he's saying, the two of them are
so close, his breath tickling her lips, that it doesn't feel like he means it.

"I need to make sure I can investigate this case impartially. I'm not
saying I think you did it, but the fact is, you've been at all three murders, and if I'm seen to be favoring a witness, I could lose my job. I
never should have started anything, but I thought we'd found our
suspect. Now we have to start again." He sounds furious, and Lauren
finds herself massively turned on by his righteous anger.

"I'll never tell," she says earnestly. She's gripped by an overwhelm-
ing desire for him to take her next to the antibacterial spray and the
lube-encrusted mops.

There's a moment of stillness between them before they lunge for
each other's faces, their lips locking over the bleach. DI Ashford pushes
her against the wall, gasping as she reaches for his belt. But as she starts
to unhook it, he pulls away.

"We can't, I'm sorry." He looks red-faced, his forehead furrowed.
"Maybe when this is over?"

It's like a slap across the face; she can feel her cheeks glowing red.
She's sick of being rejected, sick of there always being something or
someone more important than her. She's forever been last in line, with
guys, with her friends, at work. She thought she could take control,
but it's never going to end. She's always going to be the last thing to
matter to anyone.

She turns on her heel and marches off down the corridor, and
doesn't look back.

CHAPTER THIRTY-FIVE

2005 Part Three

From their vantage point on the living room sofa, the five of them watch Greg chatting up a girl in the kitchen. He's throwing out all his usual moves: the cheeky white-toothed grin, the casual hand through the hair that also draws attention to his bicep muscles, the occasional brush against her arm. He's a predator sizing up his prey with practiced precision. The target he's circling this time goes to a different school, which probably explains why she's finding him charming; she hasn't heard how he shared naked pictures of Tansy with the entire football team, or how he told everyone that one of the other girls in their year had a really baggy vagina, which isn't actually a thing. Dominica looked it up.

The five of them have been waiting for a chance to get even with him for quite some time, and tonight's going to be the night.

"Do you think this is maybe a little harsh?" Lauren asks, the only one of them unscathed by him.

"No," the others all snap in unison.

"He shared pictures of my tits with all his teammates," Tansy says. "I haven't been able to walk around school without random boys staring at me in a pervy way for months. It's like everyone's seen me naked." She's never wanted to admit it to the others, but she really regrets not listening to her friends when they told her what a shit Greg was.

"He treated Saskia and me like we were disposable pieces of meat. Not to mention what he did to Dom," Farah says.

"Can we not? Mention it, that is." Dominica gives a dry smile.

She finally plucked up the courage to tell the girls how she'd lost her virginity to Greg, in the hope that it might stop Tansy from making the same mistakes other girls had. But unfortunately it didn't. He told her she was different, special, and she believed him.

It was Saskia who came up with the plan. She's always been the organizational genius, and now she's going to use her special powers to take him down. Seeing their usually unflappable friend too humiliated to go to school, knowing that topless pictures of her were lurking on the phone of almost every boy in the year, was the last straw for all of them. It's time to act.

"What if Tansy can't get his attention because he's flirting with this other girl?" Lauren asks.

"Er, hello?" Tansy says, gesturing to herself. "Have you seen this? Also, he still messages me all the time on MSN, begging for my forgiveness."

This is news to the other girls, but they can believe it.

"It's the modesty that makes you so likable," Dominica teases.

"There's literally no way he's not going to go for her," Saskia agrees with Tansy. "And when he does, Farah, you sneak behind them and drop the crushed Viagra into his drink. After that, Tansy, wait a minute, then take him up to the bedroom. We'll all be waiting, and hey presto . . . he gets handcuffed to the bed, and we leave the door open and wait for people to find him. He will forever be known as the boy at the party tied to the bed naked with a massive erection."

"You really are an evil genius," Farah says to her.

"Well, don't praise me till we've pulled it off, yeah?" Saskia says.

"OK, we're going upstairs to hide. Farah, come join us once you've planted the seed. Just send the bat signal if you need anything." Dominica presses the little baggie of crushed Viagra into Farah's hands. "She's gone to the toilet, now's your moment!"

"Got it," Farah says putting the baggie in her back pocket. She loves a covert mission.

The other three send her and Tansy off into the kitchen, where Greg stands waiting for his next conquest to come back from the toilet, leaving ample time for Tansy to swoop in.

"Hey," she says, adjusting her top so that her boobs look bigger and more prominent. She knows unfortunately all too well that he's a boob man.

"Hey!" he says, looking pleased to see her.

"How's it going?" Tansy asks, accidentally but very much on purpose brushing against his bicep. "Oops!"

Upstairs, Dominica, Lauren, and Saskia have found hiding places, with Dominica and Saskia crushed into the wardrobe and Lauren under the bed, where Farah joins her after spiking Greg's drink. The lights are off and they're just waiting for Tansy to bring him up here so they can complete the mission.

"This one." They hear her voice outside the room. "There's no one in there."

"OK, temptress," Greg says, prompting a gagging noise from Saskia.

The sound of the doorknob twisting prompts them all into silence, and they freeze in their positions, waiting for him to reach the bed.

"Wow, someone's excited," Tansy says. Obviously the Viagra's working already.

"Yeah, man, it was getting a little too heated down there. I can't explain it, it's like he's got his own mind. I'm just so into you, I guess I can't control myself." Greg doesn't sound in the least bit concerned about his aggressive hard-on; in fact he sounds proud of it.

Tansy lets out a small snort of a giggle and the girls hear her and Greg landing on the bed. The room fills with the slurping suction noises of Greg's overactive kissing. Dominica can't believe she was ever interested in him.

"I'll go on top," Tansy says. "Here, I've got a condom."

"You came prepared, huh?"

The girls all know what's coming next.

"You filthy little slut," he says.

Dominica tightens her grip on the handcuffs and darts out of the wardrobe, Saskia in hot pursuit, as Farah rolls out from under the bed, all three of them pouncing on Greg while he's distracted.

"WHAT? WHAT'S GOING ON?!" he shouts.

Tansy stays on top of him while Saskia grabs his arms and Dominica secures them with the handcuffs. Farah turns on the light. Greg is thankfully still in his pants, though his erection is unavoidably visible. Lauren eventually crawls out from under the bed, the drama over, too scared to have participated in the main event.

"Did you really think Tansy would sleep with you again after what you did to her?" Saskia shouts.

"What? Huh?" He looks as if he's about to plead his innocence.

"And what you did to me," Dominica adds.

"Oh, come on, what is this? Are we having an orgy? If anyone walks in on this, they're going to think I'm such a legend," Greg says.

The girls stop celebrating and look at each other, realizing that he's actually enjoying the situation. They'd not entirely banked on him being such a sicko that he would actually think getting caught like this would be a good thing. Leaving him attached to the bed frame, Saskia beckons the girls into a huddle, so that they can confer on the other side of the room.

"What do we do now?" Tansy whispers.

"Nothing," Dominica says proudly.

"Nothing?" Saskia asks.

"There's no way anyone will think he's the hero he reckons he is. No way." Dominica seems to be trying to convince herself as much as anyone else.

"OK then," Saskia says.

"OK then," Farah echoes. Now that Saskia's agreed, she can be sure it's the right thing.

"Right," Tansy says, and Lauren just shrugs.

There's a groan from the bed.

"Oh God, what's he doing?" Lauren asks, too afraid to glance over.

"Christ, is he wanking?" Saskia shields her eyes.

"He seems to be in pain," Dominica says, the only one brave enough to actually look at him.

"That's how they look when they wank," Farah says, before giving a small shudder. "I walked in on Joss once. I needed trauma counselling."

"No, he's in actual pain, I think," Dominica says, rushing to the bed and bending over him. "He's unconscious!" she whispers urgently.

"What?" Saskia hurries across and takes his wrist in her hand, trying to find a pulse, while Dominica slaps his face, trying to revive him.

"He's dead." She looks up, face pale.

"As if!" Farah heads over to join the other two.

"Well, you try and find a pulse then!" Saskia says.

"I'm really good at this," Farah boasts, sure she's going to find it and that Saskia's just being massively overdramatic. But even she can't seem to locate his pulse, and as realization dawns, she drops his hand, jumping back from his lifeless body. "Fuck, I think you're right."

"How?!" Tansy asks, heading over to take a look for herself.

"The pills?" Dominica blinks.

"But old people take them. Surely they're safe?" Saskia asks.

"Maybe he had some kind of heart problem or something?" Farah offers.

"Maybe he was allergic?" Tansy, queen of allergies, suggests.

"What do we do?" Lauren whispers.

"We need to get out of here." Saskia unclasps the handcuffs.

"We can't just leave him!" Tansy says.

"What would you rather? Have an awkward meeting with the police to explain why you're in a bedroom with a dead guy and his erection?" Saskia whispers back frantically.

"Good point," Tansy says.

"Should we call an ambulance?" Lauren asks.

"Then they'll know we spiked his drink," Farah says.

Dominica thinks carefully. "No one can pin the pills on us. We just leave the room, making sure there's no trace of us having been here, and someone'll find him."

"Dom's right," Saskia says. "We go downstairs and act completely normal. Just wait for someone else to find him."

"I agree." Farah nods. "Being discovered with a dead guy would definitely mess with my uni applications. Should we leave the party altogether?"

"No, that just looks more suspicious. We'll be the ones who left the party right before the dead body was found," Dominica says.

"Please don't say dead body." Lauren has gone very pale.

"What else would you like me to call it?" Dominica snaps. "We go downstairs, keep to ourselves, act like everything's normal, and wait."

"Maybe he could still wake up?" Tansy asks, gulping.

"Why has he still got an erection?" Saskia asks.

Downstairs, the girls grab drinks and go back to the sofa where they were sitting before. They try and get into the party, but Lauren can't even focus on mooning over Joss. They feel a mixture of relief and dread when a scream comes from upstairs, followed by the shouts declaring that Greg Thomas is dead.

CHAPTER THIRTY-SIX

A week and a half after Jeremy's death, Dominica, Lauren, and Farah stand outside the West London Crematorium in black dresses, blazers, and heels, with matching black sunglasses.

"You two are the last ones who need to sign," Dominica takes an A4 brown envelope out of her bag. "I managed to get all the others done over the last couple of days. It's lucky NDAs are a standard document, meant I could cover everyone who was there fast."

She hands Lauren and Farah the non-disclosure agreements stating that they will never tell a single soul the true circumstances surrounding the death of Jeremy Bardon-Burnett. As far as the rest of the world knows, Jeremy died of a heart attack in Blackpool, where he had chivalrously driven to pick up his wife from a hen do. There is to be absolutely no mention of strippers, lap-dancing clubs, or inflatable dicks. It's important to Saskia that she protects "Jeremy's legacy," even if it's meant getting a huge number of people to sign NDAs, including strippers, venue managers, and everyone else on the hen do.

"I had to get Joss to sign one as well, because Eva obviously told him what happened before we'd come up with the plan to say it was a heart attack," Dominica says.

"Wait . . . does that mean I shouldn't have told Toby?" Farah asks faux sheepishly, but Dominica knows she's no idiot. She's a journalist. This isn't her first time at the NDA rodeo.

Dominica rolls her eyes. "God's sake, Farah! I'll get one drawn up for Toby tonight and he can swing by the office tomorrow to sign it." Not that Toby would ever say anything; unlike his wife-to-be, he understands when to keep his mouth shut.

"Thanks, babe, love ya!" Farah says, blowing her a kiss. "He can do it after his suit fitting."

"This thing's harder to contain than toxic fucking waste." Dominica takes a last drag on her cigarette and places the signed documents back in the envelope. "Where is Toby anyway? I thought he was coming to the funeral."

"Yeah, he's arriving later with Joss and Eva. He knew I had business to attend to first," Farah says.

"Do we know when Saskia's getting here?" Lauren asks, looking around the crematorium gardens to assess the other people gathering there.

"No idea," Dominica says. "I haven't been able to talk to her even in a professional capacity for days. The Holland Park yummy mummies have formed some kind of impenetrable force field constructed from Dior and YSL mourning wear. No one with less than a six-figure clothing allowance is getting in."

"Ridiculous!" Farah says. "And to think they don't even know how he really died."

"Well, quite," Dominica says. "All of this is for their benefit."

"Um, Farah, babe, do you think Saskia's still going to be able to make it next weekend?" Lauren broaches the subject gently.

Farah gets a fierce look in her eye and clenches her jaw. Already since the suspect was released she's had friends say that all of a sudden they mysteriously can no longer come to the wedding. Word seems to have spread, and people are cancelling in droves. Even though they think Jeremy died of a heart attack.

She's trying not to let it bother her. She's forging ahead, because after all this she's going to have the perfect wedding day no matter what. All that matters to her now is that she and Toby make it down the aisle and the photographer documents it. Fuck whether there are guests or not; she'll take down anyone or anything that tries to stand in her way. She wonders if she might care more about the wedding's survival than her own. And she can't believe the death of a man she hated is overshadowing her big day.

"It'll be fine," she says with a tight, forced smile.

Lauren and Dominica exchange a look. There's been a manic energy coming off Farah these last few days. She's drinking and smoking more, and her eyes have a kind of furious glassiness to them, as if behind them there's just a wedding countdown that she's clinging onto with all her might. It's quite terrifying actually.

"The service doesn't start for another fifteen minutes, but I reckon we should go in and get good seats," Dominica says, trying to avoid another confrontation.

"Good seats?" Lauren asks, looking appalled.

"You know what I mean." Dominica takes a hip flask out of her pocket and swigs from it. Farah gestures to the flask, nearly snatching it out of Dominica's hand when she passes it to her.

Dominica's phone vibrates, and the air around her is suddenly shrouded in a sense of impending doom.

"Fuck," she says, staring at the screen. "FUCK FUCK FUCK!"

"Whoa, place of worship?!" Lauren points to the crematorium doors they're about to walk through.

"Nah, it's not," Farah says.

"Is it not?" Lauren looks confused, staring up at the building.

"Just a crematorium, not attached to any religion," Farah explains.

"Look." Dominica stops them. "I need to tell the two of you something, before anyone else gets here. It's secret, like REALLY secret. I've just had word that something's about to go down. Something big."

"What?" Lauren and Farah ask, taking turns to sip from the flask.

"Has Jeremy got one of those secret families that appears at funerals, like 'Surprise, he was my daddy too!' because I would find that incredibly basic rich businessman of him," Farah says.

"No, not that. He did have some other secrets, though," Dominica says. "I had an investigator trailing him for six months. I was working on this case, a messy divorce. The husband had a fetish—he liked having little Lego characters shoved up his arse. The wife wouldn't do it, so he went elsewhere, and elsewhere turned out to be their daughter's tennis coach."

"Just men, or would he allow Lego women too?" Lauren asks, raising an eyebrow. "Does the patriarchy extend to Lego fetishes?"

"I don't think he really minded either way, but he definitely seemed to prefer it when they were wearing hats. Don't ask me why," Dominica continues, whispering furiously. "Anyway, this guy had been paying out loads of money to a company called QWERKs. At first I thought it was some kind of shell company where he was hiding his money so that he didn't have to part with it. But it turned out to be this kind of . . . club, I guess. Exclusively for men in powerful jobs or positions, providing a service for them."

"What, like prostitution?" Lauren asks, her eyes wide.

"No." Dominica shakes her head. "Say you're a member of this club and you get caught with a prostitute or doing something indecent, or someone tries to out your sexual fetish or some kind of grubby bit of gossip about you, the club gives you a kind of insurance, it protects you. They have a huge network of people, from police commissioners to TV execs, politicians, and media personnel, all looking out for each other. Once you're a member of the club, you're protected for as long as you continue paying your membership. Whatever it is that someone's about to uncover, or that you're about to be arrested for, they make it completely disappear. It gives these men freedom to do whatever they want, when and wherever they want, with absolutely no consequences for their lives, families, or careers. It's a kind of modern boys' network, but one that's frighteningly good and thorough. And it costs ten thousand pounds a month. So you know that whatever these people have done, they *really* want it kept secret."

"So it's basically a club that supports men doing whatever rank and shady shit they want and getting away with it?" Farah thinks that if Jeremy was part of this, it explains his disregard for the surrogacy laws, and how he found out about her article.

"The membership list is encrypted, so we don't know yet exactly who's in it, but the general consensus is that it includes a lot of VERY well-known people. People who are seriously high up in government institutions," Dominica adds, and Lauren feels like they're in some kind of Sunday-night BBC spy drama or something.

"But what does that have to do with Jeremy?" she asks.

"Well, turns out he was the founder of that club, the person who started it all."

Farah looks gobsmacked. If she didn't know about Jeremy's business, Dominica wonders, then what was he talking to her about down that alleyway?

Lauren stands with her mouth hanging wide open. "You knew about this and said NOTHING?" she asks. "This whole time? Does it have anything to do with why he died? And Helen and Tansy?"

"I don't know," Dominica says, scrunching up her nose. "Maybe."

Farah realizes that if she can tell Rebecca about this before it comes out, she'll get bonus points. Something else to make sure she keeps her job, and something that might distract her boss from the illegal surrogacy exposé that she's been heartlessly harassing Farah to continue with since Jeremy's death.

"The thing is, the police have all the information about the club now. We sent it to them after Jeremy died. My contact's just told me that they're planning to raid Saskia's house today. We've been talking to them, trying to see if they'll hold off until tomorrow, but if not . . ." Dominica trails off.

"It's going to happen while we're all at the house for the wake," Farah realizes out loud. "We have to warn her."

"What do you think I've been trying to do?" Dominica says. "But I can't get past the bloody Hags of Holland Park behaving like her personal Prada-wearing bodyguards."

"I wonder if the club's still going. Even though he's dead," Farah muses.

"I guess that's something the police need to establish. Along with exactly how many crimes it's covered up for people and what those crimes were," Dominica says.

"Saskia is going to lose her fucking mind." Lauren whistles.

"Unless she already knew," Farah says, wide-eyed, staring at the other two.

"What, and you think she . . ." Dominica slices her hand across her throat.

"NO WAY!" Lauren shakes her head and then looks shiftily around her. "No chance."

The three women gulp, staring into the crematorium at the gathering congregation, a huge picture of Jeremy propped up at the front of the room.

"No, you're right, there's no way." Dominica shakes her head and the others snap out of their trance. "I swear this whole thing is making us lose our minds."

"You can say that again," Lauren says as they all survey their surroundings for potential danger, as they have become prone to do.

"If she'd known, I think she'd have told me," Dominica declares with a pomposity that irritates the other two.

"Well, if she *doesn't* already know, then her husband's funeral is going to be the worst time to find out," Farah says.

"Which is why we need to tell her about it before the police surprise her with it in front of all the guests," Dominica agrees.

"How are we going to do that? We can't exactly whisper it in her ear as we offer our condolences, can we?"

"We need to get her on her own somehow," Dominica says.

Behind them, big black cars with tinted windows have begun to arrive, lining up in the lush green turning circle as they drop off consistently wealthy-looking people all dressed in black. The new arrivals start piling into the crematorium. The three friends stand in a row, watching as a long black hearse slowly approaches, a man in a top hat walking in front. Behind it come three large funeral cars containing Saskia and her entourage. Through the glass of the hearse the women can see the coffin covered in huge wreaths saying "Daddy" and "Husband."

"There's not even a body in that coffin," Farah says. "We're all about to sit in there and pretend to look sad as an empty box gets wheeled slowly toward an oven."

"Yeah, but we're the only ones who know it's empty," Lauren points out.

"Us and them." Dominica nods to the road outside the crematorium, where DI Ashford and one of his colleagues have arrived in an unmarked police car.

Lauren feels her cheeks start to color and wonders if DI Ashford feels as frustratedly horny as she has ever since their little encounter in the cleaning cupboard. She hasn't heard from Joss since his compliment spree on Saturday night, but she finds herself caring less and less. Maybe she's finally had enough of his behavior. She's found herself fantasizing far more about the detective than about Joss, which feels like a good step toward being mentally stable.

"Have either of you heard from the police since Saturday?" Farah asks as they all try not to stare.

"Not me," Dominica says.

"Me neither," Lauren says with considerably more sorrow.

The three women look over their sunglasses, surrounded by a cloud of smoke from their cigarettes, staring at the police car as if in a stand-off with the detectives inside.

"Is that why they're here?" she asks. "The club?"

"It's normal for them to be at a funeral when the death's suspicious. They want to observe the suspects and see if anyone unusual turns up," Dominica explains.

"They really think it was us, don't they?" Lauren says mournfully.

"To be fair, there's been three murders and we've been at all three of them. It would be weird if they didn't suspect us."

Farah reaches across to tuck a rogue label into the back of Lauren's dress, and Lauren's shoulders tense as she slinks away from her touch.

"We all know none of us did it, though, right?" she asks, more a question than any kind of confident statement, glancing at the other two women.

"Right," Farah says uncertainly, looking at Lauren and Dominica.

"Right," Dominica agrees, chewing on her lip as she surveys Lauren and Farah.

"Right," all three women seem to repeat at the same time as they watch Saskia through the window of the funeral car.

"I mean, it'd be nicer if the DI felt like he needed to get closer to protect me from the killer," Lauren mutters. "Rather than dumping me."

"Nah, they'd never go for you," Farah says. "You don't know any-thing, you never upset anyone. You're too pure."

"She's right," Dominica says.

I could be a killer and you'd never know, because I'm so stealthy, Lauren thinks with mounting irritation.

The three women stamp out their cigarettes and turn toward the door, checking over their shoulders with every step as they follow the other mourners past the crisp white lilies adorning the entrance.

"Does anyone else still get a strong urge to punch him even though he's already dead?" Dominica whispers as the three of them take orders of service from the somber-looking ushers, gesturing to his picture on the front.

"He's having his funeral the week before my wedding, what do you think?" Farah asks, being completely and utterly serious.

"Shh. The police might hear you," Lauren says.

"They're still in their car," Farah points out.

"Yeah, but what if they've got the place bugged?"

"OK, Miss Marple, this isn't a spy novel," Dominica quips.

They file into the back row, keeping their sunglasses firmly on so no one can see the paranoia on their faces. Dominica just needs this service to be over fast so that she can talk to Saskia and warn her. She certainly sees no need for anyone to do a long, emotional eulogy about Jeremy.

"It's weird, though, isn't it?" Farah muses, raising an eyebrow. "Whoever killed Jeremy may well be in this room right now, pretending to grieve like everyone else."

They sit watching the people around them, wondering if the killer's a few rows away, or even closer. They're so tense that none of them notice Joss, Eva, and Toby approaching.

"Lovely venue," Joss says, and the three women start. "Great day for a funeral, huh?"

They finally lower their sunglasses and peer over them at him, unamused.

"Hey." Toby waves to them all in greeting before taking his place next to Farah and giving her a kiss.

"Why're you all so jumpy anyway?" Joss asks, but his question's met with silence.

Next to him, Eva's wearing a very see-through black dress only made more modest by the addition of some kind of black cycling shorts and a bandeau bra. She greets them with kisses and hugs, leaning across the row, all without lowering her round sunglasses, then slumps on the bench alongside them with Joss sliding in at the end. As Lauren predicted, he's behaving as if he didn't confess his lust for her in those texts on Saturday. Sometimes she thinks he's a master gaslighter; other times she wonders if he's just got some kind of memoryloss issue.

"Nice dress," Farah says kindly.

"I suggested she might want to go for something a little more . . . respectful," Joss whispers.

"There's not even a fucking body here today," Eva hisses, lowering her glasses and peering at him judgmentally. "Don't tell me what I can and can't wear."

"Woman's got a point," Dominica agrees, taking out her hip flask and sneaking another sip before passing it down the row.

"This is so weird," Toby says. "What was he even doing there?"

"No one knows," Farah says a little too quickly, as Toby squeezes her hand.

Out of the corner of her eye, Farah sees to her surprise that Rebecca has arrived, wearing head-to-toe black, a tissue held to her eyes. She tries not to let the shock show on her face and hopes her boss can't find her among all the other mourners.

The noise in the room peters out and a hush descends. Saskia begins her dignified walk down the aisle, her face drawn, although if Lauren's not mistaken, she's used extra blush on her cheekbones to make them jut out just a little farther. Behind her, the pallbearers pace slowly with the wooden box on their shoulders. With the echoing of each black funeral shoe against the polished floor, the women grow more anxious. It's going to take more than a few swigs of vodka to get them through today.

CHAPTER THIRTY-SEVEN

"Oh God, I need a wee so badly," Lauren groans, jiggling her leg as a pair of thick red curtains open and the coffin begins sliding through them at a snail's pace.

"You literally went right before the ceremony," Dominica mutters, staring straight ahead.

"I know. I swear I've got cystitis despite not having had sex since last year," Lauren whispers.

They watch respectfully as the empty casket slides through to the great unknown.

"Furious masturbation'll do it," Farah offers sagely as the curtains close. Next to her, Toby holds in a snort.

Since the incident with the detective, it's fair to say that even furious masturbation hasn't helped Lauren. She's not had this many near-misses at sexual contact since she was fifteen and dating a vicar's son. A boy who was entirely banned from any sexual activity by God but constantly had a boner.

"Guess the coffin's not the only one feeling the burn," Dominica whispers.

The women snigger, just as a bereft wail comes from Saskia on the front row. Dominica feels terrible, but maybe now that Jeremy's gone, there's a chance they'll get their old friend back. In fact, while obviously she feels terrible for Saskia and the children, she can only think of positives to Jeremy's death. On the other side of Lauren, Farah's thinking almost the same thing. Wondering if this is when Saskia will come back to them, because for all her bossiness, she misses her.

Around them, the rest of the mourners sob, or at least have the decency to look bereft, but behind their sunglasses Dominica, Lauren, and Farah aren't wasting the tears. Dominica makes a note of those who appear the most upset and expects to see their names on the list when it's finally broken free from its encryption.

Lauren's leg-jiggling gets more urgent, and she wonders if she can just sneak out to the loo without anyone noticing during the final bit of wailing and crying. But just as she starts to get up, Saskia begins her slow walk back along the aisle. There's no way she could slip out un-noticed now. Everyone's nodding to Saskia on her way past, offering their hands and condolences. After what seems like an age, she finally reaches the door and other people start to leave. Lauren jumps up, rac-ing straight for the toilet, pushing past mourners as she goes.

"Sorry, just terribly upset," she mutters to one woman, who looks appalled at the speed with which she's moving. She places her hand over her face for added effect.

When she reaches the toilet, of course there's already a queue of women there and she doesn't think she's going to be able to wait that long. She peers into the men's and, seeing there's no one in there (be-cause there never bloody is, is there?), darts straight in. It won't take long because she has an awful feeling that nothing's actually going to come out. The only thing that's likely to give her any relief now is several sachets of Cystopurin and some high-strength co-codamol.

"Lauren?" She hears Joss's voice the moment she slumps down on the seat.

"Shit," she mutters. "Yep, guilty. Sorry, I couldn't wait for that queue to go down."

"Cystitis?" he asks.

"Yup," she sighs, although at least this might make him think she's got an active sex life rather than the disappointingly dormant truth of it all.

"Ah, poor you. I'm sorry. I remember how badly you used to get that," he says.

Lauren suddenly becomes pathetically nostalgic for the days when he used to go out and get her cystitis medication, then spend the day wrapped in a blanket with her watching films, tending to her hot-water-bottle needs. She rallies, stands up, pulls her skirt down, and flushes. When she exits the cubicle, she sees Joss's back and wonders what he's doing facing the wall like it's the end of *The Blair Witch Project* . . .

"OH SHIT!" she says, racing back into the cubicle. "Fuck, sorry, I didn't think."

"Oh! I presumed you'd be in there a while. It's the only cubicle. Argh! Sorry!" He wriggles about and then turns to face her, everything tucked safely away. "Finished! Sorry!"

Lauren blinks away her awkwardness and walks toward the sink, still slightly shielding her eyes. She turns on the tap to wash her hands, and Joss comes to stand next to her, increasing the awkwardness tenfold. The two of them lather and rinse in such silence that you could hear the soap bubbles popping, before turning to use the hand dryer at the same time. Their hands bump and Lauren immediately takes hers away and looks at the floor.

"Sorry," she says.

To her surprise, though, Joss takes her hands. She feels his warm fingers wrapped around hers, rubbing gently. He looks at her, searching for something, staring deeply into her eyes. Finally he opens his mouth.

"Are you OK?" he asks. "I know you don't really have anyone."

Lauren's heart turns to concrete as she registers what he's said, and she rips her hands out of his grasp. "Fine, thanks," she says, turning on her heel and walking out of the bathroom.

Of course he's only ever going to ask if she's OK. What did she think was going to happen? Did she think they were going to shag over the crematorium urinal? Hardly Jilly Cooper, is it? He's had his chance. That's the last time she'll let him stare deeply into her eyes and send her weak at the knees. The last time.

Farah waits in the crematorium gardens, hovering behind a bush. She told Toby she had to go to the loo and then raced off. Sparking up a cigarette and anxiously wringing her hands, she watches the mourners come out from afar. She knows Rebecca's read her text, but she hasn't responded. So when she suddenly emerges from behind one of the monuments, it startles her so much she lets out a little scream.

"Jesus, you scared the shit out of me." Rebecca puts a hand to her heart. "Or you would have if I hadn't had a colonic yesterday."

"Well, that's more information than anyone needs about their boss," Farah mutters. "Very happy for you and your tidy colon, though."

"Thank you. What did you want to see me about? You've turned into such a bloody secretive weirdo," Rebecca says.

"I mean, firstly, *what* are you actually doing here?" Farah asks, narrowing her eyes.

"Jeremy was a friend of many of the high-ups on the board; it's good to show your face at these events. Besides, you'd be surprised how many important conversations happen at a funeral. More business decisions get made over a sodden handkerchief than you might think."

"Christ," Farah says, marveling at the woman's callousness.

"I consider myself more of a Mary Magdalene figure, but sure . . ." Rebecca says. "Why are you so jumpy anyway?"

"Do you not think if anyone saw those texts we were sending each other on Saturday night they'd have questions?" Farah asks. Never mind the ones that Jeremy was sending her, she thinks. "And now we're standing here talking like we've got a secret."

"Yes, that does look bad for you, especially as you were there when your two other friends were murdered, but you know . . . it doesn't look bad for me. I'm just your boss, really." Rebecca lights a cigarette from the tip of Farah's. "Anyway, the good news is we can carry on with that article now. Unless you've got the money to pay the company back?"

"Aren't you even remotely nervous about going ahead with this?" Farah whispers, looking shiftily around her.

"I've not even broken the seal on a Valium packet, babe. Maybe you should, though," Rebecca says as Farah's phone vibrates, making her jump again.

She ignores it. "Look, something else is going down. Jeremy was running a secret kind of boys' club, charging members to cover up illegal stuff for them, things people would go to prison for. The police know about it and they're going to raid his house today, for evidence."

"Yeah, I know."

Farah's about to carry on with her pitch when she realizes what Rebecca's said. "If you already know, why aren't you doing an article on that?" she asks.

"Because, darling, half the men who run the magazine and pretty much every man in that crematorium was paying Jeremy to be in his club. We run that story, there's no magazine at the end of it. Besides, it's a women's magazine; stories about surrogacy get way more traction." Farah stares at her as if comprehending for the first time just how deep the dirt runs. "It sounds to me like it's time to start deleting some shit from your phone, though."

On cue, Farah's phone vibrates again, and this time she takes a look at it.

We need to go.

Guys, why are you ignoring me! I've got us an Uber! It's happening!

WE NEED TO GO!

"I've got to go!" she says, stamping out her cigarette.

"See you at the wake, darling," Rebecca calls after her, blowing air kisses.

Farah can see Dominica pacing the turning circle, waiting for the Uber to arrive. But instead of running to her, she stands hidden behind the side of the building and opens her phone. On the screen is the last message exchange between her and Jeremy.

JEREMY: *Fine, let's talk. I'm in the lap-dancing club next door. Come find me then I'll work out what I'm telling Saskia.*

FARAH: *On my way.*

She deletes the entire thread and texts Toby to tell him she has to go with the girls to find Saskia, asking him to grab a taxi with Joss. She hasn't got time to explain it all to him now.

In the garden, not far from Rebecca, crouched next to a beautiful rosebush, Eva finally snaps the perfect funeral selfie that she came out here to take. It took her a while to get the angles right on her see-through dress, but now she's pleased with it. She fires off a caption about how sad it was to say goodbye to her good friend Jeremy, and hashtags about heart health awareness before posting it on Instagram stories. Then she stands up and heads back to the crematorium. Surely Joss must be looking for her by now; he's been ages in the toilet.

CHAPTER THIRTY-EIGHT

When the Uber pulls up near the house, there are already ten cars at the turning circle waiting patiently to drop people off.

"You can just ditch us here," Dominica says to the driver as he approaches the start of the queue on the tree-lined street. It's no surprise that he's grateful not to have to join it.

The three of them tumble out of the Prius and rush toward the house, heading straight past all the much classier cars and guests waiting in line. At the front door they attempt to race past a scandalized-looking butler figure, who stops them with a snitty gloved hand.

"Please wait your turn. Mrs. Bardon-Burnett is greeting her *mourners*," he says with a sarcastic smile.

"That's fine." Dominica tilts her head, offering a smug smile in return.

Ahead of them, Saskia is standing with her children and Jeremy's parents. Every guest hugs her and tells her how sorry they are and that if there's anything they can do for her she only need ask. The three women watch her, occasionally glancing nervously over their shoulders. Wondering who's in this queue with them and what they've done.

"I'm going to whisper in her ear, tell her that the police are coming and get her to excuse herself," Dominica whispers to the other two.

"And just for your information, three people ahead of us is the Lego guy from that divorce I told you about earlier."

Lauren and Farah immediately pop their heads up, standing on tiptoe like a pair of meerkats, eager to put a face to the sexual fetish.

"Do you think he's got a little guy up there right now?" Lauren asks, fascinated.

"Probably," Dominica replies, as if completely unmoved by the whole thing.

"What kind of character do you think?" Farah wonders, and the three of them assess the back of his head.

"Policeman," Dominica says.

Farah narrows her eyes. "I think cowboy."

"Priest," Lauren offers confidently, folding her arms across her chest.

"Let me do the talking to Saskia," Dominica says. "You two cover his parents and the kids."

"Got it." Lauren and Farah nod.

As the person in front of them heads into the house, the three women move forward. Farah leans down to the kids and gives them big hugs, asking how they're doing.

"Mother brought me a new horse," Jonathan says in a way that suggests that this is all he's taken away from the situation.

"Daddy was never here anyway," Mabel sighs. "So really it hasn't been that different, except Mummy's been crying lots."

Farah tries not to show her surprise at the well-spoken bluntness of these two children, but she also can't remember a single time that she ever actually saw Jeremy interact with his kids apart from in the posed Christmas card pictures that Saskia does every year. Come to think of it, she might have even Photoshopped him into those.

Dominica grabs Saskia into a hug and whispers straight into her ear so that there can be no misunderstanding. "We need to talk, asap. The police are on their way. It's about Jeremy, there's something you need to know."

Saskia pulls away from her and looks her in the eye to check that she's heard correctly. But when she sees Dominica's stony expression, she knows she's serious. A new purpose flickers into her eyes, a steeliness that seems to have switched on somewhere in her brain, battling through grief to set her in action mode.

"Meet me in Jeremy's study, down the hall, second door on the right. Wood panelling, reeks of cigars. I'll be there in a minute," she whispers hurriedly.

They pull apart, and Dominica hustles the other two away from their tasks and into the house to allow Saskia to greet more of her husband's mourners.

"OK, I know where we're going," she says, grabbing a white, a red, and a whisky from the tray of a very bemused server. "I get thirsty when I'm grieving. It's all the crying," she tells him.

"I've got terrible cystitis and I need to numb the pain, or I'll punch something," Lauren offers as her explanation, picking up the same selection as Dominica.

"Thank you," Farah says grabbing her own drinks trio. "I'm supposed to be getting married next week, half the bridal party are dead, and I'm not getting any fucking peonies."

She downs the red wine in one and pauses to hand back the glass and grab a replacement. The waiter walks away, his tray empty, looking shell-shocked.

The women walk undetected down the hallway, in the opposite direction to all the other guests. When they find the huge oak door that Saskia mentioned, they give it a firm shove before finding themselves unmistakably in Jeremy's office. It smells of cigars and leather, and Dominica notices an "Old Library" scented candle on the huge marble fireplace. Farah imagines Jeremy in here, smoking his cigars and conducting his grubby business, protecting men from the consequences of their sordid actions.

"What if she doesn't believe us, or gets angry?" she asks. "You know how aggressive she can be when she's having a bad time. I still think it was her that shanked the Sylvanian hedgehog."

"We have no proof," Dominica notes. Even so, she pockets a small, sharp gold letter opener that's lying on the desk, and has a casual look around for anything else that might possibly be used as a weapon.

Lauren follows suit, spotting an oddly shaped metal paperweight, which she goes to hide in her bag, only realizing her error when the bag immediately falls off her shoulder and onto the floor with a crash.

"I'll put it back when we're sure she's not going to Sylvanian Families us," she explains to the others.

"Remember, we're doing her a favor. Better that she finds out from us than the police," Dominica says. "We're giving her a heads-up."

"Yes, we're doing a good thing," Lauren agrees shiftily, clutching her bag.

"Oh yes, definitely!" Farah says brightly, grabbing Jeremy's cigar cutter from his desk. She wonders if she can go to the toilet and miss the whole thing. She doesn't want any visible injuries in her wedding photos. But she's left it too late. The study door opens, and the women brace themselves for a very unnatural disaster.

"I said I needed to pop to the loo," Saskia says brusquely, closing the door behind her. She looks angrily at the three women, annoyed at her schedule being thrown off on such a difficult day. "Well? What's going on?"

"You might want to sit," Dominica says, pointing to the leather chesterfield sofa in the corner of the office. "And have this." She pours Saskia a glass of brandy from a decanter on Jeremy's desk. She's already drunk all three of her own drinks.

"What for? My husband's already dead; surely it can't get any worse than that?" Saskia looks exhausted.

The three women tense. Nothing in their years of friendship has ever been as bad as this. Although Tansy might see that differently. And Greg.

Saskia sits down and takes the brandy, while Dominica perches next to her cautiously, the other two women creeping forward. Just as Dominica opens her mouth to speak, however, the study door crashes open.

"The police are here!" The bitchy butler from earlier stands in the doorway looking frantic. "They barged in quite without invitation and now they're trying to clear out all the guests. I told them: This is a wake! This is *unseemly*!"

Dominica puts her head in her hands and Saskia looks from her to the butler, accepting that whatever it was she was going to find out from Dominica, it's far too late now.

"OK, I'm coming," she says, downing the brandy.

"I've told them it's *terribly* uncouth!" The women can hear the butler wittering away all the way down the corridor about how stressful this is for him.

"I'd better go and make sure she's OK," Dominica says. "I guess you guys should probably come out of here too. This'll be the first place they'll be wanting to look."

"Good point," Lauren says.

She and Farah down their whiskies and head out. As she's leaving the study, Lauren hears her phone beep. Joss.

I didn't express myself well earlier.

I'm upstairs in the guest bathroom, maybe come and see me?

What for? Lauren thinks. What would the point be in that? So he can ask again if she's OK because she's such a spinster? Besides, getting caught in flagrante by the police at a funeral probably isn't the classiest thing in the world either.

Best not, she types. *The police are here. They're clearing the house. Eva'll be looking for you.*

His reply is short and to the point. *WTF?*

She partly suspects the WTF is in relation to her turning down his offer of a second glamorous bathroom meeting in one day, rather than the police. Weirdly, she feels incredibly proud. Is this what finally growing a spine feels like? She can sense herself walking a little taller. She swings her bag onto her shoulder and is immediately floored by the paperweight that she'd forgotten was stowed there for self-defense.

CHAPTER THIRTY-NINE

"I can't believe it." Saskia has her head in her hands at Jeremy's desk, now littered with his papers after the police turned it over. "Am I now liable for this? For this whole grubby mess that he's created? Is that how he paid for our house in the Caymans? Oh my God, is this how he paid for OUR CHILDREN'S CLOTHES? THE NANNY?!"

Lauren passes Saskia another drink and she downs it in one again before opening a drawer and taking out a packet of cigarettes. She lights one up immediately without even so much as an ashtray and sits scrolling between the images of documents on Dominica's phone.

The police spent three hours searching the house, leaving no stone unturned, not even the children's playroom. Fortunately, the nanny is now comforting them upstairs with some hot chocolate. Lauren, Farah, and Dominica are doing the adult version of the same for Saskia. All her Holland Park yummy-mummy friends are gone; they didn't stick around long after the police arrived, seemingly whisked away by their nervous husbands as rumors spread about why the police were there. Stands to reason the men wouldn't want to hang around, and it didn't go unnoticed by any of the women that Lego astronaut man was the first out of the door.

"What happens now?" Saskia asks, tapping ash on Jeremy's prized leather desk with intent.

"Well, I guess they'll take whatever evidence they've found and then they'll work out whether you were involved in the business, and who else was involved," Dominica says.

"I absolutely was NOT involved," Saskia snaps firmly, pouring herself another brandy.

"Oh, we know that, don't worry," Dominica reassures her. "And the police should be able to work it out quite quickly too."

"I'm willing to bet that a fair few of his friends will be on that list, though," Saskia says. "And then all those wives who were sneering at me as they left this afternoon will know exactly how it feels." She takes a break to slug back more spirits. "THE SHAME! Everything that I've worked for. What about my business? There's no way people in Holland Park will want me organizing their baby showers now. How am I supposed to survive? Thank God he had life insurance, or we'd be fucked. FUCKED." She bangs her hands on the desk, making a green glass lampshade shudder.

"I'll see to it personally that it makes the news," promises Farah. "Those women won't be so high and mighty when their secrets are spread across the front page and their husbands lose their jobs."

"Thank you, that's very kind," Saskia says.

Farah knows she doesn't really have the influence to do that, but pretending she does makes her feel almost as powerful as Dominica in this scenario. Also, she'd love to take those women down.

"It'll all be OK," Dominica says, filling up Saskia's glass again. "We've got you."

Saskia looks at her gratefully before surveying the papers in front of her. "Fuck's sake, Jeremy," she mutters.

Lauren is shocked to find herself holding in a giggle. She loves hearing Saskia swear. Fortunately her phone lights up with a text from DI Ashford, distracting her just in time.

I'm still parked on the road outside, come find me. Black BMW. But don't tell anyone where you're going. X

"Just have to go to the toilet," she says, standing up cheerfully, very excited by the kiss at the end of the message.

Farah gives her a funny look, but Lauren just gives her one back and leaves the room. She doesn't know why she's tiptoeing down the hall. It's not like there's anyone out here who's going to notice anything.

Looking both ways for stealth, she creeps to the front door. There are about five locks, all with different catches that she needs to put on the latch before she can get out, making it slightly less stealthy as she slides out into the night. The security light above the front door turns on, making her jump and swear, illuminating her briefly as she rushes toward a bush. Pressed against its branches, she stalks her way down the drive, through the wrought-iron gates, and into the street.

DI Ashford flashes his headlights so that she can spot his car under a tree. Looking back to check no one's following or watching her, she heads toward it with attempted nonchalance.

"What's up?" she asks, sliding into the leather passenger seat.

"Not much, you?" he says, as if he hasn't just summoned her there.

His hands rest on the steering wheel, white shirtsleeves rolled up to his forearms. He turns his sparkling brown eyes on her, and she finds herself fumbling for words.

"Why, um, what . . . You wanted to see me?" she says, realizing that she's been silently perving on him for a full two minutes.

"Oh, er, yes, I . . . I just wanted to see you," he says sheepishly. "I feel weird, like the way I . . . on Saturday . . . and I don't want you to think that I think it's you. You know?"

"Oh yeah, no, I get it . . . I'm definitely not a murderer!" she says, wanting to shove her head in her hands as soon as the words are out.

"I'm just worried about the case and being unprofessional and if anyone finds out about . . . you know . . . anything with us, I'd be taken off the case. But I can't stop thinking about you, so I . . . um . . . when all this is over, would you maybe go for a drink with me?"

Lauren finds his nerves almost as endearing as when he's being commanding. She looks up at him, her eyes shining, and all thoughts of Joss, the man who only ever wants to see her when he's drunk in a bathroom, go out the window.

"I'd like that," she says, smiling.

"Perfect, it's a date then," DI Ashford says, smiling back.

"It's a date," she agrees.

The two of them sit side by side in shy silence, before Lauren looks over at the house, as if remembering where she is.

"I should get back . . ." she says.

"Oh yes, of course," DI Ashford says.

She starts to open the door, but he places a hand on her wrist to stop her.

"Lauren," he says, before cupping her face in both hands and stroking her cheek gently. He leans in and kisses her fiercely before pulling away. "Be careful."

"Of course." She nods.

"You should go before someone sees us," he says, but he makes no attempt to let go of her.

"OK," she replies, giving him one last kiss before climbing out of the car.

She feels shaky as she heads back through the gates, the house looming ahead of her. DI Ashford watches from the car as she opens the front door. Looking up, he sees exactly who he expected to see watching her from the window.

Not one of these women is without secrets; it's just that some secrets are worse than others. Not all the hens went to the party to have a good time.

CHAPTER FORTY

2005 Part Four

Two months after Greg's tragic heart attack, Tansy, Farah, Saskia, Dominica, and Lauren gather with the rest of the school on the sports field to watch the football team playing a charity match in his honor. After his death, rumors went around that his blood contained twice the recommended amount of Viagra, but no one could ever confirm it. So when his parents wanted to stage a football match to raise money for a charity specializing in research on young people's heart conditions, everyone attended in solidarity.

At the front of the crowd, his family weep as his teammates kick the football around the muddy field in a lackluster fashion that Greg would most definitely not be proud of, and neither is the coach by the sounds of his shouting.

The police asked minimal questions in the end, because when they did, they found out that he was a player, the sort of guy who would be open to experimenting with drugs, and him taking several Viagra, misjudging the amount, and his weak heart giving out really didn't seem that difficult to fathom.

At Dominica and Saskia's instruction, all the girls had kept their heads down and said nothing; even Lauren and her guilty conscience had managed it. Someone had told the police that the last person they

saw him with was Tansy, but she simply told them what he'd done and
that she wouldn't have touched him with a bargepole. She said that she
only went over to tell him what a creep he was before returning to
have fun with her friends. And no one else noticed anything different
because everyone was a mess.

"Does anyone else feel kind of horrific? It's just, his mum's so
upset," Tansy says.

"I feel awful," Lauren whispers.

"I feel indifferent," Farah says, secretly revising for a history test at
the same time as paying her respects. The book concealed in her
jacket.

"SHH!" Dominica hisses.

"Don't draw attention to us!" Saskia hisses back. "Greg was a bad
guy. It was an accident. There's no way we could have known." She's
certainly not going to go to prison for what was essentially a practical
joke.

At this, Lauren's eyes turn glassy and she looks like she's about to
cry, so Dominica and Saskia put their arms around her apologetically.

"Sorry, Lozzie," Dominica says. "But we did nothing wrong really.
Even if we came forward, they'd just say it was a prank that went
wrong, and we didn't have malicious intent. He had a heart condition;
something like that was going to get him in the end anyway. It wasn't
our fault."

She doesn't know if this is true, but she knows that unless she can
convince Lauren and Tansy, they're likely to lose their nerve. Farah, on
the other hand, is far too invested in getting into the best university
possible and far too dependable to ever let it get out.

"Dom's right," Farah says. "We can't be done for anything, so why
ruin our lives by saying something now. If one of us slips, we all do.
We have to keep it together."

Saskia knows they can count on Farah. Like Dominica, it's the other
two she's worried about. As usual, it's up to her and Dom, the de facto

parents of the group, to keep them in line. At least they're the last two anyone would suspect: Tansy's so pretty she could literally get away with murder, and Lauren's too much of a scared mouse to be on anyone's radar.

"How would it ruin our lives if we've done nothing wrong, though?" Lauren whispers.

"You know how people talk and how they judge," Saskia says quickly, trying to prevent a further Lauren spiral, while rubbing her shoulders.

"Exactly, people would label us," Dominica says. "And the best thing we can do right now is just grieve like the rest of the school and wait until all this passes."

"I guess the universe made a call. We couldn't have known that was how it was going to go," says Tansy, confirming that they've talked her round.

"Pass me the voddy," Dominica whispers. Saskia grabs the hip flask from the waistband of her skirt and passes it to her discreetly. Dominica takes a quick sip, disguising the bottle in her scarf before passing it down the line.

"We just need to forget it ever happened," Saskia says, placing a hand on Lauren's back as she drinks from the flask. "Move on with our lives."

After Farah drains the last of the vodka, Saskia slips the flask back into her waistband. The five girls stand in a line, holding hands, an unbreakable chain. Dominica and Saskia either side of Lauren, squeezing hers extra tight. Just to make sure she doesn't blab. She's always been the weakest link.

CHAPTER FORTY-ONE

Deep in the Scottish Highlands, the castle stands majestic against the backdrop of its lush green grounds and picturesque gardens. August sun beams from an entirely cloudless sky, as a convertible BMW trundles down the long gravel driveway. In the driving seat, Dominica watches the castle's grand turrets looming ever larger with each turn of the car's wheels. Next to her, Farah holds on to her straw hat, as she has been for most of the way, keeping her hair down. Her huge white bridal sunglasses are a thing of pure absurdity as far as Dominica's concerned, but Lauren has declared them wonderfully chic, so who knows really.

Behind Farah and Dominica in the backseat, Lauren has spent the majority of the long drive thinking about DI Ashford, replaying their kiss in his car and the way he told her to be careful. Oscillating between lust and fear, she doesn't say a word to her friends. They'd only belittle it anyway.

"I can't believe you're getting married *here*," Lauren gasps, to the irritation of Dominica, who, having heard nothing but "castle this" and "castle that" for the last two years, really doesn't want to show any hint that she's impressed by it. Though it's hard not to be.

They look up at the castle's turrets and old mullioned windows, archways and huge wooden doors. Around them butterflies, birdsong, and the far-off sounds of a lawnmower add to the ambience. Dominica dreads to think how much this is costing a woman who doesn't even own her own flat. For what Farah's paying for this, she could probably put a deposit down on a small flat in Zone 2. She will never understand why someone would want to spend all that money on one single day.

"Finally fucking getting married," Farah says, feeling a small amount of air exhaling from her lungs. She takes the huge sunglasses off her freshly Botoxed face and rests them on top of her head.

Lauren and Dominica couldn't fail to notice the shift in their friend over the last week or so: Farah's gone from being obsessed with getting every detail right to someone who doesn't seem to give a shit as long as she just makes it down the aisle.

Half of the wedding guests have now pulled out, worried for their lives—understandably, since there hasn't been another arrest, meaning the killer is still at large. That really was the final straw for Farah. Last night she made a list of all the no-shows, printed it out, and laminated it so that she will always remember to never, ever forgive any of them. Fuck those weak-willed wimps. When she's got more time, she'll unfollow them all on social media. She'd love to send them invoices for the cost of their non-attendance. She tries to bat the negative thoughts out of her mind so that they don't translate to her face, replacing them with a smile so wide it could potentially crack all the Botox. With or without those guests, by this time tomorrow she'll be a married woman, by hook or by crook.

"I was starting to think we'd all be dead by now," Lauren says without thinking. She's not talking about the murderer; she's actually referring to Farah, whose current expression certainly isn't making her look any more hinged.

No one knows what will happen to Farah after she's married, whether maybe she's gone too far to ever get back to who she was before. Can you go so bridezilla that you never come back from it? Once the stress of the wedding's over, will she look back and realize just how unreasonable her behavior's been? Dominica doubts it.

"Well, they've not caught the killer yet," Dominica quips insensitively, before catching sight of Farah's twitching eyes, her mouth still set in a wide smile as if it's all she has left. "Sorry." She makes a faux-anxious face to Lauren in the rearview mirror, knowing Farah won't want any talk of murderers today.

Farah keeps her mouth stretched, a kind of death happening behind her eyes. Lauren tries to keep her face neutral. She hasn't mentioned to the rest of them yet what Tom said to her. She knows she should—if she's in danger, surely they all are—but something is holding her back. Besides, she quite enjoys keeping secrets from them, knowing things they don't for once.

Farah sets her jaw as Dominica brings the BMW to a standstill at the front of the castle and pops the boot. She opens the passenger door and hops out onto the gravel. "You can leave everything in the car," she says to Dominica. "The porters will get it. They'll park the car as well."

"Oh right, thanks, Jeeves," Dominica says, feeling like a twat as she hands her keys to the porter.

"Where's your husband-to-be?" Lauren asks, squinting in the sunshine.

"He arrived with the best men half an hour ago. They're already all checked in," Farah says, pointedly, because Lauren made them half an hour late leaving London, fannying around.

"Are you sharing a room before the wedding?" Lauren inquires innocently.

"What do you think?" Farah's face is set in a way that Lauren thinks means she's angry, but she's had so much work it's hard to tell.

"Babe, we can't really tell if you're frowning right now, remember?"

Dominica says, gesturing to her face. "It'll be at least six months be-fore you're able to communicate with your eyebrows again."

"Haha. Very funny. Do you not think we've had enough bad luck, Lauren? Why would I do something that is actually well known to cause it?" Farah says bluntly.

"I mean . . . some could argue that you've had SO MUCH bad luck, what else could possibly go wrong . . ." Lauren regrets the words as soon as they've left her mouth.

"So nice to get out of London, please congratulate your husband-to-be on growing up in the wilds of Scotland and knowing this place existed," Dominica says, trying to distract everyone as they crunch up the gravel path toward the castle. There have been enough deaths this year. She inhales a deep lungful of fresh countryside air before lighting up a cigarette.

They reach the entrance and pass through its huge wooden door into the cool reception area, where black and white tiled flooring is peppered with columns holding beautiful bridal flowers. Dominica had thought the castle might be a little dark inside, but it feels light and airy and smells like the Diptyque room at Liberty. Everything about this place oozes money and grandeur.

The ceilings are so high that Lauren gets vertigo when she looks up at the flowers hanging down from them.

"Oh look! I thought you said they couldn't get you peonies!" she says, marveling at the soft pink flowers everywhere.

"Those are ranunculus," Farah says scornfully.

Fuck the flowers. Fuck anyone banging on about Tansy, Helen, or Jeremy. Farah's made it, she's here, and it's going to be perfect. This is her weekend, HER wedding, and frankly, Tansy never gave a shit about anyone but herself most of the time anyway. It's just that no one ever really saw through her floaty, ditsy exterior. Not that Farah would ever say that out loud. She feels her phone vibrating in her hand and looks down, expecting to see something from a family member or supplier. Instead, it's an unknown number.

> *I bet you thought you'd got away with what you did to Tansy. I've got one hell of a wedding gift for you, sweetie. I'll let you know when it's ready. Kisses.*

The world around Farah starts to spin, the words of the text blurring. How can someone know about the blackmail? Who? Jeremy's dead, and she's sure he didn't tell Saskia. The only other person she can think of is Rebecca, but she would have simply told her she knew already and added it to the list of other terrible things she knows about Farah. She feels her fists clench, her nails digging into her palms, clinging on. This isn't happening. She's not going to let it.

"Hello, Farah, darling! How's my *gorgeous* bride!" A woman wearing a white blazer and summer dress, complete with white Jimmy Choo sandals, has embraced her in a welcoming hug. The smell of her perfume chokes Farah as she feels the suffocating weight of her fawning.

"Lucie," she says, pulling herself free and greeting the venue manager with air kisses on both cheeks. "These are two of my bridesmaids: Lauren and Dominica. Eva and Saskia are on their way but aren't here yet." She doesn't mention that the last time they discussed the names of her bridesmaids there was one called Tansy, and Eva wasn't in the mix. It doesn't faze Lucie anyway. Farah's sure that brides often end up culling bridesmaids who aren't up to the task, to replace them with someone more suitable.

"Hello!" Lucie waves at them, clutching a clipboard to her chest. "We're so excited about tomorrow. And you all look *glowing*! I've made a little plan for your day, if that's OK? I thought we could get you settled in your rooms, and then I'll show you around so you can see how the preparations are going. Then I've booked you and your bridesmaids in at the spa in our west wing so that you can have the relaxing afternoon you deserve before your rehearsal dinner tonight."

"Sounds fabulous!" Farah says, but really she doesn't care anymore. Lucie can do whatever the fuck she wants as long as she makes it down that aisle tomorrow.

"Great," Dominica says, hoping that "spa" is code for booze by the pool.

"Can't wait!" Lauren agrees.

"Wonderful! Follow me!" Lucie claps her hands together. "We've got these beautiful new candles in all the corridors and rooms that were specially created by Diptyque for the castle. It's called Hylnd, and I think you'll agree with me that the scent in here is just absolutely *divine*."

Farah feels like if she inhales too deeply she might start hyperventilating, so she simply stretches her mouth into a tight smile and nods.

"Fragrant," Lauren confirms. She's never been anywhere this nice in her life and she'll probably never be again. She wants to make sure she savors every second. But despite the delicate scent, the beautiful flowers, and the perfect weather, she feels entirely on edge.

As they follow Lucie down the sunny flower-adorned corridors, Dominica wonders if the woman has a degree in superlatives. She also wonders what happens if she gets to a point where she's used all of them. Does she malfunction? Perhaps she can push her into finding out.

At least it'll be a project to distract her from remembering the interview she had with the police this week, just two hours before Jeremy's funeral, which she would describe as the *least* divine thing she's ever experienced. They'd obviously found texts on Jeremy's phone and traced them back to her. She doesn't understand why he didn't just delete them straightaway. Why risk keeping them? Unless the fucker did have some kind of heart after all. The detectives promised they wouldn't tell Saskia, at least. After all, it doesn't look great to have been sleeping with your best friend's husband. But after that, she'd had to tell them about Jeremy's club. It was only a matter of time before they found out anyway, and she couldn't risk them thinking she was in on it. And no matter what those detectives think of her for having an affair with Jeremy, she knows that everything she did, she did for Saskia.

Alone in her room, Lauren puts the second phone away in the secret zip-up part at the bottom of her case. She doesn't want to risk anyone finding it. She feels the thrill once again of having a secret from the others. Timid, pathetic Lauren isn't so timid and pathetic after all. Maybe they'll finally realize they can't treat her like she's an idiot anymore.

She looks around the lush room, wondering how exactly the bride and groom are managing to pay for all this. Anywhere that has its own Diptyque candle and Le Labo in every bathroom can't exactly be cheap. And the whole place is theirs for the entire weekend. When she went on the website, it looked as if that would come to about a hundred grand, which is more money than Lauren's ever likely to see. Surely Farah and Toby can't afford that? They must have got some help.

Married people always have much more money than single people, though, and it's not just the two incomes. People actually give them money for finding each other. Lauren thinks she deserves a five-grand check just for keeping herself alive, not to mention almost always remembering to take her makeup off before bed.

There's a businesslike knock at the door that she knows before she's even opened it is going to be Dominica. She heads to answer it, checking herself out in the fancy mirror on the way. As she suspected, she somehow looks better than normal in it. As if all that wealth has seeped into her pores by osmosis.

"Are you ready for the grand tour?" Dominica says cheerfully.

"I'm not sure Lucie needs us all—" Farah starts from behind her, but Dominica cuts her off.

"Nonsense, we're your bridesmaids. We're here to help, we need to see how everything fits together or else how are we going to be useful?"

"Honestly, it's OK," Farah says. "It's really boring, just final arrangements and things. I'll meet you both in the spa. There's Prosecco down there."

Farah knows that the best way to change Dominica's mind about something is with alcohol, and it's worked. She really doesn't need Dominica's input on things right now, or her judgment. She's already on edge enough without that.

"OK then! Spa it is!" Dominica says, relieved, because she honestly doesn't know how much more enthusiasm she can muster.

"Perfect!" Lauren replies. "Let's get pissed by the pool."

Farah heads off down the corridor with Lucie to check out the arrangements, not even caring anymore that her friends are going to have facial bloat in all her wedding pictures.

"I'm gonna go get my robe and bikini on. I'll meet you back here in ten," Dominica says.

"On it." Lauren is already reaching for the white fluffy robe on the back of her door.

At some point, hopefully she can sneakily send some spa selfies of her in her bikini to Tom without anyone else seeing.

CHAPTER FORTY-TWO

In the west wing of the castle, the spa is the most serene place on earth. The pool's the real showstopper, with a floor-to-ceiling window looking out onto the perfectly tended gardens and topiary outside. The smell of the Hylnd Diptyque candle is as prominent in here as it is in the rest of the castle, if not more so.

Lauren and Dominica are perched on opposite sides of the jacuzzi, drinking Prosecco, but neither of them is particularly relaxed. They're already on their second bottle, and they've been downing the fizz like it's water, trying to find the happy pre-wedding vibe that now seems lost to some distant pre-hen-do past. Two of the spa clinicians are hovering around in case they want treatments, but they agree it's not a good idea to do anything that might involve closing their eyes or letting their guard down around other people.

"I think someone needs to go in the plunge pool and sober up!" Dominica says as Lauren hiccups next to her.

"No!" Lauren hiccups again as she stands up. "No going in deep water when you've been drinking. That is how you DIE! Have you never watched *EastEnders*?!"

"I mean, there are a LOT of ways to DIE, if the last couple of weeks are anything to go by," Dominica slurs, squinting at her vibrating phone on the side. "It's Saskia, says she's just arrived and wonders where we are. Ah! And here's the woman of the hour!"

Farah appears in the uplit archway to the swimming pool, looking pure in her white bridal robe. She can feel the sarcasm coming off Dominica in waves despite her trying to hide it.

"HERE COMES THE BRIIIIDE!" Lauren and Dominica start singing. "HERE COMES THE BRIIIIIDE!"

Farah's annoyed that the two of them are behaving like drunken teenagers. Or maybe she's just jealous. She remembers a time before wedding planning, before debt and the threat of losing her job or, even worse, going to prison, when she would have happily downed a bottle of Prosecco without pause. Instead, the nagging memory of the text she received earlier is constantly at the front of her mind. She should be enjoying her day, having fun too, rather than feeling anxious, on edge, worried about who knows her secret and what they've got planned.

"Oh no, she does NOT look happy!" Lauren whispers to Dominica, a little too loudly.

"When does she? She's more boring bride than blushing these days," Dominica whispers back.

Farah pretends she hasn't heard them. "No Saskia yet?" she asks, clenching everything in her face.

"Just texted!" Dominica holds up her phone. "She's going to be here soon."

"Thank Christ," Farah says. At least there's one adult on her way, someone who's going to actually take this seriously. She sits at the edge of the jacuzzi, equidistant between Lauren and Dominica but touching neither.

"I think she was thrilled to get away from Holland Park," Dominica says. "All the neighbors are gossiping about her. Verity, Lavinia, and Anastasia are suddenly behaving as if they were never that close. Once the list's been released, though, I predict that they won't be quite so self-righteous." She closes one eye and points at Farah. "Worst-case scenario, I'd happily tell Lavinia about the blow job Tansy gave her husband on Saskia's wedding day, just for kicks. Can't get angry at a dead woman after all."

Dominica's secretly enjoyed the closeness that has formed between her and Saskia since her Holland Park friends snubbed her. They've been in almost constant contact since the police raid and she's loving having her friend back. There's no way Saskia can find out about her and Jeremy now; she'd never understand that it was all for her own good.

"You've seen the list?" Farah asks, suddenly interested despite herself.

"*I* haven't seen it." Dominica clutches her chest as she says it. "But I've heard things. And from what I gather, most of those investment bankers in Holland Park are on there. The richer the man, the darker his secrets. Especially the sexual ones."

"Oh my," Lauren says. "I wonder why Jeremy even needed to start something like that in the first place. I hope it's something juicy. I just can't believe you did all that without telling any of us."

"I did the same for Saskia that I'd do for any of you. I just wanted to protect her. I was hoping that when it all came out, she would be well away from it. I tried my best for her," Dominica says, thinking how they'll never know the extent of the sacrifices she made for Saskia. Mostly involving Jeremy's penis.

"You're a really good friend," Lauren says sincerely.

"You are," Farah lies. Actually, she thinks that if Dominica really were a good friend, she would have warned Saskia a little earlier, and maybe told the rest of them about it. But as usual, she had to make it all about her being the hero, and Farah's sick of it. Although she isn't deluded enough to think she herself is about to win any friend-of-the-year awards at the moment. And if the mysterious texter gets their way, they're all about to find that out.

The sound of a door opening and closing makes all three of them sit up, on high alert at the noise of footsteps approaching from around the corner.

"Prosecco!" Saskia's voice trills across the pool, echoing around the bare brick walls. When she eventually appears, she looks far perkier than the last time they saw her.

"Here she is!" Farah says, pleased to see someone who's well practiced at putting on a happy face. If Saskia can do it when she's just lost her husband and her entire world's been turned upside down, Farah really doesn't see why everyone else can't.

Dominica thinks that for someone whose husband just died, Saskia's looking really good. The hair that's been blonde since she married Jeremy has returned to its red-hued vibrancy and Dominica thinks Saskia looks more like herself than she has done in years.

"How is the bride-to-be?" Saskia asks. "NERVOUS?!"

Farah giggles. "Excited!" she lies, cracking her knuckles.

"Of course you are, darling," Saskia says, coming over and plonking another bottle of Prosecco down before hugging them all. "You're marrying your best friend."

Dominica almost laughs out loud.

"That's true," Farah says, tearing up slightly, although mostly because she knows there's yet another threat to that happening right now. A threat that might leave her not just without Toby, but also without her oldest friends. They may be annoying her right at this moment with their drunkenness, but she realizes she can't imagine life without them. They're so ingrained in her existence that she simply doesn't know anymore who she'd be without them.

"How are you doing?" Lauren asks Saskia, furrowing her brow solicitously.

"Oh darling." Saskia brushes off her concern. "After finding out that the fucker had been lying to me for so long, to be honest I'm angry. I know this is a stage of grief, but I seem to be quite stuck in it.

He can rot for all I give a shit." She plonks herself down on a lounger
next to the other women and downs a glass of Prosecco in a very un-
Saskia-like way. She's normally a sipper, not a glugger.

The other women look at her, unsure whether they should be worried, all except Farah, who honestly doesn't think she could handle yet
another thing to worry about.

"Hey, Team Bride!" Eva shouts, startling them all as she walks
through the pool area. "Final bridesmaid reporting for duty! The men
are all doing some kind of whisky tasting in the main bar, by the way,
and they are HAMMERED."

Farah finally takes a glass of Prosecco because fuck it. If you can't
beat them, join them.

Dominica eyes Eva, wondering how long she's been at the castle,
and how long she's been in the spa—she didn't hear the door open. Is
it a bit peculiar that she's become so embedded in their lives? Securing
herself as Farah's "sister-in-law" and Tansy's best friend in just a few
months? Isn't it slightly odd that for someone they don't know that
well, she's slipped into their friendship group with such ease?

Eva comes to lie on the other side of her on a lounger, grabbing
herself a glass of Prosecco.

"What're we talking about?" she asks, stretching out her long limbs,
one hand behind her head, smugly relaxing into the pre-wedding preparations.

CHAPTER FORTY-THREE

Back in her room, Lauren knows she's going to need a cold shower and a coffee if she's going to get through dinner this evening without being a slurring mess. She pulls the phone out from the bottom of her suitcase and walks into the bathroom, turning on the shower while firing off some text messages that are long overdue.

The steam from the shower clouds up the bathroom mirror and shower screen as she slips out of her bathing suit and into the water. Standing under the stream, she turns the temperature down gradually until it's almost unbearably cold. She feels like Gwyneth Paltrow experimenting for the Goop Lab, as she tries to freeze the alcohol out of her system so that she can get ready to fill her body back up with it later.

Her teeth start chattering and a tight pressure seizes her chest as she tries to breathe in through the iciness of the water. An urgent-sounding knock at the door of her room startles her just as she thinks she's mastering Wim Hof breathing, but she's relieved to have something to take her away from this self-inflicted hell. Jumping out of the shower, she throws on her towelling robe and pads out of the bathroom, dripping cold water on the castle's perfect herringbone floor. She shivers, hugging the robe tightly around her as she opens the door, only to find Joss on the other side, leaning against the door frame for stability, as saturated with whisky as she is with Prosecco.

"Whoops, I got the wrong room!" he hiccups, his mouth twitching into a cheeky smile.

Lauren knows as well as he does that he didn't get the wrong room, and he certainly doesn't look remorseful or embarrassed about it. She studies his drunken face, realizing that in comparison to DI Ashford, he's a haggard mess. For the first time in her life, her heart hasn't leaped at the sight of him.

"Oh?" she asks in a way that she hopes is playful. Coquettish even, although she's not sure why she's still bothering. Old habits die hard, but her heart's not in it. Either way she's still shivering, and it's not easy to be coquettish when you have hypothermia.

"Are you OK?" he asks, noticing her shakes. He advances toward her, inviting himself into her room, a concerned expression on his face. "You look frozen!"

She nods and points toward the noise of the running water. "I was just taking a cold shower. Trying to sober up."

Joss looks through to the bathroom and then back at her. Silently he runs his gaze over her robe, her wet hair and face. Then he closes the door behind him and takes her hand.

She follows him out of habit more than desire. He rolls up a sleeve and reaches into the shower, turning the temperature up. Steam begins to fill the room once more, and Lauren's temperature starts to rise too, without the help of the water. Fuck's sake. She can't help but still be attracted to him, especially this many Proseccos down. Staring at her, inches from her face, he begins unbuttoning his shirt, revealing his toned chest and the muscular arms she's had dreams about for years. He shrugs it off, dropping it onto the bathroom's black and white stone floor, and reaches out, putting his hands on her shoulders, fingering the towelling fabric of the robe. Rubbing his thumb along her jaw, he raises her chin to look at him. He pushes her wet hair behind her ear and trails his fingers toward her mouth, lightly brushing her bottom lip. She takes in the man she's had countless fantasies about, trying to regain those feelings but failing.

Finally Joss wants her more than she wants him. She's beaten Eva and won a prize she doesn't even want anymore. One last time for posterity can't hurt, though, can it? Leaning down, he takes her face in his hands and kisses her, the thick taste of whisky and cigars on his breath. Grabbing the belt of her robe, he slides it off in one urgent movement. Lauren wrestles with the button on his jeans and adds them to the gathering pile on the floor before he lifts her up, carrying her into the shower. She feels victorious.

In her room, Saskia checks her phone to make sure there's nothing from the nanny. She stares at the bed and the one small suitcase she brought with her. She wasn't sure how to play this weekend, whether people would expect her to be the grieving widow, but at least with everything that was uncovered about Jeremy, people will understand if she's not exactly speaking fondly of him.

She remembers the argument the two of them had the night before she went on Farah's Blackpool hen do. He was annoyed that she was spending so much time with her old friends again when she had perfectly good friends in Holland Park. But where are those friends now? She hasn't heard from Verity, Lavinia, or Anastasia since the news came out. Not one of them has even checked in to see if she's OK. Where once her phone used to buzz with constant gossip about Holland Park's elite parents, now it's completely silent, and she can only presume she's the parent everyone's gossiping about. She spent years under the spell of those women, thinking that being part of their clique and having their lifestyle was all that mattered. The lengths she went to, the things she did, just to keep that life. When she dyed her hair back to its original red, it felt like no matter what else was going on, she was regaining control, doing things her own way again.

She'll never understand why Dominica told the police, why she felt she had to do that to her. Surely she must have known it would destroy the life Saskia had left without Jeremy? But maybe that's exactly what she wanted to do. To make sure she and the others were all Saskia had left. Of course Saskia knew about the business. She'd found out and was going to leave him; she just needed to figure out a way to do it without losing everything. When he died, it felt like an easy way out. The business would die with him. It was over. At least she was free now. At her wedding she'd vowed "till death do us part," and now that death *had* parted them, she was going to move on and finally start living the way she wanted to. But Dominica had to interfere, always sticking her nose into things, trying to prove she knew best.

At least no matter what money the police have taken, she still has Jeremy's life insurance. That will provide for her and the children for as long as necessary. And the children will be fine; she's going to get them therapists, and she's going to make sure they don't turn out to be empathy-less monsters like their father.

Her phone beeps with a message from an unknown number, snapping her out of her thoughts.

> *How long do you think you can hide the truth about your children? Now that everything's out about Jeremy, how much longer do you think it'll be before your other secrets get out too?*

Saskia stares at the message, furious. Who would even know? And why would they want to do that? It would only damage her children, after they've already lost their father. Don't they realize that?

Who are you? she types. *And what are you talking about?*

The reply comes immediately: *You'll find out sooner than you think.*

A heavy knock at the door makes her jump. What if that's them now? And she's about to find out right away? Worse still, what if they want more than just to destroy her reputation? She remembers the texts Tansy was getting before she died and looks around the room for something to defend herself with, but all she can find is an iron. Holding it up in front of her face, she curses the fact that this hotel doesn't have peepholes on the doors, and nor does it have chains. The sort of combination that only a trustworthy fool would live with. A chic trustworthy fool, but a trustworthy fool nonetheless. That's not Saskia; she's no fool, despite what her husband may have thought.

There's another knock as she stands inches from the door, bracing herself with the iron held aloft. Turning the heavy key in the lock, she opens the door a crack and peers into the hallway, to see Dominica's stern face looking back.

Farah curses the decision she and Toby made to have separate rooms before the wedding. What's the point when it looks like she's going to have bad luck anyway? Her phone beeps next to her and she's hopeful that it might actually be him, missing her too. But her heart sinks when she realizes it's another text from the unknown number.

What will your friends think when they find out what you did?
What will Toby think?

Farah sits staring at her reflection in the mirror. What if she's never going to wake up next to him again? The shame and embarrassment of a cancelled wedding this size will engulf her, not to mention the heartbreak of losing Toby. Imagining herself leaving the castle without her husband or even her bridesmaids is the final straw. She's so close to walking down the aisle after everything that's happened. No matter who this person is, and what they think they know, there's no way she's going to let them take everything from her. Not when she's on the cusp of wearing Jimmy Choo wedding shoes.

What do you want? she types.

> *Meet me in the disabled toilet by the bar between the first and second courses tonight for a chat.*

She shivers, realizing that whoever it is, they are here. They're a friend, someone she's paid for to be at this wedding. She's going to confront this person face-to-face and she's going to do whatever it takes to make sure she gets to that altar tomorrow.

A loud knock at the door startles her out of her thoughts, and she stands, shaking her head before answering. She really hopes it's Toby. He's the only person she wants to see right now. But when she opens the door, it's Eva who's standing in her doorway, looking utterly furious.

"I need to talk to you, now."

CHAPTER FORTY-FOUR

2022

Eva observes from behind the big old oak tree on the other side of the road as Tansy closes up for the day. Watching as she performs the same routine she's seen her do so many times before. She's been into the café a couple of times now, wanting to hear her voice, to try and find out more about her, but she's always kept her head down. She doesn't want to be noticed, not just yet. There's so much to try and make sense of; she'd hoped that by looking Tansy in the eye, she might find some answers. But she found nothing there except emptiness, an even bigger void of information than she had before.

Tansy locks up, bringing down the noisy graffitied shutters. She's tapping away on her phone and looks nice, like she's going out somewhere. Maybe a date. Eva's sat behind a lot of her dates in the last month or so, and it seems to her Tansy's not really in it for commitment. There's a different one each time, and she always spends the night with them. One of the men talked endlessly about the guilt he felt about his wife, and how he shouldn't be meeting her, but somehow he still went home with her anyway. It doesn't surprise Eva, though; Tansy doesn't seem to notice other people's feelings. It's one of the reasons she's still so interested in her, it's really thickened the plot.

She waits a few moments after Tansy leaves, and then follows a little way behind her, being sure to stare down at her phone as much as possible, so that she looks like just another person wandering the streets of Shoreditch on their way to whatever event they're headed to.

Wannabe influencers dying to be tagged at the coolest places really get on her tits. Being an influencer came so easily to her and feels so vapid that every other content creator she meets makes her feel like she's going to be slightly sick in her mouth. Tansy stops outside Shoreditch House, which freaks Eva out slightly. There's no way she'll be able to go in there without seeing someone she knows; it's practically an influencer youth club. She might have to abandon her for the night if that's her destination. Thankfully Tansy doesn't go in, though; instead she stands waiting, tapping away at her phone, until the door opens and someone else comes out that Eva recognizes. Farah. One of the other five girls.

"Hey, stranger," Tansy says, kissing her on both cheeks.

"Heya," Farah says, without much warmth.

Eva stands outside Cowshed on the corner, looking like she's studying something on her phone while the two of them get a distance away. After enough time has passed, she continues behind them. Tansy's babbling away, but Farah's definitely frostier than Eva thought she'd be. She's personally never had friendships that lasted that long before, but she assumed that if they were still buddies, they'd be tight. Although maybe it's to do with the petition Tansy posted the other day asking people to boycott the magazine that Farah works for. She probably didn't even make the connection, the dozy cow.

"What's going on with Lauren?" Farah asks, trotting next to Tansy in a grey roll-neck sweater and a pair of wide-legged black trousers, her Veja sneakers poking out of the bottom.

"I mean, some kind of heartbreak or something?" Tansy suggests. Her long blonde hair and freckle-speckled tan always make her look like she's just come back from holiday, but Eva knows she hasn't been on holiday for at least a month. She does know that she spends a lot of money on beauty products, though, things like fake tan and Botox. The extent to which you can watch someone and get away with it when you're simply a beautiful girl staring down at her phone a lot is astounding. "I feel like there's a new emotional crisis every few weeks at the moment."

"She's still utterly obsessed with my brother," Farah says. "It's sad. She just needs to get over it and stop trying to get his attention. If she just dated people she liked for a change, rather than people he'd be jealous of or impressed by, it would be SO much better for her."

"And if she had a job where she did something more rewarding than reposting makeup memes on the internet and creating GIFs of lipsticks," Tansy adds. "Her life's purpose seems somewhat unclear."

It's not like opening a vegan restaurant is exactly saving lives, but Farah clearly isn't about to say that out loud.

"We should hurry. Dominica's probably giving her all the tough love. She'll need something a little gentler by now," Tansy titters.

"She means well. Dom's just like a mum who expects better of us all the time, and then when she doesn't get it she's not angry, just disappointed," Farah says. "It'd be better if she expected nothing from any of us. That way she'd never be disappointed, only proud that we simply managed to get up and dress ourselves every day."

The two women stop outside a small pub, waving through the window before going inside.

Eva waits on the corner. To anyone watching, she just looks like a woman waiting for an Uber, but really she's counting down the seconds and getting up the courage to go inside. In the whole time she's been following Tansy, she's never seen her with more than one of them at a time. Following them all together like this makes her nervous.

After five minutes, she pushes open the door and walks into the pub, staring down at her phone as if exchanging texts with someone she's meeting. It doesn't take long for her to get served, but then it never does when you're this beautiful. She picks a table near enough to the women that she can hear their conversation, but far enough away that she's not noticed.

"What a prick," Tansy's saying, rubbing Lauren's hand across the table.

"Terrible cunt," Dominica agrees.

"Honestly, he's not worth the worry," Farah says. "He can't be a pro surfer forever, you know; one day he's going to be too old for that and he'll have to get a real job. Then he'll be so much less sexy anyway. My advice is to start dating men in their thirties and stop messing with these boys."

"Better still, get yourself a wealthy sugar daddy who's close to death," Dominica suggests, as Lauren weeps into a large Pinot and Tansy does some kind of massage of her palms.

"What, so then she can do a Saskia on us and be too rich and important to leave the confines of Holland Park?" Farah asks.

"I would never," Lauren says, quite pathetically in Eva's opinion. "I'll always need my girls."

Eva slugs back some aggressively scented white wine, pushing the vomit back down her throat. But the silence from the others doesn't escape her notice. Maybe they're not as close as they used to be. Maybe it really is Lauren's crises that holds them all together. She expected they'd be thick as thieves, impenetrable, but maybe she can worm her way in there more easily than she thought.

"I messaged Saskia, you know, and she replied saying she was at some coffee morning and she'd get back to me," Lauren says. "Still nothing."

"She'll be busy doing some kind of rich woman bullshit she thinks is very important but is actually pointless," Dominica says. "Rich people always think they're so busy, but actually they just fill their idle days with crap while not paying their taxes and sending the rest of the world to shit."

"You OK there, social justice warrior?" Farah quips.

"I'm sure she'll be in touch when she can," Tansy says kindly to Lauren. "Oh my God, you guys, I forgot to tell you, I'm going on an ayahuasca retreat!"

Eva's ears prick up.

"Let's talk about Tansy now then," Farah mutters, and Tansy turns to face her.

"Dude, I've already apologized for the petition," she says. "I honestly didn't realize it was your magazine!"

"What's an ayahuasca retreat?" Lauren asks, trying to break the tension as usual.

"I read about those, they sound gross," Farah says.

"It's so good for you, honestly, Lauren. I reckon I can get you on it if you want," Tansy offers. "It'll make you so much less neurotic, you'll be like a new person!"

"I'm neurotic?" Lauren asks, confused.

"It'll like, totally change your personality and how you think. I'm so excited to really find myself," Tansy goes on, oblivious.

"It sounds like a lot," Lauren says. "I don't think I want to."

"We have to take risks in order to be happy!" Tansy tells her.

"She doesn't want to take mind-altering drugs, Tansy, leave her be," Dominica says sternly. "And neither should you, by the way."

"I've written way too many articles about fads like this that actually turn out to be really dangerous," Farah says. "Lauren, stay away from the shaman lady."

"You are SO judgmental," Tansy says.

Eva misses the rest of the conversation, her mind whirring. She knows there's only one retreat in the UK like the one Tansy's mentioned, and she's already been there so she knows the owner. Maybe it's the perfect place to meet Tansy face-to-face when her defenses are down. By the time she leaves that retreat, Eva's going to make sure she's the closest person to Tansy; she's going to insert herself into her world, find out what those girls did and make them pay.

After all, Tansy was the last person seen talking to her big brother at that party before he died. Eva knows that whatever she and her friends did to him when they were sixteen, they did it together.

CHAPTER FORTY-FIVE

Outside the castle, a coastal fog swirls in the cool evening air as the sun goes down. Light from the grand banqueting hall beams out from its windows as the guests take their seats for the rehearsal dinner. Among the bustle of the hundred attendees, a fire roars, keeping away the chill. Chandeliers sparkle, waiting staff tend to the guests' every need, ensuring that each course is paired with perfectly complementary wine, and a string quartet plays softly in the background, creating just the right ambience. Everything is exactly the way Farah planned it—if a little emptier than anticipated—except for the fact that the entire wedding could soon be off if things with her mystery texter don't go to plan. Far from being a blissful bride, she's on edge, scared to relax in case she misses the point where her life's turned upside-down.

She sits next to Toby at the head table with their immediate family, including Joss and Eva. Lauren, Dominica, and Saskia are close by, at the second table, with the best men and some of Toby's closest friends. Lauren can feel Joss watching her from where he sits next to Eva, but she completely ignores his gaze. She no longer feels sad and insignificant when she looks at Eva, because she's won. And now Joss is simply as disposable to her as she always was to him.

"I can't get my head round the fact that we're finally here," Farah says, trying to sound as normal as possible. She beams a little too widely at Joss and Eva as she places her cutlery together. She's aware that there's trouble between the two of them, because Eva showed up at her door earlier raging about something to do with him and Lauren, but she really doesn't have the energy to focus on it. "Can you actually believe that this time tomorrow I'll be married?"

"You know, I can't," Joss says, seemingly unaware that next to him Eva is resisting the urge to turn around and plunge her steak knife into him. "I especially can't believe that Toby still wants to marry you despite me telling him about the time you accidentally ate cat shit."

"You told me it was chocolate," Farah says, while Toby chuckles next to her.

Lauren, Dominica, and Saskia eat in near silence. Although no one notices, because Toby's lads of honor next to them are making enough noise for everyone. Dominica can't believe any of them are the same age as Toby. One of them just dared another to ask a snooty waiter for hot sauce to go on his steak tartare. They all seemed to find it hilarious, but Dominica found it lacking in comedic content.

"I should really check on the nanny again," Saskia says, putting her knife and fork down and breaking the silence between the three of them. "I'm sure Jeremy's parents are actually driving her spare by now. I need to make sure she doesn't quit."

"How long are they staying for?" Dominica asks, out of politeness rather than interest.

"Lord knows. At first I thought it would be helpful, but to be honest, all they've done since they arrived is explain to me how I'm responsible for their son dying young because I placed too much stress on him. Apparently my need for financial security was selfish," she sighs, picking up her phone.

"They still don't know how he really died then?" Dominica whispers.

"No, and I'd rather they never did. They're too old, it might shock them into an early grave, and that's far more admin than I need at the moment." Saskia pushes back her chair and stands. "I'll be back in a minute. I'm sure I'll be much more fun once I know no one's fighting about whether the children need brandy to sleep."

"Cool," Dominica says, downing the rest of her glass of red.

Over at the bridal table, Farah watches the staff start to take away the plates and knows that it's time. Whatever happens when she steps away from this table will determine whether she actually gets married tomorrow, and she's furious about it.

"I just need to pop to the bathroom," she says. She finishes her glass of wine in one gulp and stands, placing her napkin next to the plate in front of her.

Giving Toby a quick kiss on the cheek that she hopes won't be her last, she stalks off through the banqueting hall, waving and smiling to people as she goes. Whoever awaits her is about to face her full wrath, and they've severely underestimated her. She glides closer to the toilet, her smile fixed, cracking her knuckles.

"More wine?" Dominica asks Lauren.

"As ever," Lauren says.

"This time tomorrow Farah will be a married woman!" Dominica clinks glasses with her.

"And we'll be free of our obligations," Lauren says.

"Thank fuck." Dominica drinks to that.

"Spin and gin next Saturday?" Lauren asks.

"You know it, baby," Dominica says. "Finally, back to normal."

Lauren looks up to see Joss staring at her and immediately looks back down again. His unwanted attention is actually starting to feel a bit much now. Usually he'd be over her two seconds after a shag. What's wrong with him this time? Why's he behaving like this now *she's* over him?

"Going to follow Farah to the loo, I think!" she says cheerfully, jumping up and making sure to avoid Joss's eyeline.

"Maybe I'll talk to some of the best men," Dominica says.

Once Lauren's gone, though, she assesses the best men properly and realizes they're quite a bleak prospect. In the two seconds she's been paying attention to them, one of them has used the phrase "Top lad!" and patted his mate on the back, while another has mentioned twice that his bitcoin investment portfolio is really thriving at the moment. That alone is more than enough to make her cringe, but when he goes on to mention how many NFTs he purchased last year, her vagina cements shut. She takes another slug of red wine, the only thing left that will give her any kind of thrill.

"I think I'm going to join the party in the toilet," she announces, realizing that she's talking to no one because literally every single worthwhile person has left her.

Striding through the banqueting hall, she tries not to catch anyone's eye. She's really not the kind of person who likes to bump into "old friends" at these things, and frankly none of the rest of this crowd are her kind of people. Mostly they're either Farah's and Toby's work friends, or Toby's extremely extended family.

She reaches the bar and decides to make a pit stop for a quick whisky chaser. Something to take the edge off. As she downs it, her phone vibrates with a message from Saskia.

Disabled loo by the bar. Urgent.

With a sinking feeling, she rushes over to the loo. She gives the door a brief knock before pushing it open, but it only opens a crack on account of the fact that Saskia, Farah, Lauren, and Eva all appear to be crowded into what is essentially a cupboard with a toilet in it.

Dominica edges her way in through the gap, closing the door behind her and locking it for extra security. She's not sure what's happened, but Saskia looks vicious and Eva appears to be trapped, sitting on the toilet while Farah holds a sanitary bin in a threatening manner over her head and Lauren waves an unlit lighter around like she's about to burn off Eva's expensive eyelashes.

"What the *hell* have I walked into?" Dominica asks.

"I know everything," Eva says.

"About?" Dominica squints at her.

"Greg." Eva stares at her as if looking directly into her soul.

"Who?" Dominica asks innocently. She's not about to confess to something that easily.

"Greg Thomas, my big brother," Eva says.

Dominica tries not to react, despite an urge to run away. Of course, now she can see the resemblance. And who actually has a surname like "Bliss"? She should have known.

"The boy at school who died because you all drugged and tied him up. Just because he was a bit of a player. These guys have already confessed to everything and filled in any gaps I still had," Eva says smugly. "Now all I need to do is go to the police."

"GUYS!" Dominica sighs. "Are you kidding me?!"

"She said she knew everything!" Lauren says, shrugging.

"THEY ALWAYS SAY THEY KNOW EVERYTHING!" Dominica can't believe it. She should have brought more whisky with her; it might be the last decent drink she ever has.

"That's not the only thing I know either, and before I go to the police, I think there's probably some stuff you all need to know about each other. I've been gathering dirt on you all since before I met Tansy." Eva sounds even smugger than before.

"I had you on my top table!" Farah says.

"God, give it a rest. This is so not about your wedding! Despite the fact that you think EVERYTHING is." Eva rolls her eyes.

"OH YOU ARE NO LONGER MY BRIDESMAID, YOU LITTLE CUNT!" Farah shouts, advancing toward her with the sanitary bin. Dominica holds her back; she won't let her friends rise to this. She needs to think of a way to deal with the situation rationally, safely, and cleanly.

"There's nothing you know that we wouldn't know about each other," she says, hoping there are multiple things Eva doesn't know about her.

"I know about Lauren's second phone that she uses to text her secret lover, DI Ashford, so they don't get busted while he's investigating her friends for murder. But I also know that she shagged my boyfriend before dinner, so which of them is it you want, Lauren?" Eva stares at her.

"I literally have no idea what you mean," Lauren says unconvincingly.

There's a sudden knock at the door, rendering all five women completely silent.

"Lozza, it's me!" Joss's voice comes through clear as day. "Fuck, you look so sexy in that dress."

Despite not giving a shit about Joss anymore, Lauren can feel a smug little smile trying to fight its way onto her face. Farah looks horrified.

"Not now, Joss," Eva says sternly.

There's a small silence on the other side of the door, followed by a string of curses from Joss and the sound of him walking away at great speed.

The women imagine him now, looking both ways, trying to work out how exactly he's going to get himself out of that one.

"I don't even want him anymore," Lauren says, adding insult to injury.

"Lauren! Don't anger her!" Dominica hisses through gritted teeth.

"Was that the noise I heard that sounded like some kind of wolf barking at the moon?" Saskia asks. "I just thought there were wild animals about; you can never tell what might happen outside of London."

"I cannot believe you slept with my brother the night before my wedding," Farah says. "You can fuck off out of my bridal party too!"

"Oh, I'm sorry! I forgot NOTHING can happen that isn't to do with your precious wedding. The whole world stops for Farah to get married!" Lauren snaps in an uncharacteristic way, making everyone startle.

"I don't know why you're all surprised," Eva says. "Lauren pretends to be this simpering angel, but she's just as nasty as the rest of you. And I thought we were friends!"

"I have literally never been your friend." Lauren says it so harshly the others barely recognize her.

Eva simply rolls her eyes. "Anyway, Farah's done far worse. She was blackmailing Tansy for money."

Farah shrugs. "What? That's such a weird thing to say. Like, why would I do that?"

"Money, like I said." Eva looks at Farah as though she's stupid. "Because you got yourself into so much debt trying to pay for this monstrosity."

"Oh my God, Farah, it was *you*," Saskia gasps. "Tansy spent ages trying to work out what the secret was. Obviously she thought the worst. You HOUNDED her right to her DEATH!"

"All for your fucking wedding?" Dominica asks. "I'll tell you now, I will NOT be handling your divorce. You're on your own."

"What?" Lauren asks, realization dawning on her face. "Seriously, Farah?"

"Oh for God's sake, I would never actually have told Ivan anything! Tansy was going on and on about how amazingly her business was doing, I didn't think she'd even miss the money. And it's her fault for planning her wedding *right* next to mine, with a guy she'd known for

five seconds! Not to mention she got most stuff for *free* after her post
went viral, while I had to throw even more money at mine to stop her
upstaging me *again*! Anyway, she was just meant to think it was about
her Botox, not . . . the other stuff. I'd never have done it about the
other stuff!" Farah takes a breath, trying to ignore the disgusted looks
on her friends' faces. "And Toby and I will *not* be getting a divorce,
Dominica!"

"You think? *I* think when Toby finds out what a massive bitch you
are, he'll be out of there like a shot. Only a matter of time," Eva says.

"I was in trouble! I ended up taking money from work to pay for
all this, and then I couldn't pay it back. I was desperate!" Farah pleads
with the women.

"And here's where you come in, Saskia," Eva says with glee. "You
see, Farah was helping her boss write an article exposing the illegal
surrogacy clinics that operate in the UK and the people who pay for
their babies to be birthed by other people. It was the money her boss
gave her to go undercover at the clinic that she stole. Lucky for Farah
she knew someone who'd used the illegal company, right, Saskia?
When she got found out at work, she was going to force you to spill
everything so she could use it for the article and avoid getting sacked.
That was the deal you made with your boss, right?"

"How do you know all this?" Farah says in a small voice.

Saskia glares at her, her silence echoing louder than any of the
shouts that came from the other women previously.

"Huh?" Lauren finally asks, her head tilted like it's about to fall off
with shock.

"Tansy told you?" Saskia asks Farah, her voice shaking.

"No, the clinic's client list was leaked, and my boss found out."

"SO IT'S TRUE?!" Dominica asks.

"Tansy knew?!" Farah exclaims.

"WHAT'S TRUE? I'm so lost!" Lauren says.

"What's new?" Farah shrugs.

"Fuck you," Lauren hisses.

"Jonathan and Mabel were both born to surrogates," Saskia confesses.

"What?!" Lauren gasps, while Dominica simply stares at Farah, unable to comprehend how much she's fucked over two of her friends.

"Why?" she asks Saskia, though the question could apply to Farah too.

"Jeremy had some issues. He'd sustained some . . . trauma that meant he wasn't able to have children. We were going to use a sperm donor, but he hated the idea of another man's sperm . . . you know . . . inside me, so we went down the surrogacy route. We needed to make sure no one ever found out."

"Wow," Lauren mouths noiselessly in disbelief.

"So you just illegally paid someone else to have your babies for, what, Jeremy's *ego*?" Dominica asks. "I can't believe you didn't tell me."

"Or us," Lauren says, gesturing to her and Farah.

Saskia looks at Dominica. "I'm sorry, I knew it was illegal and I didn't want to put you in a compromising position."

"But you had a bump?" Lauren asks, confused.

"It was fake. I had a fake bump for every stage. I was surprised no one noticed, but the one thing it did teach me is that everyone's essentially too wrapped up in themselves to notice much," Saskia says. "Tansy only knew because she caught me when I tripped into something and the bump broke. I made her promise not to tell anyone. But then when she got those texts, I wondered if that might be one of the secrets."

"Hang on, how did *you* find out?" Farah turns to Eva.

"I overheard you and your boss, Rebecca, talking at the crematorium. Turns out Rebecca was easy to bribe once she knew what I wanted. I told her I'd do some placement ads for the magazine on my 'gram and she sang for a few hundred thousand followers. Cheap." Eva smiles.

Farah stands with a mixture of fury and shame on her face while the other women stare at her.

"I can't believe you'd betray all your friends for a wedding." Dominica looks disgusted.

"You don't know what it's been like! My whole life, everything I did was overshadowed by Tansy! And once Rebecca knew I'd taken the money and that Saskia was on that list, it was either write the article or lose my job and everything I'd worked for—maybe even my freedom if they decided to prosecute. And probably Toby as well once he found out what a mess I was in." Farah puts her head in her hands. "I didn't have a choice, I was in so deep. There was nothing else I could do. If I could take it back, I would. I'd do anything to go back and do everything differently."

"You could have talked to us," Dominica says sadly.

"We would have helped," Saskia offers, much to Eva's annoyance.

"Either way," Eva says, sick of not having all the attention on her, "*Farah* was willing to break up her friend's relationship purely for cash and throw Saskia under the bus to save herself. You lied to everyone multiple times, you're ALL liars." She points to Lauren cheerfully. "Your friendship group is *fucked*. Lifelong friends? What a load of bullshit. And now I know that you all killed my brother, it's game over for you bitches."

"So let me get this straight," Dominica says. "You stalked Tansy, pretended to be her friend, then pretended to fancy Joss purely to get closer to us and try to prove we did something to your brother?"

Farah glares at Eva, eyes narrowed. She's fucked if she's going to let this Gen Z bitch ruin her life and her wedding. "And are we supposed to believe that you did all this—held a grudge against us for this many years, hunted us down—but that you *aren't* the one who murdered Tansy, Helen, and Jeremy? Their deaths happened right after you showed up, and come to think of it, I can't place you when Jeremy was found." She sees Saskia and Dominica exchange a look that suggests the two of them were thinking the same thing.

"Didn't you go off filming for ages like right before we found him?" Lauren adds, pleased that her observations of Eva have finally come in useful for something other than feeling bad about herself.

"Plenty of time to commit a murder." Farah nods.

Eva's face pales. "I'm not the killer, it's one of *you*. You're the murderous bitches! You've got form. One of you did it and you're probably all covering for each other."

"You would say that, though, wouldn't you," Dominica says. "But literally all the evidence is pointing to you."

"So you find out that Tansy was responsible for your brother's death, you become best friends with her, and then you murder her," Saskia says.

"But why did you kill Helen? And Jeremy?" Farah asks.

"I didn't," Eva protests.

"It kind of looks like you did," Lauren says.

"I'm calling the police." Saskia grabs her phone, but Farah holds her back.

"Hang on, let's just . . ." She looks thoughtful, but everyone knows she just doesn't want her wedding ruined.

"I didn't do it," Eva repeats. "If you call the police, I'll just tell them what *you* did."

"What proof have you got? What actual evidence?" Dominica asks. "*You* murdered three people. You're going to jail."

"I didn't!" Eva shouts, and holds up her phone with a voice recording file visible. "And I've got evidence!"

Farah charges forward with the sanitary bin and knocks the phone out of her hand and into the toilet bowl. "Whoops."

To add insult to phone injury, Lauren reaches over and flushes as many times as she can.

"Are you seriously all still working together after everything I've just told you?" Eva stares at them in disbelief.

"We've been friends a long time." Farah shrugs. "We know we're bad people."

"And sometimes friendship is just about helping each other survive," Saskia says.

"And fucking up the people who try to harm us." Dominica smiles. "So I get that you had a reason to kill Tansy, but I'll ask again, why Helen and Jeremy?"

"I didn't!" Eva says, getting more and more irate. "You're not listening! I DIDN'T KILL ANYONE!"

"Helen feels random. It could have been a mistake," Saskia says. "It could have been meant for one of us. Oh my God, were you trying to kill me?!"

"It was me, wasn't it?" Farah asks. "You were going to off me before my wedding day."

"I mean, you have been a bit of a twat," Dominica mutters, and Farah shoots her a scowl.

"It was one hundred percent me," says Lauren. "She knew Joss was still in love with me."

"Oh honey." Farah turns to her. "Joss is really only in love with himself. It's time to get over that."

"I already am over that, actually." Lauren glares at her. But she can see how, having just shagged him, it may not look like that.

"I DIDN'T DO IT! WHY WOULD I DO IT?!" Eva shouts.

"Because you have this mad story in your head that we were responsible for your brother's death when everyone knows that he just took way too much Viagra. He had a heart condition and it was no one's fault but his own," Farah says.

"And as for Jeremy," Saskia says, "well, he was probably trying to protect us. Knowing him, he'd figured you out. He was a smart man, he wouldn't have let anything happen to me. He came to confront you, to stop you murdering anyone else, and you killed him."

"I didn't do anything," Eva whispers, her eyes wide. "I can prove it. And when I do, I'll tell them everything that you guys have done. ALL OF IT. If you take me down, I'm taking you down with me!"

"OK, so here's what we're going to do," Dominica says. "The way I see it, you have choices. We dob you in for the murders and you go to prison, or you can get out of our lives, leave tonight, and never come near us again. If the police ever come sniffing around to tell us they know any of our secrets, we tell them what you did, straightaway. And it's four against one."

"Could you imagine the scoop I'd get writing about the influencer I hung out with for a while who was killing my friends?" Farah asks, practically salivating.

"Content creator," Eva corrects.

"Same shit. Do we have a deal?" Dominica cuts across her. "You can leave now, save your skin, and agree to keep all the secrets secret, or you can try and fuck us over, but we'll fuck you over back, twice as hard."

"Looks like you're pretty *fucked* yourself, dear," Saskia says in a superior tone that the other women normally hate but right now are really enjoying.

"Look, second course must be about due by now," Farah says, pulling herself together and taking decisive action. "We need to go out there and finish dinner, and then you leave before morning. Or we call the police."

"Fine." Eva shrugs. "I won't tell anyone anything and I'll leave after dinner. You're all crazy and one of you did it, you just aren't smart enough to realize who."

"Stop trying to shift the blame," Farah hisses. "You're a fucking monster. And if I so much as see you looking in Toby's direction to tell him anything, you're finished."

"Just let me say goodbye to Joss properly," Eva says sadly. "I did actually like him, you know," she adds, opening the toilet door and stepping out to join the other guests.

"Urgh," Farah says, turning back to the other women. Dominica, Lauren, and Saskia are standing shoulder to shoulder, a row of disapproval. "What?"

"I think you've probably got a fair bit you need to apologize for, don't you?" Saskia says icily. Clearly all is not forgiven, despite their earlier show of camaraderie. Farah at least has the decency to look sheepish, but they all know she won't crack that quickly.

The four women exit the disabled toilet just as the waiters head to the top table with the second course. More than one of them is relieved that despite her big talk, Eva didn't know their biggest secrets after all.

On the way back through the hall, Lauren can feel Joss checking out her arse. But she doesn't turn around, she simply revels in the fact that she's ignoring him and everyone can see it. She's so sick of the way those women talk to her, treating her like an idiot. Frankly everyone can just fuck off.

In the dead of night, the four women sneak back into the castle. It was Dominica's idea for them to meet outside where they wouldn't be overheard by any of the other guests, so that they could hash things out properly. Mostly it was Farah and Saskia shouting at each other while Dominica refereed and Lauren texted DI Ashford. Once they'd shouted and screamed at each other late into the night, Saskia and Farah came up with a plan that meant Farah could write the article without Saskia being involved. And so now they're returning to their rooms. As they walk down the corridor, they hear the shouts from Eva and Joss's room before a door slams. The four of them freeze as Eva comes hurtling toward them, suitcase in hand, tears streaming down her face.

"Now you bitches have everything you wanted," she screeches, shoving past them in the hallway.

"Try not to murder anyone on your way out," Saskia whispers.

CHAPTER FORTY-SIX

Farah wakes up to the sun streaming through the window and the noise of her bridesmaids hammering on her door. She sits up in bed, stretching luxuriously and looking at the beautiful flowers, the gorgeous weather, and the crisp white sheets gathered around her. In the end she slept like a baby last night, knowing that Eva was gone and there were no more secrets to be afraid of. After everything Eva had done, she couldn't touch them, any of them. It was over, and Toby doesn't need to know a thing.

The knocking comes again, and she can hear Dominica growing impatient. To say things were strained between the group last night would be an understatement, but today, finally, it's Farah's day, and everyone has agreed to put their differences aside.

She jumps out of bed, grabbing the white silk bridal robe she had made especially for this day, and heads to the door, padding through a pool of sunshine. Everything's exactly as it was always supposed to be. She opens the door to a chorus of singing from her hens. Sure, it's not the four she'd planned, but three seems just perfect, given the circumstances. Last night she feared there might have been none.

"SHE'S GETTING MARRIED IN THE MORNING! DING DONG THE BELLS ARE GONNA CHIIIIIME!" sing the bridesmaids.

"We've come to take you to the wedding suite!" Lauren announces, all of them with their hair in rollers, wearing their bespoke silk robes and holding up their dresses.

"I'm ready!" Farah says, pulling on her own robe and hastily following them out.

The four of them walk down the hallway toward the wedding suite, a separate area near the chapel where the bride can get ready with her bridesmaids and beauty entourage. Farah has been itching to get in that room ever since she arrived.

"We've taken care of everything, so you don't need to worry about a thing today. This is your day!" Saskia says, every trace of last night's betrayals seemingly buried.

"I feel much better knowing that *she's* gone, anyway. She would have only shown me up in the pictures," Farah says as the other bridesmaids try not to be offended.

"What if she comes back and tries to kill us all? And this time she succeeds?" Lauren asks, wide-eyed with fear.

"I so don't need that thought today, Lauren," Farah snaps.

"She won't. She'd definitely go to prison then, because there's no way she's not getting caught if she does that. Besides, we know it's her now. We can look out for her, she won't catch us unawares," Dominica says.

"I'd kill her before she got within an inch of any of us," Farah says, and the women can well believe it, especially if Eva tries to do it before Farah gets to walk down the aisle.

"OK," Lauren says. "Just think I probably pissed her off quite a bit, you know. What with the whole Joss thing."

"You didn't tell him anything, did you?" Dominica asks. "He can't know ANY of it. We have to keep this contained."

"Of course I didn't tell him anything," Lauren snaps. "I'm not even interested in him anymore. It was just a one-time thing."

The women stare at her in amused disbelief, but they don't know that she spent most of last night texting DI Ashford, the messages she

KATE WESTON

received from Joss fading into the background. She actually ended up muting him, his texts more of an inconvenience than a thrill. Especially now he's been so easily won.

Anyway, she wouldn't actually have anything to tell him. When Greg died, she was simply there, she didn't do anything. Despite what the others think of her, she was far too smart for that. If these bitches go down for Greg, she's not going down with them.

Farah beams from ear to ear and Lauren grabs her arm, the two of them skipping off to the huge white double doors of the wedding suite. Flinging wide the doors, the four women pass through a welcoming arch of fresh flowers and into a spacious, lushly carpeted white room. Inside, more flowers litter almost every surface, and there's a breakfast already laid out for them so they can enjoy the calm before the extra family members and flower girls descend on them with the makeup artists and hair stylists.

"Bagsy a chocolate pastry!" Lauren shouts.

"You are literally the only one of us that can still stomach chocolate for breakfast after everything we drank yesterday." Dominica clutches her head and her stomach.

"It's impressive really," Saskia says, taking a piece of fruit.

"I couldn't eat a thing," Farah says.

"Mimosa, then!" Lauren grabs one, passing it directly to Farah, who doesn't shrug it off or make any comments about the facial bloat from alcohol.

"Thanking you," she says, and the four of them cheers excitedly to their first drink of a big day.

"This is *just* like the weddings we all imagined we'd have when we were kids, isn't it?" Lauren says excitedly as they sip the mimosas.

"I never really imagined a wedding," Dominica says.

"It's exactly the one *I* imagined," Farah says, ignoring her.

"Oh, we know," Saskia giggles. "You used to wear that wedding dress costume for every single occasion when you were five. The world's still mopping up all the tears you shed the day you realized that you'd definitely grown out of it."

The women laugh, and despite everything, Farah feels a rush of love for her friends. Finally she's getting the wedding she deserves.

An hour before the ceremony, the wedding suite is overflowing with people. Farah's mother and mother-in-law are being far too hands-on, flower girls are running around excitedly while their parents try to stop them from staining their dresses and/or injuring themselves. Other female family members have tried their best to infiltrate the room, to join in with the preparations and get a sneak peek at the bride before the service, but not one of them has actually made it in.

"Oh shit! My garter!" Farah shouts. "I left it in my room!"

"I'll go!" Lauren says, jumping up, eager to have a bit of a breather.

"Thanks, babe," Farah says as a makeup artist dusts her cheekbones with bronzer. "It's in the wardrobe."

Lauren skips down the corridor in her horrible lavender dress. At least she got to choose how to have her hair and makeup done, but she really expected better from Farah on the dress front. She's not sure what happens to brides when choosing bridesmaids' dresses, but it's as if they lose all sense of style. Though maybe that's intentional.

She slips into Farah's room, humming the bridal march as she goes. She notes that this room is much bigger than her own, with even more candles. Walking across the herringbone floor, she feels slightly bitter that she didn't get a room with a bath.

Out of the window she can see guests beginning to gather in the garden with glasses of champagne. She watches as men slap each other on the back in greeting and women squeal at each other's outfits. As she reaches for the closet handle, she wonders exactly how many people have cancelled.

It takes her eyes a little while to adjust to the darkness inside the deep wardrobe. But once they do, a small, soundless scream escapes her throat, and she clamps her hand over her mouth in shock.

Hanging from the rail, dressed in her vile lavender bridesmaid dress, is Eva. Her eyes are wide open, staring ahead, her face almost the same hue as her dress, and the bride's garter is wrapped tightly around her neck.

CHAPTER FORTY-SEVEN

The three bridesmaids stand around the wardrobe, hair, makeup, and outfits ready to walk down the aisle, and a dead body ready to send them to jail.

"What the fuck?" Dominica asks.

"AM I GOING TO GO TO PRISON?" Lauren asks, dangerously close to weeping her makeup off.

"You just found her. Why would you go to jail?" Dominica asks.

"I literally don't know anymore," Lauren says, trying to breathe in through her nose and out of her mouth, flapping her arms at her sides.

"You didn't strangle her with the garter, though?" Saskia asks.

"No!" Lauren almost screams.

"Then you should be fine," Dominica says. They need Lauren to calm down if they're going to sort this out rationally.

"*Should* be fine? I'm too nervous to go to prison," Lauren whimpers.

"You won't," Dominica says. "But someone's put a dead person in the wardrobe, and if it wasn't one of us . . ."

"Farah will kill you if you ruin your eye makeup," Saskia says urgently just as a tear threatens to spill out of Lauren's eye.

"Maybe she's already killed once today," Dominica says coolly, nodding to Eva's body.

"What? You really think . . ." Lauren's eyes turn to saucers.

"I mean, who else would it be? It's Farah's wardrobe. Eva threatened to ruin the wedding. We don't know what she was doing before we got here . . ." Saskia shrugs.

"If the garter fits . . ." Dominica adds.

"She told me to get the garter . . . Why would she do that?"

"Final bridesmaid's duty? Cleaning up the mess?" Dominica suggests.

"This feels a little beyond the job description," Saskia says, staring at the jaunty angle of Eva's head. "I can't say she didn't deserve it, though. She killed my husband, as well as Tansy and Helen." She pauses as if considering it. "No, I don't feel sorry for her."

"Why is she wearing the bridesmaid dress, though?" Dominica asks.

"Maybe she was intending to show up to the church after all and spill our secrets. And Farah found her before she could," Saskia suggests.

"Or maybe Farah put the dress on her after killing her, as some kind of twisted message," Lauren says.

"Oh God." Dominica and Saskia gasp, appalled at the thought.

Lauren shrugs. "At least we don't have to worry about her telling people our secrets anymore."

Dominica and Saskia turn to her open-mouthed.

"Are you feeling OK, Loz? Normally you'd say something like 'Oh no! No one deserves to die, not even heinous bitches!'" Dominica says, mimicking her voice.

"Maybe I've just had enough of all this shit." Lauren's sick of them pretending she talks like some fairy godmother. "I'm literally the one everyone expects to roll over all the time. I'm fed up of being so nice. It's bad for my skin to look concerned all the time."

"I mean, you're not *that* nice. You shagged Eva's boyfriend just last night." Lauren stares at her, mortally offended, but Saskia continues regardless. "What are we going to do? If we leave her here, a maid or someone might find her."

"We can't let Farah get in trouble for this, not after everything Eva did," Dominica says.

"Definitely not on her wedding day," Saskia adds.

The three of them look around the room before Saskia's eyes land on the solution.

"The wedding dress box," she says, pointing to the massive empty box the size of a huge suitcase, designed to protect the dress from any knocks in transit. "We put Eva in the box and the Do Not Disturb sign on the door. And we figure something else out after the ceremony."

"What about the garter?" Lauren asks.

"She knows she's not getting that garter," Dominica says. "Surely?"

"Unless she wants to wear it like some kind of . . . trophy?" Lauren almost whispers.

"Please, she's not Hanni-bride Lecter." Saskia rolls her eyes.

"Isn't she?" Dominica sighs. "All I know is we can't call the police unless we want to get shanked with the cake knife."

"We just wait until after the wedding and then we ask her about it," Saskia says. "We said we were in this together last night; we're still in it together this morning. There must be loads of places to get rid of a body in the middle of nowhere in Scotland."

"Yeah, like a loch, or down a hill like Janine and Barry in *East-Enders* . . . loads of places," Lauren says.

"It won't be easy, but it has to be done," Saskia insists. As if they're about to go for an unpleasant smear test rather than dispose of a body to stop their friend getting handcuffed on her wedding day (and not in a good way).

"She's out there behaving as if there's nothing wrong, and all the while she knew Eva was in here," Lauren says, her voice shaking.

"All the more reason not to disturb her," Dominica points out.

"We could make it look like she did it herself?" Saskia suggests. "After all the murders she committed, and her and Joss breaking up."

"Good idea," Dominica says. "We could leave a note saying the pressure got too much for her."

"So we're covering up for Farah, then?" Lauren asks. "Like, she's an actual killer and we're just going to cover it up? And I'm dating a police detective. Cool, cool."

"It's no worse than what Eva's done," Saskia says. "Seems a fitting end when you think about it."

Lauren sits down on the bed and watches as Saskia and Dominica move the body.

Outside the chapel, in the stone-walled waiting area flanked by more flowers and Hylnd Diptyque candles, three bridesmaids dressed in hideous lavender lace are pandering to their bride's every wish and whim. They know that just the other side of the doors are guests waiting to see a wedding. They also know that if any of them do anything that could potentially hinder Farah making it all the way to the end of the aisle, they'll find themselves sleeping in the wedding dress box with Eva.

"How do I look?" Farah asks, smiling brightly, the sun beaming down on her in an ironically angelic way.

Her three bridesmaids are trying really hard not to look at her like the psychopathic killer that she is. They nod and smile enthusiastically, throwing as much flattery into their responses as they possibly can.

"Incredible, the most beautiful bride I ever saw!" Dominica declares nervously, staring at her friend.

"A total queen. SLAY!" Lauren says awkwardly.

"You are STUNNING, darling. Honestly, I feel quite emotional just looking at you! Let's go and get you married!" Saskia ushers her forward with haste.

The four friends get into a diamond formation: Lauren, as least important, at the front, then Saskia and Dominica, followed by the bride at the back. Lauren's happy for the barrier between her and Farah. If Farah snaps, she can use Saskia and Dominica as human shields. It's what they'd do in the same position.

As the three of them clutch their bouquets and the wedding march strikes up, Saskia turns to Farah.

"Don't worry," she whispers. "We've sorted everything for you. There's no way Eva can ruin your day."

"I know," Farah says.

The doors to the chapel open and the four women start their walk down the aisle: Lauren, Saskia, Dominica, and finally the bride, with a perfect ray of sunlight shining on her crisp white veil.

CHAPTER FORTY-EIGHT

A light evening breeze starts batting around the old castle as the sun sets pink over the loch. Inside, the three bridesmaids are dancing to Cyndi Lauper while the bride is hoisted on the best men's shoulders.

Dominica looks around the party to check that everyone's suitably distracted, then leans into Saskia.

"Cigarette?" she says, and Saskia nods. They gesture to Lauren doing pretend smoking and she joins them.

Joss watches Lauren with puppy-dog eyes as she follows the other two out. He's been trying to get her attention all day, unable to work out why she's not falling at his feet. Lauren, on the other hand, is enjoying him getting a taste of his own medicine. It feels like a badge of honor using him for sex for once rather than the other way around. She's been texting pictures of herself to DI Ashford all day.

The three women walk outside without Farah. They've got business to attend to, and frankly they're too afraid of Farah to disturb her now. It takes a certain kind of bride to be able to joyfully lead a rowdy conga line around her wedding all the while knowing that the bridesmaid she murdered is hanging in her closet upstairs. They can't help wondering whether it was the wedding that turned her into a psychopath or whether she's always been one and it's been buried deep all these years. The next few months will be the deciding factor.

"Do you think she's finally at peace?" Dominica asks, watching Farah through the glass.

"Who, Eva?" Lauren asks. "Probably not."

"NO! Farah!" Dominica says, passing Lauren her lighter.

"Oh, I mean, she looks happy," Lauren says.

"What are we going to do about . . . you know?" Saskia points upstairs.

"I think with everyone down here, now's a good time to move her to Joss's room and stage the scene," Dominica says. "Apparently once the sun's gone down, they're going to be releasing a hundred light-up helium balloons with Farah and Toby's faces on them. That'll distract everyone."

"Christ," Saskia mutters. "Like the doves after the ceremony weren't enough already?"

Lauren's about to protest that she wants no part of it; Saskia and Dominica can tell just from her breathing.

"Lauren, you stay down here and talk to Joss, keep him occupied," Saskia says. "The fewer of us absent the better, and it'll only take two, I think."

"OK." Lauren smiles, relieved that she doesn't have to get her hands dirty, because really, when has Farah ever done anything for her? Although for the first time in her life, she'd rather be as far from Joss as possible.

"Let's go," Dominica says. "We CANNOT get caught. I love Farah, but I'm not about to take the fall for her."

She stubs out her cigarette and follows Saskia upstairs. Lauren stays where she is, smoking and staring out into the Scottish countryside, hoping that all this is soon going to be a distant memory. From now on, she's going to be tougher, have more resolve. She's saying goodbye to Lauren the pushover.

"Where did the others go?" Joss's voice startles her.

"Oh, just had to go and sort something out. Bridesmaid duties never end!" Lauren says cheerfully as he puts his arm around her shoulders. She immediately wriggles out of his grasp.

"That means I get you all to myself," he says. "Perfect. I've been thinking. Now that Eva's gone . . ." Lauren can't help thinking he doesn't realize just how gone Eva is. ". . . maybe you and I can give things another shot."

"I don't think so," Lauren says, head held high, shoulders back. She's had her last shag with Joss.

"Great! So we can . . . Wait, what?!" Joss says, his head tilted in shock. As if he can't possibly comprehend that she won't just come running when he calls again. That she won't drop everything for him.

"It's not worked before. I don't see what would be different now." As she says it, Lauren feels a soaring victory watching Joss crumble in front of her.

"I can't believe this. I can't believe you're giving up on us just like that."

She thinks he might actually be about to cry. He stands there for a few seconds, and she thinks about explaining to him that twenty-five years of fuckery isn't really "just like that." But then he turns on his heel, clearly not wanting her to see he's upset, and walks off back through the French doors. As Lauren watches him leave, a broken man, her face stretches into a beam.

"Where did Saskia and Dominica go?" Farah asks, appearing at her side. "I can't believe they've disappeared. We'll be releasing the balloons in half an hour!"

"They went up to sort out Eva," Lauren says as Farah takes the cigarette out of her hand.

"Eva's back?" Farah's face is suddenly filled with alarm. "I thought she left last night. What's she playing at?"

"Huh?" Lauren turns to face her, startled.

"I thought she'd left," Farah says again.

"Well, I mean, she couldn't leave, because she was dead in your wardrobe." Lauren whispers the words right into her ear, and Farah drops the cigarette. "Were you like, so filled with fury you don't remember doing it? Was it one of those out-of-body rage things?"

"Beg your pardon?" Farah asks, a haunted look appearing on her face.

"I found Eva in your wardrobe. Like I was meant to? When I went to get your garter? The garter that you'd strangled her with. We all presumed you'd left her there so that I'd find her and then we'd sort it out for you." Lauren stares at Farah's baffled face. "Wait, are you telling me you didn't know she was there?"

"I did not," Farah says slowly, her eyes narrowing. "I was kind of annoyed that you never got me my garter, though."

"So you didn't put her there?" Lauren asks again, as if Farah might consider it and come back with a different answer.

"Absolutely not," Farah says. She pauses, then whispers, "She's dead?"

"You really don't know what I'm talking about?" Lauren asks.

Farah is shaking her head. "Why would I kill her?"

"We just thought maybe the wedding had got to you, and after everything last night, and finding out she was the killer, you . . . snapped?" Lauren is sheepish under Farah's angry gaze.

"So it seemed perfectly normal to you that I would just kill her on my wedding day? So she didn't ruin it?" Farah asks.

"I mean . . . you have been kind of a bitch," Lauren says quietly.

"I'm going to choose to ignore that, because the main thing is that I haven't killed anyone yet and I'm not about to start now."

"But if you didn't kill Eva, then . . . who did?"

The two of them exchange a look of confusion and fear.

"If Eva's dead, did she maybe *not* kill the others? And maybe the person who's killed everyone else killed Eva?" Farah sounds panicked. "Where are Dom and Saskia now, did you say?"

"They'll be in Joss's room by now," Lauren says slowly. "Or yours still, retrieving the body."

"We need to get up there. What if the killer's there with the body, waiting for them to come back?"

Lauren feels prickles of urgency and fear traveling up her spine. "I don't know if . . . Should we get someone to come with us? For protection?" she asks. "I mean, I'm not really the greatest at defending myself . . ."

Farah is already running toward the staircase. "LAUREN! LET'S GO!"

CHAPTER FORTY-NINE

Farah and Lauren arrive upstairs breathless. They open the door to Farah's room first but discover it empty, the wedding dress box open in the middle of the floor. Racing back out into the hallway, they stop outside Joss's door, halted by fear.

"Should we knock?" Farah whispers. "In case we startle them?"

"If the killer's in there, we're just alerting them that we're coming, and they might finish them off sooner!" Lauren replies.

"Good point." Farah nods.

The two of them burst through the door to the sight of Eva's dead body propped on a chair in the center of the room. Dominica and Saskia jump away from the lavender-clad corpse, staring at Farah and Lauren like a pair of startled hares in headlights.

"Oh Jesus, Lauren!" Saskia clutches her chest in shock. "We thought you were someone else!"

"I didn't do it!" Farah blurts out.

"Farah didn't do it!" Lauren repeats for emphasis. "We need to call the police."

"Tomorrow," Farah clarifies, prompting the other three to glare at her.

They all take a minute to look at Eva, and the way that her body has stiffened, Farah's lacy garter still knotted tight around her neck.

Lauren's already got her phone in her hand, with her finger hovering over DI Ashford's number.

"Maybe we don't need to call the police," Dominica says, grabbing the phone from her.

"Why?" Saskia asks. "Farah didn't do it. And that means Eva's probably not the killer and the killer is actually someone who's here at the wedding."

"And we need to tell the police so that we don't end up being next!" Lauren finishes frantically.

"If the police keep everyone here, I will still be able to go on my honeymoon tomorrow, though, right?" Farah asks.

"Babe!" Lauren turns to her, having lost all her patience. "People have been *murdered,* you get that, right? Like Tansy, our friend, the friend we grew up with, the girl who used to plait your hair for you? DEAD! Actually dead, not just pretending, to inconvenience your wedding. Like, your wedding will be over and she'll still be gone!"

"If we don't do something, you'll probably be dead by tomorrow anyway," Saskia says. "Even I wasn't this much of a diva on my big day, hon."

"I WAITED TEN YEARS FOR TODAY! TEN YEARS!" Farah roars at them.

"SHUT THE FUCK UP!" Dominica screams. "SHUT UP SHUT UP SHUT UP!"

They all fall silent, taken aback.

"I'VE SPENT MY WHOLE FUCKING LIFE LOOKING AFTER YOU ALL! YEARS! DEALING WITH GREG! JEREMY! YOUR LEGAL TROUBLES!" She points to Saskia and steadies her tone. "All the times I've looked out for you and you *still* won't listen to me. We need to make it look like Eva's killed herself because she killed the others and then this whole thing can be over and we can go back to normal."

Realization slowly dawns.

"You killed Eva," Saskia says quietly, twigging first.

Dominica starts laughing. "As if—"

Saskia cuts across her, not about to be fobbed off. She knows her too well for lies.

"Why did you tell us it was Farah?" she asks.

The two women are locked in steely eye contact while Lauren and Farah stare on in utter disbelief.

"I just thought it was easier that way," Dominica says. "Farah killed Eva because Eva killed everyone else. It seemed like a solid plan."

"Unless Eva didn't kill anyone?" Saskia's eyebrows rise as she glares in Dominica's direction.

There's silence around the room as they all take in what she's saying.

"Dom . . ." Lauren starts, but she doesn't get any further. Something in Dominica has snapped.

"I've always done what's best for you all," she shouts. "Tansy was going to tell Ivan about Greg! There's no way he'd have kept the secret! Sometimes you have to sacrifice one hen for the rest of the brood. I did all of this for you. *For all of you.* I couldn't lose you."

The three women's mouths fall open, none of them quite able to process what Dominica is saying.

"But . . . Tansy?" Lauren whispers.

"You actually killed Tansy?" Saskia asks, blinking.

"I wouldn't have had to do anything if it wasn't for Farah sending her those texts," Dominica snarls. "You freaked her out. She didn't know what was going on. You should have known she would think it was about Greg; which one of us wouldn't?"

"So kill Ivan after she'd told him, for Christ's sake! He was a bell end!" Farah shouts at her. "Don't kill our friend!"

"Like she wasn't just going to blab to the next person? And anyway, don't you dare judge me. The things I've done for you all. I even shagged Saskia's husband MULTIPLE TIMES to make sure she had a way out of her marriage."

"You shagged my husband?" Saskia repeats her words slowly through gritted teeth, fists balled. "You shagged my husband and you did it *for me*?"

Lauren and Farah don't have time to take in this latest development. They've seen this expression before: Saskia wants blood. They step out of the way, out of the radius of danger.

"You weren't happy!" Dominica says. "And I'd seen your prenup before the wedding, remember? It said that if he cheated, you'd get fifty percent of his earnings, and if he had an actual *affair,* it'd be an even better deal. I was getting you out of there. When I found out about his little side business, I knew I needed to do it quickly before it all hit the fan. The night he died, he'd found out that I'd been digging into the club. He threatened me. Told me that if anything ever came out about it, or if you ever left him, he'd tell you about our affair. Show you proof. He knew what that would do to me. I couldn't let him. I couldn't lose you! Then he said that if you tried to take his money, he'd tell the police about Greg. He had proof, a recording of you telling him about it. You told us never to tell anyone, but you literally told the WORST person in the world! He'd have sent us all to prison!"

"HE WAS MY HUSBAND!" Saskia screams.

"You weren't happy," Dominica repeats. "You knew he was a prick deep down." Her voice is now terrifyingly calm.

"What do you mean, I wasn't happy? How do you know I wasn't happy. I WAS HAPPY!" Saskia protests.

"You only married him for his money!"

"How DARE YOU!"

"Just to say, he actually couldn't have sent *me* to prison," Lauren interrupts. "I've literally never done anything wrong."

"Oh God, fuck off, Lauren," Dominica says. "You pretend to be all defenseless, but you're fine. Everyone worries about you, but no one needs to. You'll always land on your feet, like a fucking cat. You're so fucking manipulative with your whole 'poor me' routine."

"Sorry to be all into the details here, but why did you kill Helen?" Farah asks, while Lauren mouths indignantly. "I assume you *did* kill her too."

"Silly bitch had too much time on her hands with all her armchair detecting. She was trying to work out who put the peach in Tansy's mug, remember? I couldn't risk her working out I'd popped it in when I hugged her. She had to go."

"Right, right," Farah says. "So just become a serial killer then, why not?"

"Like you're better than me?" Dominica snorts. "You've been fucking unbearable, Farah. You've behaved like a real prick since you got engaged."

"She's not wrong," Lauren mutters.

"Yeah, side with the murderer, Lauren, because you're so *nice*!" Farah snaps back. "Like I'm worse than a fucking serial killer just because I wanted a perfect wedding?"

"I can't believe you lured my husband to Blackpool for sex and then killed him!" Saskia shouts over them, shaking her head. "With an inflatable penis! How did you even—"

"Knocked him out, fed it into his mouth and down his throat, then blew it up a bit till he choked," Dominica says clinically.

"Why, though?" Saskia asks. "Why the penis?"

"It felt apt. A penis for a penis." Dominica shrugs. "He met Farah before he saw me, by the way."

"Fuck's sake, dobber," Farah says.

"I'm sorry, you were shagging my husband too?" Saskia asks.

"As if." Farah grimaces. "No, he was trying to stop me writing that surrogacy article. He knew I'd been blackmailing Tansy. He threatened to tell you all. But I don't think I can be judged for a bit of blackmail anymore when there's a serial killer in the room."

"I've done all this for *us*," Dominica points out, almost rationally. "And all anyone's ever repaid me with is being another fucking bridesmaid at another fucking wedding! Always the shit dresses and the tasteless sashes and tiaras. I was so scared of losing you all, scared you'd go off with your husbands and leave me, but all any of you have ever done is create more shit for me to clear up anyway!"

Lauren feels momentarily affronted: *she* never had a husband on the horizon. Clearly Dominica would literally kill not to be left behind with her. As if sensing her displeasure, Dominica suddenly launches toward her, grabbing a heavy brass lamp from the bedside table on her way past. Before she can reach her, though, Farah and Saskia grab hold of her.

"Jesus, why are you coming for me?!" Lauren asks.

"Because you're so fucking irritating!" Dominica shouts.

"Lauren?" Joss's voice comes through the door. "Loz?"

"In here!" Lauren shouts.

"WE NEED HELP!" Farah shouts.

"After everything I've done for you, you're going to just shop me?" Dominica says as they all try to restrain her.

"You killed Tansy!" Lauren shouts.

"And my husband!" Saskia adds.

Lauren and Farah kind of shrug.

"And Helen," Farah says.

No one reacts.

"And Eva," Dominica adds. "Don't forget Eva, Lauren. At least you finally got what you wanted."

"I don't need to get men by killing off the competition!" Lauren says, thanking God that's finally true. "And just to remind you, I DON'T EVEN WANT HIM ANYMORE!"

"Oh well, congratulations! That only took thirty fucking years!" Dominica says sarcastically. "Still couldn't resist fucking him last night, though, could you?"

"It was a revenge fuck!" Lauren shouts.

"Um, Loz, I don't know what you're doing in my room, but it sounds kind of intense. Are you OK?" Joss says, sounding nervous.

Lauren rolls her eyes: always with the "Are you OK?" even when she's trapped in a room with a fucking serial killer.

"COME IN, FOR FUCK'S SAKE!" Saskia yells at him. "Use your key and come in and help us."

"Er, I'm not on my own," he says.

"Well, the more the fucking merrier!" Farah sings. "It's a party. This is after all my wedding day!"

"SHUT UP ABOUT THE FUCKING WEDDING!" all the women shout at her.

"Er, OK," Joss says, opening the door and stepping into the room with DI Ashford.

"TOM!" Lauren cries, throwing herself toward the DI, but he doesn't reciprocate and he doesn't look happy.

"Does anyone want to explain what's happening with this dead body, or should I take a guess?" He barely looks at Lauren; at a guess, she thinks he definitely heard their conversation about her fucking Joss.

"Eva?!" Joss gasps, falling to his knees next to the chair. "EVA!"

"Dom did it," Farah blurts without much coaxing.

"I figured," DI Ashford says. "I just wanted to see how much you guys still protected each other."

"Dom did it," Saskia repeats.

"Dom did it," Lauren joins in, nodding.

Dominica sits shaking her head.

"Dom? Why?" Joss asks.

"Because I've spent my whole life protecting these ungrateful bitches. MY WHOLE FUCKING LIFE for nothing."

"No one asked you to, sweetie," Saskia says with venom.

"Ungrateful slag," Dominica snaps back at her, slamming her hand onto the table next to her, sending everything on it flying. "All of you are."

Farah steps out of the way to protect her dress.

"No one can prove anything," Dominica says.

"I can," DI Ashford says. "That's why I came to arrest you. I've got proof that you killed Tansy, Helen, *and* Jeremy. See, before he died, Jeremy had handed over some evidence to us. He'd been concerned about you for a while, Dominica; obviously he knew you quite well by this point, and he'd observed some strange behavior. He'd been following you, and managed to get us proof of your involvement in the murders, including the packaging for the arsenic that killed Helen, and Tansy's EpiPen. He'd watched you try and dispose of them and had sent us video evidence of you doing it. You're really not as slick as you think you are, you know. Embarrassed it took us so long, to be honest. But there were no prints or DNA, and we needed to ensure the case was watertight."

"He could have edited those videos to make it look like I did it," Dominica protests. "That's not proof! Besides, if he really suspected me, then why did he come and see me in Blackpool? I gave him a blow job in that lap-dancing club, you know!"

Saskia blinks at her, unable to believe that this is the friend she's trusted for all these years.

"Further to this evidence, he also mentioned something about a historical case involving a boy called Greg Thomas from your school," DI Ashford continues, undeterred. "We managed to get hold of the toxicology report from his death that stated that not only was there Viagra in his system, but also various sleeping tablets and anxiety medications. Today we were able to confirm from medical records that all those medications had been prescribed for your mother within the year prior to Greg's death. The doctor doing the autopsy at the time stated that Viagra on its own would have been safe. It was the combination that caused the fatal heart attack."

Lauren, Saskia, and Farah almost crumple to the ground. All these years they've believed they were responsible. It takes all their resolve not to let on to the detective that they were party to this death.

"You can't prove anything based on a historical case. It's far too long ago," Dominica replies, her superior tone full of a smugness that the women have always hated.

"Maybe not, but this combined with receiving a tip-off yesterday from someone who we now believe to be the deceased, Eva, telling us that you were responsible and that you were planning another murder was enough for us to come and take you in for questioning. And now with the confession we've just heard and the evidence from your friends, we've got everything we need."

Dominica goes to lunge toward Lauren with the brass lamp again. Joss jumps out of the way, leaving the path to her clear, but DI Ashford steps in just in time, grabbing Dominica by the arm.

"STOP TRYING TO KILL ME!" Lauren yells.

"THIS IS YOUR FAULT!" Dominica shouts. "All that flirting with the detective!"

"Yeah, like *that* was your downfall," Saskia mutters.

"Dominica Widrow, I'm arresting you on suspicion of the murders of Tansy von Weller, Helen Jones, Jeremy Bardon-Burnett, and Eva Thomas. You do not have to say anything, but it may harm your defense if you do not mention . . ."

The women stand watching as DI Ashford reads Dominica her rights and handcuffs her.

"I need everyone to clear this room, it's a murder scene," he says when he's finished, leading Dominica out. "My colleagues will take prints and statements from you all."

The room starts to fill with people in white suits, and the three women are guided out by uniformed officers into the hallway.

"My guests!" Farah fusses. "I should go and see to them! And my husband!"

"'Fraid we're going to need you to stay put for now, miss," an officer says.

"It's missus," Farah spits out.

"Farah?" Toby's voice travels down the corridor. "Farah? What's going on? We're releasing the balloons!"

"Not now, darling. Dominica's a murderer," Farah says to her new husband as he joins her outside the room.

Lauren smiles at DI Ashford, but he ignores her, heading over to his colleagues to bask in murderer-catching glory.

Joss gingerly approaches her, ready to redeem himself for jumping out of the way of Dominica's fury. He clearly still can't believe she wouldn't want to give them another go. Lauren ignores him.

"Lauren?" he asks, looking hurt. "You and the detective?"

"Yes. And?" She's poised to point out that he's no right to be upset about anything.

"He doesn't want you, you know. No one else will want you like I do. We've got history!"

"Fuck off, Joss." Lauren cuts him off.

His mouth falls open in shock. "Are you OK?" he asks, his eyes wide.

"No, Joss, no. I am not OK," she snaps before walking away to join Saskia and Farah, while Toby tries to make sense of what on earth's happened.

The three women stare straight ahead, slumped on the floor against the wall in a row. Farah's makeup is running, her dress taking the brunt of her dripping foundation and dark eyeliner. As Dominica is led away to a police car, they stare at the wreckage of their friendship, a depleted group of three. They don't know if they can survive this, but then who else could ever understand what they've been through?

. . .

Farah stands on the castle steps, bathed in blue flashing light. Mascara tracks run down her face as she turns away from Lauren and Saskia on the gravel driveway below. Most of the guests have retreated up to their rooms, out of the way, while the police wait to take the three remaining women in for questioning. Before they leave, though, they've permitted Farah to carry out this one final bridal tradition.

Taking a brief glance over her shoulder so that she knows where to aim, she raises her arms, hands clasped tightly around the bouquet she'd always dreamed of, now slightly weathered by the day's events. Then she lets it go, flinging it over her shoulder to the only two friends she's got left.

Once airborne, the bouquet starts to disintegrate, the ribbon breaking free, fluttering off in the wind, flowers falling apart mid flight. By the time any of it reaches Lauren and Saskia, all that's left to catch are a few half-dead, squashed buds. A fitting symbol for Farah's start to married life.

"Maybe my nan was right," she whispers into the night, brown petals raining down on them all. "Maybe it's bad luck after all to wear white to your wedding when you're not a virgin."

ACKNOWLEDGMENTS

The first and biggest thank-you has to go to my agent, Chloe Seager, who has championed, encouraged, and loved this book from the first moment I spoke to her about it. Even talking me through a period of MUCH moaning from me, when I'd decided that it simply couldn't be done. You're a hero, Chloe Seager, and I don't know where I'd be without you. I'm so lucky and thankful that you believe in me and my books. And thank you to all at Madeleine Milburn for everything that you do.

Big thank-you also to Hayley Steed for reading early versions of this book and feeding back on it for me. I am extremely grateful.

Huge thank-you to everyone at Random House who helped these twisted hens come to life. In particular Andrea Walker for being so wonderfully excited about it and helping shape it into the unhinged joy it is now, and to Noa Shapiro. I'm so lucky to work with such a great team with so much excitement for the book.

Thank you to my family for reading everything I write. (Sorry for swearing in this one again, Mum.) Thank you to Angus the cat, whose constant and unwavering companionship and support while I wrote this book really got me through.

Thank you to my husband, Nick, for your love, support, cheerleading, and incredible patience. I promise next time it won't be so bad (I think I said that last time). Anyway, I love you.

And finally thank you to my friends for not being like any of the ones in this book.

PHOTO: JOANNA BONGARD

KATE WESTON is the author of *You May Now Kill the Bride* and the YA novels *Diary of a Confused Feminist* and *Murder on a School Night*.

Instagram: @kateelizabethweston
X: @kateelizweston

ABOUT THE TYPE

This book was set in Bembo, a typeface based on an old-style Roman face that was used for Cardinal Pietro Bembo's tract *De Aetna* in 1495. Bembo was cut by Francesco Griffo (1450–1518) in the early sixteenth century for Italian Renaissance printer and publisher Aldus Manutius (1449–1515). The Lanston Monotype Company of Philadelphia brought the well-proportioned letterforms of Bembo to the United States in the 1930s.